Praise for *The Winter Witch*

"There's a whiff of Harry Potter in the witchy conflict—a battle between undeveloped young magical talent and old malevolence—at the heart of this sprightly tale of spells and romance, the second novel from British writer Brackston (*The Witch's Daughter*, 2011) . . . Love of landscape and lyrical writing lend charm, but it's Brackston's full-blooded storytelling that will hook the reader."   —*Kirkus Reviews*

"Brackston delivers an intimate paranormal romance that grounds its fantasy in the reality of a nineteenth-century Welsh farm."   —*Publishers Weekly*

Praise for *The Witch's Daughter*

"Lushly written with a fascinating premise and an enthralling heroine, *The Witch's Daughter* will linger long in memory after the last page has been savored. Highly recommended."
                            —Sara Poole, author of *The Borgia Betrayal*

"A beautifully written, brilliantly crafted page-turner that completely invests you in the lives and loves of the witch's daughter. A true reading event."   —Melissa Senate, author of
                                    The Love Goddess' Cooking School

"A lyrical and spellbinding time travel fantasy featuring an immortal witch who must summon all her powers to defeat the evil hounding her through the centuries."
                —Mary Sharratt, author of *Daughters of the Witching Hill*

Also by Paula Brackston

The Witch's Daughter

The WINTER WITCH

Paula Brackston

THOMAS DUNNE BOOKS
ST. MARTIN'S GRIFFIN
NEW YORK

THOMAS DUNNE BOOKS.
An imprint of St. Martin's Press.

THE WINTER WITCH. Copyright © 2013 by Paula Brackston. All rights reserved. Printed in the United States of America. For information, address St. Martin's Press, 175 Fifth Avenue, New York, N.Y. 10010.

www.thomasdunnebooks.com
www.stmartins.com

The Library of Congress has cataloged the hardcover edition as follows:

Brackston, Paula.
    The winter witch / Paula Brackston.—1st ed.
      p. cm.
    ISBN 978-1-250-00131-3 (hardcover)
    ISBN 978-1-250-02258-5 (e-book)
    1. Witches—Fiction.   2. Mute persons—Fiction.
    3. Wales—Fiction.   I. Title.
    PR6102.R325 W56 2013
    823'.92—dc23

                                    2012285580

    ISBN 978-1-250-04270-5 (trade paperback)

St. Martin's Griffin books may be purchased for educational, business, or promotional use. For information on bulk purchases, please contact Macmillan Corporate and Premium Sales Department at 1-800-221-7945, extension 5442, or write specialmarkets@macmillan.com.

First St. Martin's Griffin Edition: January 2014

10 9 8 7 6 5 4 3 2 1

For Jennie—for being slightly interesting all these years

Acknowledgments

The Winter Witch has been a joy to write, due largely to the support and input of Peter Wolverton and Anne Bensson at Thomas Dunne Books, so a big thank-you to them both. Thanks also to the design team for such a fabulous cover, and everyone else at SMP for their enthusiasm and attention to detail.

I'd like to express my gratitude to The Worshipful Company of Farriers, and to Brecon Museum, who were really helpful during my research for this book. An honorable mention, too, to my good friend Melanie Williams for checking my somewhat rusty Welsh—a real labor of love.

As always, heartfelt thanks go to my family for their continued support and understanding, and basically for not being driven mad by my near obsession with writing and all things witchy.

1.

Does the spider consider herself beautiful? When she gazes into
a dewdrop, does her reflection please her? Her web is finer than
the finest lace, her body a bobbin working her own whisper
thread. It is the web people admire. Its delicacy, its fragile strength.
But the spider, poor creature, is thought of as ugly. She repulses
some. Sends others into fainting fits. And yet she *is* beautiful, or
so it seems to me. So nimble. So deft. So perfectly fashioned for
the life fate has chosen for her. Like this one, here, in my palm.
See how she ponders her next step, testing the surface, this way
and that, her tiny feet tickling my skin, the hairs on her body
sweeping my hand as she moves. How can something so exactly
suited to its surroundings, to its existence, not be deserving of
our admiration? How can a form so elegant, so neat, so sleek,
not be recognized as beautiful? Must everything be pretty to be
adored? The ladybird has black legs and a beetle body, but girls
exclaim over the gaiety of her red wings and the cheerfulness of
her spots. Must we always bedeck ourselves in prettiness to be
thought pleasing? It would appear so. A woman must look a certain way to be worthy of a man's attentions. It is expected. So
here I stand, in a borrowed white gown, with flowers in my hair
and at my waist, gaudy as a maypole, looking how I never look,
presenting an aspect of myself that does not exist. It is a lie. How
much happier I would be to don the gossamer spider's web as my
veil. And to drape myself in my customary dark colors, the better
to blend with the shadows, the better to observe, and not to be
observed.

"Morgana? Morgana!"

Mam is impatient. No, not impatient, a little afraid. Afraid that I might slip away, hide myself in one of my many secret places, and stay hidden until this moment has passed. This moment not of my asking. Not of my choosing.

"Mor*gana*!"

Can she really wish me to go? To leave the only home I have ever known? To leave her? Surely a daughter's place is at her mother's side. Why must things change? Why will she not allow me to make my own choice, in this of all matters?

"Morgana, what are you doing?"

I am found. She peers in at me, stooping into the low entrance of my holly den. Blood hurries to her lowered head, flushing her face. Even in the dim light the prickly shelter allows I can see she is agitated. And that the rosiness of her cheeks is set against a worrying pallor.

"Morgana, your dress . . . you will make it filthy sitting in here. Come out." She withdraws and I can put off the moment no longer. I ponder the spider in my hand. I could take her with me; pop her in my petticoat pocket. At least then I might have a friend as my witness this day. But no, she belongs here. Why should both of us be uprooted?

There, little spinner, back to your web.

I return her to her rightful place. I wish I could stay with her in this dark, close space, this earth womb. But my wishes count for nothing now. My fate has been decided. I squeeze out of the den.

Outside, the sun hurts my eyes. The brash light illuminates my silly dress and showy flowers. I feel most horribly bright. Most ridiculously colored. What nonsense we are all engaged in.

"*Duw*, child, you have enough mud on you to plant potatoes. What were you thinking? In your wedding gown."

She tutts and huffs and frowns at me but I am unconvinced. I see fear in her eyes. She cannot hide it from me. She ceases beating at my skirts in an effort to remove the dirt and places her hands on my shoulders, holding my gaze as firmly as she grips me.

"You are a woman now," she says, having just this second called me *child*. "It would serve you well to behave as one. Your husband will expect some . . . manners, at the very least."

Now it is my turn to frown. Husband! Might as well say Owner! Master! Lord! I turn away. I do not wish to look at her while my heart is full of anger. I feel my bottled fury bubbling within me, and something shifts, something alters. Sounds become distant. Voices meaningless. There is such a pressure inside my skull, such a force fighting to be released. My eyelids droop. My movements become slow and leaden. The sensation of falling backward grows.

"Morgana!" The urgency in Mam's voice reaches me. Calls me back. "Do *not*, Morgana! Not now."

I open my eyes and see the dauntless determination in hers. We are, after all, alike in this way.

She turns me on my heel and all but marches me from the garden and along the lane to the chapel. With every hurried step the plain stone building comes closer. I will enter it as my own person and leave belonging to another. How can this be?

"Here." At the gate to the graveyard Mam suspends our marching to fuss with my hair. "Let me look at you." She looks, and I know she sees me. And I know that when I am away from her there will be no one to look at me in the way she does. And the thought brings with it such a weight of loneliness I have to steady myself to bear it. Mam touches my cheek. "All will be well, *cariad*," she says.

I shake my head.

"I want only what is best for you," she insists. "It is all I have ever wanted." I feel her hesitate. A jay bobs past on its uneven flight and laughs at our pain. "He is a good man, Morgana. He will give you a home, a life. A future." She sees that I do not care what he will give me; that I would rather stay with her and have none of these things. She has no answer to this.

A brisk trotting alerts us to the arrival of my betrothed. We both turn to watch the white pony stallion leaning into the collar of its harness boldly as it pulls the tub-trap up the hill, hastening the moment I have been in dread of all these months. The day is warm, and the little horse's neck is slick with sweat but it is clear he, at least, is enjoying his outing. In the trap, which is mercifully free of flowers or ribbons, Cai Jenkins closes his hands on the reins and brings the pony to a halt. He is a tall man, lean, but strong, I think. His face is angular, almost severe, but softened by a full mouth, and light blue eyes. They are startling and bright—the color of forget-me-nots in sunshine. He ties the reins and steps down from the narrow wooden seat. His wool suit is loose on his bony frame. Mam never promised him I could cook. Will he remember that, later? It is a bad idea to make assumptions where people are concerned. When he climbs down from the trap he moves easily, a man clearly accustomed to a physical life. But the hint of shoulder blades beneath his jacket suggests he does not do well. No doubt he has felt the lack of a cook since his first wife died. Three years ago, that was. He loved her, he actually told us that. Came right out with the words.

"She was all and everything to me, see? I will not pretend otherwise," said he, sitting in our parlor, Mam's best china in his hand, tea growing cold while he filled the room with his unnecessary words. He had looked at me then, as if I were a colt given to biting and it would fall to him to devise the most effective manner of taming me. "I want to be honest with you both," he said. "A drover must have a wife to qualify for his license. There is no one in my region . . . suitable."

Why is that? I wondered then and I wonder now. Why is there no one nearer his home fit to be his bride? Why has he to travel to find someone *suitable*? How am I *suitable*?

"Well," the teacup in Mam's hand had rattled as she spoke, "there is a great deal said about love and not much understood, Mr. Jenkins. Respect and kindness have a lot to recommend them."

He had nodded then, smiled, relieved that it was agreed. This was to be no love match.

Now he takes off his hat and holds it, too tight, in his hands, his long fingers turning it restlessly. His sandy hair is unruly, beginning to fall into curls at his collar, and in need of cutting. His gaze cannot settle on anything nor anyone.

"A fine morning for it, Mrs. Pritchard," he says. Mam agrees. Now he puts his eyes on me. "You look . . . very well, Morgana."

Is that the best he can do?

"Shall we go in?" Mam is anxious to get this done before I take it into my mind to bolt. She still has a firm hold on my arm.

Inside, old Mrs. Roberts stands next to the pitifully small floral displays. Mam oohs and aahs and thanks her. Reverend Thomas is all welcomes and delighteds. Mam puts me where I am to stand and Cai Tomos Jenkins stands beside me. I will not look at him. I have nothing to say to him.

The reverend starts up his words and I go to another place. Somewhere wild and high and free, untroubled by the silliness of men and their plans. There is a piece of hill above Cwmdu so steep that even the sheep won't tread there. The surface is neither grass nor rock, but shifting shale that defies the hold of foot or hoof. To climb to the top you have to lean sideways into the slope, let your feet slip down half a pace for each you ascend. No good will come of fighting the mountain. You have to work in harmony with it. Be patient, be accepting of its unsettling ways, and it will slowly bear you up to the summit. And at the summit you will be made anew. Such vistas! Such distances! Such air that has not been breathed by damp lungs, or sucked in by furnace or fire. Air that fills your soul as well as your body.

"And do you, Morgana Rhiannon Pritchard, take this man to be your husband . . . ?"

At the mention of my name I am pulled back into the chapel with a speed to make me dizzy.

"Morgana?" Mam puts her hand on my arm once more. Something is expected of me. She turns to Reverend Thomas, imploring.

He treats me to a smile so unsuited to being there I wonder it does not slip off his face.

"I know you cannot speak, child," he says.

"*Does* not," Mam corrects him. "She can, Reverend, or at least, she could when she was a very small child. At present, she does not."

She omits to tell him to exactly how many years "at present" applies.

The smile falters a little, leaving his eyes and remaining only around his wet mouth.

"Quite so," says he. Then, louder and slower, "Morgana, it is necessary that we know you consent to be Mr. Jenkins's wife. Now, when I ask again, if you agree, just nod, as clearly as you are able."

Why does he assume silent to be the same as simple? I feel all eyes upon me now. The reverend speaks a few lines more, and then leaves a gap for my response. There is a sound in my head like the waterfall up at Blaencwm when the river is in full spate. The heat of my mother's short breath reaches me. It is not the breath of a well woman. I know this. And, knowing this, I nod.

I turn and look at my husband. He smiles down at me, a faltering gesture of friendliness as he slips the narrow band of gold onto my finger.

"Excellent!" cries Reverend Thomas, hastily declaring us man and wife and snapping his good book shut with a puff of dust to seal my fate.

I grind my teeth. The door of the chapel flies open with a bang as it hits the wall. The reverend exclaims at the suddenness of the wind, of how abruptly the weather can change this time of year. A fierce rush of air disturbs the interior, rattling the hymnals in the pews, and tearing petals from the more delicate flowers.

I turn my gaze from a startled Cai Jenkins. I feel my mother's disapproval upon me.

She is younger than he recalls, somehow. Perhaps it is the white dress. At eighteen she is a woman, after all. The distance in age between them is but a few years, even if those years have been, for him, long and slow. Although not uncommon, twenty-five is young to be a widower. He thinks that she is smaller, too. Her frame almost frail. Her mother assured him she is strong, but she looks for all the world as if an October wind up at Ffynnon Las would blow her off her feet. Still, it is the start of summer now. She will have time to settle before winter comes to test her. To test them both.

After the uncomfortably brief ceremony the three ride in the trap to Morgana's cottage. The journey is short and they complete it without a word beyond the directions her mother gives him. The little house sits on the end of a row of four farm laborers' dwellings, each with a small garden to the front. Cai waits outside with the pony as the two women fetch his bride's possessions. A bundle of clothing tied with string, a wooden crate, and a patchwork quilt make up the trousseau. Cai secures them in the well of the trap and stands tactfully back as mother and daughter say their farewells.

"Morgana, remember to dress warmly, and do not venture far from the farm. It will take time for you to become familiar with the land about your new home."

Morgana nods dismissively.

"Treat the hills with respect, child." She pulls the girl's shawl tighter around her narrow shoulders. "There is not a person on God's earth cannot be beaten by sudden weather or hidden bog. Not even you." She shakes her head and ceases her admonitions. Placing a finger beneath her daughter's chin she tilts her face toward her own. "Morgana, this is for the best."

Still the girl will not meet her mother's eye.

"If you are as good a wife as you have been a daughter, then Cai Jenkins is indeed a fortunate man, *cariad*."

Now Morgana looks up, her eyes brimming with hot tears. Cai shuffles his feet, a reluctant witness to such a painful parting. Morgana throws her arms around her mother, holding her close and tight, sobbing silently onto her shoulder. Cai watches Mair close her eyes against her own tears. He sees clearly now, in the unforgiving clarity of the morning sun, and in the intensity of the woman's sorrow, that there is a deathly shadow clouding her pinched features. He wonders at the love a parent has for her child that could cause her to give her up when her own need is so acute. He remembers Mair's wariness of him when first he approached her concerning Morgana. It was understandable, the reputation of drovers being mixed at best. For the most part they are seen as wild, tough men, whose traveling sets them apart from others. Most have a name for being solitary, and even a little mysterious. After all, many living in farming communities will never venture farther than the horizon they can see from their window; who knows what mischief and shocking deeds the drovers become involved in on their journeys? And who would trust a man given to sleeping in the field with his cattle, or frequenting inns, night after night, no doubt meeting women who are charmed by the romance of their trade? It had been no easy task to persuade Mair that the head drover, *porthmon,* was different. That *he* was different. True, he is inexperienced, and this will be his first year in the role. But he has earned it. His father, and grandfather, were *porthmon* before him. It had always been accepted he would follow in their footsteps. It is not a given right, not an inheritance they could pass to him as a certainty, for there would be others who coveted the post. But tradition, habit, common sense, even, demand that the honor continues within the family. After all, if a man is left a good farm and he is known to be an able, trustworthy farmer, it is a fair foundation for the making of a *porthmon.* Ffynnon Las had built a reputation as a farm with a herd to be proud of, and had supplied cattle to feed the English hunger for roast beef for two generations. Cai assisted his father on many droves, working the herd, living the life of the traveling cattleman for several weeks every year since he was a teenager. He married Catrin, and on his father's passing it was expected that he would take over. But then Catrin had died, and everything changed. For no man can be head drover unless he has a wife, a *living* wife, and a homestead to return to. The position of *porthmon* will put him in a position of great trust in the locality. Aside from the livestock, people will place in his hands deeds of sale, items of value, and important transactions for him to handle on their behalf when he reaches London at the end of the drove. Many living in such remote areas as Tregaron will never venture beyond the parish, let alone into another country. The drove provides an opportunity for commerce and communication with a different world. Marriages are arranged. Properties change hands. Heirlooms are sold. And all proceeds are given to the head drover, to the *porthmon,* for safekeeping and delivery. Such riches might prove a sore temptation for a rootless man, the reasoning behind the law lies, but a man with a wife and farm hostage, well, he will come home.

At last his new bride steps up into the trap. She has changed from her wedding gown into clothes the color of the dry mountain earth. She looks less delicate now, but no less small. Cai registers, and is surprised by, a minute thrill at the closeness of her as she settles beside him. He turns his attention to Mair, who has about her now an air of resolute determination.

"From this moment Morgana is in my care," he assures her, "you need not be concerned."

Mair nods, handing him a cloth-wrapped cheese and some bread.

"And you?" Cai asks. "How will you fare without your daughter?"

A flash of anger passes across Mair's face. Cai knows the question is unfair, and that there is no satisfactory answer to it, and yet he could not stop himself asking. Why, he wonders. For whose benefit? To salve whose conscience?

At last Mair says, "I am content to know my daughter is settled."

"She will be well regarded at Ffynnon Las," he tells her. He sees that this gives her some comfort. He knows it is what she wishes to believe. During the months in which the match had been arranged he had made it his business to discover what he could about the pretty, silent girl who had caught his eye on the drove of the year before. He had been able to discover little, beyond that her father had upped and left when she was small, she worked with her mother at the large dairy farm in Cwmdu, and that Morgana has not spoken since she was a young child. His inquiries at the inn had yielded scant information; a few words regarding her affinity with horses, her willingness to work hard with her mother, her calming touch with the herd, and, of course, her wordlessness. But Cai had noticed something. Something telling in the responses he had gained. For each and every one of them had been preceded by a pause. No matter whom he questioned, there was always a slight but unmistakable hesitation before the speaker would deliver their opinion. As if they struggled to find the right words. As if there was something they were *not* saying. In these fleeting pauses, in these in-breaths, Cai is convinced, lies the truth about Morgana.

He picks up the reins, and with a click of his tongue the little horse sets off at a lively trot, seemingly unhampered by the extra weight he must pull. Morgana twists in her seat, waving at the lonely figure of her mother whose hand eventually falls to her side. Then the road turns a bend and she can be seen no more.

They are soon following the course of the Usk. The great river is to their left as they travel up the broad valley, the majestic mountains on either side of them. A buzzard circles, climbing on the warm, rising air of the cloudless day, its cry as sharp as its claws. Cai glances sideways. His new wife has dry eyes now, but her countenance appears stricken. He is aware there is nothing he can say that will lift the weight of her heart at this moment, and yet he falls to speaking.

"We will stop at Brecon overnight. We can reach Ffynnon Las by tomorrow afternoon easy with going like this," he says, indicating the smooth, hard surface of the track. "It is a good road. People have drovers to thank for that, see? Not that they do. No, they'll more likely enjoy complaining if it rains before the drove and the herd poach the wet ground to soup. Even that is only a temporary inconvenience, mind. Rest of the year the road is as you see it. For the benefit of all." He is irritated by his own need to fill the silence with chatter. It is a habit he knows he must break free of if their life together is to be tolerable. After all, her silence was one of the things that drew him to her in the first place. He is still unsure why. When Catrin was alive they enjoyed stimulating conversation. She had been expert at teasing him and then laughing at his blustering. He wonders if he will ever hear Morgana laugh. It seems unlikely. He slips his hand into his jacket pocket and considers taking out the small gift he has for her. The cotton and ribbon in which it is wrapped is soft against his warm fingers. He had spent many happy hours carving the little wooden lovespoon for his new bride. Tradition would have had him give it to her upon their engagement, but the opportunity had not presented itself. He had thought to give it to her on their wedding day instead, but a shyness overcomes him, and the moment does not seem right.

Their route takes them up the precipitous climb over the last of the Black Mountains through the village of Bwlch, perched on its rocky summit. By the time they have scaled the hill the pony is laboring, its pace erratic, its head low as it leans into the collar. Cai knows the animal will not falter, but will convey them safely to the top. There is a spring-fed trough at the side of the road. He steadies the pony to a halt and jumps from the trap.

"We'll let him rest awhile," he tells Morgana.

She, too, steps down, turning at once so that she can take in the final view of Cwmdu, far in the valley below. The last of home. Cai leads the pony to the trough where it drinks in deep gulps, its ears moving in rhythm with each replenishing swallow of sparkling water. He takes a tin cup from the trap and fills it, passing it to Morgana, before unwrapping the food her mother supplied. The two eat and drink in silence. He finds himself watching her and notices that she does not once look at him. It is as if he is of no consequence to her whatsoever. How long, he wonders, will it take to change that? A whisper of a mountain breeze tugs at her night-black hair. She wore it upon her head for the wedding, but now it hangs loose down her back with the sides pinned up, like a girl. From behind the hedge comes the bleating of a lamb, momentarily separated from its mother, its protestations loud and panic filled. The ewe's low reply summons it, and quiet descends once again. Cai is unaccustomed to remaining wordless in company, and yet he finds it curiously calming. Clearly Morgana does not require the near ceaseless chatter so many women of his acquaintance seem compelled to engage in. If he can only still his own mind, only learn to resist uttering the thoughts which speed through his head, perhaps he too can find peace in such quiet. Since he lost Catrin, since the body blow of grief at her passing, he has found only loneliness and lack in silence. Noticed only the absence of love and companionship. But it would be true to say, also, and this he has been all too aware of, that he has been equally bereft, equally lonely, equally alone even, when in the company of others. There is, hidden somewhere deep within him, a very small, fragile hope that with Morgana, things might be different.

Later that afternoon they arrive at the Drover's Arms on the western side of the market town of Brecon. Dusk is already tingeing the whitewash of the modest building with pink. Cai passes a coin to the lad to stable the pony, and he and Morgana carry her luggage inside. The inn has a large room downstairs furnished simply with high-backed wooden settles by the fireplace and benches running along tables. There is a low bar at one end, formed by a trestle, with barrels, flagons, and tankards behind it. It is early in the evening, so that the room is empty save for a solitary snoozing farmer by the unlit fire. The innkeeper, a genial, round-faced man, greets Cai warmly.

"Jenkins, m'n!" He grasps his hand and pumps it vigorously. "'Tis early in the season to be having a visit from the likes of you."

"Ah, Dafydd, I'm not come here as a drover this day." He knows some further explanation is expected of him, but the look on Morgana's face prevents him uttering such words as *wedding* or *bride*. He fancies she is relieved when he merely requests accommodation for the night and some supper, affecting ignorance of his friend's obvious curiosity.

They are shown upstairs to a low-ceilinged room scarcely large enough to accommodate the bed within it. When they are alone Cai hastens to put Morgana's mind at rest.

"I will spend some time with Dafydd," he tells her. "He's a keen talker who requires only to be listened to. I need not tell him of our . . . well, there we are. I will have some supper sent up to you."

Morgana looks at him, her dark eyes wide and slightly fierce, and her question as plain as if she has spoken the words aloud.

"Be at ease," Cai tells her. "I will stay late in the bar, see. I will not . . . disturb you."

She nods and lowers her gaze. He nods, too, even though she is not watching him, but is busy lifting the lid on her crate. He peers over her shoulder and is surprised to see that the box contains books.

"Oh, you can read?" He colors at the expression his question draws from her. "Of course, why not? And English as well as Welsh, I see. Very good. Yes, that's very good." He backs away, relieved to be able to leave her, already anticipating the further relief a tankard of ale will bring him.

He closes the door behind him and at last I am alone again. His earnest good intentions tire me. Mam would say I should be grateful, should be pleased to have a considerate husband. But I am not pleased. I do my best to keep my inner turmoil from revealing itself to others through my countenance, but it must surely be discernable, at least to him. And here I stand, trapped in this room, a bride alone on her wedding night. He has assured me I will not be *disturbed*. For that much I am grateful. What does he expect of me? Tonight the company of men contents him. I cannot convince myself such restraint will continue once he has me installed in his own home.

I shall look at Dada's books to distract myself from my situation. There are two candles, and still some light from the fading day. He was surprised to discover the contents of my crate. He draws the conclusion that I am able to read, and it surprises him. Indeed I can, though I am less able to write. Does he, too, consider me simple? Would he have married a simpleton? I must think not. He did appear pleased to learn I am not entirely without schooling. I was permitted to attend school for a while, and I have Mam to thank for that, as for all else. It was she who insisted I be given a place at our local elementary school.

"But, Mrs. Pritchard," the weary schoolmaster, Mr. Rees-Jones, had attempted to dissuade her, "surely the girl cannot be expected to learn, given her . . . affliction."

"Morgana is not afflicted, sir. Only silent."

"My point exactly. If she cannot form the sounds of the letters, how can she learn them? If I cannot hear her read, how can I correct her? If she cannot answer questions, how can she learn?"

"She can listen, Mr. Rees-Jones. Is that not how Our Lord's disciples learned?"

He had offered no response to this save a pursing of his thin, dry lips. I was given a place, in as much as I was permitted to attend. That was the extent of Mr. Rees-Jones's willingness to accommodate me. My seat was at the back of the schoolroom. I was equipped with neither chalk nor slate and never instructed in the art of writing. I was, however, allowed to listen, and to let my eyes follow words on the page of any book not already taken. I listened and I watched, and slowly the patterns on the paper began to reveal their mystery to me. How I longed to know their secrets. Oh, what joy that would have been. To be able to enter the minds of others, to hear their thoughts as clearly as if they were whispering in my ear. Not minds formed from a lifetime of working the fields, nor dulled by the noise of the loom, but higher minds. Minds given to ideas and imaginings beyond my small world. Mr. Rees-Jones cared not what progress I did or did not make. He had, 'tis true, no satisfactory way of measuring it, after all. But Mam saw it. She watched me curl my feet beneath me on the rug in front of the fire and read by the light of the flames. She witnessed my quiet concentration as I followed what was written and turned each page with reverent care, even though I had to struggle to decipher what was there.

"Morgana," she once said, "I declare the only time I ever see you still is when you have a book in your hand." And she smiled, pleased at my modest achievement. Pleased at such a normal talent. Pleased, I suspect, that she had been proved right.

Alas my schooling did not continue long enough for me to complete my learning. The schoolmaster's tolerance of me, it transpired, was a fragile thing. One dark winter's day when the snow lay thick on the ground, shortly after my tenth birthday, a new boy joined the class. His family had come recently into the area, his father being a well-regarded cattleman brought into the employ of Spencer Blaencwm to tend his herd of Pembrokeshires. Ifor was his only child and had clearly been indulged in all manners possible every day of his life. His body was plump with these indulgences. Beneath his garish ginger hair his face was round and red, his expression permanently expectant, as if waiting to see in what ways people might please him next. Being new to our school he encountered what must have been unfamiliar hostility. The other children disliked his overfed appearance, his self-important bearing, his evident belief that the world existed for his advantage above all else. For all their showering him with gifts and pleasures, his parents had failed to furnish him with the ability to make friends. Adrift in the choppy waters of the schoolroom, bewildered by the lack of interest he was shown, Ifor resorted to selecting a target for abuse; a child who, in his opinion, would best serve to reveal himself in a good light. For his purposes this required someone more an outsider than he. Someone apart from the others. It was his misfortune, as much as my own, that his eye lighted upon me.

For a while I endured his jibes and sneers without response. It was not, let it be said, the first time I had encountered such treatment. People fear what they do not understand, and that fear can make brutes of them. Ifor, though, had not the wit to be frightened. Better for him if he had. Each day he prodded and poked and jested at my expense. Each day he won an inch more ground in his battle for position in the class. And each day my patience grew thinner.

On that winter morning, when a weak sun glowed dully in a colorless sky, Mr. Rees-Jones sent us outside for some air and exercise to quell our restlessness. Ifor seized the moment. He was seated on a low bench beneath the schoolroom window, a thick muffler making him look even fatter than usual, his plump backside spreading widely on the snow-dusted seat. He called out to me, a sneer already arranged on his face.

"Don't make too much *noise,* Morgana. Mr. Rees-Jones doesn't like *noise,* doesn't like *talking.* Oh! I forgot—you can't talk, can you? Too stupid to speak."

One or two of the other children began to smile, pausing in their games to watch the fun. Fun made at my expense.

"Sshh, now, Morgana!" Ifor grew bolder. "You are disturbing everyone with your silly chattering. What's that you say? It can't be you because you are too dim to speak? Dim and dumb! Dim and dumb!" he chanted, his cheeks flushing. "Morgana Dim-and-Dumb, that's what we should call you. Stupid Miss Morgana Dim-and-Dumb!"

On and on he went, the chant gathering strength as others joined in, relishing the cruel song so that the air was soon full of the sound of their mocking. And Ifor's eyes grew brighter, his chest puffed up with pleasure at his own cleverness. It would not do. Really, it would not.

I wanted to be somewhere else. I might have chosen to let my eyelids fall, to let the voices grow distant, and to send my mind somewhere quiet and free. But I did not. Not on this occasion. This time my anger grew inside me, built into something hard and fierce and hot until it must come out or else I would be burned up by it, consumed by it completely. I breathed in, feeling the breath fuel the flames of my fury. I faced my tormentor, my eyes wide, holding his own gaze, a gaze which faltered as it glimpsed the anger within me. I did not once look away from him, not when the heavy snow on the roof above where he sat started to tremble, not when the other children noticed and fell silent, not even when, with a brief rumble and a swoosh, the snow slipped from the tiles, hurtled to the ground, and landed squarely upon Ifor, covering him entirely. Now the silence was broken by gleeful laughter, and the children pointed and chortled at the wretched boy—the snowboy, for such he was now. He struggled and with a wail emerged, snow clinging to his clothes and caking his eyelashes. The laughter increased. He looked wonderfully absurd, standing their wailing like an infant, the tables turned so that he was the object of ridicule. Now he could see what it felt like.

Of course, the noise brought Mr. Rees-Jones running. He threw wide the door, halting abruptly on the threshold, taking in the snow-encrusted boy. He looked first at the other boys and girls, who fought to stifle their hilarity, and then at me. He narrowed his eyes in a way I did not care for. Clearly, he did not care for the manner in which I regarded him either. He had been reluctant to admit me to his precious school in the first place. As the months had passed he had became increasingly intolerant of my presence, and my conflict with Ifor did nothing to improve matters.

Things came to a head a few weeks after the incident of the little avalanche. We had been set to work on some tedious mathematical equations, and the early spring sunshine on the tall windows was compounding our suffering, making the room unbearably hot and stuffy. One of the older girls made a plea for the window to be opened and Mr. Rees-Jones gave me the task of using the long, hooked pole to reach up and release the catch. As I crossed the room, however, Ifor stuck out his foot. I tripped and was sent sprawling onto the floor at the very feet of the schoolmaster. Again I endured mocking laughter. I snatched up the pole and, standing on tiptoe, used it to unfasten the latch. I was supposed to settle the window into the metal holding strap, which would allow but a few inches of air. However, it seemed to me this would barely be enough to sustain one of the soft grey pigeons in the yard outside, let alone a roomful of pupils. Or a roomful of pigeons, thought I. The image I conjured in my mind of a flock of the flapping birds swooping and unloading their droppings around the classroom, and particularly upon Ifor, was simply too glorious to resist. Of course, Mr. Rees-Jones blamed me for letting the window fall wide open. He held me responsible for letting the pigeons into the room. And he could not help but notice that I alone was free from the white and grey splodges the panicked birds deposited upon everyone else in the room, himself included. He was never able to say how their unusual behavior was my fault, but it didn't stop him wanting rid of me. When Mam collected me from school that day she was told plainly that I was no longer welcome to attend.

2.

As they near the end of their journey and the trees at the boundary of his land come into view, Cai feels a nervousness stir his stomach. What will Morgana make of Ffynnon Las? He is confident she will not be disappointed by the size of the house, or the scale of the farm, or the quality of his herd, but will she see the place as her home? He cannot know how much information her mother has passed on to her about his status. He cannot know, even, if such things matter to the girl. He does know, however, that she is a long way from the only home she has ever known, away from her mother, and thrown into a new life with a stranger. He does not want to remain a stranger to her. Indeed, whatever the case he put to Mair about needing a wife for his drover's license—which is nonetheless a fact—he knows that he does want, hope for, expect? No, that would be too strong a word, but *wish* for a connection with Morgana that will go beyond a contract. Beyond an arrangement.

He recalls the first time he noticed her, all those long, lonely months ago. The drove had halted overnight at Crickhowell, and had the good fortune to arrive on market day. Having settled the herd, and having no obligations beyond that of drover, rather than *porthmon,* he had wandered into the little town to divert himself by looking at the stalls. It was late in the afternoon, and people were for the most part starting for home. Some of the traders were packing up for the day. However, he found a small covered market area where several stallholders remained, their wares piled high on sturdy tables or handcarts, still hoping for further customers. In one corner was a short, low bench covered in gingham, upon which were a half-dozen rounds of soft cheese, these being all that had not sold.

Morgana was standing behind the bench. She was wearing a plain cotton dress and crisp white apron, which made her look clean and wholesome, yet there was something disheveled about her. Her hair was insecurely pinned upon her head, with dark curls escaping here and there, giving the impression the whole lot could shake loose at any moment and cascade about her slender shoulders. He remembers rather hoping it would do so. Even though she was standing still, her restlessness struck him at once. It was as if she could barely contain herself, so keen was she to be released from her post, to be somewhere else, somewhere, he fancied, freer and more open. Her eyes would not settle on anyone, and when the town clock struck five she started violently, seizing on the sound as a signal to, at last, pack away and be released from the chore of watching the stall.

In her haste to wrap the cheeses one slipped from her grasp. It rolled across the flagged floor of the marketplace, collecting dust and dirt as it wound its way between booted feet and table legs. Morgana dashed after it, the laughter and shouts of the market-goers goading her on. She was forced to drop to her knees and scramble beneath a fruit stall to retrieve the runaway cheese. Two men, clearly the worse for a day's drinking, made loud remarks at her expense. Uncalled-for comments which were both insulting and cruel, it seemed to Cai. He pressed forward through the small crowd, hastening to Morgana's aid, but before he could reach her she herself had retaliated. Grasping the ankle of the more unstable drunkard, she wrenched his foot sideways, toppling him into his fellow and sending them both crashing through the nearby fish and game stall. A roar of laughter went up from the onlookers, as the pair thrashed about amid trout heads and ripe pheasants. Morgana leapt to her feet, clutching the errant cheese. The meaner of the two drinkers lurched to his knees, spitting further abuse at her. Cai held his breath, waiting for the young woman's reaction. She narrowed her eyes, lifted the cheese high, and then brought it down with considerable force over her target's head. He reeled backward, dazed, the crumbly cheese falling about his ears in clods, the crowd revelling in the hilarity of the moment. Cai found himself laughing, too, until he realized that he was under Morgana's gaze. He turned to her then, looking deep into her dark, bright eyes, and in that moment, in that glimpse, he would swear he felt something pass between them. What? A flare of attraction? A fleeting flame of lust? He could not name it, but whatever it was, it reached him, it moved him. And he was certain Morgana had felt it, too.

He glances across at her. This morning she has chosen to sit opposite rather than beside him, the better to balance the trap, he suspects. He likes that he is able to look at her more easily, but misses the closeness of having her next to him. He found it surprisingly difficult, the night before, to stay so long talking with Dafydd, knowing that Morgana was upstairs. But he had deemed it sensible to leave her alone. He would not force his attentions on her. He did not want their coming together to be an act of duty or of right. He would be patient. When he had, at last, crept into the small bedroom, the sight of her sleeping had stirred in him not passion but sympathy. She looked so vulnerable. He had allowed himself to watch her for a moment longer before settling onto the lumpy armchair beneath a wool blanket. There was, after all, no rush. They had their whole lives together.

"There!" He is unable to hide his own delight at seeing the farm again. "That is Ffynnon Las." He points as he speaks, at a collection of stone buildings still some distance away. He watches Morgana's reaction. He is already beginning to be able to read the minute changes in her expression. She does not gasp nor gawp but her eyebrows lift a fraction, her eyes refocusing, her lips parting the tiniest bit. The pony, sensing home, quickens its pace, and soon they are turning up the driveway to the farm. Now Morgana becomes quite animated. She turns in her seat, twisting this way and that the better to take in the sloping meadows, the oak copse, the stream-fed pond with its feathery willow, the rise of the hill behind the house, the sheltered yard of barns, and, at last, the house itself.

Ffynnon Las stands as it has done for more than a century, its broad back to the mountain to which it clings, its wide frontage, two stories high, with tall windows positioned to face southeast, to greet the morning sun and shelter from the northerly winds of winter. It is not a pretty house, but a handsome one. Its proportions are not grand but are generous, and not designed for function alone. The blue-grey stone of which the building is constructed is softened by a climbing honeysuckle which scrambles unchecked above the front door, fringing the ground-floor windows with narrow leaves and blooms of palest yellow. Even the dark slate roof shimmers cheerfully beneath the summer sun. The entrance is approached through a little iron gate and along a flagstone path, either side of which are small patches of unkempt lawn, and beds of roses and shrubs apparently happy in their state of near neglect.

Cai stops the fidgeting pony outside the front gate.

"Well?" he cannot resist asking. "What do you think of the place?"

He can see by her expression that she is surprised. What had she imagined, he wonders. Some lowly longhouse, perhaps? Nothing more than a croft for her to share with the beasts? He finds he is quietly pleased by her surprise.

Morgana turns to him and he fancies she is about to smile broadly when the moment is interrupted by a raucous barking from within the house. The front door is flung wide and Cai's two corgis come scampering out, the size of their voices much greater than the little dogs themselves. They run around the trap, circling it in a woofing blur of fox-red and chalk-white fur, their short legs and bushy tails moving ceaselessly. Now Morgana looks truly amazed.

Cai laughs. "That'll do, Bracken! Meg, stop your noise! Not the sort of dogs you are used to, I suppose?"

She shakes her head, hopping down from the cart to allow the excited creatures to greet her properly.

"You won't find so many collies up here," he explains. "Corgis are heelers, better with the cattle, see?"

Cai enjoys watching her obvious delight in his dogs and it is a minute or so before he becomes aware he, too, is being watched. He turns to see Mrs. Jones standing in the doorway.

"Cai Jenkins," she shakes her head at him, "just how long are you planning to let your bride be bothered by those wretched creatures before you show her into her new home? *Duw, bach,* what are we to do with you?"

Heulwen Eluned Pryce-Jones, who has always insisted on being plain Mrs. Jones to all and everyone, is a woman as round as she is tall, and as good-natured as it is possible for a person to be. Her width bears testament to her love of good food, just as the lines on her face and dimples in her cheeks speak of her consistent cheerfulness. As always, she is wrapped in a spotless apron, her mop cap neat and crisply starched, a ready smile lighting up eyes that belie the threescore winters they have seen. Not for the first time Cai questions whether or not he would have survived the dark days following Catrin's death if it had not been for Mrs. Jones's determination to see to it that he did.

Without thinking, he reaches out a hand to Morgana. "Come and meet Mrs. Jones," he tells her.

She stops petting the dogs and stands up. She hesitates only briefly before taking his hand and allowing herself to be led down the path to the house. Cai is startled by the feel of her weightless hand in his and finds that, when the moment comes to do so, he is reluctant to let it go.

"Mrs. Jones, may I present to you my wife, Morgana Jenkins. Morgana, this is my aunt and my housekeeper, Mrs. Jones."

"Ooh, there's pretty you are! Pardon my manners," Mrs. Jones bobs a curtsey with some difficulty, her stout legs unhelpfully stiff. Morgana hastens forward to help her up, shaking her head, clearly embarrassed to be shown such deference. The two women look at one another closely. At last Mrs. Jones claps her hands together in glee. "Well, *Duw, Duw,*" she says quietly, " 'tis about time happiness came to Ffynnon Las." She beams at Cai, who looks at his feet.

"I'll fetch the luggage," he says.

"Never mind luggage!" Mrs. Jones is scandalized. "Isn't there something else you should be doing?" When he looks blankly back at her she continues, "Well, carry your new bride over the threshold, Mr. Jenkins!"

Cai opens his mouth to protest. He looks at Morgana and notices her take the smallest step backward. Would she really want him to do that? To take her in his arms and carry her into the house? Like a proper bride. His hesitation stretches the moment into awkwardness, so that now he could not make such a flamboyant gesture, even though he would like to. Instead he mutters something about the journey having been long and tiring and hurries back to unload the trap.

For a second I think he will do it; will step forward, sweep me off my feet, and transport me across the threshold as tradition dictates. But he does not. What am I to make of his reluctance to hold me? Can it be that he does not see me as a wife in all senses? Am I merely a necessity, then? A requirement of his status as head drover? Is that to be my purpose in life and no more? I might not want his attentions forced upon me, but that does not mean I wish to exist in some manner of limbo, neither maid nor mistress. What can his intentions for me be?

I confess to being astonished by Ffynnon Las. It is not the humble farmstead I had supposed it to be, but a house of some importance. And a housekeeper! It seems the lack of meat on his bones is not a result of the absence of a cook after all. And Mrs. Jones herself clearly relishes her food. Why does he remain so slight, so insubstantial, despite this good woman's care? Seeing that I am not to be carried into my new home and that my husband is occupied with the luggage, it is she who takes it upon herself to bid me enter.

"Come in, and welcome. The Lord knows it is we women who must act while men dither."

She leads me into a wide hall which has a sweeping staircase of polished wood rising from it. To all sides there are doors, so that I do not know how I will ever know my way. What use can one man have for so many rooms? I am taken into what Mrs. Jones insists is the parlor. The tall shutters are open so that sunlight floods the room. There is an ample fireplace, neatly laid, and a sumptuous couch, and a ticking grandfather clock, but the most striking piece of furniture is an enormous oak dresser which displays more china than I have ever seen in my life. The patterns and colors on each plate and cup are quite exquisite, so that I step closer, lost in the swirls and twists of briar roses, ivies, trailing blossoms, and coiling vines.

Cai comes to stand behind me.

"You like Catrin's china, then? She was so proud of it. 'Twas her mother's, see?" He pauses to gaze around the room as if seeing it properly for the first time. "I don't come in here much. I'm not given to entertaining."

An awkwardness joins us in the room and he hurries out, Mrs. Jones on his heel, both determinedly telling me of the various comforts the house has to offer. I am led from room to room until I am dizzy with gazing about me and begin to feel stifled by the stale air, longing for the outdoors. And there is something else, something which tugs at the hem of my attention. I sense it as I stand in the doorway of the master bedroom. There is a coldness in the air, and a strange heaviness to it, which seems to have no obvious cause. I have little time to consider this curiosity further, however, as my guides usher me on. At last we arrive in the kitchen. It is clear, whatever might have been the case in the past, that this is now where life is lived at Ffynnon Las. The fire in the well-equipped range is lit and throws out a welcoming warmth. There is a long scrubbed table, an assortment of chairs, a high-backed settle, hooks for meat and pots, and a smaller dresser sporting only plain pottery and some pewter. In the window there is a cushioned seat, worn and furry with dog hairs. Indeed, the minute they gain admittance, both corgis take up their positions, noses pressed against the glass, eyes brightly scanning the approach for intruders.

"Well, now," says Cai, "I must check on the stock. I'll leave you to . . ." he hesitates, as unsure as I am as to precisely what it is I am to do. ". . . Mrs. Jones could show you where things are . . ." he trails off, knowing very well that I have just seen where everything is. She attempts to rescue him.

"Perhaps Mrs. Jenkins might like to rest awhile?" she offers. "After her journey."

He looks at me and I know that he knows I am not tired. I have done nothing for two days, why would I rest? The discomfort in his eyes and the way he fidgets where he stands give him away. But still he says, "Of course. You'll want to put away your things. Rest . . . Mrs. Jones can help you prepare something for our meal." He gives up now, turning for the door. The open door. I clench my fists. The door slams shut.

"Oh!" cries Mrs. Jones. "What a draught do run through this house."

Cai looks back at me. He sees something in my face that makes him think, makes him consider. I hold his gaze. My mother's entreaties come into my head. *Do not be willful, Morgana. You must do as your husband wishes.* Must I? Must I stay in this pointlessly big house pretending I care to cook while he walks the hills? I tilt my head a little to one side, asking. Understanding lifts his features.

"Or would you prefer to accompany me, perhaps?"

I give the smallest of nods, and the door swings slowly open. Cai and Mrs. Jones stand catching flies as I stride past them, the corgis running at my feet.

We leave the house and cross the small meadow beside the house. The sun is so bright it causes the horizon to shimmer. I follow Cai and we scale the steep slope, leaning into the incline. The day is warm, but not unpleasantly so, and a soft breeze cools my skin as we ascend. The dogs scuttle ahead, noses down, big ears pricked, their tails flagging behind them. At first Cai fills our steps with chatter, but the farther we get from the house, and the nearer to the summit, the quieter he becomes. I do not think this is because he needs his breath for walking, for he has an easy gait practiced at climbing the mountains, and lean muscles I now see working beneath the thin cotton of his shirt. This is no real effort for him. Rather I think he is affected by his environment, at once calmed and stimulated by the freshness of the air and the limitlessness of our horizons. As am I.

We pass through another gateway, some distance above the house now, and the quality of the grass under our feet alters. No longer are there the lush green blades of the lower pasture. There are no flowering clovers here, but tough, wiry growth, tangled at the roots, clinging tightly to the thin layer of earth that covers the rocky hillside. The soil itself is peaty, with a spring in it that will turn to bog in places in the rains of autumn. I can smell the bitterness of the peat, almost taste it. As we at last crest the hill, skylarks whirr and flit beside us, alerting each other to our presence. Some way off to the north I hear the plaintive cry of the lapwing, its reedy upward notes seeming to ceaselessly question life and its own tenuous place in it. We negotiate a patch of sharp-edged rocks and Cai offers me his hand. Does he consider me so feeble, so fragile, as to require assistance to step over a small pile of stones? I remind myself he does not know me. It is not entirely unreasonable he should imagine me to be so . . . female. I let him take my hand. Just for a moment. Mam would be pleased.

Cai stops and raises his arm.

"Now, you can make out our boundary from here. Those Scots pines to the west, see? Then as far north as the beginning of Cwm Canon—you can see the color of the land changes where the bog starts. To the south, well, the meadows below the house you saw as we came up from Lampeter . . ."

He falls silent as he must surely realize I am not listening. I do not need words to direct me to see what surrounds me. What vistas! What landscape! Different from home, from the rocky escarpments and dramatic sweeps of the Black Mountains. Here are rolling uplands, with grazing to the very tops. We are well above the tree line, but I can see wooded valleys yonder, and here and there a tenacious rowan bush or twisted blackthorn punctuates the moorland. The ground spreads away, pale green with whiskery bents of tawny gold, patches of purple heather, clusters of gorse still flowering yellow, and whimberries low and broad-leafed, promising berries later in the year. The breeze is stiffer here, disturbing the tufty heads of the cotton grass which grows amid the damper patches of soil, where tiny streams and ancient springs will give a reliable supply of water, even in a summer drought. The only dwellings visible are far away, dolls' houses set upon the lower reaches of the hills or huddled together at the lee-ward foot of the mountains. A sudden, sharp cry above our heads makes us all, dogs included, look up. A flash of copper glinting in the sun, a fast-moving streak of color, at first too swift to be properly discerned, quickly reveals itself to be a sizable bird of prey.

"A red kite," Cai tells me. "There are plenty of them up here."

I am accustomed to sparrow hawks and buzzards but have never before seen a bird so striking in composition and color. I watch it until it has passed out of view.

"Shall we go on?" Cai asks me. "The herd will be near the dew ponds, shouldn't wonder."

I look at him and see my own excitement reflected back in his reaction to my face. I know I cannot hide how moved I am by this wondrous place. He smiles, pleased. And I smile back. He is surprised, I can tell.

"Aye," he agrees. "They are surely something special, these hills. Some people think the place bleak. Unwelcoming. Some call it 'the green desert,' 'tis so empty. For myself, well, I think no man could wish for better."

On this we are most definitely agreed. He seems reluctant to break the moment, but at last bids me follow him and continue our walk. A farther half mile brings us to another slope. Here we are traversing the side of a smaller, steeper hill, and the path is barely wide enough for a cart. At one point it turns quite sharply. As Cai walks he dislodges a stone which shoots off the track and bounces down the incline, all the way to the stony riverbed below. I had not realized how high we have climbed, and watching the rock disappear such a distance makes me feel giddy. It is not a cliff, as such, for the surface is covered in tenacious grass, but the angle would make it too steep to ride or even walk down, and to trip would mean descending the two hundred feet or so to the bottom without hope of stopping.

"Got to be careful here, mind," says Cai. "A cousin of mine lost his life being casual with that drop."

At last we arrive at the dew ponds, and the herd comes into view. I am unable to hide my surprise. These are not the large, dairy cattle I have been used to. They are much smaller, entirely black, their coats, even at this time of year, quite shaggy and rough, their horns short and sharp. They catch our scent on the breeze and raise their heads, shifting and turning to face us. As we draw closer one or two of them back away or hide themselves behind their bolder cousins. The whole group seem restless, to me, clearly agitated by the proximity of the two of us, and of the dogs, who set up a yapping which does nothing to quell the nerves of the beasts.

"Hush now, Meg! Bracken!" Cai adds a shrill whistle which quietens the little hounds and brings them to his side. The cattle wait, watching.

"They can be skittish," he tells me. "Never take their cooperation for granted, not a Welsh Black. They are hardy, mind. There's none other would do so well up here, in all weathers, on such sparse grazing." His expression softens, and I see more than pride written there. Affection, could it be? "The dogs will gather them easy enough, mind. You'll see."

I look from the comical, stumpy corgis to the powerful wary beasts and wonder that such a thing might be true. I step slowly forward toward the nearest young heifer. She snorts, lowering her broad head.

Be at ease, my crow black friend.

She hesitates, and then edges forward to sniff my upturned palm. I look back at Cai who smiles, surprise showing on his face. I find myself thinking that he is attractive when he smiles.

We leave the cattle and walk along the high ridge to where his other herd will be grazing. He did not make much of the fact that he is a breeder of Welsh Mountain ponies, but I am eager to see them, particularly if they are all as feisty and wild-looking as the little stallion who pulled our trap all the way from Cwmdu. But our journey is interrupted by the rattle of wheels down in the valley. The sound is incongruous up here, seeming to come from another life altogether. Cai shades his eyes against the sun and squints at the ribbon of road below. I, too, search and find a smart carriage and pair pulling into the driveway to Ffynnon Las. Cai's shoulders slump, only fractionally, but enough to be noticed. He catches me watching him.

"Mrs. Cadwaladr, with the Misses Cadwaladr no doubt. We must go down."

I hang back. I have no desire to leave the mountain, and certainly no wish to greet a carriage full of strangers. He pauses, aware of my reluctance. Even so he says, quite firmly, "We must go down."

By the time Cai and Morgana reach the house Mrs. Cadwaladr and her two daughters are already installed in the parlor awaiting the tea Mrs. Jones has bustled off to make.

"Ah, Mr. Jenkins. Forgive our calling unannounced. It is our natural impatience! We could not wait a moment longer to set eyes upon your new bride. And here she is! Oh! So very young. Child, step forward. Let us look at you. Well, *well*, Mr. Jenkins, what have you found for yourself here?"

Mrs. Cadwaladr, as is her habit, sports a bonnet overly decorated with ribbon, a dress overly fancy for the hour and occasion, and a quantity of rouge ill-advised for someone of a naturally ruddy coloring. Her choice of puce fabric, with her daughters dressed in paler imitations of her own outfit, is not a happy one. Cai is put in mind of a row of summer puddings. He attempts to make introductions, but is quickly drowned out by his visitor's loud exclamations.

"These are my girls, Bronwen and Siân. Young ladies of evident elegance and appeal, I am sure you will agree. Neither married as yet—'tis a mystery to us all. Say only that they are careful in their selection of a husband. Now, girl, tell me your name. Speak up, I cannot abide mumbling."

When Morgana gives no answer Cai hurries to explain.

"My wife . . . Morgana . . . does not speak, Mrs. Cadwaladr."

"Does not?" The woman is astonished. "Has she no tongue, perhaps? No capability of producing sound? Some childhood illness, maybe?" Her daughters crowd forward now, their curiosity provoked by the unexpected presence of an oddity.

"She has a voice," he tells her. "That is, she is able to speak but has not done so for many years."

This information is greeted by a stunned silence, as if everyone has now, for a brief moment, been robbed of the power of speech. Cai glances anxiously at Morgana and is pleased to see her raising her chin. The movement is fractional, but suggests courage, he feels.

"Well, Mr. Jenkins, I find this hard to comprehend. A man such as yourself, with all the qualities and attributes of a gentleman, and many an eligible young lady in the vicinity"—here Bronwen and Siân have the good grace to blush—"that you should encumber yourself with a person so . . . lacking."

Cai bristles.

"I do not regard myself as encumbered, Mrs. Cadwaladr. Nor do I consider Morgana in any way lacking. She has the ability to communicate, in her own manner, when it is required."

"Required?" Mrs. Cadwaladr is so unsettled she pulls a fan

from her bodice and begins flapping it in a way that is both agitated and agitating. "And when, pray, might it not be *required* of a wife, of the mistress of such a house, of a person, indeed, who intends taking any part in society, when might it *not* be required that she communicate? Forgive my bluntness, Mr. Jenkins, but I fear you have made a rare error of judgment, and one that I believe you will, in the passage of time, come to regret."

Cai is about to protest when they are joined by Mrs. Jones carrying a tray of tea. There is a deal of fuss as the refreshments are placed on the table and everyone finds somewhere to sit. The corgis cause some alarm by attempting to alight on Bronwen's lap. Cai sends the dogs out with the housekeeper. He catches Morgana's eye and nods at the teapot. Somewhat thrown, she nonetheless succeeds in filling cups and passing them around. Mrs. Cadwaladr does not take her eyes from the new Mrs. Jenkins for an instant.

"Ah, what pretty china. It belonged to your first wife, I believe? Such a tragedy. Catrin was so lively, so charming. I always enjoyed her company. And her conversation."

Siân and her sister stifle giggles. A frown settles on Morgana's face. Cai is not sure why, but now he feels nervous of her. She is, he decides, unpredictable. And whilst he himself does not care for his visitor or her vacuous offspring, she has a certain standing in the community, and, experience has taught him, such people can, if provoked, cause trouble. He clears his throat, ignoring her comment, and assumes the most cheerful tone of voice he can muster.

"Morgana, our guest is the wife of Reverend Emrys Cadwaladr. He is very well known hereabouts. His ministry is avidly followed. You will hear him preach come Sunday when we travel up to Soar-y-Mynydd chapel."

"Oh, you plan to take her out in company, Mr. Jenkins? Do you think that wise?" asks Mrs. Cadwaladr, her cup raised to her lips.

Cai feels the heat of anger rising within him and struggles to be civil.

"Naturally Morgana will attend chapel" is all he trusts himself to say.

His visitor smiles much, much too sweetly. "Well, if you insist. I expect she will particularly enjoy the singing," she says.

Cai cannot be certain, but thinking about it later he will believe he heard Morgana's teeth grinding just an instant before Mrs. Cadwaladr is taken by a fit of sneezing. A fit so vigorous, that she loses her grip on the teacup in her hand, causing it to upend and empty hot tea down her beribboned décolletage.

3.

Cai stirs, fitful, not asleep, and yet not properly awake. Instinctively he reaches out, his arm searching the other side of the bed. He finds only a cold, uninhabited space. Without opening his eyes he remembers, with a stab of pain still sharp after three long years. Catrin is dead. How long will his coming into consciousness each morning begin in this way, he wonders. His eyes spring open as a newer, brighter recollection comes to him. Morgana. He sighs, rubbing his eyes. Giving her her own room had seemed the right thing to do. The decent thing. The kind thing. Already he is questioning the wisdom of this decision. Last night, when he showed her to the room Mrs. Jones had taken such care to bedeck prettily, Morgana had seemed relieved, he thought. And why would she not? They live in modern times, after all. He would no more demand his rights as a husband from her than he would drag a woman in off the street. No, it is better this way. They will take time to get to know one another. She will have time to settle. Time to adjust to her new home and her new life. And, given that time, he hopes, affection will grow. But how long will such a process take? Might it have been simpler to bring her direct to the marriage bed and let proximity, the languor of sleep, and the closeness of the night assist their connection? She seems so very distant. So very shut off. Not just from him, he realizes, not particularly from him. Even so, he is concerned she will stay in her room along the hall forever if he does nothing to win her . . . her what? He is unsure of precisely what it is he expects of her. Love? Why should she love him? Hadn't he told her and her mother that Catrin had been his one true love, and that he had no romantic illusions about his match with Morgana? Perhaps the girl thinks he does not find her attractive. Perhaps she will wait for some sign from him, some alteration in his behavior, that suggests he desires her.

From outside, in the pond meadow, comes a yapping. The urgency of the bark suggests one of the corgis, Bracken, he thinks, is chasing a rabbit. But how does the dog come to be outside at such an early hour? Mrs. Jones went home after tea the previous day, her habit being to stay over only if the house would otherwise be empty. He has not heard the front door open or close, though it is heavy and customarily scrapes noisily against the flagstoned floor. Cai gets up, goes to the window, and opens the shutters.

The sight that greets him moves him in so many ways that he is left in absolutely no doubt as to his own regard for his new wife. Morgana, still in her white, sleeveless nightgown, her feet bare, her hair loose and wild, runs in the meadow, the dogs dancing with her. She is illuminated by the shimmering dawn sunlight, so that at moments her garment is entirely transparent, and at others she appears in silhouette. She runs playfully, without regard for how she might look, for how her appearance might seem to others. She runs with the joy of a free spirit, a child of the hills, a person utterly comfortable with her surroundings and her place in them. Cai has never seen anyone so beautiful. In that instant he feels such a longing for her, such an acute, basic need for her, that he is quickly ashamed, feeling both embarrassed by his desire and guilty for it. Somehow, however unreasonably, his response makes him feel that he is betraying Catrin. He shakes thoughts of her away. If he is to make a success of his marriage to Morgana, he will have to let Catrin go. And he will have to do more than wait to woo this wild creature of the elements who dances barefoot beneath the sunrise.

Hastily he washes, dresses, and goes downstairs. Mrs. Jones has left the larder well stocked. He puts a match to the expertly laid fire and swings the kettle arm over it to heat up. He fetches eggs and thick slices of bacon and sets about preparing breakfast. He cuts chunks of crusty bread and puts the board on the table. Years of living alone coupled with Mrs. Jones's determination that he should not waste away from hunger have made a tolerable cook out of him. Soon the kettle is whistling and the aroma of frying bacon fills the room. Cai grabs the kettle handle without using the quilted mitt and burns his palm. Cursing and shaking his hand he dashes across the room to the pail of water by the dresser and plunges his hand into it. He is still muttering oaths when he looks up and sees Morgana standing in the doorway, watching him, her face giving away her amusement.

"I was making us some breakfast," he says unnecessarily. The dogs scurry in to greet him, jumping up, almost knocking him over as he crouches over the bucket. "Meg, that'll do, now. Bracken, m'n, stop your nonsense." The dogs take advantage of the fact that he is so much nearer the floor than usual and persist in trying to climb onto his lap and lick his face, so that he is eventually put off balance. "Daft creatures!" he scolds them but cannot hide the laughter in his voice. Morgana comes to stand over him and he sees that she is laughing, too. Silent mirth shakes her bare shoulders, and her face is glowing. To his surprise she offers him her hand. He takes it, clambering to his feet, shaking off the dogs. Morgana takes his injured hand now and turns it over, examining the burn.

"'Tis nothing," he tells her. "My own fault. The mark will only last long enough to remind me not to be so foolish again." He does not wish to appear more stupid than he feels so he withdraws his hand, waving her toward the table. "Come, sit. The food is ready," he says, moving back to the range to dish up the bacon and eggs.

He takes his place opposite Morgana and pours her some tea. His strange new wife eats with undisguised relish. She devours every morsel on her plate, using her bread to mop up the last drop of golden yolk. Cai almost expects her to lick the platter, but she stops short of doing so. When she has finished she sits back in her chair and wipes her mouth with the back of her hand. Cai smiles, shaking his head. With her hair loose, unbrushed and tangled, her face flushed from running and from laughing, grease from the bacon smeared across her cheek, and her eyes bright from enjoyment of the meal, she looks as wild and uncivilized as it is possible to be. He has never seen a woman in such a condition.

"Well, well, my wild one, what is everyone going to make of you?"

She smiles broadly and gives a shrug that clearly says she gives not a tinker's cuss for what anyone thinks of her.

"I'm going to check on the ponies after breakfast. Would you like to come with me?"

She nods vigorously, eagerly getting to her feet.

"Whoa! Finish your tea first," he laughs, then adds, "Might be a good idea to put some clothes on, too. Don't want to frighten the horses, see?"

Morgana looks down at her nightdress, as if she has been oblivious, all this time, to her state of undress. She blushes becomingly.

The moment is interrupted by a knocking on the front door. Cai frowns, getting up.

"Who would be calling at this hour?" he asks, and goes to find out the identity of their unwelcome visitor.

He claims he is not given to entertaining and yet he has a ceaseless stream of visitors. He returns with a tall woman dressed in an expensive riding habit, complete with veiled hat. The outfit is made of a sumptuous wine-red velvet, which has the most beautiful luster to it. She is all elegance and grace and at once I feel uncomfortable. A moment before I was eating a delicious breakfast, in my new kitchen, cooked for me by my new husband, and I felt the first ticklings of happiness. Now I stand before this proud, womanly creature and feel like a girl caught somewhere she does not belong. Why did he bring her in here? Could he not have shown her into the parlor?

"Morgana, this is my good friend, Mrs. Isolda Bowen, from Tregaron. Isolda, this is Morgana," says he.

Just Morgana, is it? Not *my wife,* or *the new Mrs. Jenkins.* Not for his good friend Mrs. so-on-and-so-on. I have been demoted for her sake, it seems. What is she to him, this woman who imposes herself upon us at breakfast time?

"I am so very pleased to meet you, Morgana." She steps toward me, holding out a gloved hand which I must shake. "Please call me Isolda," says she. Now Cai is stumbling and mumbling about my not talking. Really, there are times he makes such a bad job of words himself I wonder he bothers. She still has hold of my hand and squeezes it tighter now, as if to convey some sort of sympathy or understanding, I suppose. I find her touch quite unpleasant, and am glad of the glove. There is something about her, something about this handsome, confident woman, that I do not like. There is a darkness inside her, despite her pleasing appearance.

"We were all so pleased to hear Cai had taken a new wife," says she, at last releasing my hand. I rub it against the skirt of my nightdress. Cai notices and frowns. "Your husband and I shared the affliction of grief at losing our first spouses," she goes on. "Of course my own dear husband departed this life many years ago, but still I like to think I was able to understand and to comfort Cai in his time of loss and sorrow."

The two exchange small smiles. Conspiratorial smiles. I am confused. Why did he not choose to marry his good friend Mrs. Bowen? They are clearly close. It would be obvious to a bat in a sack that she adores him. Why, then, did he not take her to be the new mistress of Ffynnon Las?

"*Duw,* where are my manners?" Cai exclaims suddenly, pulling out a chair for the woman. She sits, gracefully settling onto the wooden seat, laying her riding crop upon the table. "Perhaps you would like some tea?" he asks.

"Tea would be most welcome," says she.

Cai looks at me. I look at him. I take my place at the table and land heavily in my chair. She is *his* very good friend. Let *him* fetch her tea. He does so, clumsily. The burn on his hand is still troubling him, and he favors it awkwardly. Well, that is his fault. It is all his fault. If he had shown her into the parlor I might have been less wrong-footed, might have agreed to make the tea. She is not watching him but keeps her eyes on me. Her gaze is unsettling. Did he ever, truly, find comfort in her presence? I have the sensation of earwigs ascending my spine. This woman is not to be trusted.

"Morgana"—how I dislike my name on her lips!—"you must not think I regularly go about calling upon neighbors at this hour. The brightness of the sun woke me early. Such a beautiful morning, I decided at once to make the most of it by taking Angel out for a gallop. I've tied him up in the shade now. I think he's glad of a little rest. Do you like to ride?" she asks.

I consider shaking my head, just to stop the conversation, such as it is. Just to avoid being in any way in agreement with the woman, but Cai is watching me, and he knows the truth. I nod, but show no enthusiasm. Still this does not prevent her from treading the common ground between us.

"Then I hope you will allow me to take you out one day soon. I have a wonderful young horse that would suit you very well, I'm certain of it. Cai, would you permit your wife to come riding with me?"

"Of course," says he, putting tea in front of us. "That's a kind offer. Isn't it, Morgana?"

A nod can be surprisingly eloquent. Neither Cai nor Isolda miss the contempt in my response. I see Cai's jaw set and his eyes harden. Why does it matter so much to him that we please her? How many more people will I be expected to drink tea with while they ogle me as if I were an exhibit in a traveling circus? Did he marry me to provide a subject for gossip and curiosity among his precious neighbors? I feel suffocated by the thought. Trapped.

I begin to experience a familiar pressure in my head. There is a noise inside my skull like the winter wind through pine trees. I know Cai is talking to me, saying my name, puzzlement in his voice, but he sounds distant. I want to close my eyes, to let myself be taken to that other place, to escape. A touch on my hand brings me spinning back into the room. I shift my focus, with some effort, and see that Isolda has laid her hand upon mine. She no longer wears her gloves, and the unexpected contact with her flesh sends a burning sensation up my arm and deep into my struggling mind.

"Morgana?" Her words are syrupy with concern. "Are you quite well, child?"

I snatch my hand away. A blue bottle, fat and heavy, flies into the room. It settles on the table between us. I frown, staring at it. For a moment it merely rubs its shiny legs together, but then, quite suddenly, it rises up and hovers between myself and Isolda. She watches me closely, her head on one side, with an expression I can only name as pity. I will not endure her condescension! The fly all of a sudden swoops toward her, buzzing and darting at her face. Without being in the least bit disturbed, Isolda lifts her hand as if to calmly swat it away. At least, this is what she allows Cai to see. I, however, have a closer view, and witness her trap the fly in her hand, silencing it with a deft squeeze so that its life juices seep out between her fingers. All the while she never once takes her cold eyes from me.

I leap to my feet, my chair toppling noisily to the flagstones behind me. Pausing only to scowl at the vile woman I stomp from the kitchen, fleeing to my bedroom, Cai's irritation clear in his voice as he calls after me.

Almost an hour passes before I hear the front door rub against the stones and sounds of exchanged farewells at the garden gate. The horse's hoofbeats speed away down the drive. Moments later I hear footsteps on the stairs. I turn toward the door, waiting to see how I am to be rebuked. But Cai does not come into the room. He does not even knock upon the door. Instead he speaks through it, his voice flat and restrained.

"I'm going up to see the ponies. Mrs. Jones won't be in today. There are vegetables in the pantry for you to make our midday meal, Morgana. I'll be back at noon."

So saying he leaves, the dogs barking as they follow him. I go to the window expecting to see him striding across the pond meadow, but he does not. I wait, and shortly afterward he reappears, this time mounted on an unremarkable chestnut cob who lumbers up the hill. I watch them until they are out of sight. Midday meal indeed! I pace the room, the worn floorboards smooth beneath my feet. He knows I want to see the ponies. He invited me to go with him. And now I am not to go, all because of that hateful *good friend* of his. I shall stay in my room all day. Let him cook his own food! I will lose myself in father's books. That way the hours will pass unnoticed and I will forget about the injustice of my treatment.

And yet, the day is so lovely, I do not wish to spend it shut in the house. Was my behavior really so rude? Why can he not see that woman for what she is? The way she looked at me . . . as if I were deserving of her pity. A thing pathetic. She thinks I am not fit to be mistress of Ffynnon Las. Well, I shall show her different. I shall show them all different.

I pull on my workaday brown dress and lace up my boots. The soles are wearing so thin I can feel stones through them. On the top stair I pause, my hand on the banister. Once again I feel a chill emanating from the direction of Cai's room. There is no draft, but still the air seems to move toward me, as though icy fingers were laid upon my shoulder. I turn round, but there is nothing to see. Cross with myself for being so fanciful, I go down into the kitchen. The fire in the grate looks surly and unhelpfully low. There is a little coal in the brass bucket. I tip it on, causing a stinking plume of grey smoke but scant heat. Surely it will gather strength in a while. I venture into the pantry. There are jars of pickles and bottles of preserved fruit and bags of flour and hams hanging from hooks above my head. Mrs. Jones will not see anyone in this house go hungry, I think. I decide I will assemble a *cawl* of sorts. The staple hearty stew that bubbles away in kitchens across the land. The very idea of it transports me home. Well, this one will have to lack the lamb Mam might have put in it on fat days, but it will be *cawl,* nonetheless. Thinking of her, and of her cooking, and of home, brings a cold ache to my heart. What will she be doing now? How will she be faring without me? What would she make of my new home? I wonder if she knew how grand it is. I find it hard to believe, for she could surely never have imagined me the wife of a gentleman farmer with a housekeeper. I know Mam would laugh long and loud at the sight of me here in this larder faced with the task of cooking. The thought of her laughter brings another sharp stab of longing for her. She used to say I could burn water, left to my own devices. Well, I am a wife now. With a home of my own. And I will cook if it pleases me.

I gather an armful of vegetables and take them to the kitchen table. The smoke has dwindled, and there are small flames visible in the fireplace now. I remove the kettle from the hook above the fire and search for a suitable stewpot. The one I find is cast iron, heavy even when empty, but will serve my purpose. I half fill it with water from the pail before, with some difficulty, hooking it into place over the heat. A short search produces a worn but sharp knife and I set about peeling and chopping. It seems to me vegetables are designed to fight off our attempts to render them edible. They hide beneath mud and tough skins, knobbled with eyes or crafty shapes which defy the attentions of my blade. I have not more than half finished my chore before the knife skids off a misshapen carrot and slices into my finger. I gasp, putting the wound to my mouth, the metallic taste of blood making my stomach tighten. Enough of this nonsense. Let the boiling water finish the job. I scoop up my ill-prepared ingredients and tip them into the pot. Water splashes out, hissing as it meets the hot coals. The grey mess looks nothing like the *cawl* I had been aiming for. Finding a long wooden spoon I poke at it cautiously. The heat from the coals beneath the pot and the rising steam scald my hand so that I drop the spoon. Stepping back to a safe distance I frown at the bothersome concoction. I narrow my eyes, take a deep breath, and direct my mind to the matter. Slowly the spoon stands upright and then begins to stir. It stirs and stirs and stirs, rhythmically mixing the stew into something that might, with a little cooking, actually be fit to eat. When I am content with the results I jerk my head in the direction of the table and the wooden spoon obediently flies out of the pot and comes to rest next to the chopping board. I find a lid that fits snugly and drop it over the *cawl*. From beneath it comes a promising bubbling noise. I can see no value in my sitting to watch the thing, and in any case, the room is oppressively hot with the fire glowing on such a warm day, so I go outside.

I scan the high horizon for sign of Cai, or perhaps a glimpse of darting orange that might be one of the corgis. There is nothing. I wander to the back of the house to investigate the yard of barns and stables. They are all constructed of the same cool stone as the house, with steeply sloping roofs of slate to withstand the copious rain of a Welsh winter. I am on the point of entering the tall hay barn when the sound of running water diverts me. I find, a little to the left of the yard, set into a steep bank that climbs up to the higher meadows, a well. There is a low stone wall to the front of it, into which has been placed a trough for the animals. This in itself is not remarkable, but beside it a further circle of stonework separates another deep pool. This has been designed so that livestock cannot reach it, and is set back beneath a curving ceiling of stone, like the entrance to a cave. Mosses of surprising brightness and delicate, feathery ferns grow among the slabs and rocks. At the uppermost point, water, quick and glittering in the morning sunshine, cascades down into the pool. The combination of shade, depth of water, the color of the stones, and some unknown element make the surface appear to be the most beautiful blue. Ah! It comes to me this is what gives the house its name, for Ffynnon Las means "blue well." There is no visible outlet from either pool or trough, so the water must run on underground, presumably down to the pond in the meadow below. Leaning forward I cup my hand beneath the spout. The water is icy cold, having come straight from the heart of the hill, as yet unwarmed by summer air or sunlight. It tastes good. Slightly peaty, but exquisitely fresh and reviving. At the very top of the well ceiling there is a broad, flat piece of masonry with something carved into it. It is old and worn, but I am able to make out the faint remnant of two letters, though which they are I cannot be sure. There is something about this well, something beyond the freshness of the bubbling spring water and the prettiness of the plants. I sense, no, more than this, I would swear I can *hear* something more. It is as if the well sings to me, a high, clear note, ringing through the warmth of the day, laying its sound sweetly upon my ears.

I reach down into the pool and soak my arms, the chill of the water numbing the stinging cut on my finger. For a second I see a drop of blood swirl among the eddies before being diluted to nothing, and then the iciness works on my body to stop the flow. When I take out my hand and examine it the cut is almost invisible. Almost as if it never was.

Cai does not need to take his father's watch out of his waistcoat pocket to know that it is already past noon. The ponies were at the far point of the high grazing, and finding them took him longer than he had anticipated. The herd was in fine fettle, coats gleaming, foals playful and growing well. The minute he was among them he was sorry he had not taken Morgana. He is certain she will share his love of these fiery little horses. Now, as he urges the old ginger mare down the steep slope to home, he feels he may have been too harsh on the girl. He cannot imagine why she was so hostile toward Isolda, but then, there are many things he has yet to understand about her. It could be she felt at a disadvantage, sitting there in her nightgown. Even if she did look enchanting. Perhaps she had not slept well—it was her first night at Ffynnon Las, after all, and she had been out in the meadow to greet the dawn. As the house comes into view he resolves to be more patient with her. She must be missing her mother. Time will soften her temper and help her to settle in. Or so he must believe.

In the yard he dismounts and takes the saddle and bridle off Honey. The horse is content to pick at the grass between the cobbles while he puts the tack on its rack in the storeroom. The little stone stable is full of lovingly cleaned and well-worn harnesses for driving, ploughing, and riding, all kept at a height to deter hungry mice. Cai opens the wooden gate into the small field at the back of the yard.

"Come on, then, girl. Off you go."

Honey saunters into the field, her tail swishing lazily at the persistent flies that have been attracted by her sweaty coat. Cai gives her an affectionate pat on the rump as she passes. She is as unglamorous and homely a horse as he has ever owned, but her steady temperament and hardy constitution have endeared her to him over the years. He is doubtful, though, that she will be up to the rigors of the drove. He will have to find another mount before long, one more suited to three weeks of hard riding. Calling the dogs, who have paused to loll in the shade by the well, he makes his way back into the house. As he opens the back door he optimistically sniffs the air, hoping for some hint that a meal might be waiting for him. The overpowering stink of burnt food brings him almost to the point of retching.

"Morgana?" he calls, anxiety lending an edge to his voice. He finds the kitchen wreathed in drifting smoke from a hissing fire and a belching stewpot. "What in God's name . . . ?" Hurrying forward he seizes the coal tongs and carefully unhitches the pot from its hook before setting it down on the hearth. The corgis, who had been at his heel, retreat to find clean air elsewhere. The lid of the pot has been forced off by the boiling stew inside, which has spilled over onto the coals, resulting in a smoldering mess. The inside of the pot carries the remains of what might once have been carrots, parsnips, potatoes, and leeks, though Cai can recognize nothing.

"Morgana!" he yells. This time it is anger rather than concern that adds volume to his voice. A glance around the room tells him wherever she is, not only did she abandon the cooking but she did not so much as bother to clear away the breakfast things. The bread and milk and teacups remain on the table, coated in a layer of grime from the char-laden smoke. "Morgana!" He storms from the room and up the stairs, this time not hesitating at the door, but throwing it open. He is not truly surprised to find it empty, for he is quickly being made to realize that his new wife is not a person who enjoys being in the house. He is about to go in search of her when he catches sight of her crate of books. The lid is off, and though she has not yet had time to take them out, it appears she has been looking through the various volumes. Curiosity gets the better of him and he squats down beside the crate for a closer look. The first book he finds is a copy of *Pilgrim's Progress,* in English. It is a little dog-eared, but the evidence is of wear, rather than neglect, with no stains of mildew or signs of worm damage. He opens the cover, and inside reads, in an elaborate hand, *Silas Morgan Pritchard 1821.* He picks up the next and finds the same. And the next. All the books, it seems, once belonged to Morgana's father, for whom she was evidently named. It was her father, then, who sparked within her the love of the written word. This mysterious man about whom Mair would say no more beyond that his daughter had idolized him, and that he had disappeared one day when she was very small. Cai feels an understanding forming within himself; something so obvious, now that he has come to it, that he is amazed by his own slowness in not having fathomed the fact sooner. Morgana had ceased speaking when she was a young child, and that moment, that shutting off of her voice from the world, had been the very same moment her father had vanished from her life forever.

Cai sits back on his heels and tries to imagine how the pain of that loss must have struck the child. He recalls at once the agony of his grief for Catrin. His own response had, indeed, been to withdraw from the world. Was that not what Morgana had done, at least in the way, as a child, she was able? The door of the wardrobe is open and within it hang her few articles of clothing. Rising, he moves to look closer. There is a dress of dark blue cotton, clearly kept for best, perhaps chapel. It is pitifully plain, unfashionable, and patched in several places. The slips, pinafore, and petticoat show similar states of wear and repair. Cai feels a pang of pity for the girl. Here she is, landed up in a big draughty house with a stranger for a husband, and all manner of visitors coming to gawp at her, and she has not one decent garment in which to dress herself. Small wonder she wants to run and hide.

He senses rather than hears Morgana in the doorway, the suddenness of her appearance startling him so that he jumps. Self-consciously, he steps away from her clothes. How must it look to find him touching her undergarments and examining her linen! Embarrassment makes him sharper than is his intention.

"You left the *cawl* unattended. That was very foolish. I came home to find the kitchen full of smoke." When she shows not the slightest suggestion of remorse he adds, "You could have burned the house down!"

Her response to this is to cast her eyes down. In doing so her gaze sweeps over her crate of books, and she notices that they have been disturbed. At once her demeanor changes from sullenly defensive to furious. She rushes to the wooden box, falling on her knees beside it. She grabs the books, placing them back inside just as they had been, and then snatches up the lid and slams it in place. She leaps to her feet, standing defensively in front of her prized possessions, her fists clenched at her sides, her face dark with rage.

Cai is unnerved by the intensity of her reaction. "I did no harm," he says. "I see that they were books belonging to your father . . ."

He is not permitted to finish his sentence. Morgana runs at him, her loose hair streaming, fists raised. Instinctively Cai raises his own hands to protect himself, but she does not strike him. Instead she shoves him, hard, both hands pushing against his chest so that he is forced backward, off balance, staggering out of the room. The instant he is across the threshold she slams the door on him. All five of the paintings hanging on the landing crash to the ground, their glass seeming to smash before they even reach the floorboards, as if they were not so much shaken from their hooks as exploded. Cai stands still, his heart pounding. Only when he is convinced the storm is over does he turn and go downstairs.

4.

How dare he touch my books! He was rifling through my possessions, as if they belong to him now. As, indeed, they do. As I belong to him, I suppose. Am I to be left nothing of myself? I lift the lid from the crate once more, just to reassure myself that nothing has been taken. No, they are all here. He was looking at *Pilgrim's Progress*. Has he ever read it, I wonder? Has he any interest in stories? I have seen no books in the house thus far. Perhaps he keeps them to himself, in his room. The room he will no doubt expect me to share with him one day. What would a man like Cai read? A man who has lived all his life in one place, save for droving, what would he choose to read?

Dada selected these books. Each and every one meant something to him; his choices were never whimsical or left to fate. He had his favorites. This one, with its fine red leather binding, he never tired of—*Tales from the Thousand and one Nights*. How he loved this book! And how I loved to hear him read from it, or to recount tales from memory, as he often did. The cover feels warm, as if my dada had just this minute left off reading it. As I run my thumb across it the title spells itself out to me, cut into the leather, even though the gilding has long been rubbed away by palm and lap. A heavy sadness settles upon me, as it so often does when I recall the pain of his leaving. When I remember how he was one day there, and the next not. And how when he went away he took my voice with him.

Of a sudden I am overcome by weariness. The journey, the dragging sorrow of homesickness, this strange house, unfamiliar society, the heat . . . all have taken their toll so that now all I wish to do is sleep. And yet I fear still I will not be able to. If I clutch Dada's book close against me, tight to my heart, it may be I can bring to mind something of the warmth of his presence. Here, I will lay myself down on the rug in this pool of sunshine that brightens the colors of the woven wool. I close my eyes and wish I could go to where dear Dada is. But he is lost to me. So many times I have tried to find him, to travel as only I can to be near him. But he is gone. So completely. The only comfort left to me is to remember. To revisit those soft-edged images and remember-ings of my time with him. To recall one of those precious mo-ments my memory has entombed and preserved like an ancient treasure. A moment when he was close to me. I shut my ears to the cry of the serf's cuckoo outside. I curl myself around the book, burying my nose in the dry, powdery pages so as to keep away the bitter aroma of burnt vegetables and sulphurous coal fumes that drift up the stairs. I screw my eyes tight shut, allow-ing only the dappled dance of the sun on my lids. Slowly images appear. A dark night, still and warm. A fire, outside, at the far end of the garden. And at last, Dada, sitting beside it, his face il-luminated by the flames. He always preferred to be out of the house, much to Mam's displeasure. So long as the weather would allow it, after eating he would retreat to this quiet little place, assemble twigs and branches, and within minutes would be set-tled by a cheerful blaze, his clay pipe in his hand, an ease relax-ing his shoulders. An ease which eluded him when he was forced to remain enclosed with slate or thatch separating him from the stars. I would clamor for him to tell me a tale and, after a token resistance, he would agree, sucking on his pipe, eyes raised to heaven as if looking for divine guidance for his story selection. And then he would begin. Oh, he was an excellent storyteller! My young mind, flexible as willow, would follow the twists and turns of the adventure, pictures flashing bright before my eyes, the howls of wolves or the singing of maidens filling the night sky around me. I was enthralled. Spellbound. Indeed, most of his best-loved tales turned upon some sort of magic. Magic, he told me, was something to be taken seriously.

"Travelers understand about magic," said he. "I'm not claiming they're all sorcerers and such like, only that they know magic when they see it. Your Romany ancestors crisscrossed the globe, Morgana, and on their travels they saw many marvelous things and encountered many wonderful beings. That's how they gained their knowledge, from distant lands and strange customs of even stranger people. Traveling was my habit, my natural state, you might say, until your mother caught me in her web." He laughed. "She's a good woman, your mam, but she's not like you and me, girl." He leaned forward, dropping his voice to a conspiratorial level. "You have the magic blood in you, Morgana. I've seen it. Do not fear it, as some do. It is a gift, though there are times you may not think it so." He sucked hard on his pipe, which had gone out. He paused to light a spill in the fire and touch the glowing end to the bowl of tobacco. Abundant smoke temporarily obscured him, slowly dispersing, wisps of it curling from his nose. I was seven years old and I had a dragon for a father.

"If you are not able to travel," he told me, "the next best thing is to read. Read all you can, girl. And store up that knowledge, for you never know when you will need it." He paused, sitting straight, looking thoughtfully at me. I have often, over the years, tried to see what was behind that expression, what it was he was trying to tell me. "A person has to tread his own path, Morgana. Life will set things to pulling you in all directions, tugging you this way and that." He puffed once more, leaning back so that the light from the fire could scarcely reach him, two smokinesses rendering him faint, ghostlike. The only substantial thing about him was his voice. "Tread your own path," said he once more.

The next morning he was gone, and I never saw him again.

The memory lulls me to sleep and when I awake some hours

have passed and the room is in darkness save for a short candle flickering on the windowsill. I am surprised to find the patchwork quilt has been taken from the bed and placed snugly over me. Cai must have done it. Must have come to speak with me, found me sleeping, and thought to make me more comfortable. The man is a riddle. I might sooner have expected him to wake me and tell me to make his supper. I rise and peer out of the window. The night is bright, constellations clear, the moon aglow. It is hard to judge the exact hour, but the house is quiet, as if I am the only one awake.

I drop the quilt onto the bed and snatch up my woolen shawl instead. I take the candle and lift the latch on my door carefully. Again, as I pass the door to Cai's bedroom, I sense something out of kilter with the still silence of the night. I have the sensation of being observed. I pull my shawl tighter about me and continue downstairs. I have already identified those boards and stairs which complain at my footfalls, so I am able to descend to the kitchen quietly. The fire in the range is out. There is a faint smell of smoke lingering, but the unpleasant evidence of my calamitous attempt at cooking has gone. The table is cleared and everything returned to its proper place. Conflict unsettles me. I am glad proof of my clumsiness has been erased, but I am uncomfortable at the thought of my husband having to wash away the grime of my error. It should not fall to him. And now I feel strangely in his debt. Hunger rumbles in my stomach and I fetch a lump of cheese and a hunk of bread from the pantry. I am about to sit on the window seat when I see Cai is sleeping in the carver at the far end of the table. I wonder I have not woken him with my blundering about. How often, I wonder, has he fallen asleep down here? I remember after Dada went away I would sometimes find Mam in her chair by the kitchen range. She would explain it away as having been overtired and having drifted off. Only later did she admit to me she found her bed too lonely. Does he still miss his first wife so? Am I to compete with a ghost?

Now I notice the corgis curled at his feet. Bracken opens one eye, recognizes me, surely more by scent than sight in the dimly lit room, gives a halfhearted wag of his tail and goes back to his slumbers.

Hush, little one! Do not wake your master.

Cai is sleeping deeply. I am close enough to reach out and touch him. He looks younger, somehow. In repose his features lose something of the sternness that I see. Or at least, I see it when he looks at me. Am I so perpetually bothersome? His collarless shirt is of good quality, and that is a fine woolen waistcoat. I can see the fob and chain of a gold watch. He likes to look . . . respectable, I think. Even when at home, tending his livestock. Not the image some of the drovers have, with their long coats and rough ways. I admit, though, he has always presented himself well. On the occasions when I saw him at Crickhowell market he was well turned out, despite being on the move with the herds. Mam and I sold cheese there when we could, buying cheap milk from Spencer Blaencwm's dairy where we worked. Mam would pick wild garlic and together we would churn it into creamy rounds to sell. Business was always good when the drovers came through. That is where Cai first saw me. He could have been under no illusions as to what I was. A dairy maid with a sometime cheese stall at the smallest market in the shire. He would come to inspect our wares on the evening of his arrival, and in the morning before the drove went on its way. Then he would visit on his return journey, when he was unencumbered by his many charges. A year and a half of passing through and pausing. Snatched moments in which to convince himself he had found a suitable bride. And to convince Mam my future lay with him. I will say, he purchased a large amount of cheese! Perhaps it was that which led him to believe I might be capable of cooking. I recall he did his best to look prosperous, sensible, dependable.

And now look at him. Longer eyelashes than a man should be blessed with. Skin tanned from the outdoor life, but not yet weathered. His hair is streaked gold by the summer sun. There are several years between our ages, yet as he sleeps I see the boy in him. Unsure of himself. Vulnerable. Oh! He is stirring. I have no wish to be found standing here, watching him. He mumbles something, his eyes still closed. Both dogs lift their heads from their paws. I hasten from the kitchen and back to my own room.

✹

Cai comes blearily to his senses. His arm swings over the side of the chair, numb from sleeping awkwardly. Bracken licks his hand. He struggles to sit up. There is a fearful crick in his neck. Before he can properly open his eyes he becomes aware of a presence. A shadow falling on him, cast by a figure standing close. Morgana? He had been dreaming of her, he remembers now. In his dream she appeared like a wraith. She had leaned forward and touched his face, silently watching him, smiling at him. His own voice seems to have temporarily left him as he tries to form her name.

"Mr. Jenkins!" Mrs. Jones is not best pleased to find he has spent the night in the kitchen. Again. "*Duw*, what are we to do with you?"

"Ah, Mrs. Jones . . ." Not Morgana, then. Just a dream. Reality stands stoutly in front of him in the resolutely substantial form of his housekeeper.

"There you are again with your not bothering to get to your bed. Robbed yourself of a proper night's sleep for no good reason." She puts her hands on her hips and tutts loudly, shaking her head. "And what is Mrs. Jenkins to make of such behavior? Have you stopped to consider how it do appear to her?"

Cai opens his mouth to speak but hesitates. He was about to remind her that they did not, as yet, share a room, so that Morgana was most likely unaware of where he had spent the night. But, somehow, he has no wish to enter a discussion centering on his marital sleeping arrangements. It is too sensitive a subject, and one for which he has not yet found a satisfactory course of action. He gets to his feet, nudging corgis out of the way with his boot.

"Did Maldwyn drop you off on his way to work?"

"As he does most mornings." Mrs. Jones shoots him a look that says she will not be so easily put off course.

"He's a hard-working lad, Mrs. Jones. You've reared him well." He busies himself rattling the scuttle as if checking for coals.

"No doubt you'll have sons of your own to manage one day. Soon, perhaps, if you do treat that pretty new wife of yours properly."

Cai will not entertain thinking about what, precisely, Mrs. Jones might mean by properly. "She is exactly that, Mrs. Jones—new. And as such she should be allowed time to settle in before . . . before . . ."

Mrs. Jones waits, eyebrows raised.

Cai snatches up the buckets. "I'll fetch the coal," he says.

"The coal can wait." She steps to one side so that he would have to retreat and walk back around the table to leave the room. "I may not be a woman of the world, Mr. Jenkins, but I do know this much. Not too many sons were ever conceived while the master of the house slept in a kitchen chair and his wife kept a lonely bed upstairs."

"Mrs. Jones, for pity's sake. We've been married five minutes . . ."

"Five minutes, five years, what's the difference?"

"As I say, Morgana needs a little time."

"You may be right about that." She nods slowly. "Or it may be that *you* are the one who needs time."

"Me?"

The housekeeper's face softens, her arms falling by her sides, her hands plucking at her apron. "You lost one wife to childbirth, *bachgen,* it would take an uncommon steadfast soul not to fear for the next. At least to begin with."

Cai is taken aback. It is not a consideration that has entered his head, but now that he hears it spoken aloud, plainly as only Mrs. Jones can, he wonders if there might not be some tiny grain of truth in it. The joy of discovering that Catrin was with child and the happy anticipation of being a father had so swiftly turned to the ghastliness of Catrin's unsuccessful labor, and the loss of both wife and babe. Does he, somewhere deep and hidden, harbor the fear that a similar fate could befall Morgana? It is possible. But, of course, as long as they sleep in separate rooms, as long as he leaves her to "settle in," as long as they are not properly man and wife . . .

With mounting desperation he casts about for a subject which might divert Mrs. Jones from their present topic.

"We had a visitor yesterday morning." He is fairly certain this will pique her interest.

"Oh?" She pauses as she moves toward the pantry.

"Yes, very early it was. We were barely up." He allows this information to sink in for a moment, hoping the "we" will placate her, give her reason to hope all is well. Then he continues, "Yes, we were quite taken by surprise, having only just finished our bacon and eggs." He sees no harm in letting her assume, as he knows she will, that it was Morgana who prepared the breakfast.

"*Duw,* who would be calling at such an hour?"

"Mrs. Bowen, out riding to take advantage of the pretty morning. Indeed, she has offered to take Morgana out one day soon. Says she has a horse that she believes will suit her very well."

To this Mrs. Jones offers no reply. Her uncharacteristic wordlessness has Cai wondering if Morgana's silence is in some way catching.

"Don't you think that civil of her?" he asks.

"Oh indeed," Mrs. Jones agrees flatly. "Most civil," she says, but her face says otherwise.

Cai frowns. He knows the two women dislike each other, but surely Mrs. Jones cannot detect anything but kindness in such an offer. He feels his patience beginning to fray around the edges. Another thought comes to him, a matter in which he would in fact be glad of some assistance. "I am taking Morgana to chapel tomorrow."

"To Soar-y-Mynydd? Oh, yes! An excellent plan, Mr. Jenkins."

"I'm glad you approve," he says, not bothering to hide the barb. "It occurred to me that, having lived a quiet life, without much in the way of society, so to speak, she might not have anything suitable to wear, see? So, I thought it sensible to let her take a look at Catrin's dresses, see if she might find something. Do you think she'd like that?" He turns to look again at Mrs. Jones and is surprised to find her eyes brimming with tears. For a minute he thinks he has been horribly insensitive, judged the thing wrong, and will offend everyone with the idea. But no, they are tears of affection, and relief, he believes.

"Oh, *bachgen*! I do think she will like it very well."

"Good, then. There it is. Would you help her? Take her to the end room where the clothes are stored. She might welcome your assistance."

"No, no. It must come from you. I could not possibly . . ."

"But, another woman, in such matters . . . ?"

Mrs. Jones is still shaking her head. "It would not be right. It is for you to do," she insists.

At that moment the dogs jump up, wagging, and trot to greet Morgana as she enters on silent feet. Cai has never known anyone so capable of appearing without the slightest sound, so that even the corgis with their huge ears seem surprised.

"Good morning to you, Mrs. Jenkins. Well, *Duw,* time is marching on without us and here I am not even put the kettle on yet." The housekeeper sets about her tasks, but not before she has nodded her encouragement to Cai.

He clears his throat.

"Ah, Morgana, I was just saying to Mrs. Jones. Well, it's chapel tomorrow, see? People hereabouts like to dress up smart. Nothing showy, mind, that wouldn't do at all. No. Well, it occurred to me there's a whole trunk of dresses upstairs. Catrin's, they were. And they're not doing anyone any good locked away up there, are they?"

Mrs. Jones stares at him openmouthed, holding the empty kettle aloft, halted in her actions by the hopelessness of her employer's efforts.

Cai is painfully aware he is making a poor job of things.

"Please, come with me," he says at last, hastening from the room, a puzzled Morgana following. They climb the stairs and he leads her to the far end of the landing. The door to the room is not locked, but the lack of air inside suggests it is not often disturbed. He goes over to a heavy oak trunk at the foot of the bed and lifts the creaking lid. For a moment he remains transfixed by the sight of Catrin's dress with forget-me-nots. He had particularly liked her in that one. He gathers himself and starts pulling garments from the box and laying them on the bed.

"They are in good condition, mind. Mrs. Jones has looked after them since . . . Oh, this is very nice, don't you think?" He holds up a silk gown the color of crushed raspberries, turning to see Morgana's reaction. Her face is not difficult to read, for delight is written all over it. She reaches out tentatively. "Go on," he tells her, "take it."

She does so, a sigh of pleasure escaping her as her fingers touch the shimmering silk. Was that a sound, he wonders. Did she really utter a noise, however small? He observes her closely now, fascinated. He wonders he is not disturbed to see Catrin's things so pulled about, so scrutinized, so hungrily pored over, but he is not. He finds it . . . thrilling, he decides. So much so that after a while he becomes uncomfortable watching her. He stands, stepping away from the bed.

"I'll leave you to it then, shall I? Yes. Take your time. You are a little smaller than Catrin was, but I'm sure Mrs. Jones can be pressed into service with a needle if needs be."

She is still holding the silk dress as if she never wants to let it go. She turns to face him, eyes bright, a smile of pure joy rearranging her features.

"You'll try them on, then?" he asks.

She nods, vigorously this time. Happily. And Cai is happy,

too. It strikes him, as he goes out of the room, how happiness descends at the most unexpected of times, arriving in the most unlikely of places.

* * *

Mrs. Jones does indeed prove to be fairly expert with the needle, even more so than my mam. She approves of my choice of dress for chapel and helps me take it in a little at the waist and turn up the hem. She kneels at my feet, checking the altered fall of the skirts.

"Oh, that is much better. It could do with tucks in the sleeves, mind," she tells me, "but I think it will serve for tomorrow. I'll take a look at the others you've picked out when we've more time." She smiles up at me. "You do look a picture, *merched,*" she says, and I am grateful she has stopped calling me Mrs. Jenkins. "You'll look very fine at chapel and give all those sharp-tongued gossips something to splutter about, see?"

We finish our needlework and, a little reluctantly, I slip back into my old clothes. I admit to being surprised at how much I love my new garments. For a moment, when first Cai suggested they become mine, I was unsure. Would Catrin approve? To have her clothes worn by the woman who has taken her place? But, when Cai began pulling the dresses from their storage place, when he held them up for me to examine, when I touched them and felt the cool cotton, warm wool, and soft silk, oh! What wonderful things they are. And I detected not the slightest coolness, not the merest hint of taint accompanying them. Whatever might be the cause of the resident chill in this house, the unwelcoming presence in Cai's room, it does not, it seems, extend in any way to the clothes once owned by the first Mrs. Jenkins.

Mrs. Jones pads down the stairs, puffing slightly with the effort even of the descent as her legs trouble her so. I follow. On the kitchen table Cai has left a rabbit shot this morning. I stroke its fur. It is so soft my fingers barely register it at all.

"I'm going to make a pie for supper," says Mrs. Jones, tying a fresh apron on top of her pinafore. "Very partial to a bit of rabbit pie, is Mr. Jenkins. Do you enjoy it?"

I shrug slowly, my gesture explaining this is something I have never been offered before. Mrs. Jones's face shows first surprise, then pity.

"Well, *Duw, Duw,*" she mutters. "Would you like me to show you how I make it, or are you squeamish, perhaps?" she asks, seeing my hand on the animal.

By way of answer I snatch up a cooking pot in one hand and take the rabbit by the ears in my other, dangling it over the pan. Laughter from the doorway makes us both start.

Cai's eyes crinkle as he chuckles, his tanned skin making his pale blue irises even brighter. "I should undress him first," says he. "You might find that fur hard to swallow!" He goes out, still laughing. Mrs. Jones tutts and shakes her head, taking the rabbit from me, and the first of my cookery lessons begins.

I watch her as she deftly guts the rabbit. Mam never succeeded in keeping me long enough indoors to bother with cooking. She knew I would rather be outside, tramping the hills, or talking to the wild mountain ponies. But my life is different now, and I must apply myself to the challenges that face me. Having gutted the rabbit, Mrs. Jones takes up a cleaver and with one precise chop removes the head, as matter of fact as can be. Next she cuts neatly above each paw and then, with one swift movement, removes its skin with no more difficulty than if she were pulling off a fur coat. The wretched creature's naked body is unpleasantly fleshy and resembles too closely a corpse for me to imagine eating it. I am relieved that Mrs. Jones quickly begins to joint it, so that it is soon rendered simply meat, rather than a dead animal. She presses the blade into a leg joint, expertly finding the gap between knuckle and socket, so that the limb comes away cleanly, the bones remaining intact and without splinters. She pauses after removing the second leg.

"You try," says she. She passes me the knife.

My first attempts are too timid, so that the blade slips and the point pierces the wooden board beneath the carcass.

"No need to be afear'd of him," she laughs. "He was harmless enough living—he won't put up a fight now. Go on."

I try again, this time with more success. She nods her approval, scooping up the rabbit portions and dropping them into the cast-iron pot, which she places on the stove. She hands me an onion to chop and notices my look of consternation as I fail to hold the thing steady for cutting. It skids from my fingers, the papery skin somehow rejecting the blade.

Tutting she takes it from me.

"*Duw,* you have found the quickest way to lose a fingertip I know of. You must take a firm hold, one cut to halve it, then flat side down on the board. See? Now you can finish the job."

I do as she bids me, feeling her eyes upon me.

"Well, there you are. Not so hard is it?" She continues to regard me as I chop so that I have the sense she is weighing me up. Pondering. At length she seems to come to some manner of decision about me.

"They do say those as do not speak spend more time listening. Seems to me they might hear things as others do not."

I continue with my task. I am starting to feel uncomfortable beneath her scrutiny. "This is the right place for you, *cariad,*" she goes on. "You do fit in here like a dowel in a drilled beam. Oh, I don't doubt you do still feel yourself a stranger. A little time is all that's needed. Time and care." She gives a loud chuckle. "And, *Duw,* Mr. Jenkins certainly do care for you, *merched!*"

I feel myself blush horribly, my face burning.

"'Tis nothing to be ashamed of. I thank heavens for it. Was a time I thought I'd never see the pain go from that poor man's eyes. But you've worked some magic there, Mrs. Jenkins. Indeed you have."

The next morning I rise early, still unable to sleep beyond dawn. I hurry downstairs and spend half an hour bathing my feet in the dew before I force myself back to my room to prepare for chapel. Mrs. Jones gently suggested that now I am a married woman I ought to think about wearing my hair up. Despite her coaching and instructions, I struggle with the pins. Wisps and curls defy my best efforts, escaping from beneath my bonnet at unattractive angles. Exasperated by my own clumsiness, I close my eyes and set my hands in my lap. My mind is far more deft, and slowly I feel wayward locks and strands coiling around my head, tucking themselves neatly in place, smooth and secure. I open my eyes to check the results in the looking glass, expecting to see my mother's likeness. Oddly, it is Dada I recognize in my reflection now. I stand up, straightening the upturned brim of my straw hat, running my hands over the crisp cotton, admiring the tiny forget-me-nots of the fabric. At school, I remember Mr. Rees-Jones telling us pride was a sin. Am I sinful, then? To be pleased with how I look? For the first time in my life to wish to present myself as . . . as what? Pretty? Desirable? Is it my intention to impress the congregation at chapel, or to make myself more appealing for Cai? In truth, I do not know the answer to this.

Downstairs I find him in the hallway, waiting for me. He looks smart, though his own hair could use a little attention, falling onto his collar from beneath his Sunday best hat. He frowns when he sees me and for a moment I think we have all made a terrible mistake, and that he finds the sight of another wearing one of his wife's dresses disturbing. But no, slowly he smiles and holds out his arm for me.

"Chapel then, is it, Mrs. Jenkins?" he asks, and I nod.

The white pony stallion, whose name I now know to be Prince, gleams so brilliantly I suspect Cai may have given him a bath. The little horse trots neatly onward, the lush countryside speeding past us as we travel along the twisting lane, farther up the high valley to the chapel. Overhead a kite wheels and plunges to evade two bothersome crows. The sky is utterly cloudless and of a blue so sharp it makes me squint. The journey takes a good thirty minutes and Cai fills much of that time telling me about where we are going and who is likely to be there.

"There should be a fair turnout in such fine weather. Soar-y-Mynydd sits a ways up the mountain, and it's not a trip for the fainthearted in winter, see? 'Twas only built a few years ago and already it is known countrywide, especially now we've Reverend Cadwaladr preaching for us. People will travel distances just to hear him. There won't be enough room for everyone, mind. Some will have to stand outside and listen." He throws a glance my way. "One or two will be wanting to get a look at the new mistress of Ffynnon Las," he says. "You've nothing to worry about. Most are kind enough, and those that aren't, well . . . what do we care for their opinions?" He gives me a reassuring smile, but I am not reassured. The fact comes to me that however becoming my dress might be, and however married to Cai Jenkins, I am still a curiosity. Word will no doubt have traveled on swift, spiteful feet from farm to farm, inn to inn, kitchen to kitchen. Cai Jenkins has gone and got himself a mute wife. Dumb and dim Morgana, that's what they'll be thinking. People are the same the world over.

Prince snorts, his pace losing its easy rhythm as we crest a steep hill. We turn a double bend and the whitewashed chapel comes into view. It is freshly painted, with two young pine trees in the graveyard and as yet no headstones. Beside it flows a narrow stream, so that the front door is accessed by a flat stone footbridge. It is prettily set against the backdrop of the uplands, its tall windows drawing in the sunlight. Already there is a sizable gathering of worshipers alighting from horses or carriages or arriving on foot. I feel a tightness twist my innards. To my surprise, Cai reaches over and, very briefly, places his hand over mine.

"Courage now, my wild one," he says, and suddenly I feel stronger. Stronger because of him. This realization astounds me, but before I have time to think of it further we are arrived and a boy runs forward to tie up the pony for us.

I jump down from the trap and take Cai's arm. Together we face the crowd. I see Mrs. Cadwaladr and her daughters, dressed with surprising restraint and lack of ribbons. They acknowledge us, as do others who step forward to be introduced and shake my hand. I hear a babble of names, like a brook in autumn, all rolling into the same sea of forgetfulness, and I am thankful I will not be called upon to recall any of them. As evidenced by their lack of questioning, word has indeed reached everybody of my silence, and not one person comments upon it. Cai clearly sees this as a mark of respect and acceptance of some sort, and I notice him begin to relax, his arm beneath my hand losing some of its earlier tension.

A loud voice can be heard greeting parishioners and Cai bends to whisper in my ear. "Look, there. That is our minister, Reverend Cadwaladr," says he.

I see a stout man with a red face, dressed in the customarily severe garb of a preacher, with long black jacket and breeches and a stiff white collar apparently composed mostly of starch. He is barely taller than his equally rotund wife, but what he lacks in height he makes up for in the volume of his voice. I am several strides distant from him, but every word he utters is clearly audible to me, as it must be to everyone. Does he think God will not hear him unless he shouts? He scans the company for new faces and I fall under his powerful scrutiny.

"Ah-ha!" he bellows, causing an elderly lady standing close to him to teeter backward, "Cai Jenkins and his new bride. Welcome! Welcome, child. Here, let me look at you." He reaches out his arms toward me and the crowd parts as the Red Sea before Moses. "Ah, the innocence and purity of youth. You have come to a good place, child. All are welcome at Soar-y-Mynydd, and none more so than the mistress of Ffynnon Las." He places his hand upon my head in some manner of blessing. If he is expecting me to swoon or shake I do neither. No member of the clergy, however fervent or well-intentioned, has had the ability to move me in the slightest. This one, though, this man of God, has something different about him. Something strange. Something sinister. My instinct is to wriggle from beneath his touch and move quickly away, but I am aware there are eyes upon me, and that Cai is hoping for, at least, my cooperation. I muster what I hope is a humble and slightly grateful smile. I am mightily relieved when he lets me go.

"Excellent! Excellent!" cries Reverend Cadwaladr. For the briefest moment he is silent, though even wordless he is loud, somehow. He seems even to *look* at me loudly. It is during these few seconds, when his gaze penetrates me, that I am aware of a sense of unease wriggling its way under my skin. I shake off the sensation. He is yet another blustering preacher. I have met his like before, and none of them have approved of me. Whatever he might say, however hearty his welcome, I warrant he will prove to be no different from the rest of his calling in this.

We are shooed inside the chapel like so many sheep, bleating and jostling for position. Cai guides me to what must be his own section of a pew, to the far side, but in the front row. I recognize this as a measure of his standing in the community. The interior is unusual in that its low boxed pews run the length, rather than the width, of the space, and there is no central aisle. The rostrum is placed between the tall windows, and on it is a sturdy lectern. Behind where the preacher will stand is a broad wooden plaque with an inscription praising God and marking the erection of the building. The whole effect is one of simplicity and utility. The only pointer to any manner of connection with things heavenly is the height of the ceiling, which, whilst it is not required to accommodate an organ, will presumably lift and magnify the voices of the congregation when they are raised in song.

As I take my place a sudden chill grips me, as if the air in the room has lost all warmth. I can fathom no cause for this, and must attribute it to my nervousness at being confined with so many people. And, perhaps, my customary dislike of being preached at.

I spy Isolda Bowen entering the chapel. She is greeted by all with fawning delight. How easily people's heads are turned—fine tailoring, money, and position. For a moment the congregation has shifted its allegiance from God to altogether more earthbound wants and wishes. Cai, who has already removed his hat, signals to her with a bow. She treats him to a smile and me to a wave of a white-gloved hand. Her dress is sophisticated yet plain, and even I am able to judge it expensive. Clearly she does not have her housekeeper sew her clothes for her. Such finery can only have come from London. She sits at the other end of the front-most pew. The reverend comes in and makes a point of pausing to talk with Isolda, clearly as much charmed by her as everyone else. Indeed, by the end of their short conversation the man appears quite lit up, almost agitated. What words can they have exchanged? When all are seated the preacher climbs to his position, for once able to look down on even the tallest among us. The door is left open, so that those forced to remain standing outside might listen to his ministry.

"Brothers and sisters! Brothers and sisters!" he begins, his words bouncing off the white stone walls, forcing their way into every ear and every mind. I have heard tell of ministers such as this. Exhorters, they are called, who stir up a rousing fervor for their faith wherever they go. "You came here today to praise Our Lord, to worship Him, to show yourselves good and steadfast Christians, worthy of His love. So, then, I ask, who among you has given thanks this morning?" The congregation answer with a nervous silence. "Tell me, my devout brothers and sisters, which one of you has lifted up his or her voice, heart, and eyes to the heavens this morning and given thanks to the Lord?"

Still no answer comes, save for a fidgeting of cotton and wool on polished pew.

"What? Can this be true? Are you telling me that not one of you pious people, *not one,* has thought to thank Our Father this day for all that he has given us? You mean to say to me, that you have risen from your warm, safe beds, dressed yourselves in clean clothes and dry boots, made your way here beneath a peerless sky through fields of thriving crops and fattening livestock, greeted your good, equally pious friends and neighbors, and *not one* of you has thought to thank the Lord for all these wonderful blessings? For all the bounty he has bestowed upon us?"

Here the reverend feigns disbelief close to make him faint. He staggers, clutching the lectern for support in the face of such ingratitude.

"Shame! Shame on you, I say! That you can take so easily all the abundance with which you are blessed and not one single, solitary, humble word of thanks!" Reverend Cadwaladr's eyes start to bulge alarmingly. "Join me, brothers and sisters, join me, I beseech you, in giving thanks. Now, there is not a moment to lose!" He lifts his arms and turns his face up to the ceiling. "We thank you, Lord! We thank you for all the wondrous gifts of plenty you see fit to bless us with. We give thanks!"

"We give thanks," the congregation choruses. "We give thanks!"

A light-headedness begins to take hold of me, to add to the coldness which seeped into my bones earlier.

"Yes, my brethren, thank him. For as he nourishes our bodies, so will he nourish our souls. Give thanks!"

"We give thanks!" chimes the congregation with laudable enthusiasm.

It is at this moment I begin to feel severely dizzy. I grip the front of the pew to steady myself. Reverend Cadwaladr continues in his entreaties and the assembled company responds eagerly, but it is not the noise, nor the spiritual frenzy, which is affecting me. I glance across and find that Isolda Bowen is still sitting in her place, straight-backed and steady, watching the preacher with what appears to be rapt attention. Then, of a sudden, a terrible smell, no, a *stench,* a sour reeking fills my nostrils. It is like nothing I can place. Though it provokes some long buried memory I cannot identify it. Where is it coming from? I feel nauseous. My stomach churns, and I taste bile in my mouth. The voices of the preacher and the faithful seem to twist out of shape also, becoming a roar of noise, the words indecipherable. My mind loosens. I try to close my eyes, to let my lids fall, to let myself drift off to another place, my special escape. But I cannot. My gaze is drawn to the preacher. His shiny red face, puffed-out cheeks, and ceaseless noise make him ridiculous rather than frightening, and yet it is he who appears to be affecting me so adversely. This makes no sense to me, but I cannot deny that the source of my malady, and in fact the source of the evil stench that so disturbs my stomach, must be the Reverend Cadwaladr. Of a sudden he looks directly at me, and I am startled by the force of his gaze. No, more than force, there is a fierce *hatred* there.

Cai has become aware that I am not well and I hear him say my name, concerned. But I cannot look at him. The sickness within me builds and builds until I can fight it no more. At last, just as the congregation falls silent, I loudly, copiously, and abundantly vomit, emptying the contents of my stomach into my lap, obliterating the poor forget-me-nots with vivid splashes of half-digested breakfast.

5.

Cai stands at the foot of the stairs, his hand on the newel post, hesitating. The events of the morning have left him uncertain of how to treat Morgana. Unsure of how best to behave with her. The girl was badly shaken after her humiliation at chapel. People had been kind, however repulsed. Many had offered assistance. But Morgana had been inconsolable, had fled the chapel, rushing to kneel in the brook, scrubbing at her dress with a handful of wet moss. Catrin's dress. No, he must not think it so. After all, it did suit Morgana surprisingly well. And now it was ruined, and the girl was mortified. Indeed, when Isolda had offered to take her home in her covered carriage, affording her greater speed and privacy, his wife had reacted with what could only be described as rudeness. She had scowled at Isolda, turned her back on her, scrambled into their own trap, picked up the reins, and all but set off without Cai, who had been forced to jump into the moving cart as Prince lunged forward.

Since arriving home he has not seen Morgana, who has remained shut in her room. He cannot leave her to brood upon what happened. Some fresh air. A little time on the hills. He is confident these will restore her to good humor. Resolutely he mounts the stairs. He clears his throat and knocks on the door.

"Morgana? Morgana, are you feeling better?" There is no reply. He puts his ear against the wood but can detect no sound from within. Perhaps she is sleeping. Or sulking. He tries again. "Would you like a cup of tea? I was about to make some . . ." Still silence. One more try. "I thought I might go up and see the ponies. I want to bring the mares with foals down to the second meadow. Would you like to come and help?" He waits, knowing he has played his strongest card. And yet there is still no response. With a sigh he turns and walks away. He has not got more than halfway down the stairs when the bedroom door is pulled open and Morgana emerges. She is wearing her old brown dress and her hair is loose again. She looks pale and subdued, but at least she is willing to go with him.

He nods at her. "Good, then," he says, and together they go outside.

Cai fetches Prince from the stable, leading him with an old rope halter. "The mares will follow him down," he explains. The corgis scamper ahead as they make their way up the steep incline toward the high meadow. The day is properly hot now. Cai wonders if the weather can hold. Only three weeks to the drove, and they have had such a long dry spell. If there is rain too close to the day of departure they will have to contend with mud, which will slow their progress considerably. There is still much to be done. He has been taken up with having Morgana come to live at Ffynnon Las and he has not been giving the business of the drove sufficient attention. This will not do. He will go into Tregaron next market day and confirm agreements with the remaining farmers who wish their cattle to be taken to London. He must also arrange for Dai the Forge and Edwyn Nails to visit.

As they reach the top of the hill Prince becomes lively, fidgeting and jogging, despite the climb. Cai laughs at him. "Steady, *bachgen*. You'll see your ladies soon enough." Morgana reaches out and strokes his warm flank, but the pony swishes his tail. Cai shakes his head. "He has no time for us now, not with the scent of the herd in his nostrils." As if to underline the point the stallion raises his head and lets out a blasting whinny, calling to his mares. From some way distant comes an answering call. Prince snorts and pulls at the rope. Cai quickens his pace. Morgana shields her eyes against the sun, peering toward the horizon for the first glimpse of the ponies. And suddenly they are there, cantering toward them. At first only the front-runners are visible, three grey mares, all with foals running at foot. Then a handful of yearlings catch up, playing and biting at one another as they run. Now the whole herd, more than twenty-five ponies in all, come dancing over the springy turf on nimble hooves. Prince tosses his head, whinnying again, eyes bright, pulling at the rope that Cai holds tightly. Soon they are surrounded by the skittish, snorting ponies. There are several greys, most of them almost pure white. Cai spots his favorite bay mare, easily picked out by her smart white blaze and four long white socks.

"That's Wenna," he tells Morgana, pointing proudly. "Aye, she's a fine little mare. Getting a bit long in the tooth, but still throws the best foals, mind. See? See that one with her? That's one of Prince's colts. Look at him. Lovely straight legs, and that smart head—big bold eyes, dished face. You'll have to travel a long way to find better."

Morgana is clearly delighted by the animals. She moves easily among them, and Cai notices they are instantly comfortable with her, and not in the least bit nervous. He watches her for a moment, as she reaches out to touch the nose of one of the youngsters, ruffle the curly mane of a foal, and pat the neck of an old chestnut mare. Her face has regained its color, and she looks herself once more. He is pleased to find that she can so simply be returned to good humor and health. What does it matter, after all, if she cannot cook, has no interest in the house, and prefers not to be in the company of neighbors? How much better that she share his love of the land, and of the stock. Perhaps it will be the hills and the ponies that allow him to reach her. He finds himself smiling. She looks up and catches him watching her. He expects her to cast her eyes down, to turn away, to exhibit some sign of inhibition or discomfort. But she does not. Standing there, the little horses milling about her, the summer breeze moving her long black hair, and the love of life shining out of her face, she bestows upon him a truly beautiful, heartfelt smile. He can feel her joy, and it moves him. He is embarrassed by his own response to her, and fears she will be able to detect his sentiment in his expression. To cover his shyness he begins telling her about the herd. He explains how it was his grandfather who bought the first stallion at Llanybydder horse fair and brought him to Ffynnon Las, and how that bloodline still runs through the ponies now. He tells her how his father built up the numbers with almost ruthless care, selling off anything that did not come up to the mark, keeping only the very best stock for breeding. He recounts the winter when they nearly lost the lot to a bout of strangles, and how he remembers sitting up with the sick colts, night after night, and watching them die of the cruel disease one after the other, until his father took the only five ponies he could be sure were free of infection and walked them to borrowed pasture ten miles away. The remaining ponies all died. But his father was undaunted, and rebuilt the herd, buying in a new stallion, Prince's grandsire.

Prince has no patience for hearing his history, however, and roars at the mares, sensing more than one of them is in season.

"Hush now!" Cai scolds him. "All in good time, *bachgen*." He tugs on the animal's halter as it whirls round him in tight circles. "Ffynnon Las ponies are known throughout Wales now," he says, "and even beyond. I've to take three with me on the drove for a man in London. He'd buy the lot, old mares, straggly yearlings, every last pony, if I let him." He smiles, shaking his head. "But money's not everything, is it?"

Morgana emphatically shakes her head before leaning down to hug one of the plumper foals. Cai remembers he is trying to bring his attentions to the coming drove and all that must be done.

"I'll be going to market in Tregaron on Tuesday," he tells her. "I've some farmers to meet up with. I'm going to take some of their stock with me on the drove. We've yet to agree a price, mind. I could just take them, see, just be responsible for getting them to the buyers in London. I'd take a piece of whatever price they made. There's less risk that way—should any stock be lost I won't have paid for them, but I'll do better if I buy them here. That way I can pocket whatever I make at the end of the drove. More risk yields more profit. At least, that's what I'll be looking for. Should be a fair size herd this year. My first as head drover, so got to make a good job of it, see? I reckon two hundred of my own beasts, plus ooh, maybe fifty from Evans Blaenmelyn, and maybe eighty from Dai Cwmtydu. Watson'll want to bring his ewes himself. More trouble than they're worth, if you ask me, but they'll be his responsibility." He trails off, distracted by watching one of the foals nibble at Morgana's sleeve. He tries to collect his thoughts once more. "So, you can come along. Mrs. Jones does the shopping at the market—she'll show you what's what, and if there's anything you need . . . well, there we are, then." She looks at him briefly, registering the information, but does not seem in the smallest way taken by the idea of anything Trega- ron market might have to offer. He is a little surprised that she is not more enthusiastic—the opportunity for a diversion, a day out, market stalls, and so on. But then he remembers the events of the morning and grants that the idea of being out in public so soon might not hold great appeal.

"You look . . . much better, Morgana," he says. "I'm sorry you were distressed about what happened at chapel. Perhaps it was the rabbit pie?"

She blushes, turning away from him.

Cai feels a little worn down by how difficult it is to talk to her. One moment he thinks he is making some headway, that she is letting down her guard. The next he feels as shut out as on that first day when he brought her home to Ffynnon Las. Would it be so hard for her to meet him halfway?

"You should let others help you. People have your best inter- ests at heart, see? There was no need to be quite so sharp with Isolda . . ."

She swings round to glare at him with a look of such ferocity it silences him instantly. To his amazement, she spits vehemently on the ground beside his feet. Even the ponies draw back. Cai is aware his hold on his own temper is not as secure as his hold on the pony's lead rope.

"All right, you don't like her. You've made your feelings plain enough. I don't understand what she's ever done to make you take against her like this, but there it is. A person should be allowed to choose their own friends, I suppose," he concedes. "Come on, then. Let's get these ponies sorted. We need to take the mares and foals with us, and leave the yearlings and the barren mares up here. They'll all follow us down to the top gate. We can split them there."

He leads a now prancing Prince ahead, whistling at the dogs, who obediently fall in behind the herd, nipping every now and again at the heel of a straggler. Morgana walks beside him, letting the ponies trot along with her. Soon they have descended to the limit of the high pasture. Cai begins the job of separating out the ones he wants to move from the ones he wants to leave. It is not a simple task. The corgis are surprisingly fleet of foot and do as they are told, but the ponies are fast and dislike being herded and barked at. Prince becomes ever more agitated, rearing up in an attempt to break free from Cai.

"Behave yourself, m'n! That'll do, Bracken! Meg! Come by, Meg! *Duw,* look at those stupid creatures." He points in the direction of two young mares charging away from the gate, their foals alarmed, galloping beside them. "Bracken, for pity's sake, dog, come by!" In frustration he pulls his hat from his head and throws it to the ground. The two mares are heading for the far horizon, spooked and uncooperative and almost out of sight. The rest of the herd, sensing drama and some hidden threat, start to turn, as one, and follow. Cai knows in a moment he will lose the lot. He whistles loudly, as much at the ponies as the dogs, who are doing their best to keep the stock together. But it is a losing battle. Cai is about to give up when Morgana snatches the rope from his hand.

"What are you doing?" Cai is taken by surprise and before he can stop her she is running with the little stallion. In a single, fluid movement, she jumps, swinging her leg across Prince's back, landing lightly. Still holding the rope she takes a handful of mane and then urges him on with her heels. Cai can only watch, openmouthed, as she and the pony charge after the mares. She has no saddle, no bridle to allow proper control of her mount, and yet the two move as one. She never, at any time, looks as if she might fall off, and Prince does not fight her, but runs where she guides him, turning and circling until, amazingly, they have gathered the entire herd. She even succeeds in slowing down the agitated animals, so that by the time she returns to the gate and to Cai they are all trotting calmly. Prince is lathered in sweat, and Morgana herself looks wilder and more disheveled than ever. She also appears completely relaxed, as if rounding up a galloping herd of half-wild ponies on a fiery stallion is the easiest thing in the world to her. Cai recalls her mother telling him Morgana was a confident rider, which now seems to be selling her daughter rather short. There is not time to comment, however, as she signals to him to open the gate. He does so, and the mares and foals meekly follow Prince into the field. He shuts it firmly against the yearlings, who whinny and complain by cantering up and down the fence for a while. Soon the heat tires them, though, and they fall to grazing instead.

Morgana brings Prince to an obedient halt as she slides from his back and hands the rope to Cai.

"Well, then, my wild one," he says, grinning, "looks like you'll be putting the dogs out of a job at this rate."

Morgana shrugs, turns, and begins the walk back down the hill. He watches her go, wondering what other secret talents his wife possesses.

The next day is again fine and dry and Cai and Morgana spend it working with the foals. The better handled they are, the better price they will fetch if he chooses to sell them, or the better brood mares they will turn out to be should he keep them. Morgana is so at ease with the ponies, so gentle with them. He is struck by how quickly she earns the trust of even the flightiest youngster or wariest mare. So engrossed are they in their work that it is twilight by the time Mrs. Jones calls to them from the house, berating them for having gone so long without pausing to eat.

They stroll down across the fields in companionable silence, the dogs wagging ahead, suddenly reminded of their own hunger. Inside they are greeted by mouthwatering aromas and savory steam as Mrs. Jones ladles *cawl* into bowls. There are chunks of warm bread to dip into the tasty stew, and a pitcher of ginger cordial. Cai watches Morgana as she eats her food with such relish, mopping up every last drop of gravy with her bread, saving only the smallest crust to drop to the waiting corgis. The meal is quickly devoured, and the three settle into chairs to watch the fire for a while. Mrs. Jones has her feet up on a milking stool the better to rest her painfully plump legs.

"I did see another frog in the well today," she tells Cai, who fails to detect anything significant in this.

"What else could you expect to find there? I see them myself most days this time of year."

"*Toads,* Mr. Jenkins. You do see toads, not frogs."

"Oh," he affects mock humility, "forgive my pitiful ignorance!"

Mrs. Jones purses her lips. "You may laugh, *bachgen,* but 'tis not usual to find a frog in such deep water with no bank. They prefer ponds with shallow edges."

Cai laughs softly. "And what, then, should we read into having such an esteemed visitor in our well?" He turns to Morgana and explains, "Mrs. Jones would have us believe the well has magical properties. You see how it is? A lost frog cannot come hopping by without her reading something meaningful into it. Other than that it was looking for water and found it, see?"

Mrs. Jones frowns. "There is none so quick to dismiss what they don't understand as those who are afraid of it. And maybe with reason."

Morgana hears a story behind her words and goes to kneel at the woman's feet, her head cocked on one side, inviting more details.

"That, *merched,* is no ordinary well."

"Now, Mrs. Jones, don't you go filling Morgana's head with old wives' tales."

"Old wives know a thing or two, and you'd do well to remember it, *bach.*" She peers down at Morgana, lowering her voice to a serious whisper. "You know that the house was named after the well, but I'll wager you don't know why."

Cai puts in, "The water looks blue. Blue well—Ffynnon Las. No mystery in that."

"Aye, the color is pretty, and it is unusual. But so are the meadows green and the pond white in winter—no one thought to name the farm after those, did they?"

"Go on then," says Cai, shaking his head, "I might as well save my breath as try to stop you telling your tale."

"Oh, 'tis not my tale. The legend of the blue well is very old. Older than the farm. Some do say 'tis as old as memory." She gives a shrug. "Leastways it is most definitely older than me."

"Imagine!" says Cai.

Morgana shoots him a look that says *be quiet.* She takes up Mrs. Jones's hand and squeezes it, urging her to continue.

"They do say there are some sources of water as have special properties. *Special.* Anyone who drinks the water will know good health. In the right hands, it can effect all manner of cures and give relief from many, many varieties of suffering."

"Ha!" says Cai. "Magic water, indeed."

"Now then, did I say magic?"

"You had that look on your face."

"Tease me all you like, Mr. Jenkins. The power in that well is known far and wide, and all your mocking won't change the facts, see?"

"Oh, *facts* now, is it?"

"Pay him no heed," Mrs. Jones addresses Morgana. "There will always be those who don't want to see. But the truth is what it is, *cariad,* even if it do trouble some."

Cai opens his mouth to respond to this but thinks better of it.

Mrs. Jones, satisfied he has finished with his futile interruptions, goes on.

"Years ago, centuries, mind, the story has it that a holy man passed this way on a pilgrimage. He was not young, and had not lived an altogether holy life, so his health was poor. He was finding the journey a struggle. Well, night was falling as he reached this place, and he decided to set up camp. He went with his servant to fill their goatskin water bottles and came across an old crone sitting by the side of the spring."

"Witch," says Cai. "In the story I heard she was a witch, not a crone."

Mrs. Jones frowns. "I thought you were going to stay quiet, Mr. Jenkins."

"So long as you are dealing with facts, thought you might like to get the details right, see?"

Mrs. Jones ignores him.

"This . . . *crone* . . . was down on her luck. She greeted the holy man kindly enough and asked him to spare her some food. Just a crust of bread or a handful of porridge oats, see? So she wouldn't starve. But the holy man said he had none to spare. Well, *Duw,* this made the old woman angry, but she saw the holy man was limping and thought to bargain with him. She offered to cure his affliction, if he'd then give her something to eat. He agreed, and she took some of the spring water and poured it over his swollen leg, and muttered an incantation. And at once the pain eased! The holy man was pleased and fair skipped about, but when it came time to pay what was due he was mean, and handed over only a moldy crust and maggoty cheese. The crone felt cheated. He offered her a blessing to help her on her way. But she shouted at him.

"'What care I for the blessing of a man such as you?' she screamed. 'Call yourself holy, when you've no charity in your heart for an old woman? A curse upon you!' And so saying she scooped up water from the well and flung it over him. 'Water will be poison to you from this day onward. May you never know good health more!' The servant made to beat her, but the crone ran away into the night, her aged legs moving swifter than any could match. Well, the holy man left the next day, but he was dead before he reached the coast. They do say he could drink a dew pond dry but never quench the terrible thirst he endured, and that he wasted to nothing." Mrs. Jones sits back heavily in her chair, nodding in a knowing fashion. "Ever since, the spring at Ffynnon Las has been known as a cursing well."

Cai yawns and stretches. "A fine bedtime story, Mrs. Jones."

"It's as well you have no interest in such things, Mr. Jenkins, else people would be knocking at your door offering money for curses and cures. The owner of the well do wield its full power. Others might seek to use it, but without permission there will be a limit to what they can bring about. The master of Ffynnon Las is the master of the well. Or the mistress, mind."

Cai laughs. "*Duw,* I'd best put up a sign. We could do with the extra income."

Mrs. Jones huffs and lets her eyes close. "Mock all you like. Facts is facts. Facts is facts." So saying she falls silent, her breathing slowing almost at once, so that she is quickly asleep.

On Tuesday morning Cai stands outside the open front door of the house and calls.

"Morgana!" He cups his hands the better to send his voice up the hill, where he is fairly certain she will be hiding, and tries again. "Mor-gan-a!" Nothing. Not the slightest movement or sign of either of the dogs, who are also absent.

Mrs. Jones is already sitting in the trap, basket in her lap. Prince shakes his head to rid himself of bothersome flies. It is barely eight o'clock and yet the sun beats down from a cloudless sky, unhelpfully hot.

"Did you not tell her we were going to market this morning, Mr. Jenkins?" asks Mrs. Jones.

"Aye, I told her." He feels irritation getting the better of him.

If she hadn't wanted to come she could have said so, he thinks. He catches himself in the impossibility of this but knows that even without words she could have made her feelings plain instead of running off like a child. He steps up into the little cart crossly, causing Prince to stagger for a moment, adjusting himself to the sudden weight. With a flick of the reins they are off, joined in the trap by a tense silence in place of Morgana. Not for the first time Cai realizes how eloquent his wife's wordlessness is, for the silence that would accompany her would be of a very different quality to that provided by her absence. Particularly when her absence feels like a deliberate slight, somehow.

The road to Tregaron is twisting and narrow, but smooth enough in the dry season, if a little dusty. There is a heaviness in the air today. Beneath his waistcoat Cai's shirt is already damp, clinging unpleasantly to his back. Mrs. Jones attempts to engage him in light conversation, but he has no heart for it. His humor is not improved by the realization that it matters to him more than a little that Morgana has chosen to stay at home. While he understands her reasons he wishes, just this once, she had considered him before shunning his offer of a trip to market. He wanted her beside him as he arrived in town. He wanted the people of Tregaron to see his new bride, recovered from the unfortunate events of Sunday, sitting prettily in the trap with him, or strolling on his arm. He wanted to watch her browsing through the market stalls, selecting items for the store cupboard and perhaps a treat or two—a ribbon for her hair, or a piece of lace. He wanted to see other men watching her. He could admit it at least to himself now; he was proud of her. He wanted to show her off and now he cannot, and he doesn't know whether to feel selfish and guilty about that, or hurt and hard done-by. Either way, by the time they pass Isolda's imposing town house on the square and Prince swings into the paddock behind the Talbot Hotel his mood is blacker than the best bowler hat he is wearing as he always does when there is business to be done.

Mrs. Jones is happy to be released to go about her shopping and Cai pushes the brass-plated front door of the inn. Tregaron has long been known as the main droving town of west Wales, and the Talbot Hotel is its very center. The generous lounge bar sports a fine fireplace with polished settles and tables placed carefully to allow the privacy required if important deals are to be made. Cai greets the barman and asks for a tankard of ale. He watches the foaming beer filling the pewter mug and licks his lips, heat, humidity, and a sour temper sharpening his thirst. There is already a fair collection of farmers halfway down their first pints. Some lean against the bar, others sit in huddles, heads bowed in conversations of the utmost secrecy. Here bargains will be struck and livestock bought and sold without the assistance of the auctioneer. Promises of labor or loans of farming implements will be secured. Here men can talk business, their thoughts flowing freely after a little ale and without the encumbrance of their womenfolk, who will be engaged in their own important matters out in the square. Cai nods to an elderly neighbor before taking a greedy gulp of the strong, dark ale. He wipes froth from his top lip with the back of his hand, lets out a deep sigh of satisfaction, blesses, after all, the absence of female company, and belches tunefully.

"Duw, Duw! Sounds like you were in sore need of that, Jenkins Ffynnon Las!" The cheerful voice behind him can belong to none other than Dai the Forge. Cai turns, smiling despite himself, putting down his tankard to shake the enormous hand of the blacksmith. Dai the Forge, as he is known to all, as was his father before him, is a mountain of a man. Standing nearer seven feet tall than six, his shoulders so broad he must step sideways through most doorways, he is perfectly suited for the job he has inherited. For Dai is a drover's blacksmith. Not for him the delicate business of shoeing a lady's favorite hack, or trimming the slender hooves of Lord Cardigan's racehorses. His is a sturdier group of customers, consisting in the main of thousands of

pounds of good Welsh beef. However hardy the cattle, they cannot make the three-week journey of the drove without first being shod, every last flighty, horned, muscly one of them.

"Now then, Dai, let me buy you a pint. First of the season." Cai signals to the barman.

"Well, there's Christian of you," says Dai, slapping Cai playfully on the back, momentarily rendering him unable to draw breath. "How's that herd of yours looking, then, m'n? Ready for the off, is it?"

Cai answers hoarsely, "Aye, they're right enough. I'll fetch them down from the hill next week."

"What date are we off?"

"The last Tuesday of the month. I'll give you and Edwyn Nails a shout when we're ready for you."

"Right you are." He pauses to receive his beer from the barman, wink his thanks at Cai, and tip most of the contents of the tankard down his throat in a couple of loud swallows. "You'll be here on business today, then," he says. He indicates a wiry figure sitting by the far window. "I see your friend's in."

Cai frowns. Llewellyn Pen-yr-Rheol is no friend of his, and well Dai knows it. Once occupying the position of head drover, the man is a salutary lesson in what can befall someone who loses the trust of those on whom he depends for his livelihood. Llewellyn becomes aware he is being observed and raises his ale in salute, his smile a thin, bitter thing. Cai inclines his head half an inch but can bring himself to do no more. This was the man who took over the drove from Cai's father, when the position should have, would have, come to him, had not Catrin died. For no man, not even a widower, can hold the license of head drover without a wife. The *porthmon* must be a married householder of the district, the reasoning behind the rules being that such a man has reason to return. A rootless person, one with nothing to draw him back to the area, might be tested beyond endurance by the heavy purse of money he will receive from the London buyers at the end of the drove. Some of that money will be his, but a sizable proportion of it will belong to other farmers and townsfolk who have entrusted him with their business. A wife and a home stand as insurance against such temptation.

Llewellyn had been quick—a little too quick, in the opinion of many—to step into the position and take on the responsibility. He was not well-liked in the community, and there were those who voiced their doubts about his suitability for the task. But time was short, and many were dependent on a successful drove to survive the coming winter. Llewellyn Pen-yr-Rheol had been out to impress, to make a name for himself, from the start. He had borrowed heavily from the Tregaron bank in order to buy huge herds, resulting in the biggest drove anyone could remember seeing. Caught up in the atmosphere of opportunity and prosperity lots of farmers came forward to request their own cattle be taken to London as well, risking everything on the drove, entrusting their families' security to a man who, up to this point, few had found a good word for. Cai well remembered that drove setting off, and how plainly Llewellyn had enjoyed his newfound status. The man had even made a point of saying how, on his return, with his pockets full, he would make Cai an offer for Ffynnon Las. The idea of selling his beloved farm, his father's farm, to such a snake of a man provoked fury in Cai, but so beaten down with grief was he that he feared it might, after all, be the only sensible course of action left to him.

Llewellyn's drove had made good time, and reached the fattening fields with few losses. Fair prices had been reached for all the stock, and celebrations were already under way in the town when news reached the revelers of disaster. On his return journey, Llewellyn had been robbed of all the money he had made—his own, and everyone else's. He had been set upon by bandits crossing the Epynt, left with a cracked head in a shallow ditch, not a penny remaining. After the shock and rage had died down, and after fruitless efforts had been made to find the perpetrators, the townsfolk had, in their despair, turned on Llewellyn. As head drover, it was his responsibility, and his alone, to see that everyone's money was delivered to them. Why had he seen fit to ride home unaccompanied? Why had he not traveled by stage? Why had he not hired men to protect him and the funds? Rumors began to circulate of gambling and debts, and the possibility that he might never have been robbed at all, but somehow squirreled the money away for himself.

For all his loathing of the man, Cai doubts this. If he is sitting on a fortune he hides it exceptionally well. When he looks at him he sees someone who aimed high and fell low. His body is so thin, so insubstantial, it is as if he is being eaten away from inside by his own failure. Despite no longer owning so much as a herd, much less a farm, he continues to wear the garb of the drover, with long, ground-sweeping coat, and broad-brimmed hat. Whereas on Cai this looks workmanlike and tough, Llewellyn gives the appearance of a ghost of a man with barely sufficient strength to support his own weight. And he is not a man capable of hating himself, so that he has turned his hatred outward, first to his poor wife, who regularly sported a black eye, then his teenage son, who left home vowing never to return, and ultimately to his successor, Cai. He makes no secret of the fact that he doubts Cai has the ability to head a successful drove. He tells anyone who wants to hear it, and plenty who do not, that he is too young, too inexperienced, and will lead them all into ruin.

A small part of Cai fears he may be right. Fears that what he sees before him is his future. The town cannot stand a second failed drove. All the risks—bad weather, disease, cattle rustlers, stampedes, unscrupulous merchants, injuries, and loss—all must be planned for and overcome. He must not fail. He knows he let the farm slip when Catrin died. It has taken time for him to rebuild his own herd, and to rebuild himself, to make both ready for the coming challenge. Two seasons he neglected the farm, and financially he has not yet recovered. He needs this drove to be successful as much as anyone, to secure the future of Ffynnon Las. A future for himself and Morgana.

"*Duw,* I think he wants to talk to you, Jenkins," says Dai the Forge.

Llewellyn gets unsteadily to his feet and crosses the sloping flagstone floor. Cai straightens, putting down his tankard. The older man comes to stand uncomfortably close. When he speaks his voice is as reedy and thin as his physique.

"Well, there we are then, our honorable new head drover. What a fine *porthmon*. A man to be trusted, see?" He turns to address the room. "Wouldn't you all trust such a fellow, with his fine hat, and his gold watch at his pocket, and his new wife, bought in special for the purpose."

"Hold your tongue, Pen-yr-Rheol," says Cai. He knows he must not rise to the bait, but already his grip on his temper is slipping.

Llewellyn waves an arm expansively. "Did it for the good of all, see? Found himself a wife just so as he can head the drove and keep all your lovely money safe. Well, there's thoughtful, isn't it?"

"You're drunk. Get yourself home."

"Drunk, am I? And what's that in your tankard, then? Tea? You set yourself up very high and mighty, Cai Jenkins. Just watch you don't fall. 'Tis a long way down."

"You should know."

"Aye, I do know it well enough. Oh, don't look at me that way! I only speak out because I care about you. Your father took me on my very first drove, did you know that? A fine man, he was." He pauses, swaying, a nasty grin rearranging his features. "Good job he's not around to see how you've let Ffynnon Las go, mind."

This is too close to a nerve for Cai, who draws back a fist but finds its trajectory blocked by the bulk of Dai the Forge.

"Now then, Llewellyn, m'n. No need for that sort of talk," he says, gently but firmly turning the teetering man around and pushing him toward the door. "Go and find yourself a shady spot. Sleep off some of that ale."

Llewellyn allows himself to be guided away from Cai, but

calls back over his shoulder as he leaves, "We'll all be watching you, Cai Jenkins. The whole town'll be watching you. You think you can be the man your father was? You want to be head drover, then? Well good luck and welcome to you, *bachgen,* you'll need every bit of it!"

Early this morning, from my lofty hiding place I watched Cai and Mrs. Jones down in front of the house, trap ready, dressed in their market day best. I heard my name called, but the word was snatched away by the mountain breeze. Moments later the clip-clop of Prince's hooves echoed up the valley as he conveyed his grumpy passengers toward town. Let them go without me. I have no wish to be paraded in town as I was at chapel. Who knows what further humiliation might await me? If there is the slightest chance I might have to endure another moment in the company of the Reverend Cadwaladr I would sooner not risk it. The day is too bright, too golden, to sully with the company of strangers. I would so much prefer to be here, listening to the heartbeat of the hill.

Up here, in the high pasture, I have found a perfect spot. A shallow dip in the ground worn by years of sheltering sheep. To one side are three boulders, smoothed by the weather, and leaning over the top is a sturdy blackthorn, its low, twisted branches and tough leaves providing shade. If I crawl forward and peer over the rim of this grassy bowl I can observe all that goes on at the farmhouse below without fear of being seen myself. Today the corgis have joined me. Bracken fidgets, and I stroke the little dog's dense copper fur, soothing him, and he relaxes once more, stretching out to rest his nose on his white paws. Behind him Meg yawns lazily. I smile at them.

We three will not be going to market today.

Bracken responds by beating his bushy tail lazily against the mossy ground.

I imagine how Mam would scold me to see me lying here

instead of setting off with a basket on my arm and coins to spend like a good wife should. I roll onto my back on the warm grass. The fractured sunlight that the blackthorn allows dances on my closed lids and makes me drowsy. Here, safe, free, away from people, where nothing is expected of me, I can consider things with a steady mind. And what I must consider, while I can put my best wits to the subject, is indeed not a *what* but a *who*. Reverend Emrys Cadwaladr.

I still see clearly the expression on his face as he reveled in my humiliation at chapel. It is as if he instantly judged me, the moment he met me, judged me and found me wanting. His sermon was vague enough—I cannot say that any of it might be directed at me, and yet I feel that his disapproval, his anger, they were meant for me. I cannot explain it properly yet. I know only that I have made an enemy without even trying. I cannot believe he was able, in that brief introduction, to detect that there is something . . . different about me. Something that, I confess, no preacher has ever been comfortable with. What puzzles me most, however, is that I lost my singular ability to be in another place, to travel in my special way in order to escape a situation not of my liking. I have been doing it all my life, and yet at chapel I was utterly trapped. I had lost the gift for witchwalking.

I have only ever in my life known one person other than myself who could witchwalk. Dada. I remember the first time he put a name to it. I did not realize then that this was something other people could do, but thought it peculiar to me. It was spring, I recall. I was not more than four years old. We had been to Crickhowell, I forget why. Mam was not with us, but this was not unusual. Often Dada and I would set off on errands together. Errands which, more likely than not, would end up at the White Hart. Dada sat me outside on a bowed wooden bench and bid me wait for him. I quickly grew impatient, but would not think of disobeying my father. I had been told to sit and stay, and sit and stay I would. At least, in body. I remember as if it were days rather than years ago, how my eyelids grew heavy and drooped, how the rough stone of the inn wall pressed itself through the thin cotton of my dress against my back. I wished I was in Spencer Blaencwm's hayfield, playing with his collie puppy. I wished to be there and wanted to be there and thought of being there and then, in less time than it takes for a bumble-bee to flap its wings, I was transported to that very place. The tall grasses and feathery fescues tickled my bare arms as I ran. I called the puppy, in my high, clear child's voice, called him until he appeared. And together we skipped and jumped through the flowering meadow, two young beings enjoying the late spring sun. And then I became aware of Dada's voice, urgent and cross, and his hands on my shoulders. I remember the confusion of that journey back to myself, how everything seemed to turn in on itself. And then I was outside the inn once more, and Dada was gripping me tight, looking at me long and hard. He said nothing more until we were away from the curious ears of his fellow drinkers. Striding home he had asked me where I had been, and I had told him.

He nodded thoughtfully, then said, "Witchwalking is a serious business, Morgana. Stray too far, stay too long, and you might never find your way back. You remember that."

And I did remember it. I do. Even now I am aware of my limitations, of times when I have touched the fringes of danger, almost going beyond that point of no return.

My daydreams coupled with the heat make me lethargic and slothful so that I am soon asleep. When I awake, the sun has begun its descent. Groggy from our slumbers, and hot despite the shade, the dogs and I stumble from our den and walk down to the house. There is not a whisper of a breeze now, and the air has become heavier, as if thunder might not be too many days off. I hurry to the well, drawn to the shimmering water as the dragonflies that flit about the small plants which surround it. I sit on the stone wall and lower my feet into the pool. The water is blissfully cool and I begin to come to my senses properly. I am on the point of going indoors, mindful of the fact that Cai must be making his way home by now, when a coldness not caused by the water chills my body. I hear hoofbeats upon the dry road heralding the approach of a small trap or cart. At once I know it is not Cai returned, but someone else. Someone who has the ability to inspire unease in me even before I can see them. I climb from my perch and turn, shielding my eyes against the sun to try to make out who it is. I see an unremarkable grey mare harnessed to a modest but good quality gig. As if from nowhere a cloud passes in front of the sun and in its shadow I can clearly discern the solid, unfriendly form of Reverend Emrys Cadwaladr.

6.

Both dogs stand beside me, clearly agitated by the man's presence, as am I. What can he want of me? Was it not sufficient that he see me humiliated in front of all our neighbors? He must know he will not find Cai here on market day, so why has he come? Why would he wish to see me alone?

He pulls the mare to a stop and ties the reins, casting about for signs of anyone other than myself. Quickly deciding that there is no one, he does not bother with so much as the pretense of a smile, nor with the formal pleasantries of greeting. Such behavior would be false. He and I both know it. Whatever performance he might put on for his congregation, it was plain to me upon our first meeting that he has taken against me. My sickness in the chapel was brought on by him, I am certain of it. And the nauseating smell, though fainter now we are outdoors, follows him still. I am on my guard. Bracken rushes about, barking. Meg stays close, her lip curling to reveal sharp, bright teeth as the minister draws nearer.

I stand still, steady. I will not be intimidated by this preacher. This is my home now.

"Well, *merched*," says he, "it is good I find you alone. It is as I hoped. What I have to say to you would best be kept between us. Of course, how you choose to act will determine whether or not the content of our conversation remains private." He gives me such a look of loathing as I have never received before. Truly, I must disgust him. He speaks in what is, at least for him, a low voice, though there is no one to overhear us.

"You are not welcome here. I know what you are. *I know*. I

have sought God's guidance on the matter. Would it be un-Christian to shun you, to denounce you, even? I have prayed. I have wrestled in my mind with the principles at stake, the case for and against. What is right, and what is against God. I have also, make no mistake, taken into consideration your husband. It is clear to me he is blinded by his obvious infatuation with you, enchanted by your youthful appeal. Bewitched, one might almost say." At this he allows himself a slippery smile. "But then, he is a young man still, widowed, and in need of a wife. I cannot condemn him. Nor do I believe him to be aware of your true nature. Of what you are. To publicly declare the truth, what I know to be the truth, well, it would mean ruin for him. He would be finished here. Forced to leave, I shouldn't wonder. Leave Ffynnon Las, give up the farm, everything . . ."

He pauses to sneer at Meg, who is still snarling at him. Bracken has come to sit nervously behind me now. Can they, too, smell the awful odor that seeps from this man's pores? It is acrid, sour, curiously familiar. Suddenly I know where I have smelled it before. Once, when I was a small girl, I was roaming the hill on a particularly hot day, the sun making me clumsy in my movements. As I scrambled over some smooth rocks I disturbed a nest of sunbathing vipers. I recall now the exact same smell, the smell of warm reptiles. How can such a stench emanate from a human being?

The minister has resumed his sermon.

"Well, then, what to do? In the end it was the Good Book which gave me the answer I had been seeking. As is so often the case, the guidance I needed lay within those beloved bindings." He leaves off restraining the habitual inclination of his voice to ring out loudly, so that now he booms and bellows as he delivers his verdict upon me, his face reddening. "The words it gave me left no room for doubt, no space for prevarication or misinterpretation for there I read: 'Suffer not a witch to live!'"

I am openmouthed now. It is many years since anyone has applied that word to me. I realize now, that I had hoped here, at

Ffynnon Las, I might have the opportunity to begin anew; to be accepted as a young woman from another place, nothing stranger than that. When I was growing up there were whispers, of course, and Dada made sure I knew as soon as I was old enough to be told that I had the magic blood in me. But the word *witch* was not lightly used. I do not like to think of myself this way, for the title fills others with fear, and garners, at the very least, unwanted interest. What causes him to label me so? He has no knowledge of my witchwalking, he cannot have. And in any case, Dada could witchwalk, but he was not a witch. I can harness the power of my anger sometimes, and direct it where I will, but this is not spellcraft or some ancient art. It is simply in my being to do these things—a natural part of me. And how would he know of these things? He has not seen them.

I feel my mouth dry and my stomach tighten, as I take in what he is saying. Not only is he accusing me, to my face, here and now, of being a witch, but surely he is threatening my very life with his statement.

Before I can respond in any way he goes on, "There is no home for you here, no place for you. The people of Tregaron are Godly and devout, and would not tolerate a witch among them. Were I to expose you they would hunt you down and, if you were fortunate, drive you out. If their fury at your being here took hold, they might demand the magistrate try you. Or, and I cannot vouchsafe their restraint, they may simply choose to . . . *deal with you* in their own way." He shakes his head slowly. "A mob is a terrifying thing. It is my calling, and my sincere belief in Our Lord's compassion, that has compelled me to seek you out alone and present you with the opportunity to leave. Vanish. Disappear into the night. Take yourself away from Cai Jenkins, away from Ffynnon Las, away from my parish, and never return!"

At my feet Meg starts a rumbling growl. A dragonfly dips by, turns, and has the bad judgment to alight on the edge of the gig. The iridescent green and blue of its body dances in the bright sunshine. The loathsome minister reaches out his pink, plump hand and snatches it up, trapping it in his fist. He stares at me as he deliberately crushes the life from the hapless jewel of a creature, before carelessly letting its broken body fall to the ground.

"Remember, *Mrs. Jenkins,*" says he, mockery in his voice, "you could be as easily dispensed with, should the need arise."

Something in his tone, or perhaps it is the very blackness of his heart, finally provokes Meg beyond endurance. With a roar far greater than her size she charges forward and seizes the reverend by the ankle, sinking her teeth deep into his abundant flesh. He gives a scream and kicks out at her, struggling to free himself from her painful grasp. Bracken barks furiously but is too timid to actually take hold. Reverend Cadwaladr grabs his hat from his head and beats at Meg with it.

He shouts at me to control her, but I will not. Why should I? I would bite him myself if I didn't fear to do so would be to taste poison.

At last he shakes her free, his other foot catching her a vicious thump in the ribs. She yelps and retreats long enough for him to scramble into the driving seat of his conveyance. Both dogs continue to bark and leap. The minister takes up his whip and cracks it at them, catching Bracken a stinging stripe across his back, causing him to yelp and whimper. Meg is not so easily put off. With a scowl in place of farewell, the reverend picks up the reins and roughly hauls the mare about, whipping her forward. Still Meg runs after him, and then, too late, I see what he is going to do. He waits a few strides for the dog to come close to the front wheel and then wrenches on the left rein of the horse's harness. The painful jab on the animal's mouth causes it to swerve violently to one side.

I gasp, my hands flying to my face, as I watch Meg disappear beneath the wheels of the gig. She does not make a sound. She does not have time. As the cart moves forward she is revealed, broken and inert, on the dusty road. I dash forward, scarcely registering that the reverend has pulled the gig to a halt. It is only as I throw myself over Meg's lifeless body that I hear more hooves upon the lane and become dimly aware that Cai and Mrs. Jones are returned.

Cai calls out a greeting to the reverend, but as he draws closer he sees me on the ground and in distress. He pulls a startled Prince to an abrupt stop, throws the reins to Mrs. Jones, and springs from the trap, running to me, taking in a scene that must make no sense to him. He cannot see his poor little dog at this point, only myself on my knees weeping and distraught, behind the wheels of the carriage. On reaching me he sees that I am unharmed and I recognize relief as it alters his expression from one of fear to one of puzzlement.

"Morgana? What is it? What has happened?" he asks gently.

Now he sees Meg, and is not quick enough to mask his own sorrow. He puts a hand gently on her head, his shoulders slump. He is lost for words, even when Mrs. Jones calls anxiously from the trap wanting to know the cause of such obvious anguish.

Reverend Cadwaladr climbs down from the gig, his manner most solicitous and pastoral.

"Oh, my dear Mr. Jenkins. What a sadness, what a wretched accident. Please, accept my apologies . . ."

Cai shakes his head. "'Twas not your fault, Reverend."

"Nevertheless, I feel partly responsible for the poor creature's fate. I came out here to offer Mrs. Jenkins my best wishes in her new home, to assure her of her place in our flock, and now . . . this."

Cai masters his emotions and thanks the minister, seeing in my distress only grief and upset for Meg, not having any way of telling what else could possibly lie behind my agitation.

"Well, if there is nothing to be done, I'll take myself off," says Reverend Cadwaladr. "Leave you to attend to matters."

Cai nods, muttering a response. Mrs. Jones has stepped down from the trap to join us. She lays a steadying hand on my arm and, though I cannot be certain, I fancy her look seems to me to reveal a broader understanding of the situation. We watch in silence as the skinny mare pulls the gig unevenly up the lane and away from us.

Cai takes off his hat and runs his hand through his hair. Mrs. Jones sniffs loudly. Bracken comes to sit beside his sister, tips back his head, points his nose skyward and begins a high, mournful howling. Cai gently scoops Meg up in his arms and carries her toward the garden, the rest of us forming a woeful procession behind him.

Cai grunts with the effort of swinging the axe. The morning is horribly humid, the air thick, but there are no clouds and the sky offers no promise of rain any time soon. He has stripped to the waist to let what air there is cool his skin, but sweat continues to trickle down his back until his body is glistening with it. He can taste salt on his lips. With every fall of the iron axe head into the blocks of wood he asks himself, *What happened?* He has been splitting the dry oak rounds for over an hour and still he has no answers. There was something about Meg's death, about Reverend Cadwaladr's presence at the farm when he must have known Cai would not be there, something about Morgana's distress that does not quite fit. He does not understand why, but he finds this mystery unsettling. Troubling.

He pauses in his work, straightening up, stretching his tired muscles before leaning on the axe handle for a moment. He looks up at the cloudless sky. The weather is set fair for now, but must surely break in the next few days, and no doubt when it does so it will do it suddenly and with some drama. This is not what is needed. After such a long dry spell the ground will be baked hard, and heavy rain will wash over it, running in rivers down the mountain, moving too quickly to soak in and be of any use. The result will be a thin layer of slippery mud without much benefit to the parched soil and plants. And if the rain were to be prolonged, the weight of the cattle would poach the ground to soup or sucking clay bog, depending where they trod. Best to get them off the hill ahead of time, he decides. Herding the beasts down the steep slopes in such conditions would be a perilous task, posing danger to the legs of cattle and horse alike. He had hoped to gain a week or two more from the high grazing, but it is not worth the risk. Better safe than sorry—it is far too near to the date of the drove to risk losing any stock. With the perilous state of the finances of Ffynnon Las, each head of cattle counts, and none can be wasted. He leans his axe against the woodpile, pulls on his cotton, collarless shirt, and goes in search of Morgana.

He finds her kneeling at Meg's grave. Together they chose a sunny position in the garden to the front of the house. Morgana is busy planting a Welsh poppy in the freshly turned soil. Cai approves of her choice of flower—its golden yellow petals so perfectly echoing the sunny brightness of the dog's coat.

Morgana hears him approach. She turns to look at him, but does not rise.

"Just right." Cai nods at the spindly plant. "Good growers, those poppies. There'll be lots more there come next summer, see?" He steps closer. He can tell how upset she is and he is swamped by a desire to crouch beside her, take her in his arms, and comfort her. Assure her the pain of her loss will ease in time. Hold her close. But he hesitates and the moment is lost. Morgana turns away from him, back to the grave. She presses the earth around the stem of the flower, and as she does so Cai notices a single tear dash down her cheek and drop onto the brown earth. The teardrop sits for an instant upon the fine, dry soil, and then melts into it, watering in the tender plant.

Cai clears his throat.

"I've decided we should gather the cattle. Today. Now." When Morgana does not move he realizes he has not explained himself sufficiently and goes on. "I'll need your help, Morgana."

At the mention of her name she starts and gets up, her head a little on one side, questioning.

Cai shuffles his feet. He does not want to put things baldly, but there is no avoiding the facts. "I've only one dog now. Bracken will need a bit of assistance."

Morgana considers the remaining corgi which is sitting beside the grave, looking as sorrowful as it is possible for a dog to look. She nods, understanding.

"Right you are," says Cai. "I'll take Honey. We'll find you a saddle for Prince."

Together they fetch the horses and tack them up and are soon urging them to climb the steep hill behind the house. Bracken is at last stirred into action, seemingly pleased to be put to work.

Cai tips his hat back on his head. He has chosen to wear it for the shade its brim provides, but his scalp is prickly with the heat and the stickiness of the air. He digs his heels into Honey's flanks but the old mare, too, is feeling the heat and swishes her tail stubbornly. By the time they reach the gate onto the hill both horses are slick with sweat. This does not, however, dent Prince's enthusiasm for the place. He begins to prance and fidget, eager to run. Morgana sits still, unperturbed by his behavior.

"He thinks we're going to see his mares," Cai says, tying the gate open behind them. "Not today, *bachgen*. We've other business to take care of today."

They press on toward the dew ponds, the thunder tracking their steps. They canter along the track as it narrows above the steep, rocky drop and twists still farther upward. At last they crest the hill and the moorland opens up before them.

"There!" Cai points as he sights the herd some half a mile distant.

It is as they approach the herd that a curious change occurs. Much to Cai's astonishment, the sky, which had until now been a flawless blue, smudges and darkens. Clouds gather and swirl with unnatural speed so that soon they form a heavy mass, blocking out much of the sunshine, casting an eerie gloom over the moorland. Cai is accustomed to the capricious nature of the weather on the hills, but even he has never witnessed such an abrupt shift in conditions. Before they reach the herd the next rumble of thunder, like the snoring of some distant giant, vibrates through the air. If that giant should wake before they have the cattle off the hill, if the storm should break . . . he does not wish to consider the danger further. As if the rain would not make the task of gathering treacherous enough, Cai knows that the open mountain is no place to be when lightning begins its dance. He looks at Morgana and reads unmasked concern in her expression. She is a child of the hills, after all. She cannot be unaware of how strange and threatening this sudden storm is.

The animals shift and turn, unsettled by the curious behavior of the elements. They jostle for position within the group, none wishing to take up a place in the exposed outer circle. By the time Cai and Morgana reach the cattle the clouds have begun to empty their heavy load with such force that the water bounces back up a yard or more when it reaches the parched earth. Almost at once the quality of the air changes, becoming markedly fresher and cooler, filled with the scent of wet grass and heather. Cai whistles and calls to the cattle. His cries are not commands so much as communications, indistinct words and sounds to at once calm and cajole. To reassure the herd, and to remind them to whom it is they belong.

"Ho! Hup! *Dewch! Heiptrw ho!*" he calls, before whistling again, this time at Bracken, who instantly recognizes the signal and speeds off in a wide curve so as to arrive swiftly at the rear of the herd. The rain is falling so hard and so heavy now that the noise of it half drowns his words as he turns to Morgana. "Go to the lower side. Keep below the cattle. Not too close. We must bring them down steady, not running, mind."

Morgana nods and leans her body to turn Prince, giving him his head so that he willingly canters across the wet turf. The cattle lower their heads as he and Morgana pass. Their horns are short but sharp and shining in the rain. The bolder of the animals snort, and one or two dig at the ground with a hoof, their eyes wide.

"Ho! Come on, then! Ho! Ho! *Dewch!*" Cai waves his arm as he shouts, and urges Honey into a thudding trot, taking the higher ground, so that he is near the front of the herd, but just above them. He knows they need to gain forward movement before he can take up position ahead of them. They will follow him well enough once they are settled and resigned to being moved. For now he must assist Bracken in pushing them forward, and, with Morgana's help, keep them straight and headed toward the track that will lead them off the hill. Already he is wet through and knows Morgana must be, too. It has been so hot, and his body is so coated with sweat and dust, that the warm rain is a blessed relief. Even so, it is worrying. Beneath Honey's hooves water has even now begun to bubble and flow as the baked soil rejects it. Within minutes the terrain will become slippery, with the dusty track turning to slick mud before they can descend to the farm. He snatches off his hat, waving it as he yells at the cattle, eager to get them, to get everyone, off the mountain. For now the storm is fully upon them. Thunder crashes with such volume that sensible thought is impossible. Simultaneously the sky is illuminated by sheets of lightning which momentarily replace the slate-grey storm clouds, bleaching all color from the sky, revealing the landscape in a jittery, preternatural brightness. The cattle begin to give voice to their nervousness, so that even between the cacophonous growls of thunder the air is filled with noise. Water and noise. Cai squints through the rain coursing down his face. Morgana and Prince are a single, blurred shape moving back and fore, keeping the herd tight together, deftly retrieving a stray steer. She is more capable than he could have hoped, and he is profoundly glad of her help, but a part of him wishes she were safely back in the house. As long as there is only sheet lightning there is no real danger, but Cai knows the mountain weather well enough not to be complacent. If the nature of the storm shifts, which it could in an instant, forks of lightning will start striking down from the heavens, searching for the highest objects, which can conduct them to the wet earth. And, on this treeless hilltop, there is nothing higher than the cattle, the horses, and the riders.

"Ho! Bracken, steady, m'n!" Cai cautions the dog, who, without the calming influence of Meg, and barely able to hear his master's whistles and commands, is quickly becoming overexcited, pushing the herd too fast. "That'll do!" Cai hollers, but his words are completely erased by an almighty crack of thunder directly above their heads.

When the first spike of lightning splits the sky it does so with such ferocity that at first Cai thinks he himself has been struck. There is a ringing in his ears followed by a calamitous roaring of the cattle. Time seems to stop, and in that frozen moment he sees the celestial fire find its route through the three rearmost cattle. He sees the jagged light reach them, encompass them, and enter them. He hears the nerve-splitting crack as it hits them, hears the agonized cries of the surrounding beasts, and the terrible hissing of unimaginable heat on wet bodies. Later he will swear he could smell the aroma of sizzling skin and cauterized flesh as the unstoppable power of the lightning seared its way through the cattle, like hell's merciless branding iron held in place until meat, muscle, and bone yield beneath it.

Three young bullocks are dead before their superheated bodies thud to the ground. A fourth is left senseless and immobile. A fifth and sixth sustain vicious burns to their backs. Terror travels through the herd as quick as the lightning itself. If time had, for a moment, paused, now it speeds forward as if at twenty times its normal pace. Cai watches in horror as the cattle, moving as one terrified mass, raise their heads and begin their stampede. He digs his heels into the old mare's flanks, urging her after the disappearing stock, but she knows her own limitations, and is clumsy and wary of such a reckless descent. He shouts after the cattle, calling them back, knowing that his words are lost amid the thunderous drumming of their hooves on the stony ground and their petrified bellowing as they run. Bracken, however fleet of foot, is left behind, an ever-widening gap opening up between dog and herd. Cai whistles frantically to send him below the beasts to try to turn them back up the side of the hill. The corgi's oversized ears serve him well. Picking up his master's command this time he darts downward, quickly catching up with Morgana and Prince. Morgana is doing her best to maneuver the animals, but with little effect. Cai can see her attempting to steer Prince alongside the outer cattle, using him to lean into the panicked creatures to guide them upward. But the pony is too small, and the cattle too terrified. Prince is surefooted and willing, but he is no match for the muscled cattle, and, were he to trip and fall, such close contact could easily result in both pony and rider being trampled. Cai, being above and now almost completely behind the stampede, is reduced to the status of an appalled observer. If the cattle are not turned, but are allowed to descend the narrow pass at such speed there is no possibility of them all surviving the descent. The track is too narrow to accommodate the shape of the herd as it is, and with the beasts so panicked they will not step into place behind one another but charge blindly as one. They must be turned.

"Morgana!" Cai screams at her, waving his hat madly. "Morgana! You must turn them! They will go over the edge. Send them up! Up!"

Morgana gallops on beside them, Prince slipping and stumbling on the waterlogged ground but never once balking or slowing his pace. She is keeping up with the herd, but cannot turn them by her presence alone. Bracken is with her, barking wildly now, but to no avail. It is not enough.

"Call to them, Morgana!" Cai shouts as loud as he is able but he is already too far behind to connect with the cattle, all force and authority taken from his voice by the rumbling of hundreds of hooves, the bellowing of the beasts, and the relentless, deathly music of the storm. Still he prays she will be able to hear him. "Use your voice, Morgana!" he begs. "They will listen to you. You must call to them! Morgana, for the love of God . . . speak!"

But she does not. She looks back at him, her face stricken, her mouth open in silent torment. At the last minute she pulls hard on the reins, causing Prince to throw up his head and wheel around, for the way forward has become too narrow for them to proceed farther. In seconds the herd has moved ahead of her and is charging along the track that follows the side of the mountain down. Cai forces his reluctant horse after them. He reaches the brow of the hill, Morgana slightly in front of him, just in time to see the calamity reach its inevitable conclusion. The cattle charge on to the slender pass, and, too late, the front-runners realize there is insufficient room for them all. They swerve and push and scramble in an effort to stay on the track, but the force and speed of the stampede make such changes in direction and pace impossible. Cai watches in disbelief as his livestock plunge over the edge and disappear down the lethally vertiginous and rocky mountainside. On and on they go, like a seething torrent, pouring in a black waterfall, relentless and unstoppable. The doomed cattle charge to their deaths as if the devil himself is driving them on, on and on until all save a handful have gone, vanished, stepped into nothing and dropped, silent at last, to the stony valley floor two hundred feet below.

7.

He despises me now, I am certain of it. How can he not? He watched me let his herd rush to their end. Watched me fail to stop them. Watched me, Morgana dumb and dim, who could not make a sound to save them. *Could* not. But he will not understand that. *Would* not, he surely thinks. Thinks that it was my choice to leave them rumble on to meet their deaths, his marvelous cattle, his livelihood. Did he but know that I summoned every morsel of my energy, in whatever shape, to try to save them. But my will was of no use; it would not work for me when I needed it most, for my mind was in such turmoil, all happened with such speed, and the beasts were too strong and too possessed of their own terror for me to be able to affect them.

And more than this, it was as if some unseen force was resisting my attempts to control the herd. I sensed a strong presence, even over and above that elemental force of the storm. For that was a storm the like of which, in all my years of knowing and loving the mountains, I have never encountered before. It was not born merely of nature, I am certain of it. It was as if there was something, or someone, provoking and directing the very weather about us. The notion that such power can be bent to the will of any one being terrifies me. But who? And how? And, for this is what torments me, *why*? Why would anyone wish to ruin my husband? To see Ffynnon Las fail. Or to do him harm? Or was *I* the intended victim? I have no answers to these questions, and but one small clue as to where the truth might be found. For when we were on the point of losing the herd, when the storm raged at its most fierce, when the animals were in the grip of terror, and when I proved unable to change the calamitous course of events, something strange tweaked at my attention. Something altogether out of place. Only now, away from the turmoil and the desperation, have I been able to identify what it was that further perplexed me. It was a singular, memorable, and nauseating stink. The exact same stench that had turned my stomach in the chapel.

And what has my husband left to take on the drove now? Only a handful of the herd were able to stop themselves falling. A handful will not turn about the fortunes of Ffynnon Las. Has he purchased sufficient beasts from farmers to even make the long journey to London worth his while? He will not talk to me of these things, and why should he, when he holds me responsible . . . ? I failed him, that is the truth. These past two days, since that terrible moment on the mountain, he has scarcely said a word to me, and none that was not necessary. His face is clouded with anger, as if the storm still rages deep inside him. Anger and grief, too, I believe, for I think it not an exaggeration to say he loved those fine, fearsome animals. 'Tis true, their fate was to be slaughtered one day, but not all of them, and not in such terror, not so brutally, not in such anguish. And not for nothing. For most lie rotting at the bottom of the precipice, their value decaying for want of access. The exultant cries of the buzzards and kites can be heard even now as they feast upon such bounty as they have never seen before. Foxes, too, will come and gorge themselves, tearing limbs from their sockets, devouring flesh and drinking blood and crunching bones until nothing is left but food for the worms.

If only he knew that he cannot hate me more than I hate myself. I have not slept but the roaring of those poor panicked cattle fill my dreams. Last night I forced myself to visit them, witchwalking to the very place where they lie. It is not a place of peace. I could still taste their fear in the wet air. Even the sky continued to weep, it seemed to me, the rain not having ceased since the weather broke. The tempest has passed and been replaced by a dull greyness and melancholy rainfall.

And now I must dress in more of Catrin's finery, drag a brush through my knotted hair, tie a bonnet on my head, and accompany my husband to chapel once again. The idea of it fills me with dread. The memory of my humiliation there has faded; it is not that which sends a chill through me at the prospect of returning to Soar-y-Mynydd. No, it is the knowledge that Reverend Cadwaladr will be there. If it were in my power to do so I would choose never to be in his terrible presence again. He made his opinion of me plain. He delivered his ultimatum. He crushed Meg beneath the wheels of his gig without hesitation. I know he will destroy me just as coldly if he decides to do so. But I am not so easily put out. What proof has he against me? None. What actions of mine can he show as evidence that I am a witch? None. What witnesses can he call to my being anything other than a young woman whose strangeness lies only in my having come from another place, and in my wordlessness? None. This is my home now.

I know also that I have caused Cai enough trouble thus far. He needs me, for without me he cannot be *porthmon*. To leave him now would be to cast him to ruin, I am certain of it. I would prefer not to have to face the monstrous Cadwaladr at all, but Cai requires me to be with him at chapel, on his arm. He needs me beside him today, for all to see. It must cost him to look at me now. How he must replay the terrible events of the storm in his mind, and how he must see so very clearly my sorry part in it. I must do what I can to help. To make amends. However much I would prefer to stay away from the reverend, I cannot refuse Cai, not now. Oh, how I wish Mam were here to guide me, to help me be what he needs me to be. I am fortunate indeed to have Mrs. Jones to assist me as much as she does.

Cai is waiting for me in the trap and barely glances at me as I climb in beside him. I have found a modest bonnet for the occasion and am wearing a somber green dress, the plainest I could find. Mrs. Jones stitched up the hem for me and showed me how to pull my stays tight to draw in the extra width about my narrow frame. The rain has slowed to a fine drizzle. As we set off I cannot help thinking how different our mood is from the first time he took me to chapel. Prince trots onward just as briskly, but now Cai is as silent as I, and it is not a comfortable quietness. It is as if he does not trust himself to be civil to me. I confess I am surprised at how much his displeasure affects me. I had not thought to care so much for his opinion. I had not realized how much I have come to take his approval as a given. And how much I have come to value it.

As we approach Soar-y-Mynydd the first person I see is Isolda alighting from her carriage. She is as elegantly dressed as ever and has dignified smiles for everyone she greets, but I find myself as always unsettled in her presence. I admit I do not understand my own dislike of her, beyond it being instinctive, and that she has the ability to make me feel awkward and unsuited to my position.

"Morgana?" Cai's voice startles me from my thoughts. "Are you ready to go in?" he asks.

I nod and he helps me step down from the trap. As we make our progress through the worshipers people offer words of sympathy and support. We may live in isolation at the farm, but bad news travels even through the empty fields.

"The worst kind of luck," says an elderly farmer, shaking his head slowly.

"Aye," another agrees, tipping his cap back to scratch his forehead. "'Tis a real shame. A fine herd, you had, Ffynnon Las," says he to Cai, but can offer no further comfort.

Cai allows them to tender their condolences and offers of help as if a close family member had died. I see now why it was important for him to come here today, and for me to be on his arm. We must show everyone that he is not finished. He will still lead the drove in two weeks' time. He is still a man to be trusted in charge of cattle. It was extreme bad luck caused his loss. The sort of ill fortune that could befall any man, and not a measure of his ability or determination. His cattle might lie rotting at the foot of a ravine; theirs he would take, good as his word, to London to secure their incomes for the coming winter.

I sense his arm beneath mine tense, and he draws himself up to stand very straight. There is a man walking toward us I do not know, but it is evidently he who has caused such a reaction in Cai. The man looks down on his luck, ill-fed, and sports a grin displaying more gaps than teeth. Even at this early hour I can smell liquor on his breath.

"Well, well, Cai Jenkins," there is slurred mockery in his tone, "seems you are not so perfect after all. But *Duw,* there's a pity. Your whole herd lost, they do say, or the better part of it. Well, well."

He sways on his feet just as the crowd parts to allow the reverend to emerge. At the sight of him my palms dampen with nervous sweat. I feel my whole body tighten, as if I am readying for flight. I fear my consternation is evident on my face, but Cai is too occupied with the drunk to notice my reaction to the minister.

"Come now, Llewellyn. Our Lord's garden is no place for your spite," says he with his customary force and command, but the man is intent on goading Cai further.

"Won't be much of a drove to take east now. Hardly worth the bother, see? Might as well stay at home, m'n. Leave droving to those as knows how to keep a herd of cattle on a path, is it?"

Cai shows admirable restraint. I wouldn't have blamed him for boxing his tormentor's ears and sending him on his way howling, but he does not. Stepping forward as if the man does not exist he nods good morning to Reverend Cadwaladr, doffs his hat to Mrs. Cadwaladr, and leads me into the chapel. He has done the right thing. We are carried through the narrow door on a gentle current of approval from those watching and waiting to see what action he might take. He has risen above the impulse to thump one who would mock him, and he is the bigger man for it. And I am thankful we have not been engaged in discourse with the reverend. I cannot bring myself to look at him, knowing what he thinks of me. Knowing that it was he who so callously brought about Meg's death.

The service passes without incident. Cai joins in the acts of worship attentively and I wonder if he is praying for guidance and for better fortune in the coming weeks. I feel horribly helpless, guilt still tasting sour in my mouth, loathing of my own failings which have so added to his difficulties making my mood as grey as the sky outside that blanks out the tall windows of the chapel. On top of which I must master my discomfort at being beneath Reverend Cadwaladr's gaze. His sermon is harmless, and does not mention anything I might take to be aimed at me. How long, I wonder, will he allow me to act upon his demand that I leave? How long before he decides there is no course open to him other than to denounce me to the parish. No course, that is, save for one.

As we are leaving the crowded little building Isolda Bowen steps forward to speak to us. Or rather, to speak to Cai. She scarce acknowledges me, her attention focused squarely upon my husband.

"I was so sorry to hear of your misfortune," says she to him, her face a picture of concern.

Cai mumbles some sort of acceptance of her condolences. He becomes restless in her presence, I notice. Ever the riddle, I cannot fathom his reaction to her. At least I am not expected to make polite conversation—what a mercy that is!

Isolda puts a hand on Cai's arm and asks, "I wonder if you would both like to return to my house to dine. I know you do not have the help of the good Mrs. Jones on Sundays, but I have my cook and she will not be stopped in her quest to see me double my size." She laughs lightly. "There is always more food than I can eat, and the waste is sinful. Please, say you will both come."

Cai is hardly in the mood for socializing and hesitates.

Isolda appeals to his compassionate nature. "I pass so many hours in solitude," says she in a small voice. "I would be profoundly grateful for your company."

He might require time to consider the offer, I do not. To make my feelings plain I pull hard on his arm, stepping toward the waiting pony and trap, frowning at him. He can be in no doubt of my response to Mrs. Bowen's invitation, nor can anyone observing our conversation. I see that I have managed to do precisely what I had so fervently wished to avoid—I have drawn attention to us, and am in danger of humiliating myself once more. Myself, and, by association, him.

"Really, Morgana, why must you behave this way? Mrs. Bowen has generously invited us to dine with her." He leans down to me, lowering his voice. "It would be rude to refuse. She is being gracious. You are not to make a scene, do you hear me?"

There is a bossiness, a shortness, in the way he speaks to me that I do not care for. Why do I so often find myself in these impossible situations because of him? I am doing my best to be how he wants me to be, to do what he wants me to do. But I cannot spend time in the company of a woman who belittles me and clearly still has designs of some sort upon my husband. And I will not be chastised for refusing to do so. If he is too stupid to see her for what she is, let him dine with her. Alone. Pointedly, I let go of his arm. I dig my fingernails into my palms as I muster what little dignity the circumstances allow. I am keenly aware that Isolda is enjoying my discomfort, and that we are still being watched by members of the congregation. I will not be bullied. Too late I realize my anger, my hurt, is seeping out of me, as my passions are wont to do. The damp stillness of the day is abruptly bestirred by a swirling wind which snatches at bonnet ribbons, tugs kerchiefs from pockets, sends hats tumbling from heads, and raises skirts to undignified levels. At once, amid much squealing and gasping, all the women present have their petticoats and undergarments indecently on display as they flap at their unruly dresses, frantically trying to pin them down and spare their blushes. All the women present . . . except me. It does not pass unnoticed that I am the only one not so affected by this unexpected and disrespectful wind. I am aware of how undesirable this manner of notice is. I know how people are given to gathering little scraps of suspicion, hiding them away in a fearful part of their minds, until they have sufficient for a feast of accusation and blame. The reverend has made his feelings toward me plain enough. I must take care not to give credence to his claims.

"Oh!" cries Mrs. Cadwaladr as her daughters squawk and reel about her. "What wickedness is this? Oh! Husband, save us!" she shrills, in a manner which is, to my mind, excessively dramatic.

The menfolk, the reverend included, do their best to restore the dignity of their wives, mothers, and offspring, but are soon scampering after their own hats or ushering their women back inside the shelter of the chapel. Reverend Cadwaladr raises his voice, appealing for calm. Isolda, her own gown merely billowing attractively, retains her poise. Even as I try to return myself to the tranquil state necessary to restore order I feel Cai's gaze upon me. Now he is properly angry. He might not, indeed, he *cannot* understand what is happening, but I sense that, even without realizing it, he connects the disturbance in some way, some way he could not possibly so much as voice to himself, connects it to me.

"Morgana!" he growls at me. "Take the trap and go home! I will dine with Mrs. Bowen and I will return . . . later. Go home now," says he, pointing the way back toward Ffynnon Las as if I were a dog that required directing. I do not need telling twice. I march past Isolda, her smug expression lingering horribly in my mind as I pick up the reins and urge Prince homeward at a canter.

Not until we are well out of sight and sound of the chapel do I ask him to slow to a steadier trot. I do not know whether I am more angry than I am stung by Cai's harsh words, or if I am simply disappointed in myself. Either way, here am I, returning home alone, in disgrace once more, whilst my husband, of his own volition, goes to spend time in the home of that woman. Why does she persist in her pursuit of him, even now he has chosen to marry someone else? She is a woman of independent means and standing in the community, however misplaced, what can she want with Cai? Why does it matter so much to her to be the mistress of Ffynnon Las?

The rain has set in again in earnest now, and my bonnet begins to sag about my ears. We are not half a mile from home when Prince shies, dancing sideways and then standing still as stone. I cannot see what has spooked him, and flick the reins gently, asking him to continue, but he will not. His eyes roll and he snorts at something in the hedge just ahead of us. Now I can hear a flapping sound and see that the undergrowth is disturbed by some erratic movements. I climb down from the trap and tie the reins to a sturdy hazel branch before creeping forward. The source of the minor commotion reveals itself to be a young barn owl, fallen into the ditch. I quickly put my hands over his golden wings to stop him thrashing about for fear that he might hurt himself. Examining his snow-white body and sharply taloned feet I can find no signs of injury.

What, my little feathered friend, are you doing out in the glare of daylight, poor thing? You are small. An inexpert flyer, perhaps.

He seems both puzzled and calmed to hear my thoughts placed in his head. His pearly plumage is soft as cotton grass beneath my fingers. The bird looks up at me with enormous eyes and blinks slowly. He seems confused, and I think that he may have bumped his head as he crashed to the ground. I fold him into my shawl and carry him back to the trap. I resolve to make him a nest in a quiet corner of the house. Somewhere he will not be disturbed, and where I can tend him until he is recovered enough to go free again. For the remainder of the journey I allow myself the pleasant diversion of imagining the snuggery I will construct for him in the parlor when I reach home.

After a delicious meal and some particularly fine wine, Cai at last begins to feel the tension of the morning, and indeed the trial of recent days, melt away. He leans back in his chair with a sigh, swirling bloodred claret in his crystal glass. The room, typical of Isolda's home, is opulently yet tastefully furnished, with an impressive table dressed with the best quality silverware, tall candles flickering at its center, and a warming fire blazing in the hearth. There are no rustic pieces of furniture here. Each article or artifact has been selected for its quality and beauty first and foremost. There are imposing oil paintings on the walls, drapes of Chinese silk at the windows, a mirror of dazzling size and decoration above the marble mantle, and glorious Turkish rugs covering the floor. This is a town house built to impress and to house the very best of everything. Isolda smiles at him from the other side of the table.

"I am pleased to see you looking a little less perplexed, Cai. Your demeanor at chapel had me concerned for your well-being," she says, licking red-wine stains from her lips.

Cai is struck, in this moment, by the differences between his hostess and his wife. He recalls the first breakfast he cooked for Morgana and her uninhibited enjoyment of it. It is difficult to imagine Isolda with bacon grease smeared across her cheek. She is so self-contained, so in control of herself. And so remarkably beautiful. The room is lowly lit with candlelight and the dancing illumination from the fire, but the effect is not in the least gloomy, rather it is comforting. It is easy to forget, at least for now, the greyness of the day outside and the worries of his own life.

"It has been a testing week," he says, then shakes his head, not wanting to think of the woes and demands of the mundane, preferring instead to savor the pleasures that are on offer. "That was a splendid meal, Isolda," he says.

"Such a shame Morgana did not feel inclined to join us."

"I am sorry . . . for her behavior." He struggles to find an excuse for her. "She is not yet . . . settled, in her new life. In her new home." He knows this sounds feeble and takes a deep swig of his wine, avoiding Isolda's gaze.

"She is very young," she offers. "I'm sure, given time . . ." She lets the statement drift.

When he looks up from his glass he finds she is watching him and for an instant their gazes meet. Hers is unwavering, bold even. Not for the first time he feels a stirring of desire for this strikingly beautiful woman. There were occasions, since Catrin's passing, when he questioned himself as to why he did not ask Isolda to be his wife. He is quietly certain she would have accepted him. Was it her considerable wealth that stopped him? Did he feel unequal to her, and worry that he would always, were they to be married, feel himself inferior? Or was it that, for all her elegance and charm, for all her beauty, there is something he finds curiously unlovable about her? He cannot imagine ever being intimate with her. Taking her to his bed, yes, he can imagine that. She is undeniably attractive and desirable. But closeness, real togetherness, such as he had found with Catrin? No. It is true, he enjoys her company and conversation, and that this enjoyment was for a time heightened by the element of sexual possibility that existed between them, but on the whole this is something that makes him feel bad about himself. He is not the sort of man to enjoy a physical relationship with a woman without love; it is simply not in his nature. He does not enjoy, in fact, being reminded of his baser needs and desires.

And now he has Morgana as his wife, and his feelings are further confused. He runs a hand through his hair. He is tired. Tired of how complicated his relationship with Morgana is proving to be. Tired of trying to ignore, or make sense of, his wife's strange ways. Tired of trying to do the right thing, and be patient and understanding, and struggling to deal with her wordlessness. A characteristic that has, in part, resulted in the loss of almost his entire herd. And he is tired of having to make all decisions regarding their future on his own. Whilst it might fall to him, as husband, as master of Ffynnon Las, and as head drover, to make difficult choices, he wishes, somehow, that he felt less alone in all these things. He had hoped, despite the obvious obstacles, that he would find a companionship with Morgana that would remove the loneliness he has suffered these past three years. And yes, there have been moments when he has felt close to her;

when he has glimpsed a possible warm, supportive, loving future for them together. But now he feels defeated by the mountain he must climb to make his marriage work. To make his business work. To make anything in his life work.

"I should go," he says, more abruptly than he intended. He stands up, and finds he has drunk more wine than is good for him, causing his head to spin as he rises. Isolda is quickly at his side.

"Must you leave? It is still early, not yet dark," she points out.

He turns to face her. She is standing very close to him now, so close that he can feel the warmth of her, sense the powerful desire within her. They stand in silence, but it is not a quiet moment, filled as it is with unspoken thoughts and needs and wishes. She lays a hand upon his chest and he can feel his own heartbeat pounding beneath her palm. His desire frightens him, so that he casts his eyes down, affecting a protective formality.

"Forgive me, I thank you for your hospitality, but I must leave. Morgana will be waiting for me."

"Do you think so? Do you really believe she is even now at the window, watching the empty road, eagerly awaiting your return?"

There is a note of scorn in her voice which he does not care for. Her words are all the more unpalatable because he fears she is right; that Morgana is not missing him, but indeed is glad of his absence. Relieved by it. He knows Isolda is challenging him, daring him to speak truthfully of the problems in his marriage. Willing him to turn to her, to find comfort, to find passion, with her. Whether or not she sees the refusal in his eyes he cannot be certain, but what she says next takes him completely by surprise.

"Besides, Cai, there is another matter I wished to talk to you about. I am astute enough to know that any farmer, any *porthmon,* suffering such a loss of livestock as yourself, well, he would struggle to produce a financially viable drove under such circumstances. I am no businesswoman, but I understand a little of these things. Being a widow, on my own, I have had to learn the ways of the world, and that includes some of the harsher facts concerning money. I am fortunate that my late husband left me well provided for. More than that, in fact. I shall come to the point. I want to make you the offer of a loan."

Seeing his shock she holds up her hand before continuing.

"No, please, do not turn me down without considering the proposition. I am prepared to lend you what you need to purchase sufficient stock to turn the profit you had been anticipating before the tragedy which befell you."

"Isolda, I couldn't possibly . . ."

"*Please,* do me the courtesy of at least pondering the proposal for a day or two. I only wish to help you."

Cai marshals his whirling thoughts. The money would be a godsend, that is the first thought that comes to him. It would indeed ensure the best chance of a profitable, successful drove. That he does not wish to put himself in a position beholden to Isolda is the second thought that darts about his mind. What, he wonders ungallantly, would she expect in return? And what would others think of such an arrangement? Indeed, what would Morgana think? He is surprised to find that this last consideration matters to him almost more than the others. At last he nods, a little stiffly.

"It is a kind offer," he says, "and one I promise to think about sensibly before responding." He lifts her hand and bows over it briefly, avoiding her searching gaze, before taking his leave.

Outside the rain has stopped and he is grateful for the cool, fresh air, and the long walk home. He wants to arrive at Ffynnon Las with a clear head and his humor improved. With each stride he attempts to shut his mind to the very real temptations Isolda has put before him, and to train his thoughts to home, to Morgana, to the life he has made and must now take responsibility for, however difficult. His head is still fuzzy from the wine, and his temper disconsolate. At once the uncertainty of the future weighs upon him. He had started to feel foolish for having drunk and dined in the grandeur of Isolda's home when he should have been applying himself to the question of how to ensure the coming drove is not a complete failure. And now he has been offered a solution precisely because he had done just that. Even in his befuddled state he knows the fact remains: If he does not succeed in turning around his finances, there is a very real danger he could lose Ffynnon Las. The idea is unthinkable. Could his own weakness, the time he spent wallowing in his grief for Catrin, his poor judgment in moving the herd in a thunderstorm, could these things, could *he* really lead to the end of all his father and his grandfather had worked for over so many long, hard years? It seems even in choosing a wife he cannot be relied upon for sound decision making, for had not Morgana been, in her way, also to blame for the situation in which they now found themselves? And had not he chosen to overlook her *lack,* as Mrs. Cadwaladr had called it? These thoughts swirl round and round in his head so much that by the time he reaches home, the grubby sky bruising under the touch of twilight, he has a fearful pain behind his eyes.

Inside he finds the house in darkness, no fire burning in the kitchen hearth, nor any lamp left lit to welcome him home. Bracken jumps down from the window seat and wags a gentle greeting, but Cai brushes past him, helping himself to the brandy from the top of the dresser. Such is his mood he does not even trouble to find a glass, but slumps on the settle and swigs directly from the bottle. With each mouthful his desperation increases. How has it come to this? Is he to finish up like Llewellyn Pen-yr-Rheol? What sort of wife has he saddled himself with, that has neither conversation nor any social graces? Why must he accommodate all her increasing strangeness, when she gives so little in return? On impulse he gets up and strides from the room and up the stairs. He does not go to his own bed, but crosses the landing to Morgana's room. He turns the handle and pushes open the door. He has not taken care to be quiet, but, for once, she is sleeping deeply and has not heard him. He steps over to the bed and looks down at her. At once all his anger, all his rage, all his blame and harsh judgment of her disappear. She looks so young, so pretty, so fragile. He feels such a loathing of himself for harboring unjustly critical thoughts of his lovely, innocent wife, that his eyes fill with tears, so that her soft, sleeping form blurs. He resolves to do right by her, to make a success of their farm. He will not let her down. He will not be defeated by a bit of weather and some bad luck.

Unsteadily, he leans forward, overcome with the need to kiss her. Not a passionate kiss driven by desire and lust, but a chaste act of deep affection; the sealing of a silent promise. He bends over her and lets his lips touch her forehead.

It is at this moment that Morgana wakes up, opening her eyes to find him looming above her.

Cai sees the terror in her eyes.

"Morgana!" he says, attempting to straighten up. But he is caught off balance and falls forward. Morgana wriggles beneath him, pushing at him, determined to throw him off.

"Be still!" he tells her. "There is nothing to be afraid of. Morgana, calm down . . ."

But she continues to writhe and strike at him. He grabs her wrists in an effort to quieten her, to explain, to reason with her, to reassure her that he was not attempting to force himself upon her. As soon as she feels his grip tighten on her she lunges upward and sinks her teeth into his hand.

"Argh!" Cai shouts, instinctively swiping her away. The back of his free hand connects with her face, sending her down onto the bed. Cai staggers backward. Morgana has bitten deep and drawn blood. He clutches at his wounded hand, shocked by what she has done and appalled at his own behavior. Never in his life before has he struck a woman. She leaps from the bed and stands, her back to the wall, fists clenched, defiant even now. The pain in his hand has a sobering effect on Cai, so that he becomes acutely aware of how badly he has behaved, and how much damage he may have done to his delicate relationship with Morgana.

He wishes he could find words that would undo what has happened, but he can only mutter apologies as he hurries from the room.

Without moving from her place against the wall, Morgana slams the door behind him.

8.

A noise wakes me and I scramble from my bed. Has he returned? Has he come back to my bed to demand his rights as a husband? I thrash about, but I am alone. It is morning. The noise that woke me is being made downstairs—a terrible crashing and smashing. It seems to be coming from the parlor. Oh! The parlor!

I hurry from my room and reach the top of the stairs in time to see Cai pull open the door below and gasp as he stands on the threshold.

"*Duw,* what . . . ?"

He dashes inside and I hear his cries and shouts.

"*Diawl, ydych chi!* Get out! Get out!"

From the kitchen Bracken sets up a barking and scrabbling, but the door is firmly shut.

I run down the broad stairs and into the parlor to witness a scene of mayhem. The owl, it seems, has regained its senses and, finding itself trapped in an unfamiliar place, set about seeking a way out. But I had not thought to leave a window open and the poor bird is swooping and screeching, hurling itself about the place, hitting the walls, reeling backward from the grandfather clock, trying to alight on the dresser shelves, its wings flapping frantically, sending Catrin's beautiful china smashing to the ground. Cai runs back and fore, grabbing at the bird, which only increases its terror, causing further chaos, breaking more and more of the delicate plates and cups. First a serving dish, now a milk jug, next the lovely teapot and two saucers tumble to the floor, shattering on the unyielding flagstones.

I hasten forward, dodging the falling crockery, stepping this way and that to avoid Cai as he blunders about, snatching at the wretched bird. Can he really believe his actions are helping? Why would the owl listen to him as he charges and thunders like an ogre? It lands on the mantle and hesitates, searching for an escape. I dart past Cai, ducking beneath his outstretched arms, and lay my hands upon the trembling bird in the second before it can spring into the air again. As soon as it feels my touch it ceases to struggle, giving itself up almost gladly to my care. I hold it close to me, stroking its silken feathers, fearful that Cai will kill it in his rage.

He looks from the bird to me and back to the bird, taking in its altered demeanor. Now he spies the nest of hay in an old crate in the corner of the room. He narrows his eyes. He looks terrible. It is clear he has slept in his clothes. His hair is wild. His skin pale. The smell of stale wine is strong on his hot breath.

"You." His voice is hoarse. "It was *you* brought that . . . *thing* in here. Don't you know never to fetch a bird into a house? Don't you know of the ill luck that will follow? Are you an idiot girl after all? Look!" He waves his arm, fist clenched at the end of it. "Look at the . . . *havoc* you have caused!"

He takes a step toward me and I move back until I am in the corner of the room. I am not afraid of his temper. I will not let him strike me a second time. But the owl is in such a nervous state I fear its galloping heart will give out if it is subjected to anything further. I can do nothing but stay where I am and control the fire that rises in my own belly. Cai looks at me with such desperation. When he speaks he is no longer shouting. His voice is low, almost a whisper, and his words are full of dismay.

"Calamity surrounds you," says he. "Destruction is ever at your heels. What manner of wife are you? What manner of creature have I taken into my home?"

Abruptly the front door is pushed open and Mrs. Jones breezes in.

"Good morning," she calls out. "And a beautiful morning it . . . Oh! *Duw,* Lord in heaven, what has happened here?" She stands at the entrance to the parlor, her hands flying to her face as she takes in the scene. Catrin's precious china in pieces. Me crouched between dresser and hearth like a cornered rabbit. Cai leaning over me, his face displaying a dreadful combination of heartbreak and disgust.

He turns to her but says nothing, merely striding from the room, pushing past her, snatching up his hat from the hall table, and leaving through the front door. We watch him go, and as he draws level with the window he pauses, his attention taken by something new. I rise slowly from my hiding place, the bird still in my hands, and move closer to the window. A bewildered Mrs. Jones instinctively follows me. Now we see what Cai has seen. Meg's grave. Only days ago we laid the little dog's body beneath the dark soil, and to mark the spot I planted a glowing, yellow poppy. A *single* yellow poppy. Now, though not a week has passed since that sad afternoon, the mound shows not an inch of soil, but is covered in a mass of flowers, fourscore at the very least, their bright petals open to the morning sun, dew glistening on their leaves.

Cai stares at the impossibility in front of him, struggling to believe the evidence of his own eyes. Sensing he is being watched he swings round to find us both at the window. Beside me, Mrs. Jones stands openmouthed, shocked to silence. The owl swivels its soft head, its eyes closed against the sunshine. I stand straight, holding my feelings tight inside me lest they escape and cause further turmoil. Cai looks at me. Looks *into* me, I fancy. And in this moment I know that he sees me. Sees me in the way Mam used to see me. There can be no more hiding the truth. No ignoring the way things are. No more pretending I am not as I am. He holds my gaze for a long moment, his face, for once, unreadable. Without thinking about what I am doing, my action a reaction to the confusion in his expression, I step forward and raise a hand, letting my palm rest on the cool glass of the window between us. He hesitates, as if he might return to the house, but instead he turns away, heading off across the meadow.

I watch the lonely figure that is my husband walk swiftly away from me, climbing the hill toward the freedom and sanctuary of the open mountain, and I wish, more than I have wished anything for a very long time, that I was walking with him.

I feel a gentle hand on my arm.

"Cariad?" Mrs. Jones's voice pulls me back into the room. "I think we'd best put your little friend outside." She nods at the bird. "Don't you agree?"

Together we pick our way through the debris which litters the room. At the front door I kiss the owl briefly before holding it high. It stands on my hand for a moment, stretching its wings, blinking in the brilliance of the daylight. It rotates its head, as owls are given to doing, almost completely, scanning the area for possible dangers. Finding none, it makes a low, purring hoot before leaping upward, wings wide, and flies swiftly toward the trees at the far side of the pond meadow.

We have no sooner retreated inside and closed the door than Bracken tears into the hall, having finally managed to push his way out of the kitchen. He scrabbles frantically at the front door, leaping and whining, desperate to follow his master. I lift the latch and allow him to go, watching his foxy shape, nose down for the scent, tail up for balance, as he charges up the slope in pursuit of Cai.

"He'll be all right now," Mrs. Jones assures me. "Come inside, *merched*. I'll wager a pound to a penny you've had no breakfast. *Duw, duw*, what are we to do with the pair of you?" she mutters, shaking her head as she leads me into the kitchen. "Nothing do feel so bad after hot tea and some of my Welsh cakes, you'll see."

I sit beside the unlit range. I am numb. It is as if when Cai stormed from the house in such a passion he took all my feelings with him. How could I have brought about such destruction? Catrin's beautiful china . . . it is as precious to Cai as it was to her. I watch Mrs. Jones bustle about taking a spill to the kindling in the grate and working the bellows to encourage flames.

"Now, don't you fret, *merched*," says she without pausing in

her work. "Cai Jenkins is a good man. He has it in him to forgive. A walk will calm him down."

But what if it does not, I wonder. What if by my thoughtless-
ness I have broken whatever fragile connection there might have
been between us, just as surely as I have broken Catrin's china?
Smashed. Beyond repair. And how will he treat me now that he
can no longer ignore my . . . strangeness? *What manner of wife are
you?* he asked me. What answer will he find up there on the
mountain?

Mrs. Jones swings the kettle over the burgeoning fire. Water
slops from the spout causing a deal of hissing steam. She continues to chatter on, words of reassurance and consolation, all the
while fetching teapot and cups, and a basket of her flat, sugary
cakes from the pantry. I do not have the will to rise from my chair
and help her. Seeing my deepening despair she at last pauses in
front of me. Hands on hips she smiles, kindly but determined.

"Mrs. Jenkins," says she, her stout legs firmly planted, her
head nodding slowly, "I think the time has come for you and me
to have a talk."

I frown, trying to understand what she can mean by this. She
has been talking nonstop for the past twenty minutes. She knows
I cannot contribute to the conversation. What can she expect of
me? I put my head on one side, questioning. Her answer is to
turn and pad across the flagstones to the old dresser.

This is a very different piece of furniture from the grand,
gleaming one that, until now, safely housed Catrin's china collection in the adjoining room. This is a workaday construction, its
wood darkened by smoke from the fire, its size and age causing
it to sag somewhat in the middle. With difficulty, Mrs. Jones
bends to her knees and pulls open the lower left-hand cupboard.
From this she removes pots and pans and boards and platters until she has the thing quite empty. Next, to my amazement, she
all but crawls inside. Indeed only her own expansive girth prevents her from disappearing altogether, so that her aproned
rump and broad feet remain in a most unflattering pose. When

she calls to me her voice is muffled and her burrowing causes the entire dresser to rock, so that I fear it might topple.

"I do need your assistance, *cariad*. Seems I can't . . . quite . . . reach." With a gasp of exasperation she wriggles backward, turning to sit, flushed, with her plump legs outstretched in front of her. She takes a moment to dab at her brow with her apron and right her skewed mop cap.

" 'Tis no good," she puffs. "My arms have grown too short or the hole has grown deeper, one or the other." She points into the darkness of the empty cupboard. "You will have to fetch it from there." She waves me into the uninviting space. "Crawl to the back, *cariad*. Feel for the gap in the wood."

I scramble inside, marveling that Mrs. Jones did not find herself stuck fast, so tight is the space. There is indeed a piece cut from the wooden back of the dresser, so that I can feel the cold stonework of the wall behind. Mrs. Jones's efforts have already in part dislodged a smooth, square stone.

"Do you have it? You must pull the block out fully," says she, "and then reach your arm right inside, far as you can go."

I do as instructed, firmly banishing from my mind all possibility of disturbing a nest of rats. However at ease I am with countryside creatures, I still have a childish loathing of rats.

"Can you reach it? Have you found it?" Her voice has an edge of excitement to it now.

Had I words at my disposal I would mention that it is easier to tell if you have found something when you know what it is you are looking for. As it is I am left to grope about the gritty space. And, yes, my fingers have found something. Something that cannot be wood or stone, as it yields a little as I probe. It feels almost padded. Wrapped, perhaps. I fumble and scratch at it until my fingers hook the string with which the object is bound, and I am able to pull it free.

As soon as Mrs. Jones sets eyes upon the package she snatches it from me and holds it to her breast, her eyes closed, as if it were the most precious treasure returned to her. When she recovers her senses she smiles at me, holding out a hand.

"Well then, help an old woman to her feet. Not doing my poor bones any good sitting on these cold flags."

With some effort I set her up on her legs and we take to chairs either side of the fire. The flames have caught the larger chunks of wood and are beginning to claim the coal now. The kettle is making faint but promising noises. Mrs. Jones tugs gently at the string, her plump fingers surprisingly nimble as they undo the bows and knots securing the parcel. With great care she removes the wrapping, setting it down on the floor beside her chair. In her lap there now sits a large book, its leather cover worn and showing signs of age, the gilding on its page edges rubbed bare in places. She strokes, no, *caresses* the book tenderly, and her face as she does so appears to lose some of its sags and lines, almost to regain a trace of her lost youth, so that her complexion glows with a secret joy. What can be written on these pages to bring about such a transformation? I lean forward in my chair to better examine the book and notice Mrs. Jones instinctively tighten her hold upon it. It is clear she will not give it over to me just yet.

"Now, *cariad,* where to begin? Ah, the poppies. Yes, I think we should start with the poppies."

At this I cast my eyes downward, feigning interest in a loose thread on my nightgown.

"Oh, there is no call to be wary. Not with me, not now. You see, I do understand you, Morgana."

Even though we have grown easy in each other's company since my arrival at Ffynnon Las, it feels strange to hear her address me thus.

"When your parents named you, did they know, right when you were born, what talents you held? I wonder if they were recalling another who lived long ago, who was one of the most powerful and gifted witches that ever did live?"

The use of the word *witches* startles me into meeting her gaze.

My father chose my name. And yes, Dada knew of its origins, for he often told me tales of the magic wonders performed by my mythical namesake. I have always imagined my sensible, earthbound mother would have fought against the choice, but Dada could be stubborn when it suited him.

"But, to return to the poppies," Mrs. Jones goes on. "I do know you planted a single bloom but a few days ago. And now we can all see the cheerful abundance of flowers on poor Meg's grave. I do believe you were almost as astonished as poor Mr. Jenkins at first sight of them, weren't you, *cariad*? Think back, child. Might you have wept upon that flower as you planted it? *Duw,* there's some strong magic in the tears of a witch. No, stay, don't jump from your chair like a hare from a gunshot. 'Tis only a word." She sighs softly, looking at me with great fondness, so that I find I am not afraid. I find instead that I am reminded of the way my own mother would look at me. "I knew what you were, what you could be, the first time you touched me, *merched.* Do not be frightened. No other living person will hear your secret from me, I do promise you this. For how could I denounce one as is the same as me?"

At this I cannot say what shocks me more—that she has just called me *witch,* or that she has declared herself to be one. In either case, my hands start to tremble. Before I can react further she continues, eager to dispel my fears.

"There are different kinds of witch, mind. And we are not cut from the same cloth, you and me, *cariad.* I am a hedge witch, plain and simple. Everything I know I learnt at my mother's knee, same as she did from her mother, and her mother before that as far back . . . ooh, as far back as any can remember, and then maybe a little further again. All the special recipes, all the cures and blessings, all the healing, all handed down through generations." She pauses to reflect for a moment and I fancy there is a tear in her eye when she tells me, "I did yearn for a girl of my own. Near broke my heart that I was not blessed with a daughter. I do love my boy, of course, but . . . well, he do make a fine farmer, and would have made a very poor witch!" She chuckles at the thought. "My mother did say I had some talent, and she taught me well. Over the years I have done what I can to help people who needed me. Sometimes what I had to offer did ease suffering. Other times, as when poor dear Catrin was stricken with childbed fever . . . well, other times I was not able to help. My talent is but small magic, for small wants and needs. But *you, cariad,* well, you have such a strength in you, such a power . . ." She shakes her head slowly. "I do imagine it must scare you sometimes, isn't that so?"

At this I nod, and then stop suddenly, realizing that I have just admitted to . . . to what? To being a witch? To using magic? I have never confessed such a thing in my life before. Not even to Mam. It was unspoken between us, but understood. My magic came from Dada. He alone could advise me, guide me in this. But then he went away, and as far as Mam was concerned, that was an end to it. Having magic blood was dangerous. Even in these modern times, plenty suffer accusations of witchcraft. At best they are driven from their homes and drummed out of the parish. At worst, well, a mob is a terrifying thing. Some pay for their gifts with their lives.

"'Tis a wonder," says Mrs. Jones, "as others do not see the magic fizzing out of you."

Some do. Sometimes. My schoolteacher thought he saw it, though he could never prove anything. And the children, did they detect something . . . different, too? Others in the village had their suspicions. There were things I did that caused whispers, and then Mam would chide me and warn me not to be so reckless. And so I have become adept at hiding the light that would shine out of me. Until now. Here, with Cai, I have let down my guard. Mrs. Jones has recognized me for what I am. Reverend Cadwaladr was quick to form his own, fierce opinion of me. And now Cai has seen the poppies, and he knows that we saw him notice them. Now the secret no longer sits between us, blocking our view of each other. What will his response be? In what state of mind will he return from his walk?

Mrs. Jones shifts in her seat, trying for a more comfortable position, but not for one second loosening her grip on the book in her lap. The kettle at last begins to sing. We exchange glances.

"Would you mind, *cariad*?" is all she has to ask.

I jump up, full of restlessness brought about by the subject of our discussion, and happy to be given something to do. I set about making tea while she talks on, finding it easier to mask my reactions to her words whilst I am occupied.

"You do know what lies inside you, mind. How could you not? It must be hard for you, keeping the best part of yourself buried. Well, *merched,* you cannot hide the truth from your husband any longer. No more can he deny it. 'Tis fortunate indeed that you have come here, to Ffynnon Las, for this is a place built on magic. There is witching wisdom in its very stones." She looks down at the book again, and, out of the corner of my eye as I pour tea, I see her start to open it. Gingerly, warily almost, she begins to lift the thick cover, the aged spine crackling minutely as she does so. I long for her to throw it wide open and reveal the contents, but it is as if she does not quite dare, does not quite have the courage. Or is it that she does not yet trust me sufficiently to share what is written? Is that what makes her yet hesitate?

"I have told you of the well, of how any who own it own the power it possesses. If they do know how to use it. Well, there is something more. Something that makes this cursing well different to others. Sets it apart. Something that does make it a great deal more powerful. The origins of the well are widely known, hereabouts. What few people are aware of, mind, is what happened many years after the spring was first used to curse, after its magic was first called upon. The story was told to me by my mother, and before she spoke she made me swear a witch's pledge never to disclose the secret to any save another witch, and then only if I was certain, *certain,* mind, that witch was to be trusted." She looks up at me. "Well, *Duw,* don't stand about letting that tea get cold, here, give it to me."

I hand her a cup of the steaming drink and she slurps noisily. I sit opposite her once more but have no interest in my tea. I am far too taken up with her tale.

She closes her eyes the better to savor her drink, drains her cup despite the considerable heat of the liquid, places it on the floor, leans back in her chair, and then, with her eyes remaining closed, she speaks again. When she does so her voice has about it an unsettling flatness, as if she is reciting something. Or, even, as if it is not entirely her own voice.

"This is the *Grimoire of the Blue Well*. All that is written here was set down by a true Witch of the Well, and none other may read it or use it. She who seeks to use its wisdom must first prove herself worthy, must demonstrate her mastery of the craft, must adhere to the code of the Witches of the Well, and must pledge to preserve and protect the well and spring water from those who would destroy it, or would abuse its magnificent power." Her eyes spring open and the sight of them makes me drop my cup which shatters noisily as it meets the floor. What a sight! Gone are the milky but bright brown eyes of my friend and housekeeper, and in their place sit brilliant orbs with irises of gold! Light shines out of them. I am unable to look away, and feel their unearthly gaze searing into my mind, into my soul. I am laid bare before them. I am being judged, I sense it, and not by Mrs. Jones. I have the sensation of heat entering my body, flooding it, until I fear I will be burned up. There is a distant sound of bells, high pitched, notes I can scarcely make out, but clear and beautiful and resonant. Then, as quickly as it started, the examination is over. The heat is replaced by a hollow chill, so that I am surprised to acknowledge to myself that I am bereft at its leaving. For that brief moment I felt . . . complete. At this instant I would give anything, *anything*, for whatever it was that inhabited my spirit to return.

At once Mrs. Jones's eyes return to their normal state. She gives a little cry, and I wonder if she, too, is grief stricken at the loss of such heavenly company. She takes a moment to steady her breathing and attempts a reassuring smile.

" 'Tis well done, *cariad*," says she. "Very well done."

Yet even now she does not pass the book to me, nor open it. I find that I want desperately to hold it. I want it with such a fervor I cannot resist reaching out to take it. Mrs. Jones's smile vanishes instantly.

"Not yet." Her voice is sharp, but unmistakably her own. "You have a way to travel yet, *merched*. But I will help you on your journey, and the rewards will be, oh, so very marvellous, *cariad*! I do know of the wisdom in these pages. I have been entrusted with the keeping of the book, but I am not witch enough to use what is written here. Nor was my mother, nor my grandmother. Rare is the witch who can hold such magic, who can take such knowledge into herself and use it without being destroyed by it. I do believe you are witch enough, *cariad*. *You,* Morgana, you are who the *Grimoire of the Blue Well* has been waiting for, all these long years. But you must prove yourself worthy. Demonstrate that you are ready to be instructed in the ways of the Witches of the Well. And the first step you must take is that you let your own sweet magic out. Give it free rein. Allow yourself to feel your own strength."

I look at her, shaking my head, wanting to do what she asks, but not knowing how. And not knowing if I dare.

"All will be well. You have been *seen, cariad*," says she, and I know what she means by this, though I long to know, *seen by whom?* She looks suddenly very tired, and I see that acting as she did, as some manner of conduit, has exhausted her. She lifts a hand and waves it feebly in the direction of the door. "There is something you can do. Something you should do. I do think you know what it is." With this her eyes close and she drifts into a deep sleep, all the while clutching the *Grimoire*.

Unsteadily, I get to my feet. She is right, I *do* know what it is I have to do. Or rather, what I must try to do, for I am not in the least confident that I will succeed.

I return to the parlor. The dresser is decimated. Most of Catrin's china lies broken on the floor. I tread carefully and find a small clear space so that I am able to kneel down. I hold a fragment of a tea plate in my hand. The shard shows part of a wild strawberry plant, its tendrils brutally cut, its fruit split in half, the rough innards of the china exposed at the newly formed edges. Cai told me how much Catrin treasured the collection, and how strongly it reminded him of the wife he loved. A good wife. A proper wife. Not a wife who brings chaos and disaster with her. Not a wife who causes her husband to take to the hills to escape her. Not a wife with strange ways and abilities, none of which serve any useful purpose. Not a wife such as I.

For is he not correct? Is it not true I have brought him only trouble? He should not have struck me, 'tis true. But then, I should not have bitten him. He only raised his hand to me instinctively, as a person would to swat a stinging wasp. I cannot berate him for it. And had he not chosen to return home to me, rather than stay with Isolda? He came to my bed, as a husband has a right to do, having shown more patience than I deserve, and how did I repay his kindness? With violent protest. How can he view what have I done since I arrived here at Ffynnon Las? The cattle died because I could not call them from their fatal path. I have humiliated him at chapel twice in as many weeks. And through it all he has striven only to make me feel at home. He has not forced himself upon me. He has not cast blame in my direction, though he could have done so. And he has not questioned the curious, some would say unnatural, occurrences which, at times, my will provokes. Until now. He cannot pretend he has not seen Meg's grave. We can none of us pretend any longer. And, that being the case, I can, surely, put what meager and whimsical talents I have to some good use. Mrs. Jones tells me I must let my magic out. Whatever it was who visited me through her, whatever it was that stole into my soul and examined me, whatever it was needs me to prove I am mistress of my own magic. This is a test I must not fail.

I look at the piece of china in my hand. Slowly, merely by willing it to do so, I cause the door of the parlor to swing firmly shut. Mrs. Jones said there is powerful magic in the tears of a witch, but at this moment I have no tears. What else do I have to offer, to sacrifice in order that the spell might take? I run a finger along the sharp edge of the broken plate and it slices into my skin. A thin line of blood wells up in the tiny wound. I watch the blood ooze and trickle down the length of my finger, holding up my hand, turning it, so that the crimson rivulet travels to my wrist, twisting around my arm like the tendrils of the strawberry plant. At last a thick, glossy droplet falls from my elbow onto a tiny chunk of broken china on the floor in front of me. I close my eyes. I feel the air in the room stirring, growing colder, the force of it whipping up my hair and my nightdress, gaining strength, until it begins to rattle the window latches and lift the rugs and wobble the candlesticks on the mantelpiece. Soon the entire space is in motion, a swirling, whirling muddle of dust and ash from the hearth and slivers and crumbs of china. I keep my eyes tight closed and raise my arms. Blood continues to seep from my finger, and with each drop the pressure in the room builds like the coming of a storm. I sway now, letting the maelstrom move me, my head dizzy, my chest tight, my limbs starting to shake and twitch with juddering tremors. I have no conscious notion of what it is I do, only the sense of doing it. Only the will. My will. I feel the power of it envelope me and everything in the room, until all is connected and pulsating with the thrilling force of it, so that I feel the walls cannot withstand it and must surely burst outward. But they do not.

High above Ffynnon Las, morning cloud sits heavily upon the mountain. As Cai walks the dampness settles about him and he can see no farther than a few yards in any direction. But he knows these hills well and could walk them blindfolded if he had to. He is familiar with the rocky stretches of path, the precipitous drops, and the sucking bogs, and even in his current, distracted state can navigate between them without danger. A curlew, its song muffled by the water-filled air, sets up its whirring call which rises to questioning, upward notes. Cai does not hear it. His mind is occupied with attempting to reconcile what he knows to be good sense with what he can no longer ignore or deny. There is something about Morgana which defies explanation. Her strangeness goes beyond her silence and her wildness, he knows that now. There is more behind Meg's death than she is able to make him understand. Then there are the sudden winds, the slamming doors, her enviable, almost unnatural, rapport with the livestock . . . and now the flowers on Meg's grave. Flowers which should have taken two or more years to become so abundant, and yet he saw what he saw. She had planted a solitary flower and watered it in with a single tear and now there grow a multitude of blooms. What is more, he can no longer hide what he knows about her from Morgana herself. She saw the moment of his epiphany. All pretense must cease. He must admit, first to himself, that she is . . . what? Possessed by demons? A conjurer? A sorceress? A witch? Even hidden inside his head the words sound preposterous.

When he was a boy he heard talk of such people, of course, the legends of the land seethe with them. But they were spoken of with either fear or loathing. These were bad people, if people they could be called. Beings to inspire suspicion and hatred. Conjurers were tricksters and conmen. Sorcerers gained their powers from the devil. And a witch would be no man's choice for a bride. Why had he not seen the extent of her strangeness sooner? Was he blinded by lust? By love? By his need for a wife? Why had nobody who knew her thought to warn him? And now he remembers how the villagers where she lived had spoken of her carefully, even kindly, but with those telling pauses. Those small hesitations. Now he understood what lay in those unspoken thoughts. For how could they speak to a stranger of such a thing as magic?

He walks on, tramping over the wet ground, not letting the uneven surface disturb the comforting rhythm of his pace. At least up here he is able to think. Able to order his tangled thoughts. For aside from Morgana, there is the drove to attend to. He still has the cattle he will purchase from neighboring farmers to take, and a handful of his own stock. Others will bring their sheep, and he has the three ponies promised to the London breeder, but it is not enough. The simple fact is, as it stands, he will lose money. The cost of borrowing to buy, added to the expenses of the drove itself—the fodder, shoeing, grazing, accommodation, labor, and, of course, the tolls he will have to pay to use the roads—mean he will not clear sufficient funds to break even, let alone make a profit.

Unless he accepts Isolda's offer of a loan. She did not speak of terms, but he assumes they would be more favorable than those the bank might offer him. But what would it cost him, truly cost him, to accept such assistance from her? The idea of being in her debt does not sit comfortably with him. And yet, he is not in a position to dismiss it out of hand.

With or without a loan, from the bank or a benefactor, another stark fact remains unchanged. If the future of Ffynnon Las is to be secured the ponies must be sold. All of them. Cai knows the London buyer will gladly take every last leggy yearling of the Ffynnon Las bloodline, and at a fair price. It will break his heart to do it, but his heart has been broken before and he has survived.

He reaches the dew ponds and, as if summoned up by his decision, those ponies still on the hill step forward from the dense mist, emerging as if spirits from some ghostly realm. Cai stands still and lets them approach him. They are youngsters and sniff nervously, necks stretched long, ears alert, ready to whip round and tear away should a threat present itself. Which it does, in the wet and panting form of Bracken, who has at last found his master and comes barking through the miasma, scattering the snorting ponies. Despite himself, Cai laughs, and stoops to ruffle the soggy fur of his remaining corgi.

"Now then, *bach,*" he says, "you'd best save your energy.

There'll be more than enough work for you to do this year." He knows the truth of this. In fact, he knows that one dog will not be sufficient to work the drove, not with so many ponies to manage as well as the cattle. Cai watches the skittish youngsters disappearing back into the slowly rising cloud and a realization comes to him. The person most suited to herding the flighty little horses on the long journey is Morgana. He stands up, shaking his head at how convoluted are the twists of fate that life delivers. He has only this morning admitted to himself that his wife is a woman apart, a creature full of mystery and miracles, and here he is planning to enlist her help on a three-week drove that will make or break the farm and any possible future together they might have.

"Dewch," he bids the dog at his heel, and together they start to descend. His chosen route takes him to the lane on the far side of the hill, so that he will have a steady hour's walk home still. He is in the act of climbing the neatly laid hedge onto the road when he hears hooves nearby. There is no cloud at this level, so that he can clearly see the small, raggedy funeral procession as it makes its way along the lane toward the old chapel at Llanwist. Cai steps out of the way and takes his hat from his head as they pass. The cortege is strangely silent, save for the steady hoof beats of the hairy-heeled horse, and the slow creaking of the wheels of the old cart it pulls. The coffin is small and plain. Ahead of the deceased a minister Cai does not recognize leads the way. There are four men following in tall hats, and these he takes to be pallbearers. There is a handful of mourners, no more than six in all, two of them elderly, shuffling women. The somber party drifts quietly on. Cai feels a chill travel up his spine and puts it down to the damp of the morning getting into his bones. He waits a respectful moment before continuing in the other direction, following the lane toward Tregaron.

He has not gone half a mile when he comes across a farmer of advanced years mending a gap in the hedge. For all his age, he is able to deftly raise the short-handled chopper and split the hazel branches before bending them to weave a tight seal for the hole. Cai recognizes him as Dai the Forge's uncle. They exchange pleasantries and pass the time of day for a few moments before Cai thinks to ask about the funeral.

"I had not heard that someone had died," he says. "Do you know who they are burying up at Llanwist today?"

The old man's eyes widen and he stares hard at Cai.

"There's not been a funeral up at the old chapel for years," he tells him slowly. "Not since Reverend Williams moved to the coast."

"Well there's one there this morning," Cai assures him. "You must have seen it come past. I had to step out of the way to let it go by, see?"

The old man has paled noticeably. He shakes his head.

"I saw no funeral," he says.

Cai is puzzled and not in the mood for nonsense.

"Well, *Duw,* you'd have to have been asleep in the hedge not to notice! A big ugly horse they had, pulling the cart. Smart enough bearers, mind, proper top hats . . . The mourners were not many or young, but . . ."

The old man repeats slowly, "I saw no funeral. And no more did you."

"Are you saying I'm a liar?"

"I'm saying you are mistaken."

"Don't be daft, m'n. I know what I saw. How can I mistake a whole funeral?"

The old man points with his hatchet as he speaks to underline his words.

"I'm telling you they don't hold funerals up at Llanwist no more, and not a horse nor a cart nor a coffin went by me here to-day." He leans forward, his walnut face screwed up, his voice low. "What you saw was a *toili*."

"A *toili*?" Cai laughs nervously. "Have you been supping ale for breakfast, granddad?"

"Aye, call me a fool or a drunk if that makes you feel any easier about it, but there's no getting by the facts."

"Facts, is it? You are telling me I've nearly had my toes trod on by a load of ghosts, and you're talking about facts?"

For Cai has heard of a *toili* before. Many years ago, when he was no more than a boy. He remembers his grandfather telling him of how Jones Heol-Draw witnessed a spectral funeral, horses with black feather plumes and all, over near Pontrhydigiad, one bright August afternoon. No one would believe him. Cai recalls hearing how the man had been scared half out of his wits and was adamant about what he had seen.

The hedger goes back to chopping at the hazel branches to finish his repairs. "No good denying it," he says, not bothering to look at Cai any more as he speaks. "Not for us to decide these things. A *toili* comes as a message from the spirits, from those passed over. 'Tis a message for him as sees it and none other. Someone is in danger," he states, baldly. "Someone close to you is going to die, and there's not a thing you or anyone else can do about it."

Cai opens his mouth to argue further with the man, but a coldness has gripped his heart. He knows the superstition well enough. And he knows what he saw. He is tempted to retort that there is no one close to him any longer; that death has already claimed the woman he loved. And then he remembers Morgana, and a fresh pain stabs through his heart as keen and as agonizing as anything he felt for Catrin. Morgana!

He runs. He runs so hard and so fast that even Bracken is left trailing behind him. He runs though the air sears his lungs and his chest might burst from the effort. He runs though the muscles in his legs scream and his head becomes giddy from the doing of it. His hat flies from his head but he does not pause to retrieve it. He can think only of Morgana, and that he has judged her harshly. He sees now that it is unfair of him to take against her strange ways—they have always been a part of her. He has simply been choosing to ignore them; how can she be to blame for that? The realization comes to him that he does not care, not about magic or mystery or things he cannot explain. He cares only about her. Morgana, with all her wildness and her curious gifts. Such talents as she has cannot be bad, he reasons, because they are part of her and she is a good person, he is certain of that. Why should these gifts not be God sent, after all? The thought that she might be in danger, that something might happen to her before he can reach her, drives him on.

He runs until at last he can see Ffynnon Las, and then he runs harder up the drive, past the pond meadow and into the house itself, flinging wide the front door.

He all but collides with Morgana as she emerges from the parlor. Standing in the hall, panting, fighting for breath so that he can speak, he grips the startled girl by the shoulders.

"Morgana! Morgana, you're all right. Oh, thank God. Thank God!" With one more gulp of air to sustain him he pulls her close, pressing his mouth over hers, kissing her with the passion and longing of a man starved of love for a very long time. A man who has only just realized what he has. A man shaken by the fear that he might lose what he has finally found. He stops kissing her but does not loosen his hold on her. Mrs. Jones has come out of the kitchen and is staring at him in astonishment, but he doesn't care. Morgana looks shocked. He tries to explain, gabbling on about the *toili* and the old man in the hedge, making no sense at all. In the end he gives up and pulls her close, kissing her again, this time more slowly, with less desperation, savoring the sweet moment.

When she pulls back it is to look at him, questioning still, her expression uncertain.

Cai smiles and says gently, "Well, at least you didn't bite me this time. I call that progress, my wild one."

Morgana smiles now, her whole body relaxing, a deep sigh escaping, a sigh of letting go. She hesitates for a moment and then takes his hand, leading him into the parlor. Cai follows meekly.

For a second he cannot see what it is she is trying to show him. The room is as it has always been. Now he recalls the chaos in which he had left it not three hours before. Order has been restored, pictures righted on the walls, cushions and rugs straightened, and there, on the dresser, every piece of Catrin's china restored to perfection.

He steps forward and touches the teapot, searching for signs of breakage or mending, but can find none. Every cup and saucer, every plate, everything that was broken is now as new. Whole again and perfect.

Cai looks at Morgana who is watching him nervously, clearly unsure what reaction to expect. He is only glad he took that time on the mountain to think about his extraordinary wife and to consider how best to cope with the aspects of her nature he can no longer ignore. There could certainly be no more pretending now. Not for any of them. He gives Morgana's hand what he hopes is a reassuring squeeze. He calls to the housekeeper.

"Mrs. Jones! I think we could all benefit from a cup of tea."

"Oh, right you are, Mr. Jenkins."

"We'll take it in here. In the best china, if you please."

"Oh, yes!" she cries, more than a little breathlessly, before disappearing to do as he bids her.

Cai looks at Morgana. He is still holding her hand and feels no inclination to release it. Instead he raises it to his lips for the softest of kisses and says only, "Thank you, Morgana. Thank you."

9.

At every available opportunity, Mrs. Jones and I now engage in the practice of magic. What joy it is, at last, not only to be freed from the burden of my secret by sharing it but to be actually encouraged to use my gifts. Of course we must take care not to be observed, and are even cautious when it comes to revealing what we are about to Cai. I still tremble when I recall the moment I took him into the parlor to show him Catrin's china restored. I had not been certain I would succeed, and my attempt to control my gifts so very specifically, so very precisely, felt childishly haphazard and blundering. And more than a little frightening. Never before have I sought to muster my strength in such a way. Up to that moment, all my efforts to direct what powers I have, to harness the strength of my will and send it out into the world, they have been more . . . instinctive, brought about as an immediate response to something. This time was different. This time I paused, considered, shaped my thoughts into something so much more particular. Even as I felt the familiar tempest surging out of me and connecting with the elements in the room I was uncertain as to how to proceed, or as to how successful my efforts might prove. I admit, I surprised myself. It was as if a hundred elves had worked their magic over a hundred nights to produce flawless results. I could not have wished for better.

And yet the notion of revealing my work to Cai terrified me. I knew there could be no turning back from such a path. This was my way of laying myself open to him, naked, vulnerable. No more hiding. No more pretending, to him or to myself. *This is what I am,* I was saying to him, *will you still have me as your wife?* I half expected him to put me out. Send me on my way. But he did not. Of course, the moment was in no small part eased by the kisses that preceded it! What mysteries men are. He had left the house in a fury, calling me a creature, lamenting ever having brought me into his home. He had returned, but a few hours later, fearing some calamity might have befallen me in his short absence, holding me to him, and kissing me with such fervor that had I been given to speaking I would have been dumb-struck. As was Mrs. Jones! The picture of her face, first witnessing Cai's behavior, and then setting eyes on the china . . . Well, I shall recall the image whenever my spirits are in need of lifting.

Still, we must not press his acceptance of my talents too far too fast. He has seen what I can achieve; he has held Catrin's re-perfected china in his hands and stood and gazed at the poppies on Meg's grave, but he knows nothing of the *Grimoire,* nor of the Witches of the Well. It is one thing for him to accept me, whom he loves—I am sure of that now—for what I truly am. It would be quite another for us to hope that he will consent to Mrs. Jones instructing me in the ways of an ancient order of witches, using a book that holds power even she is more than a little afraid of. She and I have agreed that there is no call for him to be both-ered by each and every thing that we do in this regard. It is enough for me that he is content to let me be as I am, without secrets, without judgment, without fear.

Meanwhile, Mrs. Jones is proving to be a formidable task-master. She was quick to inform me that restoring a few plates was not considered sufficient evidence of my abilities, and that my mettle, my talent, and the seriousness of my commitment to the Witches of the Well must be tested further before she would consider letting me read one word of the *Grimoire.* Thus far she has had me transport objects about the kitchen without leaving my chair (an exercise I found almost tedious in its simplicity), ignite a spill for the fire with my breath (which I will admit proved more troublesome than I had anticipated), and summon a mouse and his family to the pantry to feast on breadcrumbs on the floor. This last activity did not run precisely according to plan, so that within minutes the shelves were riddled with the tiny rodents, and it took us much longer to persuade them all to leave than it had done to invite them to dine in the first place. It was a lesson, as my mentor repeatedly reminds me, in how too much magic can be as unsatisfactory as too little when spell-casting. I was only grateful my clumsiness with the spell had not brought rats running to us, else I might have lost my nerve and fled.

And today we are to work with the well as we attempt to expand and develop my witching skills. Cai is absent. He has an appointment with Mr. Evans at the bank and left for Tregaron half an hour ago. We shut Bracken firmly indoors to spare us from his enthusiastic help, and go out to the well.

Mrs. Jones leans over the mossy wall of the pool and scoops up a palmful of the cool water. She takes it to her mouth, sips, and nods at me to do the same. As my fingertips break the glossy surface ripples fan out in hypnotic circles. The day is already warm. The curved wall above the pool is in deep shadow, so that as the water pours from the spout between the stones it remains out of the sun's reach and retains its mountain chill. Only as the day progresses will the edge of that coldness be blunted by the summer warmth. This early, the temperature is both shocking and refreshing. Even with scant light, the water yet retains its characteristic blueness—a rich indigo, full of mystery and promises.

Mrs. Jones closes her eyes and lets another handful of water fall softly back into the pool as she speaks. "We ask for the protection and blessing of the well. We come to this sacred place with open hearts, bearing no malice to others, wanting only to act in harmony with the wishes of the Witches of the Well, followers of the *Grimoire of the Blue Well*." She opens her eyes once again, and we two stand in silence for a moment, a silence broken only by the gentle trickle of the spring water and the lapping of the pool against the ancient stones which surround it.

I find I am nervous, no, not quite that . . . excited, at the prospect of further testing my magic. For so many years I struggled to conceal this part of myself, for fear of what I might do. And for fear of what others might do. It is thrilling to have the freedom to explore the wonderful gift that magic can be. Dada would be so happy for me, so proud.

"Take off your shoes, *cariad,*" says Mrs. Jones.

I hesitate, surprised at the instruction, but my teacher is in no mood to give what she clearly considers unnecessary explanations.

"Take them off," says she.

Once my feet are bare she bids me climb up and stand in the well pool. If the spring water was shocking to my fingers it nearly takes my breath away as I lower myself, waist deep, into it. My skirts billow about me, tugged by the current where the water leaves the pool on its underground journey to the pond in the meadow below the house.

"A Witch of the Well can work with water like none other," Mrs. Jones tells me. "It will be your element, Morgana, if you learn how best to persuade it of what you want. Never force it. Do not attempt to govern, only to guide. All the elements resist arrogance, mind. Remember that, *cariad.* Now, there are words you should use. No, don't fret that you have no voice. It does not matter. Speak in your mind, and with your heart, and you will be heard. So, arms by your sides. No, not like that, *Duw.* You look like a scarecrow. Down low, loose, there." She leans forward and shakes my arms to encourage them to flop. "That's better. When you utter the chant slowly, *slowly,* mind, raise your arms. Raise them all the way up until they are above your head, where you clasp them together and hold them, as if you are joining two ends of a rope together. Are you ready? Well, then, repeat, over and over, as you move . . . 'The circle of water has not beginning nor end. The shield of water holds me safe.' Stand straight, *merched*! Right, on you go. No! Don't wobble. Stand firm." She prods me sharply in the stomach so that I flinch before I am able to compose myself properly again.

At last she is quiet and I begin the chant, repeating it as I gradually raise my arms. It is a curious task, indeed, to carry out instructions without having the first idea of what it is one is trying to achieve. I feel more than a little ridiculous, standing fully clothed in the pool, moving my arms as if in some manner of dance. A blackbird comes to the well looking for a drink, sees my curious behavior, and changes its mind.

To begin with nothing happens, save for water running down my sleeves and a deep chill setting into my feet. Seeing this lack of success Mrs. Jones berates me.

"You do need to think the words *clearly,* with sincerity. Again. Do it again."

My actions are similarly without result the second time, and the third. Mrs. Jones tutts and shakes her heads, repeating the chant to me to make certain I have it right, pushing me to try again and again, over and over, until my legs are become numb with the cold and my arms ache. Then, suddenly, something does happen. On what could be the fifteenth attempt, I am aware of a change, a subtle alteration in the air about me. A slight ringing, or singing, perhaps. I recall the bells I heard when Mrs. Jones first showed me the *Grimoire* and wonder, with real hope, if we will be visited by whatever heavenly presence came that day. But no, we are alone, we two, save for the well and its own special magic. And now that magic begins to show itself. This time, as I raise my arms, the water rises with them. The effect is somewhat alarming, so that I have to fight to control my urge to stop what I am doing. The look Mrs. Jones gives warns me against any such notion. I continue to lift my arms, and the water, and now I can see that I am being encased in a complete bubble! A thin layer of glistening water, transparent but colored in parts by fractured light falling through it, envelopes me, so that I am soon totally surrounded. I keep my hands clasped above my head, scarce daring to breathe lest I break the spell. I am indeed inside a shield of water, totally enclosed and held, with plenty of air, and not a bit of wetness. What an astonishing feeling it is. I see my own glee reflected in the delighted expression on Mrs. Jones's face. I experience such a wonderful sensation of both safety and exhilaration at one and the same instant that I cannot help laughing, and the second I do so the spell is broken. The bubble bursts with a loud pop and the water around me falls to the pool, soaking me as it does so. I am a silly sight, water dripping from my nose and coursing down my face, my dress sodden, giggling like a lunatic. For a moment I think Mrs. Jones will chide me for my lack of seriousness, but she, too, is taken up with the playfulness of the moment, and with my modest success.

She smiles broadly, her face dimpling.

"Da iawn, cariad," says she with some satisfaction. "Well done indeed."

Two days later and the morning of the shoeing arrives, and with it another spell of testingly hot weather. There is still moisture in the air, making it sultry and uncomfortable. As I kneel beside Meg's grave, leaning forward to plant a sprig of honeysuckle, I can feel perspiration tickling the back of my neck as it runs. Cai has found a piece of slate to act as a headstone and cut Meg's name onto it. He seemed pleased with his work, but to my eye it is too somber for such a cheerful spirit. The honeysuckle will soon cover it. Very soon. I will make certain of it, just as I have brought about the speedy proliferation of the poppies. At my side Bracken pricks up his ears. He has heard something I have not. I stand and shade my eyes with my hand, squinting down the road. Now I hear the sound of an approaching wagon, and soon a sturdy covered cart comes into view, drawn by a piebald cob possessed of a lazy trot and a walleye. Two men sit in the conveyance, and, as they come nearer, I cannot hide a smile at the comical sight they present. For the driver is a mountain of a man, with shoulders broad as a butcher's block, his great chest straining at the buttons of his shirt, sleeves rolled up to show his arms, hairy and brown in the sunshine, muscles bulging like wool sacks. He favors a cloth cap, which is noticeably too small for him and is jammed onto the back of his close-cropped head providing neither shelter nor shade. His companion is a slender youth sporting a mass of dark curls that bush out from beneath his felt hat, which is of a size more suited to the driver. He is as slight as the other man is substantial, and as tall as he is broad.

Cai has heard them, too, and appears from the yard, where he has been making preparations. The cattle, what few we are to take with us, are already in place, milling about the cobbles, disconsolate at the lack of grass. The ponies we gathered yesterday and are waiting now in the paddock behind the barn. I have not yet reconciled myself to their being sold. When Cai explained to me that this is the only option left to him if he is to turn a profit on the drove I understood his words, his reasoning, but I could not believe he meant to do it. All of them, save for Wenna and one other aged mare, neither of whom are strong enough to make the journey. But the rest of the herd must go. The herd which his father and his grandfather spent their lives nurturing and expanding. I cannot bear the thought of all these wonderful, wild creatures being wrenched from their home, from all that they know, to be taken to a far-off place, tamed, broken, and used as driving or riding ponies among the fearful noise and clamor of London. I know it pulls at Cai's heart, too. Just as I know that had the cattle not died the ponies would not have to be sold. Once again the sour taste of guilt flavors the memory of that awful day. To his credit, my husband has done his utmost to assure me that he directs no blame toward me for the loss of his herd. That the past cannot be undone. That we must work together toward a secure future. And that I am to accompany him on the drove. This decision he delivered as matter-of-factly as if it were a passing thought of no consequence. But, oh, it is of great consequence to me! I, who have never been farther than an overnight journey from my home, to be traveling across counties into the heart of England, guiding and caring for the ponies. If go they must, I would rather it be me taking them, seeing to it that the drove is as safe and gentle an experience for them as it is possible to be. Cai says I am to have Prince to ride, and I shall treasure the hours I get to spend with him before we must part forever, for even he is to be sold. Cai will have to make do with Honey, which is a matter of some concern, he tells me. She is, in truth, too old and too slow for such work, and will not make the testing task of *porthmon* any easier, but he cannot afford to purchase another. She, too, is to be sold at the end of the drove, and we are to return home by stagecoach.

The hefty piebald reaches the house and comes to a clumsy halt, regarding me warily with its startling light-blue eye. The men greet each other as old friends, and there is much back slapping and good humor. At last the giant man, who is, if it were possible, even more imposing once he has climbed down from the cart which creaks under his shifting weight, spies me. I stand up, awkward beneath so many eyes, still clutching a handful of honeysuckle.

"Well, *Duw,*" says the man mountain, "who is this vision of loveliness? Queen of the May, is it?"

The younger, slighter man says nothing but steps forward and puts me under such intense scrutiny that I blush horribly.

Cai smiles, pleased, it seems, at their interest in me. Will he never tire of me being a curiosity? Perhaps it will be worse now, in our newfound life together which includes all that I am able to do. All that I am.

"This is my wife, Morgana." Cai is enjoying making the introductions. "Morgana, this is Dai the Forge, and Edwyn Nails," says he.

Dai snatches his cap from his head. "Well, Jenkins, m'n, you didn't tell me as you had taken an angel for a wife! 'Tis a pleasure to meet you, Mrs. Jenkins."

Cai explains, this time without awkwardness I fancy, "Morgana does not speak."

"Well, *Duw,* you are a lucky man, Ffynnon Las. A beautiful bride who chooses to be silent. There's doubly blessed you are!"

says he, before letting out a bellow of laughter. He jams his cap in place and gives Edwyn Nails a slap on the back that sends him teetering. "Come on with you, m'n. Stop staring like a stoat at a hen. There's work to be done."

Edwyn contents himself with nodding in my direction and joins Dai in fetching what they will need from the wagon.

Dai sets up his portable forge, pumping at the bellows until the coals glow first red, then orange, and ultimately white. The fumes of the burning coal oil fill my nose and sting the back of my throat. The cattle cluster nervously on the far side of the yard, but they need not concern themselves, for they will be cold shod. The ponies, however, must have iron shoes heated and beaten to fit their neat little hooves. Prince and Honey will have a full set. The foals, young stock, and most of the mares will go without, the breed having naturally dense and durable hooves. Only some of the older mares whose feet are given to mud cracks or splitting will also need to be fitted with shoes. Edwyn assists Dai in stoking the forge and placing anvil and tools so that they can be easily reached. The three men exchange easy banter and teasing, and the mood is light, filled with a sense of purpose and the pleasure of shared work. All the while, however, I am aware of Edwyn's eyes upon me. No matter that he is occupied with the task in hand, he finds time for furtive glances and even outright stares. Cai seems not to notice, or if he does he makes no comment. I soon become uneasy beneath such unceasing interest, however, and find his behavior bothersome. If it were not for this attention I should be enjoying the day, for here I feel useful, included, valued as a part of Ffynnon Las, given that Cai trusts me with the ponies. When they are gone, I wonder, will he find me useful still?

The first to be shod are the old mares, who stand quietly enough. After these come Honey and Prince. Both tolerate the rasp and paring knife without complaint, standing calmly whilst Dai folds himself almost double to trim and file their hooves. Prince provides a particular challenge, being so small, so that Dai is at one point reduced to kneeling. Once he has shaped the feet he selects a set of shoes nearest to the required size and throws them into the furnace. Edwyn works the bellows, and the thick iron curves slowly change color. When they are ready, Dai uses a pair of heavy pincers to pluck them from the coals. He lifts up Prince's off hind, pulling it through his legs so that it comes through the split in his tough leather apron to rest on his knee. With the utmost care, he positions the shoe onto the hoof, which sends up a plume of pungent smoke as the heat burns into the insensitive layer. When he lifts up the shoe the black print that remains shows him how close he is to the desired shape. Dropping Prince's leg he carries the shoe to the anvil where he beats it with a bouncing *one*-two-three, *one*-two-three rhythm, wielding the heavy hammer as if it were no weight at all. He repeats the procedure twice more until he is satisfied and then plunges the shoe into a pail of water, which bubbles and steams as it cools the iron. Edwyn steps forward now, nails gripped between his teeth. He takes the warm shoe from him, lifts Prince's leg, and tap, tap, taps the iron slipper into place. The work is slow and necessitates care, for a badly shaped or ill-fitting shoe will lame a horse within a mile.

I stroke Prince's snowy neck, sending the pony into a doze despite the attention his feet are receiving. Looking across the yard I catch Cai watching me. He smiles, and I feel my heart speed a little. The memory of the way that he held me, with such sincerity, with such, could it be, passion? He has not kissed me since, but then our days have been filled with the business of preparing for the drove. I wondered if he might come to my room and found myself unable to sleep, but it seems I am still not to be "disturbed." As if I were not already! I find his affection heartening. Soothing. Reassuring. If only we can make a success of the drove, then it may be that I shall know happiness with this curious husband of mine.

"Right, that'll do him," declares Dai, waking Prince up abruptly with a slap on the rump. "You can take him away, Mrs. Ffynnon Las. Let's get to those cattle."

I put Prince in the low stone stable with Honey while the men dampen the forge, more steam rising as Edwyn empties the water bucket over it. Where shoeing the ponies was a pleasantly sedate business, fitting *cues* to the Welsh Blacks is another matter entirely. Cai, Dai, and Edwyn select a beast, corner it, with the unasked for assistance of a barking Bracken, and rope it. It is now that I see why Dai's size so perfectly equips him for his chosen trade. The bullock (for such this one is) must be turned. This involves Dai leaning shoulder to shoulder with the anxious, leaping beast, picking up a front leg, and pushing the whole of his considerable weight into it, his own strength and bulk pitted against that of the muscular animal until it is unbalanced, tipped over and falls to the ground. Cai sits on its neck, holding its head by the short, sharp horns, whilst Edwyn ropes its feet. Now Dai deftly places the thin shoes over the cloven hooves so that Edwyn can nail them in place. He must work fast, as the longer he is held the more the bullock will struggle and its captors tire. Within minutes it is done, the ropes untied, and the beast springs to its feet and rejoins the herd. I marvel at the thought that, come the drove, this process must be repeated with perhaps two hundred head of cattle. We have scarcely more than two dozen remaining, but even this seems an exhausting task. In order to be of use I employ Bracken to help me select those already shod and let them slip through the yard gate into the rear meadow. They buck and leap as they reach the turf, testing out their new footwear.

It is midday before we are finished. The moment the final steer joins its fellows Mrs. Jones appears in the yard with welcome refreshments.

"Here we are, *bechgyn*," she calls to us, as if we were children played too long in the sun. "*Duw,* there's dusty you are!" This is directed at me, and I notice now that my bare arms, and indeed my face and neck, are coated with a fine layer of grime kicked up by the cattle, stirred through the air by the heat of the furnace and the sunshine, and stuck to me by my own clamminess.

While the others help themselves to ale, bread, and cheese, I step over to the well and dip my hands into the pool of glossy water. The shade has kept it cool and I feel goose bumps rising on my skin as I scoop up the water and splash it over my arms and neck. I hear laughter behind me.

"Half measures are no good," Dai tells me, still chortling. "Best to go the whole hog and climb right in."

Mrs. Jones feigns shock at the idea. "Mrs. Jenkins will do no such thing." She flaps her teacloth at the farrier. "Bathing in front of you ruffians indeed! It would not be proper."

I smile at her, but the thought is tempting. To climb over the mossy stones and lower myself into the dark pool until I am completely submerged and could come out refreshed and rid of this grit and filth . . . it is an enticing notion, audience or no.

Cai drains his tankard and shakes his head.

"Mrs. Jones is right," says he. "Besides, we don't want you contaminating the spring now, do we? Cattle might not drink from that trough again if they see a woman swimming in it." He is struggling to keep a straight face as he speaks, but the others are less certain than I that he is joking, and their breaths are held. I put on my most charming smile and crook my finger at him, beckoning.

"Oh, look out," Dai cautions, wiping foam from his top lip. "I reckon your wife thinks a wash would improve you, too, Ffynnon Las."

"Oh a wash, is it?" Cai puts down his drink and walks toward me, his eyes crinkling at the corners. "Well, there's the pot calling the kettle black," says he.

As soon as he has ventured close enough I scoop an armful of water out and fling it at him. And then another, and another. The men laugh at the sight of him dripping and splashed, water making clean tracks through the grime on his skin. He dashes forward, shoveling handfuls of water at me until my hair hangs wet about my shoulders. Dai the Forge laughs fit to bust, the sound bouncing off the stone walls of the stables. Even Mrs. Jones cannot

contain her mirth. Faster and more furiously we splash one another until he catches hold of my arms to stop me. But I continue to wriggle, and as I attempt to escape he grabs me around
the waist.

"You'll not get away from me so easy, my wild one!"

In one swift movement he has lifted me off the ground and
makes to drop me in the pool, but I clutch at his soaked shirt and
pull hard, putting him off his balance. There is a second's pause,
I hear him shout, and then we both tip over the wall and into
the pool. Even as I fight the urge to gasp at the coldness of the
water I am aware that he does not let go of me, but makes sure
I come quickly and safely to the surface. We emerge to raucous
guffaws from Dai and Edwyn, and shrieks from Mrs. Jones. I
find I do not care how ridiculous I must appear to them, or how
indecent. I care only that we are standing here together, wet to
the skin, laughing, close, happy. It is as intimate a moment as I
have experienced in my life.

The cool of the early evening finds Cai and Morgana sitting at
the kitchen table. Mrs. Jones lowers her bulk into the chair by the
stove. The fire in the hearth has served its purpose for the day
and is being allowed to fade.

"Well, *Duw,*" says Mrs. Jones. "'Tis nice to have peace and
quiet once more now those boys have gone."

Cai smiles. "Dai's the best farrier for miles around, mind.
They are a good team."

"Good and rowdy." She makes a poor show of hiding her
affection for them, and for the fun of the day. "Encouraging Mrs.
Jenkins to climb in the well," she tutts, "and you no better, Mr.
Jenkins," she says, wagging a finger at him.

Morgana grins. Her hair has dried, and she has changed into
clean clothes, but she still looks like a person who has recently
taken a dip, her curls flowing unchecked about her shoulders,
and her feet bare.

Cai finds himself gazing at her. "We were all in need of a bath," he says.

"Maybe you were." Mrs. Jones stretches out her legs stiffly. "But the well is not a place for horseplay and nonsense. Not *that* well."

A look passes between her and Morgana that Cai cannot quite make sense of. It seems the two women have some shared secret, and one that he is clearly not to be told about. Part of him is pleased that they are becoming such good friends—it matters to him that Morgana not be lonely. And part of him, he is surprised to find, is just a little bit jealous of that closeness.

"Well, Mrs. Jones," he says lightly, "who knows what wonders that magic water might do to a person who bathes in it."

The old woman tutts and purses her lips before closing her eyes and settling deeper into her chair. "Make fun if you must, Mr. Jenkins. One day you might be forced to admit the truth of that well. One day."

She falls silent briefly before setting up a deep, rumbling snore. Cai smiles at Morgana and shrugs, beckoning her to the table. "Come," he says, "I've something to show you."

He stands up and takes from a small pile on a high shelf one of the maps he inherited from his father. He unfolds it and spreads it out on the table before them. He leans over the faded charts, pointing out the route the drove will take.

"We will set off from Tregaron early and head directly west," he tells her. "I want to make it through the Abergwesyn Pass and up to the Epynt on the first day. Won't be easy, mind. Takes a while for the herd to settle. They're unnerved by leaving their farms and being put together with new stock. Not to mention the muddle the sheep and ponies are bound to get into for a few days." He looks up from the map for a moment. Morgana is intent on learning everything, he can see that. The way she frowns trying to make sense of the lines and squiggles in front of her. The way she is uncharacteristically still. As she bends forward her loose hair swings down, revealing her neck. Cai has to fight the urge to plant a kiss on that tender part of the nape which he finds so alluring. He recalls how beautiful she had looked with her hair wet and her clothes clinging to her as he held her in the well pool. If they had not had an audience he would have kissed her again. Even now the memory of their first kiss stirs him. He clears his throat and returns to his explanations.

"The warm weather will have dried the ground again, so the going should be good. We'll pass through Brecon and follow the main road toward Abergavenny. It will mean paying tolls. I'll avoid them where I can, of course, but I have to find a balance, see? Too many turnpikes and we'll be broke before ever we reach the fattening fields. Too many mountain routes or rocky paths over difficult ground and our progress will be awful slow, and the animals will lose condition." He puts his finger under the name of a small town. "We can spend the night here," he tells her. "Do you recognize the place?"

Morgana shakes her head.

"Why, 'tis Crickhowell. I thought you might like to ride up to Cwmdu and call on your mother."

She turns to him, eyes wide with delight, a smile transforming her face. She nods keenly.

"Well, there we are then. Only one night, mind. Can't afford more. The grazing's a bit costly in that area, see? Right, then we continue west, oh . . . we're onto the next map now." He folds up the first one and opens another. "Not that I'll be taking these with me." He gives a short laugh. "I should know my way by now. Might be my first drove as *porthmon,* but I've been on plenty, man and boy. Not likely to get lost!" He straightens up, looking at her again, and says, "I think you'll make a fine drover yourself, Mrs. Jenkins. For a woman, that is."

Morgana punches him playfully on the shoulder.

"Course, there are those as say 'tis bad luck to employ a woman. Oh, they're happy enough for them to follow behind on foot, knitting stockings to sell, earning a few pennies weeding along the way. But working the herd . . ." He shakes his head. "There will be one or two will complain, no doubt. You just leave them to me. This is my drove, and I'll decide who works it. You'll be paid a drover's wage, same as the others." He hesitates, then adds, "There's no one could manage those ponies better than you. That's the truth of it."

She meets his gaze. This is not something she is embarrassed to hear.

From the hearthside comes the low rumbling of Mrs. Jones's snore. Bracken stretches out on the cool flagstones at her feet. It has been a tiring day for all of them, but a satisfying one. A successful one. A good one. Cai feels they have taken an important step, he and his strange little wife. A step into their new lives together. He bites his bottom lip, contemplating what to do next, uncertain.

At last he folds up the maps, quickly putting them away.

"Wait there," he says. "I've something for you." He leaves the kitchen, running up the stairs to his bedroom and returning two minutes later. He stands in front of Morgana awkwardly, shuffling his feet, a small parcel in his hands.

"I want you to have this," he says, not yet giving her the paper-wrapped object. "I meant to give it to you a long time ago. Well . . . on our wedding day, in fact. 'Tis traditional you should have one, and I know we did not have a proper courtship. It has bothered me, sometimes. You've been . . . very fair . . . about that. Here." At last he all but shoves it into her hands.

Morgana unwinds the wrapping and finds inside a small, carefully carved lovespoon. The wood is dark and smooth, the bowl of the little spoon worked into a shallow dip the size of her thumbprint. The handle is of a barley sugar twist, beautifully carved. The end of the handle is fashioned into a curious hollow block which rattles when she shakes it. There is a fine leather thong threaded through the handle so that the spoon can be worn around the neck.

Seeing her confusion Cai finds it necessary to explain further, chattering on, nervous about what her reaction to the gift will be.

"I made it for you while we were engaged, but had not the opportunity to give it to you before our marriage. And then, on the day, well, the moment did not seem quite right. . . . And since . . . As I said, 'tis a tradition, a token of my . . . affection, if you like."

Morgana turns the spoon over and over in her hands, letting her fingers glide over its polished surface, examining every detail. Her mouth is a little open, her cheeks a tad flushed, but he cannot quite gauge her response.

"There is something else about it. See, here." He takes it and surprises her by putting it to his mouth. He blows into the top of it and produces a clear, loud note. Morgana gasps. He does it again. "It's a whistle, see? I added this bit after . . . well, I added it later. I thought you mind find it useful, on the drove. If you need to call me, to signal, I don't know, something about the herd, or if you are in trouble, or . . . Here, you try." He passes it back to her.

Morgana takes the spoon as if it might bite her and stares at it.

"Go on," says Cai. "Give it a go."

Slowly she lifts it to her lips. Her first attempt is so tentative that the whistle makes only a breathy gasp.

"Go on, my wild one, put some effort into it!" Cai teases.

Morgana takes a deep breath and blows, this time producing a shrill blast that surprises her so much she drops the spoon. Mrs. Jones wakes shrieking from her slumbers.

"*Duw!* What in the Lord's name was that? Heaven protect us, Mr. Jenkins, I swear I heard the last trumpet sounding!" she cries, her hands clutching at her racing heart. Bracken leaps and barks around the room. Morgana stands as if turned to stone. Cai bends down, picks up the spoon, and hands it back to her.

"Well, will you wear it, Morgana? For me?"

By way of answer she snatches the gift from him and throws her arms about his neck, hugging him tightly.

Cai laughs and twirls her around and around, holding her close, luxuriating in the feel of her body against his, and the knowledge that she has accepted the gift gladly, understanding the caring that lay behind its invention.

"Well, well," says Mrs. Jones, barely recovered. "A person shuts their eyes for five minutes and when they wake up the world has gone mad!"

Eventually, above the noise and gaiety in the room comes the sound of a carriage approaching. Cai lets go of Morgana and steps over to the window.

"Isolda," he says simply, feeling his shoulders droop. He knows it is an uncharitable thought, but he does not welcome her arrival, and would give a fair amount for this moment, this mood, with Morgana to be left uninterrupted by the formality of entertaining a visitor. What is more her arrival forces him to turn his mind to the matter of her offer of money. His visit to the bank a few days earlier had been both humiliating and fruitless. His options are few. It is becoming obvious to him that he has little choice but to take the loan from Isolda. The thought fills him with unease.

Even so, he goes to the front door to welcome her, Morgana following him with the dark expression she seems to reserve solely for Isolda Bowen.

Outside, the driver helps his mistress from the carriage, and now Cai sees that Isolda's black thoroughbred is tied to the rear of it.

"Cai, Morgana, please forgive the intrusion at such an hour. I had planned to call earlier in the day but had business to attend to which delayed me." She strides to the horse, unhitches it, and leads it forward. "Now, I know you will protest, but I shall hear no argument from you, Mr. Jenkins. I want you to take Angel so that you are suitably mounted for the drove." She holds up a hand to stave off his response. "No! Do not deny me the chance to do this small thing by way of thank you for all the kindnesses you have shown me over the years. You cannot pretend that your old cob, dear as I'm sure she is to you, is up to the work. Angel is fit and strong and I am certain he will go excellently well for you."

Cai glances at Morgana and is a little cast down to see open loathing on her face now. Why does she hate the woman so? He still cannot find a satisfactory answer to this question. He looks at the magnificent horse before him, with its sleek black coat, its strong, lithe limbs, its powerful chest and noble head. It would, indeed, be an asset to him.

"'Tis true, Honey is a little beyond her best years . . ." he says.

"Then you'll take him? Marvelous!" Isolda declares, flinging the reins at him and clapping her hands in delight.

Angel whirls about and whinnies, seeming to sense he has been passed from his mistress's care.

"Hush now, *bach*." Cai soothes the anxious animal. He turns to Morgana, about to encourage her to come forward and inspect the wonderful horse, but her expression stops the words in his mouth. It is as if the closeness between them that had felt so enduring only moments ago has been broken somehow by Isolda's brief presence. Morgana folds her arms across her chest, swings around, and marches back into the house. He sighs and turns back to Isolda, but before he can form an apology or excuse for his wife's behavior she puts her hand gently on his arm.

"Do not concern yourself, I am not offended. Morgana is your wife, she is young, she has not yet learned to mask her feelings. I am pleased, in fact, to have the opportunity to speak with you alone."

Cai knows what is coming. He finds himself looking at the horse, minutely adjusting its bridle, in an attempt to cover his own awkwardness.

"I had planned to call on you," he confesses.

"Ah, then you have reached a decision about my offer of a loan?"

"I have."

Isolda waits, eyebrows raised. Cai clears his throat, the words catching as he speaks, as if deep down he is fighting against what he knows he must do.

"I would be most grateful . . ." he begins, "that is, it would be of great assistance to me . . ." At last he faces her. "If your offer still stands, I would like to accept." Seeing how pleased she is he hurries to explain himself, so that she be in no doubt about how he has come to allow himself to accept her help. "I approached Evans the Bank," he rushes on, "I put my case to him. He knows I'm good for the money, but still he would not take the risk, he said. What risk, I wanted to know. How was my proposition anything other than sound business? Any man, any farmer, can suffer a loss, a misfortune. That does not, surely, render all his future enterprises risks."

"It doesn't matter. Mr. Evans was shortsighted. I know you will make a fine *porthmon*. I have every confidence in you, Cai. I have always believed in you."

"It will mean the difference between success and ruin, nothing less. But your money will be safely returned to you, with fair interest, I promise you that."

"I do not doubt it."

Cai nods and feels the tension go out of his shoulders. Perhaps he need not have worried. Perhaps, after all, Isolda is merely being both neighborly and business-minded and nothing more is expected of him than to honor the debt.

IO.

Cai holds the reins of Prince's harness lightly, letting the little pony steer the trap himself as they make brisk progress along the lane toward Tregaron. Despite their haste, he knows they will arrive late. Morgana sits beside him, her cape covering Catrin's best evening gown, her hair, tamed for once by Mrs. Jones and a deal of effort, covered by the deep velvet hood which falls low over her brow, so that when Cai glances across at her he cannot see her eyes, cannot read her expression. Neither of them is looking forward with pleasure to the evening ahead. The prospect of dining at Isolda's house in the company of the Cadwaladrs brought on a burst of temper from Morgana when he insisted they both attend. It was only when he took her hand in his, kissed it gently, and asked her softly to go with him that she sweetened and agreed to do so. In truth, he would far rather be spending the evening in front of his own fire, but he knows he is bound to attend. Already he feels the obligation of accepting the loan from Isolda beginning to chafe. How many polite dinners will he be required to endure, he wonders. How many times must he answer when she calls? He promises himself the minute the drove is complete and the money is in his possession he will pay her what is due. Pay her and be out of her debt.

When they arrive at Isolda's house a stable boy springs forward and takes hold of the pony. Cai helps Morgana down, his hands on her slender waist. Her hood falls back as she jumps from the seat of the trap and for a moment he is captivated by the sight of her. Her hair is pinned high on her head, her complexion a little flushed from the speed of their journey. The dark red silk suits her well and, thanks again to Mrs. Jones's expertise, shows off her trim, girlish figure to best effect. He wants to pull her close. To kiss her. To reassure her. But here, away from the sanctuary of Ffynnon Las, exposed to other eyes, he feels inhibited. How will she fare spending a formal evening in such company? He is conscious of his own nervousness about how she might behave. He has been so at ease with her at home; they have grown close, especially now that the previously unspoken matter of her curious talents is no longer a barrier between them. Now they are honest and open with each other. At least, that is how he wishes to be. He has not yet found the moment to tell her about the money he has accepted from Isolda. When he announced he was going to Carmarthen to purchase more cattle to take on the drove she and Mrs. Jones assumed the bank had agreed a loan. He knew this, and he allowed them to believe it, so that now an untruth exists between them, and he is sorry for it. He must put it right. He knows Morgana dislikes Isolda, and is certain she will disapprove of him taking her money, but business is business. He has done what he believes is best. He will look for the right time to tell her the truth, and will be relieved when he no longer has to swallow down the lie.

Isolda greets them in the hallway.

"Mr. and Mrs. Jenkins," she purrs, "I can't tell you how pleased I am to have you both here." She offers her hand to Cai, but for once her attention is taken by Morgana. Cai experiences a rush of pride at her reaction to his wife. "Why, Morgana," she says, "what a transformation. That gown is perfect for you. I always thought the color a little overpowering for Catrin." She smiles broadly as she leads them to the dining room. "Come, we were on the point of going to table when you arrived."

"I am sorry not to be punctual," Cai says, hoping he won't have to provide an excuse. He does not wish to recall the cajoling necessary to compel Morgana from the house.

"There is nothing to apologize for." Isolda moves closer to him and lowers her voice to a conspiratorial level. "We should happily have waited, but Mrs. Cadwaladr declared herself faint and it was suggested she might be in need of something to eat, unlikely as that may seem."

Cai is uncomfortable to be sharing a joke at the expense of his neighbor, and would rather not have Isolda loop her arm through his. But she is their hostess, this is her house, and he is determined the evening will go without mishap. He pauses to take Morgana's hand and give her what he hopes is a reassuring smile.

The long dining table has been impressively set with the finest silver, china, and cut glass. Four elegant candelabras hold tall, tapering candles down the center, between abundant arrangements of roses and orange blossom. Dozens of additional candles and sprays of delicate ferns decorate the room. New curtains of shimmering Chinese silk, the cost of which would be beyond the purse of anyone else Cai knows, gleam at the darkening windows. A fire glows in the expansive hearth. The whole effect is opulent and extravagant. Amidst it all sits Mrs. Cadwaladr, whose best efforts at sophistication have not come off well. Reverend Cadwaladr rises to his feet. His face is even ruddier than usual, a fact Cai attributes to the glossy claret in his glass.

"Our Ffynnon Las friends have arrived." Isolda signals to the servants to fetch the first course.

Cai notices immediately that Morgana stiffens at the sight of Reverend Cadwaladr. He takes her hand and leads her to her chair as greetings are exchanged. He is surprised to find that the reverend, for his part, barely acknowledges Morgana's presence. He supposes the preacher might share his own nervousness at his wife's unpredictable nature. After all, on each occasion the reverend has encountered her at chapel there has been some manner of scene or upset. As Morgana takes her seat Cai has the wearying feeling that the evening will be a long one.

As if to compensate for his reserve toward Morgana, Reverend Cadwaladr's manner toward Cai is effusive. "Mr. Jenkins, a pleasure indeed to have the opportunity to dine with you before the drove," he says. "Mrs. Cadwaladr and I wish you the very best in your endeavor, naturally. As do all in Tregaron. A great deal rests with you, young man. Your first drove as *porthmon,* and the hopes and livelihoods of many hereabouts in your hands. . . . 'Tis a burdensome responsibility, is it not?"

"I try not to see it as such," Cai tells him. "I prefer to put my attention to the practical matter of the drove itself. I must not allow myself to be distracted from the task at hand."

"Ah!" Mrs. Cadwaladr leaves off plucking grapes from the silver platter beside her to express her concern, "but I hear that your wife is to accompany you on the drove. Will that not, in itself, be a distraction, Mr. Jenkins?"

"I value Morgana's support. And she is a capable horsewoman. I know of no other who could manage the ponies as well."

Mrs. Cadwaladr shakes her head. "But is it seemly? Your own wife, the mistress of Ffynnon Las . . . I mean to say . . . working as a drover . . ." She leaves the thought unfinished, her expression clearly showing how distasteful she finds the idea.

Cai glances at Morgana and can see that she is already tiring of being discussed as if she were not present. She frowns at him darkly.

Isolda is quick to support Cai. "I'm sure Mr. Jenkins has given the matter considerable thought," she says. "It is not for us to tell him how to organize his drove. Nor his marriage."

There is something mocking in the way she says this, but there is nothing in her words at which to take offense. Nonetheless, Cai senses a needling, a lurking criticism which only increases his discomfort. He has little time to dwell on her tone, however, as the reverend has chosen another subject to voice his opinion on, with his customary volume and lack of tact.

"I hear you have acquired some fine new cattle to replace the ones lost. I am told they look very well indeed and stand to make you a fair profit. How fortunate you are, Mr. Jenkins, to have found such a kind benefactor in Mrs. Bowen."

Cai can feel Morgana's gaze burning into him. How could

Isolda have spoken to Cadwaladr of what he understood to be a private arrangement? He is too shocked to be angry.

"Oh," Isolda laughs lightly, "I would hardly call myself a benefactor, Reverend. My loan to Mr. Jenkins was merely a neighborly gesture, and sound business sense. I have every confidence I will receive a good return on my investment."

Cai forces himself to respond, though he can feel himself coloring beneath Morgana's scrutiny. This is not how he would have had his arrangement with Isolda revealed, but it is too late now.

"I am, of course, extremely grateful for Mrs. Bowen's generosity," he says as levelly as he is able. "I will indeed see to it that her faith in me proves justified."

Their conversation is temporarily interrupted by the arrival of a fine game soup. The servants attend the diners with smooth efficiency. Mrs. Cadwaladr slurps noisily and declares the soup the finest she has ever put to her lips. Isolda tells them the pheasants and partridge were a gift from Mr. Evans the banker, who keeps a well-stocked shoot. Cai listens to the harmless dinner table chatter, but his eyes are on Morgana. She dips her spoon into the bowl in front of her, but does not raise it to her mouth. Instead she closes her eyes, putting her hand to her brow. Cai is horrified to see her turning pale as he watches. Has she been taken ill again? Is there to be a humiliating repeat of what occurred the very first occasion he took her out in society, when they attended chapel for the first time? Will he only ever be able to be off his guard with her when they are at home? Is he never to take her from the farm without this attendant disquiet?

Isolda has also noticed Morgana's pallor.

"Why, Mrs. Jenkins, are you feeling unwell? Here, sip some water."

"What is the matter with her?" asks Mrs. Cadwaladr, not allowing her concern to for one second keep her from her soup.

"Morgana?" Cai leans across the table, but cannot reach her through the array of silver and flowers. "Morgana?"

She opens her eyes, panic showing in them. She drops her

spoon and snatches up her napkin, pressing it to her mouth, swaying slightly in her chair. Cai springs to his feet and hurries round the table.

"My wife is feeling faint. Is there somewhere she could lie down for a short while, perhaps?"

Isolda gets up, snapping her fingers at her servants. "Of course. Poor thing. It is a little warm in here. I ought not to have had the fire lit. I will have Anwen take her to the chaise in the morning room."

"I will go with her," Cai says, but even as he does so, Morgana all but pushes him away.

"There is no need." Isolda puts an arm around Morgana as she hastens from the room, passing her into the care of her maid who has arrived at the door. "Anwen will take excellent care of your wife. I am certain she would not want you to disturb your meal. Stay with us. A woman needs time to compose herself in these circumstances and does not require a man fussing about her while she does so. Is that not the case, Mrs. Jenkins?"

Before Cai can protest further Morgana is led from the room, the door shut behind her, and he is ushered back to his seat. He takes a long gulp of wine, and as he does so he catches sight of a somehow significant look passing between Isolda and the reverend. Puzzled, he tries to rekindle his appetite, reasoning that the sooner the meal is eaten, the sooner the tortuous evening will be at an end.

Mrs. Cadwaladr finishes her soup before anyone else and falls to regaling Isolda with account of her daughters, a subject upon which, it seems, she could enthuse all night. Cai feels a hand on his sleeve and turns to see Reverend Cadwaladr regarding him earnestly. For once, he speaks quietly, so that their conversation does not disturb that of the women present.

"Mr. Jenkins, I feel compelled to raise a delicate matter with you."

Cai drains his glass and waits.

"It is difficult indeed to talk to you on such a sensitive subject . . .

please be assured, I have only your very best interests at heart." The reverend pauses, but if he hopes for encouragement, Cai can find none to give. He goes on, "It has been brought to my attention that, well, there are details concerning your wife of which you may not be aware."

"Details?" Cai watches the servant refill his glass and resists the temptation to drink deeply.

"As I say, it is a delicate matter . . ."

"Then please speak plainly, Reverend."

"Mr. Jenkins, you are a good man, of that there can be no doubt. I knew your father well, and have always had the greatest respect for your family."

"But?"

"Let me come to the point . . ."

"I do wish you would, Reverend."

"How much do you know of your wife's background?"

"I met her mother several times. I am aware she comes from humble beginnings. Her father . . . is no longer with us."

"And in the parish where she lived, where she grew up, did people speak well of her?"

"I prefer to form my own opinions."

"Quite so, and yet, it is often among the community that we find out best how a person is regarded."

"No one spoke ill of her."

"But did they speak *well* of her?"

Cai fidgets, half wishing Mrs. Cadwaladr would see fit to include him in her conversation. He knows, deep down, what it is the reverend is fishing for. But he will not bite. This is dangerous ground to tread. He knows Morgana's gifts, her singular qualities, would, at best, sit badly with a man of the church. At worst, well, however modern the times might be, he cannot imagine a minister tolerating the notion of magic.

Reverend Cadwaladr reads Cai's silence as some sort of agreement and is emboldened to continue.

"I have heard that her father was a Gypsy of sorts, and that he disappeared into the night leaving his own wife to rear the child. A child who was not quite the same as other children in the parish. Oh, you are a young man, Mr. Jenkins, and your wife is undeniably pretty, with all the charms of youth, but I must urge caution. Watch her carefully. Do not let prettiness and guile blind you to her true nature. And know that the church does not abandon those who seek help."

A coldness, despite the heat of the fire and the warmth of the summer evening, spreads through Cai's body. What can he have heard? When Cai gently questioned those who knew Morgana he learned so little. Who has he been talking to, and why? What might have made him suspicious in the first place? Morgana's behavior in public might have been unruly and lacking social graces, but what could he have seen to make him suggest something more? Something . . . unnatural? Cai recalls Morgana's very first meeting with Mrs. Cadwaladr, and remembers the poor woman's sudden fit of sneezing that had resulted in her upended teacup emptying its contents down her dress front. Had she thought that was Morgana's doing? Had she scuttled home to her husband and whispered magic? Surely not. It was too slight a thing, too easily explained away. It is with some relief that Cai hears Isolda questioning him on the route he is to take on the drove, so that the conversation moves on, and he is not required to discuss his wife further.

I am taken to a small sitting room where Anwen, Isolda's lady's maid, bustles about settling me upon a chaise. I am too occupied with managing the sickness in my stomach to protest. I fear I may begin retching, but, mercifully, the sensation begins to lessen as soon as I am removed from the dining room. I lie down, my head spinning, and close my eyes, as much to shut out Anwen's whittering attentions as to rest. My thoughts are in turmoil.

How could Cai have accepted a loan from Isolda and then lied to me about it? 'Tis true, he did not actually tell me where he had obtained the money for the new cattle, but he let me think it came from the bank. There can be as much of a lie in silence as in words. I, of all people, should know this.

But it is not this slight, this unwelcome news, this deceit, I might call it, that has made me feel unwell. No, once again, the proximity of Reverend Cadwaladr has made me sick. The whiff of serpents filled my nostril as soon as I was seated opposite him. And the way he looked at me, on the brief occasion where he could bring himself to do so . . . it is clear his loathing of me remains unabated. I have been fooling myself to think he might have forgotten about me, might have decided against bothering with me. He wants rid of me still. And I am yet here. What will he do next? What might he be saying to Cai even now, as I lie here, weakened and excluded?

I risk a glance at my carer. She is putting a match to the neatly laid fire, but her attention is only momentarily diverted from me. I know she will not let me leave this room without alerting her mistress. Fortunately, I have more than one method of absenting myself. I quickly close my eyes again and steady my breathing, striving to give the impression I am sleeping. Only when I am content that Anwen believes this do I let my mind drift, my limbs become weightless, and my soul step lightly from my body. There is such a freedom in witchwalking. Gone is the revolting sickness that beset me. Gone is the churning of my stomach and the pounding in my head. Painlessly, noiselessly, effortlessly, I leave the room.

My intention is to return to the dining table and secretly observe and listen. It is said eavesdroppers do not hear good of themselves, but I will chance being offended. At least I will know what poison is being spat into my husband's ear. As I make my way across the broad, imposing hall, I glimpse a door I had not noticed earlier. It is unremarkable, plain, and tucked away in a corner, but there is something about it that alerts my interest. From beneath it there is a curious glow, unlike either natural light or the illumination candles might throw. I hear a distant sound, too. With my senses heightened as I witchwalk, I am certain I can hear . . . what? A susurration of some sort. Could it be whispering? I glide closer, and as I do I am once again struck by the now familiar reptilian stench. Whilst I am out of my body it cannot make me feel ill, but it is unmistakable, and stronger the closer I come to the door. This makes no sense to me. If the smell emanates from Reverend Cadwaladr, why is it also coming from whatever lies beyond that door?

I am on the point of investigating further when Isolda and the reverend suddenly emerge from the dining room.

"Forgive my interrupting your meal, Reverend," says she to him. "I would have had Mr. Evans witness the documents himself, but I left the bank without doing so. A trifling matter concerning some of my smaller investments, but I would be so grateful if you could stand as witness. I dislike leaving matters unfinished."

"A pause in our feasting will sharpen my appreciation of courses to come, Mrs. Bowen, rest assured."

Isolda calls back through the doorway. "We will be but a moment."

Together they go to the drawing room. I am torn. The strangeness of the unexplained door and whatever it might reveal must wait. If the reverend is intent on stirring up ill feeling against me, he may well wish to put his case privately to Isolda. I must know what is said in that room. I quickly travel to stand beside the brocade-draped window next to the drawing room hearth, so that I am able to both watch and hear. I do my best to ignore the intensified odor which lingers about the place now, thick enough to taste.

Isolda dismisses her servant, and the second the door closes her demeanor undergoes a dramatic alteration. As does that of Reverend Cadwaladr. She rounds on him, all but hissing in her fury.

"You pathetic wretch!"

"Forgive me!" pleads the reverend.

"What use are you? I issued you with one simple task, and you have failed utterly." Isolda strides about the room as she castigates the preacher, who is now weeping pitifully. She passes so close to me I feel the disturbance of the air as she moves. I have to fight my instinct to flee, determined to hold my place, reminding myself that she cannot see me.

"You are the minister of this parish, a preacher of note and standing—you should command respect. Obedience. I told you to warn the girl off. To rid me of her. What manner of man are you? What manner of preacher, that you let that slip of a witchgirl better you? She should be long gone from here."

"I tried, mistress, believe me. I sought her out. I made my case plainly . . ."

"Not plainly enough, evidently."

"She is not easily frightened. She has a strength about her beyond her years."

"Strength! She is a child, who has no knowledge of her own capabilities. She is newly arrived, married to a man whose good sense has flown at the sight of her dark eyes and smooth skin. You have allowed her to remain."

"I warned her. I told her to leave. I explained what would happen if she did not." The minister slumps onto a chair, taking a handkerchief from his pocket with which to mop his brow.

I am stunned by what is being revealed. The fearsome Reverend Cadwaladr under the rule of this terrible woman? What hold can she have over him to reduce him to the sniveling, broken man I see now?

Isolda looms above him.

"You warned her, but you did not follow through your threat, did you? I told you then that you needed to act, to press home your case, as forcefully as necessary. Yet you did nothing."

"I was waiting, hoping she would leave, I . . ."

"She has no intention of leaving! All this time that has passed, time that *you* have seen fit to grant her, has merely allowed her to grow more secure in her husband's affections. Why did you not act? Last time we spoke of this I expressly told you to do more, to move against her in a way she would be powerless to resist."

"But, mistress, to publicly denounce the girl as a witch when she has done nothing wrong . . ." wails the reverend.

At this Isolda loses whatever hold she had upon her temper. She raises an arm as if to snatch something invisible from the air. There is a loud crack and the smell of singeing as some tufts of the cowering minister's hair catch light. He yelps, slapping at his head until the flames are extinguished, clutching at a patch of burned scalp behind his left ear.

"I am the one who decides what is right and what is wrong. It is not for you to make judgments in this matter." She pauses, collecting herself, and stands straight, composing herself once more, her expression now one of revulsion rather than fury. "I told you what would happen if you did not assist me in this. You were warned."

"Oh, please . . . I beg of you, don't . . ."

"Stop your whining. I have not the time nor the inclination to make your simpering girls suffer for my displeasure. Not on this occasion, at least."

Upon hearing this the reverend falls from the chair to his knees in front of Isolda, hands clasped together, as if in prayer. I cannot help but wonder what his congregation would make of it if they could see him thus.

"Oh, thank you! Let . . . let me try again. I'm sure this time I can persuade her to go."

"It is too late for that, they are on the point of departing on the drove. She won't be separated from him now. No, it is obvious I must deal with her myself."

"What is it that you plan to do?" asks the reverend, his voice betraying the fear she fills him with.

Isolda opens her mouth to speak but then hesitates.

"Get up," says she. "Compose yourself, man. We must return to my guests and not give them reason to suppose anything . . . untoward has occurred. As I say, I will handle the matter myself."

He scrambles to his feet and hurries out of the room ahead of her. At the door Isolda pauses. Pauses, and turns, and looks directly toward the place where I am standing. For one dreadful, bone-chilling moment I feel that she sees me. But she does not speak, nor react to my presence, but steps across the threshold, firmly closing the door behind her.

My head is swimming, my mind racing to make sense of what I have learned. Isolda has been forcing the reverend to do her bidding. It was she who was behind his telling me to leave. And he is clearly terrified of her. Who could have imagined such a transformation in the man? What terrible threat toward his daughters can she have made? I can only imagine. But I know that he would have believed her capable of fearful deeds. *Witchgirl,* she called me. She has seen the magic that lies inside me. She knows what I am. Just as surely as I can see what crouches inside her, and oh, it is a dark and terrible thing! The power that set fire to the reverend came from somewhere unspeakably wicked. Now I understand the reptilian stench. It was the stink of an evil enchantment, attached to someone, forcing them against their will, and though it clung to Reverend Cadwaladr's being, it had its origins in Isolda.

Things are clearer to me now. Whilst I am wary of all men of the cloth, this evil woman is the person I have true cause to fear. It is not Cai that she wants, but Ffynnon Las. And she wants Ffynnon Las because of the cursing well and the power it would give her. Oh! Can she know of the existence of the *Grimoire*? She must. Yes, that would explain her determination. It is plain to me that she is determined to get what she wants, and she will trample any who stand in her way. But I have glimpsed the power of the *Grimoire of the Blue Well*. What terrible havoc could Isolda Bowen wreak were she to possess it? Whatever happens, whatever I have to do, I must see to it that she is *never* allowed to have it.

11.

At last the moment is come. We were up before dawn mustering the stock and arrived here in Tregaron with the brightening of the day. The ponies were excitable, in particular the youngsters, but I kept them close by me and they proved biddable enough. At the very last minute Cai had a change of heart and decided he would keep two of the older brood mares. With luck they are both carrying foals for next year, so that, his reasoning went, we will have some core stock with which to rebuild the herd. If the drove goes well and we have money to do so.

It pains me to acknowledge that this decision is in part due to the loan he accepted from Isolda. That creature! Had he known what I now know, he would never have taken money from her, however desperate the hour. It hurts me that he kept the arrangement secret, and learning of it at that dreadful dinner, amidst such company . . . I thought I was beginning to understand him. I thought he was beginning to trust me. And yet he did not think to share this important decision about the future of the farm—about our future—with me.

Had not other events overtaken the matter in both importance and urgency I would no doubt have dwelled upon it. As it is, such a small slight has paled beside the awful truth of what Isolda Bowen is, and of what terrible actions she is responsible for. For as I have had time to think, to examine the events of recent weeks, I have recognized some terrible facts. Not only did she compel, by threat and by cursed magic, Reverend Cadwaladr to further her aims, but I am convinced she was behind the thunderstorm that killed Cai's cattle. The weather was too extreme, too swiftly changing, to be natural. And I sensed a presence on the mountain that day, an evil presence. I now know whose it was. No doubt she thought to ruin Cai by robbing him of his herd. Then, when she saw he would not be so easily cast down, she lent him money to tie him to her. She is playing with him. She has no interest in him, I see that now. It is the farm she wants, for the well. And the *Grimoire*. My main concern now must be what she may do next. I believe we are all of us in peril on the drove now, for how much easier it will be for her to cause mayhem amid the melee of the herds, away from the watchful people of Tregaron. I must be ever on my guard.

At the same time, there is the practical business of the drove itself to occupy us all. The livestock whose fate lies many miles from here have so far proved easy to herd along. Of course, this may not be the case a few hours from now when they are part of the whole drove. For now they are content to graze in the paddock behind the Talbot Inn. I think Cai is pleased with how I have managed them. Thus far. I confess I am excited about what lies ahead—being in charge of the ponies, traveling farther from home with each passing day, seeing new places, meeting new people. And, not least, the chance to visit Mam. Oh, how good it will be to see her again! It feels a lifetime ago that I sat in the garden in Cwmdu watching her tend the vegetables, or listening to her chat over the fence with our neighbors. I will hold her so tight she will plead with me to be released, but then she will squeeze me every bit as hard.

I have never seen so many people as are come to Tregaron this day. The streets teem with bonneted ladies, squealing children, red-faced farmers, and all manner of persons. Reverend Cadwaladr is holding court in the town square, waiting his moment to bless the drove. How different he looks to the wreck of a man I saw at Isolda's house. I confess my loathing of him has in part turned to pity. It is clear his actions were driven by fear for his family. Fear of Isolda. How can it have taken me so long to see her for what she really is? My instinct recoiled from her the first time we met, but I thought my feelings were those of a new wife faced with her husband's beautiful friend. I should have known. I should have looked deeper. Dada would have done. Could it be that she was, in some way, masking her true self, beyond simply presenting herself as a respectable neighbor? Was I, too, bewitched, so that she has only now revealed herself to me because it suits her purpose to do so? For the more I have thought about it, the more I have come to believe that she *did* see me that night, in her drawing room. That she knew full well I was there, and her treatment of the reverend was for me to witness. It must be so, for a witch is visible when witchwalking only to another witch, and such Isolda has shown herself to be.

Mrs. Cadwaladr and her daughters are besporting more ribbons than a Maypole, and clutch parasols designed, it seems to me, with the express purpose of startling livestock. There are stalls selling pies and toffee apples and cakes and ale, so that the air is filled with a stew of smells so savory and sweet my stomach growls at it. Everywhere people stand in animated conversation, about what I cannot imagine. How can they find so much to say to one another? Are they so interested in the condition of the cattle, or the size of the drove? I think not. The snatches of chatter which have reached my ears have been of so little point I wonder that sensible people bother to engage in such nonsense. But then, I confess, I am entirely taken up with my own concerns. Ahead of us lies an immense challenge; one that will either secure the future of Ffynnon Las, or see Cai forced to sell his beloved farm. The drove will take three weeks, if we make good time. We are to hope for fifteen miles progress each day, but expect less. I worry that some of the older mares will suffer at these demands, and some of the foals, too. Cai has promised he will call a rest day if necessary, and that he has chosen a route with particular attention to the quality and abundance of the grazing, so that mares with foals at foot will be able to continue supplying milk to them.

Dai the Forge and Edwyn Nails have been here two nights

already, shoeing all the cattle that are to be taken, so that the holding fields outside the town are a shifting mass of black beasts. Cai told me that our newly purchased cattle together with those he is taking for other farmers there will be near 260 Welsh runts, as they are so unflatteringly known abroad. 'Tis a poor title for such valued stock—the English might name them so, but it is these runts that will feed their desire for roast beef for many Sundays to come. For nowhere in England do farmers produce their equal. We may be thankful for the fact, for it is this that keeps the droves running, year after year, taking the prized meat on the hoof to London.

And there will be Watson's one hundred sheep, bleating and stinking and no doubt giving us all a deal of trouble. And our precious ponies—thirty-five of them, if I include Prince, which I know I must. Cai has patiently described to me the workings of the drove, so that I will know what I am to do. I so want to prove an asset to him. Around my neck, tucked beneath the cotton of my blouse, I am wearing the lovespoon he carved for me. I have never owned such a thing; never had such a gift made especially for me. I can feel the smooth wood warming against my breast. I will admit I was at first alarmed at the idea of the whistle. I am accustomed to being silent. I have never, in all my long years of wordlessness, found the need to make a noise of some sort in place of speech. On first seeing it I feared that equipping me with such an instrument demonstrated Cai's concerns over my . . . *lack,* as Mrs. Cadwaladr so succinctly put it. Am I not, then, sufficient as I am? But I know him better now. Had he given it to me on our wedding day, with the whistle already in place, I would have thrown it back in his face. But I am content that the gift shows a thoughtfulness, and a concern for my wellbeing, which I find . . . touching. Whether or not I would be able to bring myself to use it in public is another matter! Time, and circumstance no doubt, will tell.

It is not yet nine o'clock but the heat of the day is building. I find a wooden bench in the shade at the front of the hotel and sit. Cai is occupied with the final deals and tasks to be fixed before we leave. For he is not simply a man who will move livestock and sell it at the best price he can secure. He is emissary, taking important letters and documents from the great and the good of this parish to the center of commerce that is London. Some will send deeds of sale or covenant for land or property. Others wish investments to reach the city banks. Still others wish their sealed letters to be placed in the hands of distant relatives, or prospective brides, perhaps. All are entrusted to the *porthmon*; a man of honor, integrity, and worth. And such he certainly looks today. Even though he is dressed in the habitual drover's garb of stout boots, woolen stockings, tough cord breeches, plaid shirt, and wide-brimmed hat, he has about him the bearing of a man apart. There is something in his demeanor, something in his deportment, that suggests, yes, here is a head drover. Here is someone with whom our livelihoods will be secure. Here is someone who will make something of all our hopes and dreams for the future. When the rains come, as they surely must on any drove at this time of year, Cai will put on his ground-sweeping coat, so that even in silhouette he will be recognizable as a drover. Over days and weeks he will accumulate a patina of grime and a weathering to his skin, but still he will be instantly recognizable as Cai Jenkins Ffynnon Las, *porthmon*.

I, on the other hand, may very well draw only gasps of shock or stifled giggles from onlookers. My husband took some persuading that my choice of garments would not lay me open to ridicule. I stood my ground, however, and let him argue so long that he defeated his own objections. I must be dressed for practicality and comfort, not fashion nor acceptability. I must prove my worth to all on this drove, not just him, and to do so I cannot be hampered by ridiculous corsets and skirts. Mrs. Jones and I have been working in secret for some time, so that my outfit would be ready, and so that Cai could not gainsay either its decency or its suitability for the job in hand. My blouse is of soft cotton, the color of ripe hazelnuts, for white would be foolishly difficult to keep clean. I have a second identical blouse in my saddlebag, along with a washcloth; a light chemise that will serve as nightdress or extra layer if need be; a pot of lavender cream for cuts and bruises and to ward off biting flies; and a brush for my hair, which Mrs. Jones insisted I include and which, I confess, may not see a great deal of use! I am wearing a single, specially adapted petticoat, for modesty and comfort. I have not room for another in my pack, so I must look for an opportunity to wash it when I can. It is my skirt that caused Cai to balk, and which now garners curious glances from passersby. The idea for it came to me watching Dai the Forge with his split leather apron. At market, with a deal of mime and insistence, I purchased a quantity of tough brown cotton of the sort used for men's breeches. Further lengthy demonstrations and false starts allowed me to instruct Mrs. Jones to fashion me a skirt with a divide running the length of it. Either side of this gap the edges are strongly sewn, so that they will withstand weeks of rubbing against the saddle and the pony's sides without chaffing or wearing through. When I stand, it is almost impossible to detect the construction of this garment, save for it being also somewhat shorter than the norm, as it scarce covers my calves. However, as I move, or indeed when I sit astride, the unusual feature of the skirt becomes apparent. Its divide means it falls into two, wide trouser legs, modest but practical, which is what will prove invaluable in the coming weeks. As a matter of necessity against sun and rain I also wear a black felt hat, its brim broad enough to give shade but not obscure my vision. A leather thong tied from it beneath my chin prevents it blowing off. It is irksome that people feel they have a right to stare and sometimes to pass comment on how I choose to dress myself, but it is not as if I am unaccustomed to being an object of curiosity. At least, in this case, I am become so by my own choosing, and with good reason. It is a small price to pay if it enables me to do my work better.

At last I see Cai making his way toward me through the crowds. His progress is slowed by people stopping him to shake his hand or even touch their caps as they wish him well on his journey. I stand up, smoothing my unfeminine skirt, momentarily ill at ease about appearing plain. He sees me and, noticing my discomfort, I fancy, gives me a warm smile. A smile that says, I care not about the strangeness of your clothes, or the strangeness of your ways; you are my wife, and all will be well.

He is on the point of reaching me when Isolda Bowen steps forward from the throng, firmly setting herself between us. The Cadwaladr women do not stand the comparison well. Nor, I fear, do I. I hasten to build barriers in my mind, as I now do whenever I am in this woman's presence. I feel her looking at me differently now, or is it only now that I have the truth of her I see her differently? No, I am sure of it, I sense her looking right into me, probing, testing for weakness, like a hungry wolf clawing at the peasant's door.

"Why, Mr. Jenkins," says she, a soothing softness to her voice, "you are every inch the *porthmon*. An exciting day indeed."

"Isolda, it is good of you to come to see us off. And I am pleased to have the opportunity to thank you once again for the loan of your fine horse. It is exceptionally kind of you."

Kind! I doubt the creature knows the meaning of the word.

"Think nothing of it." She gives a dismissive wave of a hand. "I'm sure the work will be of benefit to my dear Angel; he loves nothing better than to be occupied. As I have said, I am confident he will go well for you."

"Having a fit horse will be a godsend," says he.

God, I venture, has nothing to do with it.

Nor he did, Morgana.

Oh! She is here, inside my head! I hear her words as clearly as if they were spoken aloud.

Get out! I will not converse with you—leave me alone.

I will leave you alone when you leave Ffynnon Las, not before.

Even as she torments me she continues to talk with Cai, commenting on the brightness of the day and the cheerful mood of the well-wishers.

I will be watching you, witch-girl. My eyes will travel with you. Know this, I will make sure that by the time you return from the drove everyone will know the truth of what you are, and your husband will realize the mistake he has made in choosing you over me!

I want to turn and run, to get away from this vile woman, but to do so would color this moment, Cai's moment. I will not let her spoil it. I will not! I stand my ground, letting my determination show in my expression, filling my head with snatches of Dada's stories so that there is no room for her poisonous words. Summoning my courage I move forward and take Cai's arm. He appears a little surprised, but pleased, placing his hand on mine before addressing the crowd.

"I thank you all for your good wishes, neighbors," says he, removing his hat and effecting a bow. "When next we meet, God willing, I will stand before you with gold in place of beasts, and we shall all face the winter with full coffers."

There is much cheering and ribaldry. Cai leads me through the archway to the rear of the Talbot and we fetch our mounts. Prince is already wide-eyed, all too well aware that something momentous in his life is about to take place. Angel is chewing at the bit in his mouth producing foam, his ears set back in a warning to all to keep their distance. Still, he allows Cai to spring into the saddle on his back. We trot through the small paddock and into the holding field, where the other drovers are waiting.

"Morgana," says my husband quietly, "watch me. I will set the pace. If you need me, use your whistle, or come forward if you must. If the ponies start to move too quickly you must slow them, or they will push the cattle to an unnatural pace, and that way accidents lie." As if seeing the recollection this statement brings to mind he adds with a smile, "Show them, my wild one. Show them there are two drovers from Ffynnon Las working this herd."

I smile back briefly and then urge Prince into a brisk canter so that we might take up our position with the ponies. I pass Edwyn Nails, who gazes at me in a manner that almost brings a blush to my cheeks; a manner that should not be employed to look upon another man's wife, I feel. Cai checks that everyone is in place, sitting securely even as Angel spins around, prancing and snorting. The horse is excitable, and sweat already lends a sheen to his arched neck, but Cai is not perturbed by such antics and holds the reins gently. At last he raises his hat high and gives the mustering cry of "Ho! *Heiptrw ho!* Hup!" and the drove starts on its lumbering, noisy, perilous way.

What a procession we comprise! Cai rides at the front, his calls serving both to lead the cattle onward, and to warn people up ahead of the approaching herd. For any cattle encountered loose along the way will be compelled by instinct to join the others, and, as Cai told me, it would be the devil's own job to separate them from the drove once again. The beasts themselves are even more jumpy and boisterous than is their habit, now that several farms' worth have been brought together. They bellow and blast, stirring up a perpetual cloud of dust with their newly shod hooves, jostling and buffeting one another for the safest position or the best mouthful of grass. Bracken is in his element, dashing about to nip the heels of slowcoaches, tail wagging, boundless energy willingly put to use.

There is one other mounted drover, a wiry man known simply as Meredith. I am told he appears for this drove each year, regular as a harvest moon, always on a different horse of doubtful provenance, never encumbered by wife or offspring, his two preoccupations being the cattle and the ale, both of which will be available to him in abundance for the coming three weeks. He rides behind the beasts, pushing them along, cutting off the path to retrieve any strays, wearing his long duster coat despite the warm day.

Walking with him is Edwyn Nails, his height giving him a long easy stride so that he has no difficulty keeping up with the moving herd. He looks for all the world as if he would snap like a twig if he found himself on the wrong side of a Welsh Black's temper, but I have seen how he handled the beasts at the shoeing. He is a cattleman, every skinny bit of him, and as such will be an asset. Even so, I find his constant ogling of me disquieting and resolve not to be alone with him.

Behind him are the ponies. They are shocked to find themselves part of such a rumbustious cavalcade, and there is a deal of whinnying and uncalled for bucking. The older mares are steadier than the rest, but those with foals are understandably anxious. The babes themselves seem to view the whole exercise as a game and flit about, curly tails over their backs, heads high, giving their mothers the bother of calling to them all the time. Prince and I cut among them, cajoling and admonishing. He is crucial to their cooperation. As herd leader they will follow him; as parent the youngsters will respect him; as stallion the mares will, however reluctantly, go where he bids them. I scarce have to tell him what to do, but am merely a passenger offering occasional caution or encouragement through hand or heel.

Next in this curious carnival come Idwal Watson and his sheep. The noise they make with their continual bleating drowns out even the cows. They sound to me like so many old women, all complaining about their sore feet and empty bellies, and rolling their unholy eyes at the two black-and-white sheepdogs that run back and fore beside them, tongues lolling over sharp teeth, grandfather wolf glinting in their eyes. Watson himself is distinguished as shepherd by the long wooden crook he carries and the melodious whistling with which he controls his collies.

The creaking wagon of Dai the Forge follows on. His piebald cob clops along, blue eye half closed, mane trembling, and back twitching against the attention of irksome flies, his great feathered hooves demonstrating a remarkable economy of movement. In the driver's seat Dai lets the reins lie loose in one hand, leaving the other free to whip off his cap so that he might wave it above his head when the mood takes him, with a booming cry of "Get on, you slovenly creatures!" or *"Duw,* there's some ugly backsides to be staring at for weeks on end! Ho, hup!" It is well known he has no time for sheep.

Padding quietly on foot, forming the rear of the procession, are the women and boys. There are four in all; Cerys, the wife of Dai the Forge (who is never allowed to ride in the wagon), and their twin teenage boys, Ieuan and Iowydd; and Spitting Sara, her skin weather worn, her eyes heavy lidded, of indeterminable age but an appearance that suggests she has seen more droves than anyone else present. She has earned her nickname for her fondness for chewing tobacco and the resultant need to frequently fling phlegm and brown juice from her mouth The women and boys knit as they walk, and will sell their stockings in markets along the way. Spitting Sara has already started up a song, the words of which she sings out all the while continuing to chew.

We move up, away from the town, winding along the lane that takes us past Soar-y-Mynydd chapel and on up, up, up until we are atop the highest hill in the area; the limit of the horizon that can be seen from the mountain behind Ffynnon Las. This is not a route I am familiar with, having arrived via Llandovery. Next we ascend and descend the twisting steepness that is known hereabouts as the Devil's Staircase, and with good reason. By the time we reach the riverbed and the ancient pass of Abergwesyn we are all showing early signs of fatigue. This is a marvelous place indeed. I can almost hear the footsteps of the thousands of travelers over hundreds of years who have trod this path. The gap between the hills is narrow, dropping down steeply to follow a slim river bordered by marshy grass and a firmer, drier track. The riverbed is stony, with many flat boulders of immense size, worn smooth over centuries, gleaming slick and cool beneath the summer sun. I see a Kingfisher dart from its perch and snatch a minnow from the fast-moving water, its wings an iridescent flash of brightness against the cloud grey of the stones.

We work to keep the livestock out of the water, but it is too tempting for them after the climb. There are no deep bogs here, but having the cattle dawdle in the shallow water and the ponies pause to splash about slows the forward movement of the drove horribly. Cai has said that we will not pause today, but continue straight to our overnight stop. His reasoning is that it is better to have a short first day than to face the confusion of stopping and starting when the animals are as yet unaccustomed to travel, and no proper rhythm has been achieved. We are all pressed to get them going again, putting the dogs to work harder and drawing louder and more commanding cries from the men. At last we turn away from the stream, through the village itself, which comprises only a few houses and an inn, which makes us all lick our lips. We must content ourselves with swigs from the skins tied to our saddles, however, and urge our charges on farther.

By the time we reach Llanwrtyd Wells it is clear to all of us that a rest is crucial. Sound as Cai's planning was, the beasts have their own opinions. The heat of the day has tired them terribly, and in their fatigue they have become stubborn and quarrelsome. Cai directs us to push them into a pasture on the edge of the village.

"We'll give them an hour," says he. "No more, mind. We've the worst climb up ahead."

The cattle settle meekly to grazing in the meadow, as do the ponies. The sheep make a pretense of being too scared to feed, but greed soon overcomes them and they too put their heads down. Within minutes the small field is full to bursting with stock, all, happily, too tired and hungry to bother with each other. Cai sends the women to fetch ale and pies from the nearest inn and people quickly avail themselves of shady spots. Dai calls to me as I lead Prince toward the trough by the gate.

"Well, Mrs. Ffynnon Las, how do you like the droving life so far?"

I smile back at him and give a little shrug. We both know it is too early to tell how successful I might prove to be at mustering the ponies. We have not yet been properly tested. No doubt the time will come.

"Morgana." Cai takes Prince's reins from me. "We can tie the horses under that oak. Come, sit with me." He hitches Angel first, leaving his rein long enough that he can nibble the grass at the base of the tree trunk. Prince flattens his ears against his head and goes to bite his new stablemate. "Now then, Prince!" Cai berates him. "Show some manners, *bachgen,*" says he, looping the pony's reins over a low branch a short distance away. We loosen their girths and find our own cool patch beneath the outstretched arms of the aged tree. Cerys arrives with foaming ale and warm meat pies and we sit in companionable silence, intent on our refreshment, quietly pleased with the way the morning has progressed. It strikes me that this is the most relaxed we have been together for some time. Can it be that, away from the farm, away from the notion of being husband and wife at home, we can find a new ease together? We have a shared purpose, and that must be our focus, instead, perhaps, of the scrutiny our marriage has so far come under at Ffynnon Las, whether we are alone or in company.

All too soon our respite is at an end. We push the lethargic cattle through the gate first, and there is a certain amount of fuss and bother with both ponies and sheep before they are organized into their rightful places once again. The road is rougher here and the ponies slow their pace, picking their way over the sharper stones. The most noticeable change, though, is the steepness of the incline. Whereas the trek out of Tregaron was uphill, we climbed it over some distance, making the task less arduous than this unforgiving pitch. Now the cattle move laboriously, effort obvious in each step. The landscape falls away from us in far-reaching vistas to the north, but we have our backs to such glory and are intent only on the summit, so that the area around every one of us shrinks to the patch of track ahead that can be reached in one pace or two at most. Even the sheep have ceased their bleating to conserve energy. As the animals toil in the afternoon sun they give off a malodorous stench of sweaty skin, hot urine, warm feces, and belching breath. The Procession starts to stretch, so that Cai must keep halting the front-running bullocks, and the ewes at the rear must be pushed on firmly to keep up. The slower the drove moves, the more apt beasts are to break off on their own, so that we are all engaged in the tiring business of coaxing wanderers back to the body of the herd. Through it all I spy the women plodding ever onward, still knitting, as if the needles work entirely on reflex alone. I notice, though, that Spitting Sara has no breath left for singing.

Shortly before six o'clock, a shout from Cai indicates we have reached our destination. The ground has flattened now, as we arrive on the wide plateau of the Epynt mountain. There are no farmhouses here, but a single, lonely building, with only a handful of Scots pines for company. A wooden sign, its paint paled by many winters, declares it to be the Drover's Arms, and for all its shabbiness it is to us the most wonderful inn we have ever beheld in our lives, for never was a group of travelers so sore in need of rest and refreshment.

Spurred on by our own desire for the day's work to be done, and that of the animals to be left in peace to graze and doze, the herds are quickly penned in the holding enclosures behind the inn. I remove Prince's tack and take him over to the water pump to fetch a pail of water. He stands patiently while I pour it over his body. Steam rises, and the little horse gives a sigh of contentment before shaking vigorously, sprinkling me with sweaty droplets. I catch sight of Cai laughing at me quietly. As soon as I slip the halter from Prince he kneels in the dust and rolls with enthusiasm, ridding himself of itches and loose hair. By the time he scrambles to his feet he is covered in dry mud and looks a sight. He tolerates having his ears rubbed and then trots off to graze.

The women fetch pots from the rear of Dai's wagon and set about putting some *cawl* to boil over the already glowing campfire. The men move swiftly into the inn in search of ale.

Cai comes to stand beside me. For a moment we simply watch the herd grazing, sharing the satisfaction of seeing work completed for the day and our charges brought safely to their enclosure.

"A good day, Morgana," says he. "I couldn't ask for better for the start of the drove. No mishaps, and we've made good time."

He waves his arm at the cattle. "They are tired, mind, but they'll rest well here tonight. The walking will come easier to them as we go on, see?" He smiles at me. "You did well, *cariad*. For a beginner."

I am too pleased by his public use of such an expression of endearment to mind the implied criticism.

Cai bids me follow him inside. The interior of the building is blissfully cool, its thick stone walls keeping out the summer heat. I follow him up a twisting stone stairway to a low-ceilinged bedroom. There is a sagging bed and a washstand with jug and bowl.

"This is for you," says he. "I won't leave the herd on the first night. With the breeze in the right direction they're still close enough to smell home. They might take it into their heads to return, see? I'll camp out with them tonight." He shuffles back to the door, a little hesitant. Is he waiting for me to protest? I wonder. "There will be supper downstairs when you're ready," he tells me, and then disappears. I am reminded of our wedding night, and another lonely bedroom, in another lonely Drover's Arms. As I ease my aching feet out of my boots I am aware my weariness is not entirely due to the physical demands of the day. I take advantage of the washstand. It is heavenly to feel the cool water against my skin. I rinse my blouse and hang it out of the window to dry, before slipping into my second one. I might not always have the opportunity of such comforts, so I had best make the most of them where I find them.

Later, after a tasty supper shared with the other drovers, I retire to my room once more and take to my bed. It feels even more comfortable than I could have anticipated, and I imagine I will be asleep within moments. But though my body is weary my mind and my spirit are restless. It does not feel right to be in here, separated from the ponies. Separated from my husband. I want to go outside, take my blanket and put it on the ground beside him, so that we may sleep side by side, listening to the rhythmic munching of the little horses as they crop the grass, but I cannot. To do so would seem so . . . forward, somehow. I know this to be ridiculous, and yet I do not know how to go about changing the situation. Now my mattress has become rocky as a riverbed. I turn this way and that, but can no longer find comfort. At last I decide that I will not rest unless I gain some air. I slip my coat around my shoulders, pad on silent bare feet down the stairs and, unseen, out of the back door.

Outside, it is a perfect night. There are no clouds, so that the stars glow like sparks from God's own campfire, flaring and fading as they are apt to do. The air is close and full of the scents of evening; the pulsing bodies of the beasts, the smoke from the dwindling fire, the spent tobacco in the still-warm bowls of clay pipes, the fragrant needles of the pine trees. The night is so still, tiny sounds are able to make themselves heard. I notice not only the hooting of a solitary owl but the rustling of its wing feathers as it swoops from a high branch. I make my way to the ponies and move among them. As always, they are comfortable in my presence. They consider me friend. There is great solace to be found in the company of creatures when they are at rest. Their acceptance of me makes me feel at ease with myself.

I see Cai sleeping beneath the tree nearest the boundary wall. He has his head against his saddle and a rough blanket draped over him. His hat might have started the night tipped to shade his face but has fallen to the ground. He looks so very . . . *gentle,* in repose, and wears the cares of life lightly on his sleeping features. I step closer, drawn to him, wishing I could lie with him, snug against his back, so that we were both lulled to sleep by the muted noises of the night.

A sudden coldness makes me start. I turn and find Angel has come to stand behind me. He is neither grazing nor dozing, but looking at me, and I know he sees me in a way that is different from the other horses and ponies. He is Isolda's favored mount, after all. I should not be surprised that there is something of her about him; a fraction of her own presence, even. A shadow

moves out from beside him, a darkness not created by the blocking of the bright moonbeams falling this night. The shadow
shifts, takes shape, and emerges. Isolda!

"You should not be so shocked to see me, Morgana," says she,
her voice a low, hissing, whisper, such as a snake might use to
transfix its prey. "Did you really believe I would allow you two
to travel together without me? I told you, by the time this drove
is at an end Cai will want rid of you. You will no longer be welcome in Tregaron, nor at Ffynnon Las."

I fight to keep my mind empty. I will not have this woman
violate my thoughts. I confess I am astounded at the distance she
is able to witchwalk. Will we never be beyond her reach?

"No, Morgana, you cannot step beyond the limit of my powers." She smiles as she speaks and it is as chilling and frightening
a smile as any I have witnessed. She leaves off making a fuss of
her horse and steps closer to Cai. I fear for him and hurry to put
myself between them. She laughs mirthlessly. "Your willingness
to place yourself in the way of danger to protect him is touching.
Touching, and stupid. Do you think there is anything you could
do to stop me if I chose to turn my strength against him? You
may be a witch, but you have little control over your abilities.
Scant expertise in the way of directing them. Why, you have
spent your entire life denying you are what you are, even to yourself, it seems."

I put my hands on my hips, feet firmly planted. Let her bluster
and goad. I will not be scared away by her threats. It may be that
she is right, that I am useless against her. But I will make a stand.

"How feverishly that callow mind of yours works, Morgana.
There is no need for you to trouble yourself to make sense of
what you cannot possibly understand. You have led a simple life;
you see things in simple terms. What can you know of me and
my kind?" She walks past me, and I know there is nothing I can
do to stop her. She bends over Cai, gazing down at him. I want
to drag her away, to claw at her, to pick up a stout stick and beat
her with it. But it is only her phantom stands before me. How

can I do anything to influence it? A pain grips my heart as I watch her plant a kiss on my husband's brow. He murmurs in his sleep but does not wake.

Isolda considers me, her head on one side, eyebrows raised.

"I almost pity you," she tells me. "I suppose you are not to blame for the position in which you find yourself. However, it is still your choice to stay. My patience is nearing an end, witch-girl. If you do not leave of your own accord, I will have rid of you, by any means necessary."

The sound of the words is still hanging in the air but her shape has vanished. Angel goes back to his grazing. Somewhere a dog fox barks. From behind the wall comes the purring of Dai the Forge's snore. Isolda has gone, and it is as if she has never been, save for the dread she has placed deep inside me.

12.

Cai opens his eyes to a glorious dawn breaking over the distant Beacons at Brecon. The sky is hill-fire orange with slashes of scarlet fading to the yellow of candle flame at its uppermost reaches. Skylarks trill and whirr. A family of crows add their raucous argument to the sweeter sounds of marsh tits and robins. He lies still for a moment, letting the sky and the birdsong bring him slowly to his senses. He does not recall a dream, only a sense that his night was disturbed somehow. Whether by memories or something outside himself he cannot be sure. He looks for the familiar ache of loneliness within but, strangely, does not find it. He acknowledges a change in himself, a significant shift in what moves him. Time was, for a long time, his waking moments were filled with longing for Catrin, and his arms ached to hold her once more. Slowly that grief melded with loneliness into a dull pain of emptiness, a yearning for someone to make him complete again. Now such vague wishes have altered to be highly specific. Now it is Morgana he longs for, Morgana for whom his arms ache, Morgana's name on his lips when he wakes, troubled and full of desire in the slow, hot hours of the night.

He sits up, rolling his stiff shoulders in an attempt to shrug them into suppleness. The mountain ground is a hard bed, and already he is aware of pains and discomforts that will only be added to in the weeks to come. Standing up he brushes down his clothes and puts on his hat. There will not be the luxury of a wash today. He thinks of Morgana in her cool, quiet room and pictures her, for a vivid moment, standing before the washbowl, pouring water over her slender body. He feels shameful at such a thought, and then, at once, cross. She is his wife, after all. As if he has summoned her up he finds her standing in front of him, though he never heard her footsteps. Bracken wakes up to greet her, too, wagging his tail and snuffling at her feet.

"Ah. Good morning, Morgana. Did you sleep well?"

She gives a gesture which suggests she did not.

"Well, a strange bed . . . perhaps you would have preferred the lullaby of the foxes and owls out here." He says it as a joke but, seeing her face, realizes that, of course she would rather have been outside. When has he known her ever to choose to be indoors? He shakes his head at his own shortsightedness, silently cursing himself for missing the opportunity to share the night with her, however publicly. However hard the bed.

It takes far longer than it ought for the livestock to be mustered and the drovers and followers to be assembled. Cai is irritated by how slow everyone is, and how disorganized. Even Bracken is bad tempered and gets into a scrap with one of Watson's collies, leaving him with a bleeding ear.

Cai knows they cannot spend their mornings like this, in such disarray. He must make certain of an earlier start tomorrow, he decides. And then he remembers tomorrow is to be a rest day. It is early in the journey to call a temporary halt, and he knows to do so will raise some eyebrows. He is resolved to stick to his reasoning—the stock are unused to travel, he will say, let them have a day to recover from hauling themselves over the mountains. Better to keep the condition on them than to rush. It is flimsy logic, and he knows it, but it will be worth it. They will camp for an extra day and night outside Crickhowell so that Morgana might visit her mother and spend time with her. He has promised her this, and he will be true to his word. He knows how much it will mean to her.

Having scaled the Epynt the previous day, the journey to Brecon is comparatively easy. The general downhill gradient helps the animals overcome their reluctance to press their aching limbs into action. In Brecon they pass the Drover's Arms where

Cai and Morgana spent their wedding night. It shocks Cai to realize how many nights have passed since and still he has not taken Morgana to his bed. Suddenly he feels stupidly slow, like some tongue-tied teenager. And now they are on the drove, and he knows the opportunity to do anything to cross the distance that remains between him and his wife may not present itself for weeks. He twists in his saddle, seeking her out among the moving mass behind him. The wide street of the town narrows over the bridge to cross the Usk and he can pick her out, urging Prince between the mares and the sheep, nudging them along to keep up with the cattle. She appears so at ease on the little horse; completely confident, her signals to her mount barely perceptible to the onlooker. The pony goes well for her. Cai is saddened at the thought that he must be sold when they reach London. Morgana will take the parting hard.

People have come out to watch the procession. Children run alongside Angel, admiring the fine horse, a little in awe of the *porthmon* riding at the front of the drove, his hat brim shading his eyes, his curious calls summoning the herd behind him. The beasts set up a bellowing as the buildings grow taller and the number of spectators around them increases. One of the younger foals panics and darts down a side street, leaving its mother to whinny frantically. Cai sees Morgana and Prince fly after it, cutting it off before it can become lost or hurt, gently directing it back to the herd. Watson's sheep provide the most noise, bleating like some discordant choir, a senseless, tuneless racket that serves only to wear the nerves and strain the voices of those who must control them. The two sheepdogs work swiftly, one becoming sufficiently agitated to nip at the nose of a sluggish ewe, drawing blood. Watson emits a stream of curses at the dog, which slinks away to the far side of the flock, tail down. The heat of the day and the excitement of the beasts provoke a powerful stink which seems to both precede and follow the procession. It is with some relief to all that they finally leave the town and press on toward the high pass at Bwlch. After more plodding hours they crest the hill. Cai signals to Morgana who hurries forward to join him.

"Look." He points down into the wide valley below. "You are nearly home." As soon as he says it he wishes the word unspoken. He does not want her to think of anywhere but Ffynnon Las as her home now. But when her face fair lights up with joy at the sight of the village where she was born and raised, Cai feels only pleased that he has been able to give her this small happiness. It is as they are descending the steep slope from Bwlch that he notices an unevenness in Prince's gait.

"Bring him over here," he tells Morgana. "Let me see what's troubling him."

They dismount and he lifts the pony's off hind, cleaning it out gently with his pocketknife.

"Ah, he's picked up a stone. There it is." He flicks away the sharp piece of sandstone and tests the sole with his thumb. Prince flattens his ears, swishes his tail, and tries to pull his hoof away. Cai shakes his head. "He's bruised his foot," he says. "You'll have to lead him, Morgana. It's a good thing we've a rest day tomorrow." Seeing her concern he adds, "Don't worry. Dai'll take a look at him. He can fit a special shoe if needs be, see?"

She nods, stroking Prince's neck thoughtfully before gazing in the direction of Cwmdu. Cai puts his hand on her arm. "I'll take you up to your mother's cottage on Angel. He's fit enough for a bit of extra work."

She smiles her thanks, still managing to give Isolda's horse a filthy look. Cai marvels that her hatred of the woman should extend even to her horse.

By the time the livestock are safely installed in the enclosures just west of the tollgate at Crickhowell the sun is dipping toward the horizon. Cai could happily ride Angel right into the nearest stretch of river for a swim before heading to the inn to sit with an ale or two, but Morgana has other ideas. With Prince put out to graze, she plants herself firmly beside Angel, her intentions plain.

"Come on then." Cai reaches down to her. "Let's go and surprise your mam."

She grasps his wrist, puts a foot on his boot, and springs up to sit behind him. He cannot suppress a smile at how sensible she was to design a garment that allows her such mobility whilst maintaining her modesty. Just about. He calls to Dai to tell him to keep an eye on the herd in his absence, growls a command at Bracken to stay behind, and they set off at a gentle canter along the narrow valley road that leads to Cwmdu. Morgana sits lightly, her natural balance making her an easy passenger. It may be his imagination, but Cai believes that she holds her arms around his waist just the slightest bit more tightly than is truly necessary. He enjoys the closeness of her, and wishes he could carry her off to a secluded, shady spot somewhere, instead of delivering her to her mother. All too soon, for him, the short terrace of stone houses comes into view. They have barely reached the garden gate when Morgana slips from Angel's back and runs to the front door. She is perplexed to find it locked. She knocks loudly, but there is no answer. She peers in through the window. Now Cai notices that the tiny front garden is more neglected than he remembers. A cold feeling of foreboding settles upon him, dispelling the warmth of the day, creeping through his bones. Morgana turns to him, and he sees real fear in her eyes.

The door of the neighboring cottage is dragged open and an elderly woman pads out into the sunshine. Cai recognizes her as Mrs. Roberts, who was a witness at their wedding.

"Morgana, *cariad*? Is that you?" Her voice is feeble, cracked not just with age, but with anxiety, too, Cai is sure of it.

Morgana hurries to her neighbor, taking her hands, searching her face for answers.

"Oh, *cariad*. My poor *cariad*." The old woman is close to tears. Morgana stares at her, openmouthed. The moment is filled with horror at the story that is about to be told. "She was so poorly, your mam," says Mrs. Roberts. "We thought she should send for you. Bryn Talsarn offered to fetch you, he did, but she wouldn't hear of it. Even when she was fading . . ."

Morgana snatches her hands away and takes a step backward, shaking her head.

"She didn't want to pull you from your husband, from your new life. She told me, *cariad,* she told me she wanted the best for you. Didn't want to be a burden, see? She'd known for many months that she was unwell. She knew her time had come. Said there was nothing to be done. No point in the both of you suffering . . . oh, *cariad,* don't take it so hard. I stayed with her, see? She wasn't alone at the end . . ."

Morgana runs to the door, pulling at the handle, hammering on the wood fit hard enough to break her hands. Cai jumps from the saddle, looping Angel's reins over the gatepost.

"Morgana, stop . . ." He hurries to her, putting his hands on her shoulders, but she shrugs him off, her expression wild, desperate, refusing to accept the truth of what she hears.

Mrs. Roberts steadies herself on the low garden fence.

"I planted flowers for her, Morgana. I'll not let her lie untended," she says.

Morgana backs away, staring at her neighbor as if she were a madwoman. Cai reaches out to her, but she swings round on her heel and runs for the chapel.

"Morgana . . . wait!" She is away before he can stop her. He takes Angel's reins once more. The horse is unnerved by the commotion and will not stand for him to remount.

Mrs. Roberts struggles to her gate.

"She wouldn't even let us fetch Morgana for the funeral. 'Let her be,' she told us. 'Let her be in her new life'—she was adamant . . ."

The old woman falters at the look on Cai's face, for he is recalling the *toili,* the ghost funeral he witnessed, the vision the old man had told him was a portent of the death of someone close to him. Not Morgana, then, but Mair!

"When did she die?" he asks.

"A week last Tuesday" comes the reply.

Just two days after he had witnessed the spectral coffin being carried to its phantom resting place. Cai shivers as he pulls a fidgeting Angel down the road at a run.

He finds Morgana prone atop a new grave. It is marked by a small bed of pansies and a simple wooden cross. The earth shows brown between the inadequate patches of turf. Morgana's whole body shakes, convulses almost, with silent sobs. She clutches and claws at the ground, digging her hands into the dry soil, pulling at the gritty surface as if she would dig her mother up and cradle her body in her arms. Cai hesitates. He cannot bear to see his dear wife in such pain, but still, even after all these weeks, even though a closeness has built up between them, he does not know how she will respond to his attention and care. Gingerly he kneels beside her.

"Morgana, *cariad*. Don't . . . Morgana, I am so sorry. Please, stop . . ." He takes hold of her hand. She shakes him away, and then starts beating at him, furious, despairing, her mouth open in a soundless scream of anguish, her face awash with tears. "Oh, Morgana . . ." he says, his own vision blurring. She flails with her fists, shaking her head, her hat fallen from her head, her hair escaping its ties and falling wild about her shoulders, her eyes unfocused. Cai wonders if it is true a person can be driven mad with grief. He recalls all too clearly how close to insanity he came after losing Catrin. It tears at his heart to see Morgana suffering so and to be powerless to help her. So he lets her beat him. Lets her rail and thrash and throw herself about until she is spent and exhausted. Then he takes her in his arms and rocks her back and fore, back and fore, murmuring her name into her tangled hair. Slowly her sobs subside and the two of them stay where they are, huddled on the pitiful mound of earth, clinging to one another until the light of the day goes out and the more fitting darkness of evening envelops them.

When I awake I am in a strange bed, in an unfamiliar room. I sit up, gasping as if drowning, throwing the covers from my sweltering body. The soft glow of moonlight through the open window gives dull illumination to the room, and slowly my eyes adjust, bringing shapes into being. A simple bed, in which I lie alone. A roughly made table and stool. A worn rug on the floorboards. In the corner a low armchair, and in it Cai, sleeping, his chest rising and falling slowly, a comforting rhythm. Now I recall the events that brought me here senseless, and the pain knocks the breath from me as surely as if I'd been kicked by a carthorse. Mam. Dead. Gone. Forever. Just like Dada. One day a living, breathing, warm person. The next a cold corpse. At least this time I have a grave to visit. Why did she not send for me? *Why?* Could she really have believed she would save me suffering by allowing me to find out about her passing this way? Did she not think I would want to be at her side, to comfort her, to hold her one last time? It seems she did not even want me at her funeral, and what a pitiful affair that must have been. Were there any mourners present save for old Mrs. Roberts? Of course I knew she was ill. And her illness was the reason she agreed to give me to a stranger. She was thinking of me, of what was best for me. For my future. But I had always imagined she would call me back . . . when she neared the end. That she would want me to be with her.

I cannot recall getting here. My last clear memory of yesterday was weeping as Cai held me. Weeping until I'd no more tears left in me, and I fell past sense in his arms. He must have brought me here. Taken off my boots and my heavy skirts, and laid me in this bed. He, at least, has not abandoned me. He sleeps but a few paces away, my slumbering guardian. He is all I have left.

There is a persistent buzzing inside my head. Ordinarily I would succumb to it, drift from my sleep-heavy body, and travel to another place. Somewhere free and open. But I have not the heart to do it this night. For where would I go? Could I step in a single place of my childhood hereabouts and not think of Mam? Would I not wait to see her rounding the bend at the top of our lane on the way back from milking? Or emerging from the cottage with a basket of cheeses for market? Or calling for me in the woods behind the house? Or find her sitting in her wooden rocker by the fire? And yet, she will not be there. Not now. Not ever again. She is lost to me, as Dada is lost. I searched for him for so many years, witchwalking the hills and meadows, visiting inns in my phantom form, in a restless quest to find him in whatever guise he chose to present himself. But he is not on this earth anymore, I convinced myself of this fact a long time ago. Will Mam find him now, I wonder. There is some solace to be had in believing she will.

A distant growl of thunder momentarily distracts me from my sorrowful thoughts. I shake away another difficult memory. Climbing from my bed I stand at the window. We are lodged in a scruffy inn beside the enclosures, and from here I can see the herd resting peacefully. Tomorrow was to be a day spent with my mam; a day of togetherness and joy. Instead I shall be at a loss. Will Cai change his mind about tarrying here and order us to move on? If Prince's foot is recovered I hope he chooses to do so, for what point is there in lingering now? How can I hide my grief when I am surrounded by whispers from the past and see only an absence where there should be the one person left in this world who loved me. No. That is not quite true. Looking back from the window, standing aside to allow the moonbeams to drift across the room, I contemplate the warm, strong figure of my husband. What a confusion of emotions stirs within me! Even as I am swamped by a wave of loss and sadness, I cannot deny that the realization that I am yet loved, yet wanted, yet cared for, heartens me. I will prove myself worthy of him. I will apply myself to the task ahead and put aside my grief. There will be time enough to revisit it later.

A grey morning greets us when we emerge from the inn, with a sky as heavy as my heart. Cai is sensitive to my mood and does not subject me to pointless chatter. We examine Prince's hoof and I am relieved to find him sound. Cai gathers the company and informs them that we will not be having a rest day as planned. There is a token resistance to this news, but no one is able to raise any sensible objection, and we set about our duties to prepare the herds for the off.

While I am tacking up Prince, Edwyn Nails finds his way to me. He shuffles his feet, whipping off his battered hat before he is able to find any words.

"I was sorry to hear of your loss, Mrs. Jenkins," says he. "It must be terrible, to find out a parent has passed like that . . . My own parents are both dead," he tells me suddenly.

I stop what I am doing and face him. Such a revelation, of such a personal nature, demands my full attention.

"Oh, it wasn't sudden, mind," he goes on. "Not like . . . well, Mam died of the scarlet fever when I was seven. Caught it from us, she did. Rare for an adult to go like that, the doctor told us, but there it is. My father, well, he had a weak chest. Saw one too many hard winters . . ." He stops stretching his hat out of shape and looks me steadily in the eye. "I know it's not the same, not the same as it is for you, but . . . well, I wanted you to know that I understand. How you feel. How it is to be without parents, Mrs. Jenkins. Morgana . . . can I call you that? Morgana?"

How can I deny him this small thing when he has gone out of his way to help me carry my burden of grief? I nod, and he relaxes his grip on his hat a little more before shoving it back on his head.

"Very good. Well, best get to it," says he. He pauses to do nothing more than look at me for a long minute. It is a look not wholly appropriate to the moment, and something in the way he regards me, so boldly, so intently, unsettles me. And then he is gone, lost among the throng of cattle and people as the drove is mustered once more. Only then do I notice Cai has been watching our exchange.

By the time we are heading east once more it is to the accompaniment of steady drizzle. We stand for what seems like an age whilst Cai pays the toll for the drove. I see now why he wishes to avoid as many turnpikes as possible, for they are ruinously expensive. There is talk about that if something is not done to lower these tolls, many of the poorer people will be unable to pay them, unable to travel or trade, and many will know hunger and real poverty this winter.

The pace is slow and the mood of the drove somber without the sun to cheer us. Gone are the bright kerchiefs and head-scarves, replaced by stout hats and oilskin coats that give the drovers their distinctive outline. I insisted on being given just such a coat and am glad of it now. It is a weight, and I feel Prince adjust his pace to accommodate the heavy material. At least it keeps the rain off his back, too. Rain that, before we are out of sight of Abergavenny, has become forceful enough to beat out the sound of hooves and bellowing and bleating, so that soon we progress only to the music of water. Water falling upon us. Water falling upon the road. Water falling upon the cover of Dai's wagon. Water falling upon the beasts. Water flowing in ditches beside us, and swelling the streams and rivers along the way. I think of the raindrops as tears for my mother, and try to imagine the sadness I feel washing away from me with each passing mile. But it is a vain hope, for there is now within me a cold misery that I must carry no matter where I go. I cannot imagine, at this moment, that there will ever come a time I am free of it.

13.

Even as we leave Wales and cross the border into England the rain follows us. I recall setting off with such excitement inside me at the prospect of leaving the one country I have known all my life, but when the moment comes all the color of it is washed out by the grey light of the weather and by the manner in which my heart shrinks within me, as if to hide from any further blows. Cai sees my suffering, I know he does. I should allow him to comfort me, but how can I risk exposing myself to more pain? Everyone I have ever cared for has been taken from me. Am I a jinx, then? Would caring for Cai, would letting myself feel for him what I had begun to believe I could feel, put him in danger somehow? Perhaps, after all, he would be better with one of the awful Cadwaladr girls. Perhaps he was right when he said calamity surrounds me. For have I not also brought the wrath of Isolda into his life? If he had never met me, never chosen me, he might have settled upon her as a wife, and then she would have had no call to harm him. But, no, the idea is unthinkable, for then she would have access to the well and the *Grimoire*. I cannot let that happen. The second we return I must find a way to explain everything to Mrs. Jones. If I am not to be beaten by Isolda, I will need her help.

I am numb to the prettiness of the landscape, or the curious construction of the houses, or the novelty of hearing an unfamiliar language spoken around us. Cai manages English well enough, as he must, but few others among us are so able. I have heard Meredith mutter a few blunt words when called upon to do so, and Spitting Sara converses with surprising fluency, a talent no doubt acquired on her many droves. The rest are content to keep to themselves. It is not until we are nearing the end of our second week that the sky brightens. Watson fancies himself something of a weatherman, and warns this is but an interlude, and yet more rain will follow shortly. All the more reason for us to take advantage of the warmth. Cai calls a rest day, so that we might all succeed in drying our clothes, and, indeed, our damp bones.

We find good grazing for the stock and settle them into two generous enclosures. There is even a capacious barn the farmer is prepared to let everyone bed down in. It is decided that during the next day, Dai and Edwyn will attend to the feet of those cattle and ponies who need it. There is a grassy paddock leading down to a broad stream behind the barn. After a deal of activity a campfire is soon burning, stew pot bubbling, various items of clothing draped in the low sun or steaming as close to the flames as is sensible. Everyone eats together, making the most of extra ingredients bought at market that afternoon as we passed through a small town of redbrick houses. Spirits are lifted by the sunshine and the prospect of a few hours of rest, so that the atmosphere in the camp is convivial. Were I not nursing my own chilling grief, there would be much to enjoy.

Dai settles himself against a low wall with a sigh and takes out his clay pipe.

"Well then, Mrs. Ffynnon Las," says he, "those ponies of yours are looking fit as fleas. Mr. Ffynnon Las will be pleased with your work." He laughs, a gulping guffaw of mirth. "You might find an extra shilling or two in your pay, see?"

Meredith swigs off his ale and gives a pointed belch. "Days were you wouldn't see a woman on a drove," says he.

Dai waves his pipe at his own wife and Spitting Sara. "Aye? And what are these, then, Meredith, m'n? Fairies, is it?"

The fairies laugh at this, particularly Sara, who finds it so amusing she spits out her well-worn lump of tobacco and celebrates the moment with a fresh piece. Edwyn grimaces and then smiles at me.

"You know what I mean," says Meredith. "Some used to think it bad luck to let a woman work the herd." He pauses to tip more ale in his jug. "Some still do."

"You tell me who the man is as could do a better job of keeping those ponies in hand than the lovely Mrs. Jenkins here," Dai challenges him. Getting no reply he gives a hearty grunt. "There you are, see?"

"Handsome is as handsome does," puts in Spitting Sara, which leaves everyone a little puzzled. Cai, who has been talking to the owner of the farm, reappears. He comes to sit beside me. Meredith mutters into his ale. Edwyn sighs and looks away from me now.

"Let's have a song!" says Dai. "Come on, Watson, start us off."

"Oh, I don't know . . ." Watson puts on a poor show of reluctance before being persuaded by everybody to sing. He stands up and clears his throat dramatically. There are a few seconds of silence and then he begins in a clear, graceful tenor to give a subtle rendition of *Calon Lan*! The words work their spell, causing all to fall quiet, lulled by the music, carried away by the sentiment.

> *Nid wy'n gofyn bywyd moethus*
> *Aur y byd na'i berlau mân*
> *Gofyn rwyf am calon hapus*
> *Calon onest, calon lân*

> *I ask not for ease and riches*
> *Nor earth's jewels for my part*
> *But I have the best of wishes*
> *For a pure and honest heart.*

At last the other men cannot hold back. Edwyn joins in, providing a passable second tenor, while Dai and Meredith reveal themselves to be fine baritone and bass, respectively. They sing together in close harmony, finding their notes as if they were born to such sweet music, which of course they were.

Cai gives me a small smile and moves close to my ear to tell me quietly, "'Tis the *hiraeth*, Morgana. The yearning for home every Welshman feels when he is away from it. They cannot help themselves." Indeed, only a few seconds later he gives in to this longing himself and joins the song, adding a gentle baritone of his own, the notes pitch perfect and melodic.

When they have come to the end there is a silence filled with thoughts of home. Sara, unable to stand the sight of such melancholy descending on the evening, claps her hands together abruptly and begins a bawdy song of her own that soon has me blushing and everyone else yelping with laughter. Even Bracken joins in with a discordant howling. I only wish I had the heart left to feel such joy.

After supper Cai leaves us to check on the cattle, taking the tired corgi with him. I myself slip away, following the flow of water downstream until I find a private spot. The riverbank is grassy and slopes gently into a bend in the stream which provides a natural bathing pool. The thought of washing away the grime of the journey is a soothing one. The pastures here are small and gently sloping, with many small copses, so that there are no vistas, but instead pockets of tranquil grazing. The place of my choosing is wonderfully secluded, with hazel trees and willows lending shade and screening short stretches of the water from view completely. I find a broad, flat rock at the water's edge and quickly undress. My blouse, being one of a pair, is still in reasonable condition, and my slip is tolerably clean as I have been able to rinse it on occasion. My heavy divided skirt, however, has fared less well. It reeks with the smell of horse sweat and the dung of the various livestock kicked up as the cavalcade advances, is stained with muddy rainwater, and is altogether coated in filth. Nonetheless, it is serving its purpose well, and I am glad of it. I stand naked, hesitating for only a second before stepping off the rock into the deepest part of the pool. The coldness of the water is shocking but wonderful. On tiptoe I am just able to keep my head above the surface, so that I have only to bob down to completely submerge myself. I take a breath and disappear into the glorious peacefulness of the underwater realm, reveling in the sensation of the current tugging through my hair, caressing my skin, washing away the toil and effort of the preceding weeks. If only the ache in my heart were so simply eased.

I break the surface, my eyes closed, water coursing down my face. Even sightless, however, I am instantly aware of another's presence. My eyes spring open, and I shake droplets from my face, squinting into the trees and bushes on the riverbank. I can make out a figure. A man. At first I think it is Cai, and am not alarmed. The deep water is maintaining my modesty, at least, and, I am surprised to realize, I do not feel resistance at the thought of being naked with him. In fact, quite the contrary. It comes as a shock, then, to see that it is not my husband who stands watching me. It is Edwyn Nails.

Instinctively I cross my arms over my chest. I cannot reach my clothes without getting out of the water. I cannot leave without fetching my clothes. I am trapped. I think at first he must have stumbled upon me by chance; been following the river perhaps in search of a place to bathe and heard sounds of splashing. As I watch him, though, as I study the wideness of his eyes, and the tension in his body, I see this is not the case. He has come look-ing for me, and he has found me. Here. Unclothed and alone. My anxiety increases as he steps onto the rock where my clothes lie. He stoops and picks up my thin cotton slip, holding it against his cheek, smiling. The love spoon whistle falls from its folds, landing on the stones hopelessly out of my reach. I feel panic ris-ing within me.

A memory, sharp and painful, comes unbidden into my head. A memory of another young man, some years ago. A memory of another lonely place. Another instance of my being trapped. That time I had been only thirteen, a girl on the cusp of wom-anhood. I had been out walking, roaming the hillside behind my home as I was wont to do. Tired from the heat I had rested in the corner of a ripening hay meadow. The field was full of grasses tall and soft, and bespeckled with cornflowers, poppies, and buttercups. Lying among their cool stems I had near drifted off to sleep when a shadow fell across me. The sun behind the figure who towered over me made it difficult to be certain of the identity of my attacker. Before I had the chance to as much as get to my feet I felt the weight of the young man on top of me. He was so lumpen, so hefty, that he winded me as he pinned me to the ground. The sun illuminated his hair in a copper red halo, so that I knew him then. For there was only one lad in the village with hair that color. One who had been a brute as a small boy, and had grown to be a brute as an adult. Did his assault on me stem from resentment for what I had done to him in the schoolroom all those years before? Or was he merely driven by the animal inside him, wanting what he would not be given, so taking it instead? I will never know.

Nor did anyone else ever have the opportunity to ask him.

Edwyn takes his shirt off over his head. I cast about for a way out, but still cannot overcome my reluctance to emerge naked from the river. He hops around pulling at his boots and then sits down to remove his breeches. He barely takes his eyes off me to do so. I shake my head firmly, holding up my hand in a gesture that can only mean *No!* He pays no heed. In seconds he is standing on the rock naked. I look away, turning to wade out toward the opposite riverbank. I hear him splash into the water behind me. I move as quickly as I can but cannot outpace his long limbs, even through the stream and over the uneven rocks. He grabs me around my waist, pulling me back against him.

"Cai calls you his wild one, I've heard him." His voice is harsh, his words urgent. "Seems to me you need a good man to tame you," says he, doing his best to spin me round to face him, despite my furious struggles. "I know you like me," he goes on. "I've seen you looking at me, Morgana. We are alike, you and I." He is panting now, with the effort of restraining me and with his mounting desire. I feel pressure building inside my head. I will not let him violate me. I do not believe I have encouraged him to think that this could possibly be what I want. Indeed his behavior at this moment is so at odds with the character he has shown to this point I barely recognize him as the same man. The man trusted by Cai. The man known locally as honest and hardworking, recommended by Dai the Forge, recognized by all as someone likable and fair. How can it be he is so changed? So altered, that he would try to force himself upon me?

In my desperate attempts to wriggle free of him I lose my footing and unbalance us both. We topple as one, the silky water closing over our heads. In the unearthly muffled depths he continues to pull at me. I kick him away and break the surface, gasping. But I am not free of him yet. His rough hand seizes my wrist. He stands before me again, grinning.

"A fine game, Morgana. If it makes you feel better to pretend you don't want me, I don't mind." He tightens his grip on my arm and pulls me toward him. I shake my head again as plainly as is possible. Now his other hand finds my left breast.

This will not do. Really, it will not.

I fix him with my gaze. He continues to grin. He is still grinning when the water about him starts to swirl. It takes a moment for him to become aware of something curious occurring. Only when he finds himself at the center of a whirlpool does his expression change. He starts to lose his balance; to be sucked down by the unnatural force of the maelstrom. He shouts out in fear. Now he lets go of my wrist. Or rather, he tries to let go of my wrist, but he finds he cannot. His face becomes colored by panic. Frantically he tries to unfurl his fingers, to draw away from me. He looks at me in utter bewilderment. When he sees how calm I am, when he sees that the water around me remains undisturbed, when he sees that the level of the whirlpool is ever rising about him, he gives way to terror and starts to scream. It is a terrible sound. The sound a snared animal might make, perhaps. Or an unwilling girl brutally used to satisfy a man's lust.

"Morgana!" he shouts as the water reaches his chin. "Morgana, help me! Please! I'm sorry . . . please!"

I do not enjoy seeing him suffer so. I do not wish to torment him. I want only to repel his advances. Will he try to impose his desire on me again, I wonder. I think not.

I release my invisible hold on his hand and he disappears beneath the water. Swiftly, I leave the pool and snatch up my clothes. Behind me the whirlpool is subsiding. As I step into my garments I see Edwyn clambering from the river, dragging himself gasping and spluttering onto the far bank where he lies, stunned and wheezing, coughing up water. I admit there is satisfaction in seeing how my actions have tamed him. Humiliated him. Given him pause for thought. And there is something else—I am aware of the subtlety of my power on this occasion. Yes, my response was born of fear and of anger, but it felt somehow different this time. As if I were more in control. As if my will could be more focused, and my magic more carefully directed. The knowledge that my abilities are ever increasing gives me some strength, some comfort.

Something catches my eye and I turn quickly to see a figure standing, silhouetted against the sun. I narrow my eyes to see more clearly, but already I know who it is. Isolda. Now the alteration in Edwyn's character is explained. Is there no one she will not use, will not bend to her will?

My hair still dripping, my clothes sticking to my wet body, I pick up my boots and run barefoot back to the barn.

❦

Content that the stock are settled for the night, Cai makes his way back to the camp. There is a certain nervousness within him, one that he chides himself for. He knows its cause. He has not secured a room for Morgana, so she will spend the night with the rest of them in the barn. The thought that she might lay beside him through the soft hours of darkness is thrilling. Stupidly so, he tells himself, for with so many people sharing the space it is hardly a night for privacy or intimacy. Even so, the idea of having her close, of watching her sleep, perhaps, moves him. He busies himself clearing a space in a corner of the barn, making sure there is sufficient room for two, so that she might naturally take her place next to him.

It is as he is arranging the saddles for pillows that she returns. It is obvious she has been bathing, for her wet hair hangs heavily down her back and her feet are bare. She sees him and he smiles at her. She looks wonderfully fresh and young. But she does not return his smile. Indeed, she seems agitated, irritated almost, by the sight of him. She looks at the cozy bed he is constructing and, instead of falling happily into it, snatches up a blanket and disappears to the other side of the barn to be with the women. Cai does his best not to let his disappointment show on his face. He must not read anything into her actions. After all, Cerys has also chosen to stay with the women rather than join Dai in the wagon. Perhaps Morgana considers it would not be proper for her to lie with him. He must be patient. He is resigning himself to another restless night when he spies Edwyn returning from the same river path from which Morgana emerged. He, too, is wet, his hair slick against his head, his shirt clinging to his damp body. He, too, has been bathing.

Bathing with Morgana?

The question reverberates around Cai's mind. Could it be true? Would she do such a thing? Spurn him, in favor of a young lad she barely knows? Make a fool of him here, now, on the drove, of all places? He cannot believe it. He will not believe it. Not of her. Surely she is not capable of such betrayal? And yet, she is several years younger than him. And she has not shown any inclination to take to his bed. Has not shown affection. Does she find him so unlovable? Has her head been turned by a youth, by a boy who has nothing, is nobody? Has all his care and patience been for nothing, just to be made a fool of? Anger chokes him. Anger, hurt, and confusion. He contemplates a flagon of ale Meredith has missed. But no, if he has been found wanting as a husband he will not fall short of what is required of a *porthmon*. Without a backward glance he strides from the camp across the meadow, not caring where his route takes him, knowing only that he must put distance between himself and Edwyn. Between himself and Morgana. Enough distance, enough walking, enough time, for his temper to cool and reason to return.

It is an hour later when he makes his way back to the barn and flops grumpily onto his blanket. Beside him, Dai lies, eyes closed, hands behind his head. He speaks without opening his eyes or troubling himself to sit up.

"Enjoying married life then?" he asks.

Cai hears friendly mockery in his tone, but is in no mood to joke about the matter.

"Is it a thing to be enjoyed? I had not noticed."

At this Dai laughs heartily. "*Duw, bachgen,* you've a deal to learn about women yet."

"And you are an expert on the subject, no doubt."

"Doesn't take a wise man to recognize love when he sees it. Takes a fool to pretend it isn't there, mind."

Cai busies himself rearranging his bedding, not trusting himself to give a civil reply. Dai raises himself up onto one elbow and frowns at him.

"You've a fine young woman there, Mr. Jenkins. A woman with love in her heart for you, if you'd only let her show it."

Cai pauses in his fidgeting. He wants to believe that Dai is right, that the idea of Morgana favoring Edwyn is ridiculous, that her strangeness will not prevent them from ever living a contented, normal life together. He dearly wants to.

"You think she . . . loves me, then?"

"Course she does, m'n! Plain for everyone to see. Everyone except you, mind."

Cai shrugs and shakes his head slowly. "I do care for her . . ."

"*Duw,* spit it out. It won't kill you. You love the girl. Nothing to be ashamed of. She is your wife, m'n."

Cai finds himself blushing. And smiling. Such faith in the obviousness, in the simplicity of his situation, is reassuring. Of course he was wrong to doubt her. He knows that, in his heart.

It all seemed clear enough when they were at home. It is only the pressure of managing the drove, the tragedy of finding Mair had died, worrying about Morgana's grief . . . She needs him to be strong and he has responded with muddle-headed thinking. He nods decisively.

"Aye," he says. "So she is. My wife."

Dai lies back down, chuckling to himself. "Well," he mutters, "there's a thing. A man in love with his own wife, and her in love with him. *Duw, Duw.* Who'd have thought it? Who'd have thought?"

The next morning is damp again with the promise of yet more rain. Cai feels better after the few words he shared with Dai. He must pull himself together and be the husband Morgana needs him to be, as well as head drover.

"Right you are, *porthmon.*" Dai is his usual hearty self, despite the greyness of the day. "Let's take a look at these beasts of yours, shall we?"

Cai nods, looking over his shoulder for Morgana. She was up early checking the mares' feet, so he has hardly glimpsed her. Edwyn has been fully engaged in preparing the forge with Dai and assembling nails and tools. He has not, Cai is certain, had the opportunity to be alone with Morgana again. If he ever had, he reminds himself. He is certain now that nothing happened, save for what his own tired imagination dreamed up. He tells Dai, "We'll put the cattle in the small meadow. Bring the ponies in here to check first." Morgana arrives leading Prince. She gives him a spontaneous smile, and he is touched that the sight of him can, however fleetingly, lighten her grief.

He smiles back. "Fetch the others into the yard," he says.

Morgana opens the broad wooden gate. Prince whinnies to his mares and the herd trots meekly through, milling about the narrow cobbled yard. There is barely space for all of them. One side is bordered by a high stone wall. The far end comprises a lower wall and the gate out to the lane. The far length is the front of the barn, its heavy doors shut. The meadow end, aside from the gate, is formed by a short run of pigsties. Morgana shuts the gate behind the last yearling, looping the rope over the top to secure it. At once Meredith moves the cattle into the meadow, Bracken nipping at their heels to urge them into the small space, and soon they are pushing and jostling, annoyed at having been ushered into an inadequate area. He cusses them, telling them to behave and wait their turn.

"They don't like being cramped in like this," he tells Cai.

"They'll have to put up with it for now. The ponies won't take long," he says.

"I'm just saying"—Meredith shakes his head—"they'll not settle in here."

"Just watch them, m'n. They'll stay where they're put." Cai does not need anyone finding fault or making problems where there are none.

Dai wastes no time but begins the backbreaking work of bending low to inspect the ponies' hooves. Edwyn's skills are not required yet, so he steps aside, leaning against the wall in an effort not to have his feet trodden on by the wandering little horses. Morgana holds Prince so that Dai may fit new front shoes. From the meadow comes lowing and snorting. Meredith is right, the cattle resent being so confined. They have grown accustomed to moving off each morning and dislike the change in their routine. Added to which, the ponies have cropped the meadow, so that there is no grazing left to distract them. Twice already Meredith has had to take a bullwhip to some of the more boisterous bullocks to stop them stirring up trouble in the herd. For all his efforts, they will not be quietened. Cai wends his way between the ponies toward the enclosure. If the cattle are not calmed the rising tempers among them could easily spark panic, and the fence on the far side, leading to the river field, is flimsy in places.

"Meredith!" he calls. "Don't let them get the better of you. Keep them still."

Rather than find a sharp retort the cowman keeps his attention on the stock, for he, too, is aware that they are becoming worryingly agitated. One young bull, in particular, is behaving in a way that is alarming the others, pawing at the ground, shaking his head, emitting low bellows. Some of the smaller beasts try to run from him, seeking safety. Finding none they push against the others, shoving them against the wall and the fence. Cai knows something must be done before they lose control of them completely. He puts a hand on the wooden gate and springs over it.

"Let them back into the other field!" he shouts to Meredith. But there is such a noise and commotion his words are lost. "Meredith! The gate back to the other field, m'n. Open it now!" He signals frantically at the stockman who at last understands, but his path is blocked by the pressing youngsters who will not move for him. Cai fights through the melee. The cattle bump and jostle him with increasing force. At one point he stumbles, righting himself only by clutching hold of an elderly cow who tolerates his using her to regain his footing. To fall beneath the herd when they are so disturbed would be dangerous indeed. He presses on. The cattle have become a moving mass of sweaty hair, lean muscle, and sharp horns. Being in their midst requires nerves of iron.

"Ho! *Duw,* steady now," Cai tells them, but he knows they are not listening. The far gate must be opened quickly, so that the pressure in the enclosure can be released through it into the empty field beyond. The herd are looking for a way out and will take the first opening they find; one of their own making if necessary. It is as Cai is twisting and shoving his way through the animals that he glances back toward the yard. Morgana is still holding Prince, who, sensing the drama close by, is refusing to stand. Dai has straightened up and pushes his cap back on his head, regarding the maddened herd with a deep frown. Edwyn is nowhere to be seen. One more thing snags Cai's notice. The gate into the yard is untied. One push from the cattle and they will pour through into the bottleneck of the yard, into the ponies, crushing anyone in their way. Cai opens his mouth to shout, to scream at Morgana, to warn her. As he does so a frightened bullock barrels into him, knocking the wind out of him, and with it his voice. Gasping, he waves his hat in the air, signaling to any who might see. Somewhere in the silence of that instant Cai glimpses what it must be like to be Morgana. What it might be to have no utterance with which to communicate, neither to man nor beast. He is taken back, in a flash, to that terrible moment on the mountain when the lightning robbed him of his herd. Now he is powerless again, and calamity is unfolding before him. He grabs hold of the nearest set of horns and hangs on, knowing that to be knocked to the ground now could prove fatal.

"Morgana!" he gasps.

As if everything has slowed to the speed of a nightmare, two bullocks lean into the yard gate and bump it open against the nervous ponies on the other side. Morgana now sees what is happening. So does Dai. He screams at her to open the gate onto the lane. She lets go of Prince and runs to do so, but the latch is broken and the gate has been tied with frayed rope. She darts over to Dai's tools for his paring knife. In the few seconds that stretch to an eternity it is clear to Cai, as it must be to Dai, that Morgana will not have time to get back to the gate and cut the rope before the stampede of terrified ponies and unstoppable cattle is upon her. The beasts will trample their way out, over fallen ponies, over the gate, and over Morgana. Cai watches helplessly as Dai turns to face the cattle, feet firmly planted, fists raised, and lets out a roar that is as loud and as terrifying as anything Cai has ever heard. As anything the cattle have ever heard. The ponies swerve around Dai. The cattle hesitate. The alarm the front ones feel at the sight and sound of this giant madman halts them in their tracks for just a few seconds before the momentum of the stampede, the weight of the bulk of the herd, pushes them on once more. In those few seconds, Morgana has cut the rope, and the path to freedom is open. She springs through, throwing herself behind the far side of the wall. The cattle reach Dai.

Back in the small meadow the rest of the herd thunder after the front-runners. Cai finds himself barged to the side, a horn piercing his arm, goring it from shoulder to elbow as it passes. He screams, but does not fall. He watches in horror as Dai is lifted off his feet, his arms still raised, fists beating the air, roaring as the beasts carry him on with them. For an instant he is borne aloft on a thundering mass of blackness, his cap still fixed to the back of his head. But even his immense bulk is no match for the irresistible force of the herd.

"Dai! Dai!" Cai screams, pain making his words rasp in his throat, shaking his head in despair at the sight of his friend being carried away by the frenzied horned beasts.

And at once, Dai is gone, disappeared beneath the charging cattle, vanished into the darkness of the bellowing stampede, swallowed up by their terrible crushing weight.

14.

I pick myself up, my mouth full of dirt, my body bruised from the sudden impact as I threw myself to the ground to escape the galloping cattle. I knew the ponies would not tread on me; that they would swerve or jump to avoid setting a single hoof upon me. But cattle are different. They do not possess such athletic abilities, and would simply plow forward, running over a person as if he or she were nothing more than a mound of earth or pile of stones to be scrambled over. Spitting grit I squint through the still swirling dust the stampede has left in its wake. Slowly shapes come into focus. Cai, clutching his arm, blood seeping out between his fingers, running across the empty yard. Cerys hurrying through the gate, her hands clasped to her face, the twins close behind her. Edwyn standing staring at the ground. There is something odd about him, as if he has a shadow standing next to him. I rub dust from my eyes and look again and am shocked to see that Isolda stands beside him. No, not beside, almost overlapping somehow, as if her insubstantial form is shifting through him. As she moves away she pauses to whisper in his ear and I see his face clearly stricken, though he does not appear to be aware of her presence. What hand has she had to play in all this?

Now I see Dai, inert, lying heavily on the hard cobbles, horribly still. I limp over to them, my left ankle complaining as I put weight on it. It is terrible to see such a strong man, a man so full of vigor and life, reduced to a crumpled, bloodied wreck. His legs are at awkward, unnatural angles to his body, clearly broken and useless. His arms are bloodied and do not move. His face is a mess of gore, his nose smashed, teeth missing, his jaw misshapen. Even so badly broken he manages to stir, opening his mercifully undamaged eyes. He tries to turn his head, searching for his loved ones.

"My boys?" he gasps. "Where are my boys?"

Cerys is on her knees beside him. She touches his cheek tenderly. "They are here. Right here, see?"

The twins fall to the ground beside their father, their faces already wet with tears, looking suddenly so very young, nearer children than grown men. Dai struggles to lift his head.

"Shh now," says Cai, "don't trouble yourself to move, m'n. Save your strength."

"For what?" Dai wants to know. There is a silence filled with regret and sadness, filled with the knowledge that there will be no more time for Dai, that he will have need of his great strength no longer. *"Bechgyn,"* says he, his voice strained and weak, "look after your mam, see? Iuean, you must be man of the house now. Work the forge. Iowydd, support your brother . . . you are good lads . . . good lads . . ." His words fade and his eyes glaze. From Cerys there is a small cry, such as a bird might make when startled, nothing more. Then all is quiet, and Dai lies dead.

We stare at his body in disbelief. How can such a force, such a presence, be snuffed out in an instant, rendered nothing more than memory and a body soon to be laid waste by corruption? Must life ever prove so fragile that even the strongest among us cannot withstand a fateful collection of circumstances? At last the silence is broken by the pitiful whimpering of Bracken, who has come to stand beside me.

Cai puts his hand on Cerys's shoulder. "Come away, *cariad,"* says he. "We will take him into the house."

She stands on unsteady feet, her boys supporting her, as now they must do in all things.

Edwyn's voice strikes a harsh note in the shocked stillness of the moment.

"It was Morgana," says he. "It was Morgana left the gate untied. 'Tis her fault the cattle got through. This is her doing!"

Now we are doubly stunned. I shake my head vehemently. This is untrue. I tied the gate, I know I did. I look desperately from Cai to Cerys and back again, still shaking my head, imploring them to see the truth. But already I feel the others regarding me with loathing. Meredith steps forward, his face grim.

"No good can ever come of letting a woman work the herd. Everyone knows that," says he. "I've said as much before, and I stand by my words."

"You are speaking nonsense!" Cai insists. "Both of you. And you, Meredith, you are old enough to know better than to spout superstitious rubbish."

But Edwyn won't easily be silenced. "That gate wouldn't have come open if it had been tied, that's the fact of it. And 'twas Morgana who shut it last, bringing the ponies into the yard."

"Be quiet," says Cai.

"You don't want to see the truth. You're just protecting her . . ."

"*Cauwch eich ceg,* I tell you!" He regains his temper and lowers his voice. "Now is not the time for recriminations. We must do right by Dai." He stoops down and slips his hands beneath his friend's broad shoulders. Only now do I see how badly he himself is injured. His shirt is torn to reveal a deep wound, still pouring blood. He mutters a curse as the pain of it stops him from lifting Dai's body. I whip my scarf from around my neck and bind the wound for him as best I can. Briefly he lays his hand over mine. "Thank you, *cariad,*" says he before quickly returning his attention to the sad task of moving Dai. "Help me," he instructs the others. "We will put him to lie in the farmhouse."

Meredith, Watson, and Edwyn help him carry Dai inside. The twins make as if to follow, but they are still holding their mother and she pauses, looking directly at me. And in that look I see such heartbreak. Heartbreak that seems to say, 'How could you? Your carelessness has made orphans of my children.' But she does not voice her thoughts. Instead silent tears begin to run down her cheeks, dripping unchecked onto the dusty cobbles. I shake my head, my eyes expressing my sorrow, but she turns and makes her trembling progress to the house.

I stand where I am. Everything has changed. In a few dreadful moments a husband, father, friend has been snatched away. And Edwyn would have me blamed. How dare he! Is his pride so great that he would have the world hate me because I spurned him? Cai defended me, but his reaction was instinctive, I think. Does he believe me? How can I offer another explanation for the untied gate when I have none? Then it comes to me. Edwyn. Edwyn must have untied the gate himself, deliberately. How quickly desire can turn to hate! That he should risk his friend in order to get at me. But I remind myself his will is no longer his own.

When Cai emerges through the front door he finds me where he left me. The other men trooping out behind him. He gestures to Meredith.

"Fetch back the cattle," says he. "Watson, you go with him. And you, Edwyn. Morgana and I will recover the ponies."

No one argues at this. The men set off, Meredith on his horse, the others on foot. Cai fetches Angel and pulls me up to sit behind him. The animal jibs and even bucks in protest at having me on his back again, but Cai pays him no heed, ignoring his antics. We take off at such speed I am forced to cling to Cai to prevent myself falling off. I can tell his arm is troubling him, but he will barely acknowledge the wound, so intent is he on what we must do. I sense anger and grief in the way he kicks at the thoroughbred's sides and urges him on down the lane at a canter. Bracken runs behind us but struggles to keep up. We find the ponies a short mile away, grazing the lush verges, their angst forgotten. Spotting Prince, his halter still in place and rope trailing, I slip down from Angel, glad to be away from Isolda's pet. Cai catches my hand, the pain in his arm making him wince.

"Morgana," says he, "you did tie the gate, didn't you?"

I nod emphatically.

"You are sure of it? It is very important you be certain."

I nod again, fighting back tears, and I see that he believes me. He hesitates, and I know there is something else.

"Yesterday, I saw you come back from bathing in the river. I saw Edwyn, too. You were both wet. I . . ." he stutters, struggling to meet my eye. "I doubted you, Morgana. I'm sorry. I know I was wrong. I couldn't understand . . ." He shakes his head. Suddenly, as if a new thought has struck him hard, he looks at me squarely. "What happened at the river? Did he find you there? You were alone. Morgana, did Edwyn . . . did he try to, to force himself on you?"

I close my eyes, in part to hold back yet more maddening tears, in part not to see the look of fury and hurt on his face. When I open them again I see that he has his answer.

"By Christ, I'll swing for the bastard if he so much as laid a hand on you!"

I shake my head, taking his hand in mine and holding it to my heart. My eyes, my gesture, tell him *no, he did not touch me. He tried, but he did not succeed.* The rage and tension sigh out of Cai, leaving only grief and weariness.

Later, when the herds are safely recovered and accounted for, we all gather once again in front of the farmhouse. Cai has made the necessary arrangements. Dai's body, now in a simple coffin, is loaded onto his own wagon. The piebald cob rolls his walleye as the casket is slid into place as if sensing all is not well, as if searching for his master. Iuean and Iowydd help their mother up onto the seat in front, one of them taking up the reins, the other keeping a protective arm around their beloved parent. Already they seem changed, childhood lost to them now, their future uncertain. They are to take Dai home on the stagecoach, which they will pick up at the nearest stop some five miles hence. There a man has been engaged, at Cai's expense, to drive the wagon back to Tregaron for them.

Cai holds the cob's bridle, looking up at Cerys.

"I will see you right, you know that," he tells her. "You will have Dai's full pay when I return. Perhaps the boys will come up to Ffynnon Las. There's work there for them if they want it," he promises.

"Maybe." Cerys struggles to hold her emotions in check. "Or maybe they won't want a daily reminder of who was responsible for their father's death," says she.

My mouth hangs open. Still she does not believe me! She takes Edwyn's word that I was careless. How can I make her see, make her know the truth? Edwyn looks openly triumphant. This is so unfair! I clutch at Cai's sleeve. He knows I am innocent, surely he can convince them. But when he looks at me I see doubt in his eyes. No! I point at Edwyn, my accusation plain. Cai narrows his eyes, his head cocked, thinking, considering what it is I am trying to tell him. When I look at Edwyn again he has his arms folded, eyebrows raised, in an expression of such smugness, such self-satisfaction. Is Isolda's control over him so strong that he can be so completely altered? Can he have cared so little for Dai? Is all that matters to him my humiliation at any cost? My fury escapes me before I have time to check it. A whirlwind whips up dust, dirt, and stones, rendering the air choking, stinging grit assailing our faces. Sara starts to wail and scream. The piebald whinnies in fright. Edwyn flies backward as if he has received a body blow from some invisible giant. He is knocked off his feet and sent skidding across the yard, only stopping, winded and shocked, when he comes up against the very gate in question. As quickly as it started the wind subsides. Edwyn gasps for air, pointing a trembling hand at me, shouting his accusations.

"She's evil!" he shrieks. "I tell you she's put a curse on the drove! Everywhere she goes bad things happen."

Cai lets go of the horse and turns to stand tall beside me.

"Morgana did not leave that gate open," says he, his voice level and full of contained rage. "When I vaulted it to help Meredith with the cattle in the paddock it was tied shut. It must have been, else it would have swung open under my weight, see?"

"I'm telling you," coughs Edwyn, "she left it open."

"The only person anywhere near that gate before the cattle

went through it was you, Edwyn," says Cai. Suddenly his expression changes, realization and understanding enraging him anew. "It was you! You untied it."

"Why would I do such a thing?" Edwyn scrambles to his feet, shaking his head all the while.

Meredith puts in his halfpenn'th. "Thought the world of Dai, he did."

Cai's fists are clenched. "Dai was not your target. It was Morgana you wished to harm."

"You're bending the truth to protect her. You don't see her for what she really is—wicked. There's bad blood in her. You don't know her."

"I know her. I know she wouldn't leave a gate untied when it mattered. Just as I know her to be a true and faithful wife." He shakes his head. "Oh aye, you made me doubt her. I'm ashamed to admit it. But judging her wrongly is my fault, not hers. She has done nothing to be ashamed of. But *you*! She spurned you and you wanted revenge for your bruised pride."

Edwyn appeals to the others. "He's lying, making things up to protect her. Everyone can see she's bad luck. He lost his herd because of her. And his dog. Now Dai's dead and it's her fault."

Cai takes two strides forward and for a moment I think he will beat Edwyn, unleash his anger without restraint. But he does not.

"Get your things and go," says he. "Get out of my sight before I show you how I'd like to deal with the sort of man who would force himself upon another man's wife!"

The tension crackles in the air between the two men. Edwyn is young and tall and defending his reputation; Cai is stronger and powered by hatred for the youth who stands before him. Nobody moves. All of a sudden Edwyn pushes past, shoving his way through the watching group, stomping toward the barn where his few possessions remain.

Cai regards Meredith, Watson, and the two women.

"Anyone else thinks Morgana should not be working this drove can leave now."

Watson shrugs. Sara shakes her head.

"What say you, Meredith? I mean to complete this drove, with all the stock, and I mean to do it with my wife in charge of the ponies. I'll not succeed otherwise. So if you've a problem with that you'd best follow Nails and get yourself home."

Meredith's face is grim but it is clear where his loyalty lies.

"I signed up for the whole drove. A drover doesn't go back on his word."

Cai nods, satisfied, but still he adds, "Not a word more against my wife, mind. From any of you." He waits for his words to be considered and then picks up his hat from the ground, dusting it off against his leg. "Right, we are two men down, and we'll have to find a forge along the way. We've a job to do."

Watson voices everyone's surprise.

"You mean us to continue today?" he asks.

"I do. This minute. Now we've no wagon we have need of packhorses. Morgana, get Sara to help you sort two of the quieter mares. We leave on the hour."

And so we do. And a sorry and sadly depleted parade we are. Dai's absence is like a piece cut out of the sky, or a sliver from the heart of each of us. I even miss the sight of his ugly cob and tatty cart. I do not miss the overbearing presence of Edwyn. I wonder what Cai will do, when we return, regarding the sly creature's part in Dai's death. Will he talk to the magistrate? Who will people believe? By the time we are in Tregaron again many will have attended Dai's funeral, and Edwyn will have had weeks to spread his story; to blacken my name; to chisel away at Cai's credibility.

We trudge through the grey afternoon. Each mile feels twice its natural length. Gone is the usual chatter and laughter. Even the beasts sense the somber mood and plod meekly along the tracks. The day dwindles into evening, and I begin to wonder if Cai plans to make us trek through the night. By the time we find an inn with a suitable enclosure for the livestock, bats flit about our heads, swooping and flapping at insects we humans can no longer see in the fading light.

I find I am so tired, so drained by the events of the day and the long journey, that when I dismount, my legs give way beneath me and I stagger. Cai is suddenly at my side, an arm around my waist to steady me.

"Come, Morgana. Enough for one day." He slips the tack off Prince and lets him wander off to join the herd. Despite his injured arm, he shoulders both saddles as if they were no weight at all and bids me follow him. We go into the inn where he instructs the landlord to supply the others with a place to sleep, a hot meal, and as much ale as they require. He also asks for a needle, thread, and scissors. We are taken up to a room at the back of the redbrick building. It has high ceilings and long windows, and the furnishings are quite fine, but I am in no condition to appreciate such things. I stand in a daze until I become aware of how awkwardly Cai is moving. His arm must be paining him dreadfully. How taken up I have been with myself! I hurry to him, leading him to sit in a chair by the window, but there is no light left in the day. I light a candle while he takes off his shirt. Kneeling before him I cautiously unwind my scarf from his arm. It is so caked with dirt and dried blood it is beyond saving. When I pull the final remnants of it from his wound he gasps. The sight of the gaping slice in his flesh makes my stomach boil. Cai peers down at it, though it is not easy to discern detail in the gloom of the room.

"No real harm done," says he. "The bleeding has stopped." He nods at the washbowl on the stand. "It must be cleaned. Can you do that for me, Morgana?"

I nod and fetch the bowl, setting it at his feet. I pour water into it and tear a strip from a washcloth. He flinches as I bathe the fissure, and I know it must be difficult for him to remain quiet and still. I am as gentle as I can be, but the dirt of the journey has worked its way into the exposed meat of his arm, and I must be persistent if it is all to be removed. At last the gash is cleaned. Cai points at the table now.

"Pass the needle through the flame of the candle before you thread it," he tells me.

I stare at him. He means me to sew up his arm! My mouth dries. For a moment I think I cannot do it, but I look into his eyes and know that I must not fail him. The injury is a lucky one—no bones need setting, and the bleeding has stopped—but if it is left so open it will not heal. It may even go putrid, and he could lose his arm. Or his life.

"Can you do it, Morgana?"

I take a steadying breath and pick up the needle. Once I have cauterized the point and coaxed the thread through the eye I move the candle to the table so that as much light as possible falls on Cai's arm. The wound looks dauntingly long now. How many stitches will be required? How many times must I force the point of steel through my husband's flesh and tug it out again? How will he endure such a lengthy, painful process? He sees me hesitate.

"Courage, *cariad*. It must be done." I feel him struggle to sit up straighter. "Would you have me ask another?"

I shake my head firmly, placing my hand on his to still him. He nods, satisfied that I am up to the task.

I choose an area of skin that looks firm and in good health. I have no wish to go deeper or farther from the opening of the wound that is absolutely necessary, but if I am too timid, if I select flesh that is damaged or thin, it will not be strong enough to hold, and the thread will tear through it, reopening the cut. The horn of a bullock is a blunt, brutal instrument when applied to a man's arm, and the injury is not neat or regular but jagged and ripped at the edges. The needle enters the flesh easily enough. Cai remains motionless, his breath held against the anticipated pain. Now I must push the needle hard to work it through. Fresh blood emerges in its path. I grit my teeth, compelling myself to keep to my task. But it is hard! To so slowly and deliberately inflict pain on one who matters to me so. As I tug at the needle to draw the thread through I hear Cai curse, feel him turn his face away from me. To extract the needle fully from his flesh I have to pull with some strength, as it is gripped by the wetness that lies beneath his skin. I am too timorous in my movements, so that it is only on the third attempt that the needle frees itself. It does so with such sudden speed that I stab my left hand with the point. I raise my palm to my mouth to stop the flow, but not before a drop of my own blood has fallen into Cai's gaping wound. And now I recall Catrin's china. Now I think of how I mended so many cracks and breakages. Could I do that now, for Cai? I am no healer. I have not talent to make the sick well or banish their pain. But I can move things. I can stir their composition. I can shift and alter the arrangement of things. My lessons with Mrs. Jones must surely have increased my ability and my control where my magic is concerned. But what if I were to produce a bad result with my unruly skills? How badly might Cai fare were I to mismatch and confuse as I worked? I have never attempted such a thing before. Never sought to produce a mending upon a living person.

"Morgana?" Cai's voice is tight with effort and pain. "Are you able to go on, *cariad*?"

I give him a gentle smile. I sense his confusion as I take the scissors and snip the thread, before putting down the needle. He watches me closely, as if he is somehow aware of what I am about to do. Does he now recall my mending skills, I wonder.

I hold my palm above his cut and let three more drops of my blood fall into it. Then I place my hands over the vivid pinkness of his wound. I close my eyes. I put all my attention, all my will, all my heart, into the challenge I have set myself. Very soon I have the sensation I am falling backward. I feel a lightness in my head, and hear a noise in my ears like the flapping of the wings of a giant bird of prey. Whoosh, whoosh, whoosh, they beat. My body begins to heat up. The temperature rises, starting with my feet and hands, working inward toward my heart in no way that follows any sensible pattern. Soon I am almost overcome with the intensity of the heat, and fear I may be burnt up from the inside. But still I do not move, I do not release my grip on Cai's arm. I will not stop! Now I find I cannot open my eyes. There is a blackness swamping me, as if I am interred in some deep, underground place, from which I may never escape. My breathing becomes rapid and shallow. Will I lose myself in this endeavor? Will I be able to find my way back?

And now, far in the distance, I hear someone softly calling my name. Slowly it becomes louder. At last I recognize Cai's voice.

"Morgana? Morgana?"

Of a sudden I am able to see again. I blink away blurriness from my eyes and look down at Cai's arm, which I still grip with both my hands. Cautiously, I remove them, to reveal his wound sealed shut! The join is not pretty, and the flesh looks angry and inflamed, but it appears strongly melded, and I know it will hold. Cai touches my cheek.

"You did well, my wild one. You did very well, see?"

I find I am almost too weak to stand. I try to get to my feet, but fall. Cai catches me and sits me on the edge of the bed. I am shaking, my whole body gripped by tremors. Cai kneels in front of me, his hands on my shoulders.

"'Tis the shock," he tells me, settling to the task of unlacing my boots. "Here you are looking after me, but you yourself have been through an ordeal. Had you not been able to cut the rope on the far gate and jump behind the wall . . ."

He leaves the words unspoken, but we both know what it is he is trying to say. It could have been me lying trampled and broken in that yard. Indeed, it most likely would have been, if it weren't for the brave actions of a generous-hearted man, a man who now lay cramped in a coffin on his final journey home. In truth I do not know what troubles me the most—my brush with death, my overwhelming feeling of guilt that Dai died saving me; my loathing of Edwyn; or my fear that no one but Cai will ever believe the truth of what happened.

Cai takes off my boots and helps me out of my outer garments.

The stump of candle flickers and dies, so that the room is lit only by the dull twilight through the windowpanes. He empties the washbowl out the window and refills it. There are clean cloths on the tiled stand, and he selects one, dipping it in the water and then wringing it out. He kneels before me once more and gently bathes first my face, and then my hands. I feel as a child, soothed by a loving parent, and yet there is something else his tender touch ignites within me. Something sweet and sharp at the same time. Something powerful which has lain dormant.

"My poor wild one," says he, washing my fingertips. "You need rest, see? You'll feel stronger in the morning."

At last the trembling subsides, though I feel flimsy as a new-born lamb. I let him lift my feet and settle me on the blissfully soft mattress. He walks to the far side of the bed and I hear his boots drop, one, two onto the floor and then his clothes.

He climbs into the bed and moves to lie close behind me. His body curves around mine but the contact is oh so very slight. Yet I feel the heat of him; his bare chest against my back, his smell of spice and earth, his breath warm and half-held against my neck. His heartbeat echoes in its cage of ribs, the beat strong enough to interrupt that of my own, faster and more nervous. I feel at once terrified and exquisitely alive. I realize it is not him I fear, but the unpredictable nature of my own response to him. To his nearness. To his restrained strength. To his desire.

He touches my brow, gently moving a stray lock from my forehead, settling to stroke my hair softly.

"Sleep now, *cariad*. Fret no more today. Only sleep. I am here. Sleep."

But now I am far from sleep! My senses are astir and ablaze. How is it possible to feel such things and to sleep? If we are always to share a bed I may die for the lack of it. His presence is so powerful. It disturbs me to acknowledge how he agitates me. He is so vital, so astonishingly full of life. There is something comforting in the extreme, certainly, to know such protection, for I am confident nothing would induce him to use his strength against me, only in my defense. The thought allows a kernel of hope to form inside me, set to grow with a spark of . . . what? Affection? Love, even? No, I cannot conceive of allowing myself to love, not now, not when I am raw from the loss of it. What, then? What is it that stirs my blood, that hastens my heartbeat, that causes my breath to catch in my throat and my mind to float at his touch? Is it desire, then? Is that what this is? Desire for him? Desire for him.

"Shh, *cariad,*" he soothes, all too aware of my restlessness. "Shh," he whispers, and, despite the heavy weight of all that has happened this day, I smile. For never in my life before has a person had cause to urge me to be quiet!

I5.

By the following morning the temperature has dropped and there is a feel of autumn in the wind that accompanies the drove as they progress ever eastward. Cai directs the young cattleman he has engaged to work the rest of the way to follow the cattle on foot, and to be ready to help Watson or Morgana if they have need of him. His name is John, and what he lacks in experience he makes up for in enthusiasm. Indeed, his energy and cheerfulness are at odds with the rest of the company, but then he has not recently lost a friend. He does not notice the absence of Dai and his family. He does not struggle, as the others do, to shut out the heartbreaking image of Cerys and her boys weeping over Dai's shattered body. Still, Cai reasons, it is as well to have at least one person on the drove whose every action is not colored by grief. Cai's own heart is leaden in his chest. When he thinks of Dai the memory is tainted by the rage he feels toward Edwyn. The matter is not yet at an end, he knows it. Knows that upon his return to Tregaron he must visit Cerys, must make sure she understands the truth, must see that justice is done for Dai.

At least he has something else to fill his mind with; something that gives him hope for the future instead of regret for the past. The exquisite closeness he enjoyed with Morgana is still fresh in his mind. She allowed him to care for her, allowed him to step closer. He closes his eyes to savor the recollection of that closeness. The hours he spent with her sleeping in his arms were the most wonderful he has passed in many long, lonely years. How could he ever have doubted her? How could he have thought that she would let Edwyn . . . ? Not for the first time he feels ashamed at how quickly and how harshly he has judged her.

They journey another taxing day, the cold rain forcing everyone into their long coats, collars turned up, hats pulled low. Even Bracken's fur is sodden to a dull brown. Neither song nor banter speeds the passing of the miles, only the knowledge that each footfall made, each hour ridden, moves them nearer to their goal and the completion of their task. And ultimately, nearer to returning home. For there is no delight among the drovers now. They must all draw upon their reserves of will and strength, driven on by a common cause, and by the need to succeed if they are to avoid poverty in the coming winter months. Finding no inn come six o'clock Cai settles for a farm with ample grazing. The farmer, sensing an opportunity to turn a speedy profit, charges over the odds per head of livestock. Were Cai not so weary he would have haggled further, driving down the price, but he is tired in his bones, and can think only of rest. Sara cooks up a thin stew for supper and a small quantity of ale is found. The mood is dark, and John's chatter is jarringly bright. When someone halfheartedly suggests Watson give them a song the shepherd merely shakes his head and sucks hard on his clay pipe.

They are billeted in a drafty barn, the roof of which has more gaps than tiles, so that it is hard to find a dry space to bed down upon. Cai comes upon some old woolsacks and does his best to fashion a tolerable sleeping space for himself and Morgana. When he has finished he calls to her.

"Not much comfort tonight, I'm afraid. Most of us are tired enough to sleep standing up, mind."

She gives him a small smile and then picks up the blanket and holds out her hand to him. Puzzled, he lets her lead him out of the barn and away from the farm. Bracken trots behind. They walk some distance in the rain, climbing over a rickety stile and crossing a sloping meadow, before coming to a little stone barn in the corner of a fallow field. There are no doors, only an opening on one side and two narrow windows. Cai cannot see how such a place would provide better accommodation, but he follows her inside. Morgana points out an old wooden ladder which leads up to a hay loft. He goes in front, testing each rung carefully. Once up on the broad boards he reaches down a hand and helps her up. The space is small, but dry and warm, with the additional benefit of sweet-smelling hay as bedding. From below comes a squeak of protest from the dog, who eventually gives up and settles to sleep.

For a moment Cai and Morgana stand where they are, the sound of the rain falling on the slates above them, both dressed to keep the weather out, their coats skimming the wisps of hay on the floor, water dripping from the brims of their hats. Cai thinks he could stay gazing into Morgana's wonderful face forever. He lifts a hand and touches her cheek. Her skin is so soft and his hands so rough from his farming life he can scarcely feel the contact. He takes hold of her water-sodden hat and lifts it from her head. Her hair, as ever, is only partially tied back, and for the most part is wet, making it even curlier and glossier than usual. He gently removes what few pins there are so that it swings forward, thick and loose. Shyness overcomes Morgana and she drops her gaze, lowering her head. Cai puts a finger beneath her chin and tilts her face up once more.

"Do you know how very beautiful you are, my love?" he asks. At this she blushes, but also allows herself a smile. Now she takes his hat off, letting it drop onto the hay beside her own. She unbuttons her coat and he does the same. Next they unlace and tug off their boots. Now Cai sees Morgana's confidence desert her. She stands before him hesitating, uncertain. He steps closer, takes her face in his hands and kisses her lightly on her slightly open lips. He kneels before her, pulling her gently down onto the hay beside him. For a long while they lie close to one another, reveling in the tenderness of the moment. Her fingers explore the contours of his face. He places the briefest of kisses on her throat and neck, finally tasting that treasured spot in her nape he has for so long wished to touch. He finds he is horribly afraid of upsetting her, of moving too fast. He wants her, his desire for her fierce and urgent, but above this, above everything, he wants her to want him. He has waited many weeks so that this moment will be right, will be a culmination of their growing affection for one another. She is such a wild, unfathomable creature, he fears if he overpowers her, overwhelms her, she might instinctively retreat, recoil, and turn away from him. Slowly he removes her clothes and his, one button, then another, one garment, then another, taking infinite care. At first she merely allows him to do this, neither resisting nor assisting. Then, gradually, she becomes bolder, slipping his shirt from his shoulders, running her hands over his lean chest, nuzzling into his neck, tentatively tasting the salty skin of his throat. He kisses her deeply now and feels her respond. Quickly their movements and faltering touches become more urgent, more driven. He pulls her to him and feels her wrap her arms and legs tight about him. It is as if after all they have been through together, and after all the waiting and watching and wanting, at last they can abandon themselves to the heat of their mutual desire. He is both surprised and pleased by how responsive she is. How eager. How passionate. Later he will wonder how he ever thought she could be otherwise; such a wild instinctive creature would surely know how to give her all to the act of love. But now he is lost in the moment, unable to form sensible thoughts, conscious only of the sweet harmony of such shared intimacy, and of the exquisite pleasure they are both able to enjoy.

❦

I wake to the sound of rain beating upon the roof of the little barn. It is not yet dawn, and all hint of moonlight has been obliterated by the weight of water in the clouds above us. I am unable to see so much as an outline of Cai, so complete is the blackness. But I feel his heart beneath my ear as I lay my head on his warm chest. I smell the sweet saltiness of him mixed with the hay we crush under us. I hear the faint sigh his breathing makes as he sleeps. I taste, still, his mouth upon my mouth, his tongue upon my tongue, his skin upon mine. The memory of our lovemaking stirs me now, hurries my blood through my veins, causes my head to spin and my body to soften and yield at the very thought of him. That such sensations could exist! I feel I have lived in a dream all my life until now, until discovering what the passion between a man and a woman can mean. He was at once so gentle and so fervent. Did I please him? He told me that I did, said I was his bliss, his heart, his everything. Do all men say such things when they are enraptured, I wonder. I want it to be true, now, more than anything, I want him to feel for me what I am feeling toward him.

Oh, within me there is such a struggle twixt sorrow and joy. The deep pit of loss where my mother once stood. The shocking recollection of Dai's terrible death. The fear that I will not be believed, but always held to blame. And now the uplifting, light-filled delight of this powerful loving. How strange are the ways life seeks to test us.

Cai stirs and I pull away, not wishing to restrict his movements as he sleeps. Instinctively he draws me back to him. I luxuriate in his embrace. Never have I felt myself so safe, so accepted. My fingers find his mouth in the darkness and I place a kiss on his lips. He is not, it seems, as deeply asleep as first I thought. He returns my kiss twofold, slipping his hands down my spine, stroking my flesh, sending flashes of heat through me. Desire charges my blood once more and though I should be tired I am filled with such an energy, such a longing and a need, that I forget my fatigue, forget what might be seemly or proper, and follow only what my heart and body bid me do.

Cai murmurs into my hair, "Well, my wild one, seems I never knew how fitting that name was when I gave it you." There is laughter in his voice, as well as something hungry that thrills me.

I need little by way of encouragement to show him how happy I am to be his lover. No one can weaken the bonds we have formed. We are truly husband and wife now. Let any who care to

try to take him from me or send me from him—I will not surrender him to anyone, nor suffer to be parted from him, ever!

Later the drove continues at a steady if somber march. The
company is downcast at the loss of Dai, weary from the colder,
wetter weather, and generally fatigued by weeks of travel and
camping. I confess I find my own demeanor at odds with the
mood of my fellow travelers. 'Tis true, I still grieve, and carry
with me the dull ache of loss, but the joy my love for Cai brings
me makes me want to dance. He feels the same, I know it. For
not only has he told me so, often and with, I believe, sincerity,
but it is there in the tender glances he gives me as we move the
herd; in the way he touches my hand, however briefly, whenever
he can; in the snatched kisses we exchange when chance allows.

There is something, alas, which continues to trouble me. I
sense a growing distrust among the other drovers. Despite Cai's
insistence that I was not to blame for what happened to Dai, and
that it was Edwyn who must accept responsibility for what he
did, they are not convinced. After all, why should they side with
a newcomer? Most of them have known Edwyn all his life,
watched him grow into a fine young man, a hard worker, and a
skilled assistant to the farrier. Why should they take my word
over his? My silent word. For therein, I fear, lies the basis of their
mistrust. Yet again I am set apart, I am different, and in that difference people see something frightening, if they allow themselves. And I know, if I am to face the truth of it, that my silence
alone would not be sufficient to kindle such suspicion. They
have all, now, watched the result of my anger released upon another. They were all present when Edwyn was knocked from his
feet by the maelstrom caused by my fury. They saw him skit-
tered on his backside across the yard and slammed against the
gate. They tasted the dust in their own mouths as it swirled about
them in spiraling clouds. They were able to discern for themselves the origin of this phenomenon. They know that it came
from me. What will they be calling me now? Conjurer? Sorceress? Witch? Of course, not one of them has stepped forward to

voice their opinion, neither to myself nor to Cai. They hide behind their frowning looks and nervous watching to whisper in corners. But I know what they are thinking. I have seen such behavior before, though both Dada and Mam did their utmost to protect me from it. The gossip lessened a little after my father left. Perhaps I was deemed less of a threat on my own, for had I not obtained my magic blood from him? For a while I was better tolerated. But, as I grew from small child to girl to young woman, so their anxiety grew. The schoolmaster did his bit to fan the flames of their fear. The rent collector was one of the most outspoken, claiming I had visited a curse upon him after he pressed my mother for overdue rent. Ha! I had never heard of the acquiring of rent involving pinning a woman to the floor of her own home and demanding her affections before. I was but twelve years old, else he might have fared worse. I interrupted his attempts at *collection* by rushing into the room and beating him about the head with a besom. It wasn't until a full day later that the boils began to appear. First on his face, then his back, then his stomach, until his whole filthy body was covered in them.

Mam always knew it would be hard to find me a husband who lived local.

How many times she had to explain away my behavior, defend my innocence, convince the people of the parish that all was circumstance and coincidence and nothing more, I will never know. But she was a clever woman, and resourceful. She was driven to protect the one she loved most in the world, and I see how that drives a person to overcome all variety of difficulties and obstacles. And now I see that she chose well for me when she trusted me to Cai. How hard it must have been for her, to send me away, knowing as she did, that she had not long to continue her footfalls on this earth. Knowing so little about the man, seeing only a heartbroken drover with a kind smile and a need for a wife. Or did she see more? Did she detect something in the way in which he regarded me, something in his manner, perhaps, that gave her to believe he would care for me? If I ever have a child, could I be so selfless, I wonder. How I wish she were alive now, so that I might tell her she was right, that I am able to love this man, and that I am so well loved in return.

And now I must fight for my reputation in my new home. And what an unfair fight it is. For beyond the injustice of not being believed, beyond the villagers' instinctive fear of what they do not understand, there is Isolda, and her determination to see me damned. She warned me she would see to it I will not be welcome in Tregaron by the time the drove is over. This was clearly no idle threat. For I saw her moving through Edwyn. It is evident to me she pulls his strings as a puppet master works a marionette. It was her evil ambition that lay behind Edwyn's actions, both at the river, and in untying that gate. But none other than me can see her for what she is. They are either charmed by her, or under her spell in a more frightening way. In either case, the effect is the same. No one will hear a word against. Least of all the silent word of a girl who can whip up the wind. A girl who, many will soon believe, was responsible for the death of Dai the Forge.

Five more days bring us at last to the fattening fields. The herds are put into three large enclosures, each with grazing aplenty and shady trees. The rain has stopped at last, but summer has gone away. Everyone is wrapped against the chill autumn winds, and already the beasts show signs of growing their warmer coats. Cai is leaning on the wooden gate into the cattle field, considering the condition of the stock. They look well, and he is pleased. I come to stand beside him and he smiles at me. He takes my hand in his to slip it into the pocket of his long coat to warm it along with his own.

"We did well, Morgana," says he. "Better than I could have hoped. Look. Look at them. All those miles, and they are still sound and sleek and have meat on their bones. They will fatten quickly here. You and I will bide a week with them. Watson will stay with his flock. I will pay the others and send them home. No one has the heart to linger without Dai . . ." He pauses, the name catching in his throat. "Come Friday next we will be ready to meet the dealer. They should fetch a fair price." He catches me turning my head in the direction of the ponies and squeezes my hand. "The ponies will go the same day," he tells me, and I cannot meet his gaze. He knows how hard it will be for me to part with them, and if I look at him now I will see my struggle reflected in the blue of his eyes. "We will have a new beginning on our return, my wild one. All will be well, see?"

I nod and lean against him, letting him slip an arm around my shoulders, drawing comfort from the warmth and strength of him.

After being paid, Meredith leaves without saying good-bye, disappearing to wherever it is he goes between droves. Before she leaves, Sara exchanges a few words with Cai but for me she has only a sidelong glance. Watson will stay on a smallholding on the far side of the pastures and not bother us. When we are alone I feel a weight lifting from me, and only now do I realize how heavy was their opinion of me, and how that heaviness dragged me downward. Now it is just the two of us, passing the few days that remain with the herd, waiting with hope and a little anxiety to see if all our efforts will prove sufficient.

I am on my guard for Isolda. At the moment her malevolent presence seems less strong than at other times, though I can discern no pattern to her menace, save that it continues, and that Angel can act as a conduit for her. I make a point of tethering the ill-tempered horse as far as possible from where we sleep. I will not have its mistress sully our nights together with her sour aura. What will happen when we return to Ffynnon Las? Will she see how close Cai and I have grown and accept defeat? No, she is incapable of such a course of action. If she insists on pursuing him, persists in her demands that I leave, I will have to face her. I must stand my ground. Cai is all and everything to me now. What life could I live without him?

We could be accommodated in the Merchant's Arms, a busy inn, the owner of which also has the tenancy of the fattening fields. The food is of good quality, if a little pricey, and the rooms comfortable, but we would scarcely be in it, for it would be folly to leave the stock unattended. Instead we sleep in an old shepherding hut placed in the pasture for the very purpose of keeping watch over visiting herds. It is snug and dry, and affords privacy if not comfort. We pass the days checking the stock and doing our best to instill some manners into the ponies. The youngsters, in particular, are in need of some instruction. The more biddable, the calmer, the easier to handle, the better price they will fetch. It is a joy to be able to spend time with them, uninterrupted by the demands of domesticity, and without the bother of society. Would that I could ban all callers from our own home to make it such a haven! Imagine, no tedious taking tea with the Cadwaladrs. No unwelcome visitations from Isolda under the guise of friendship. I would be inclined to allow Mrs. Jones to continue coming to Ffynnon Las, however. Despite her tireless patience, I am still not much of a cook.

There is no one to disturb us here, and nights in our little wheeled room are blissfully peaceful and intimate. Strangely, I have not seen Isolda for some days now. At first I thought we might have traveled beyond her reach, farther than she herself is able to witchwalk. But I have come to another notion. It cannot be coincidence that her visitations ceased the first night Cai made love to me. Is there, then, a power in our intimacy, in our loving connection, that shields us in some small way? It comforts me to believe so, but I cannot allow this to make me complacent. She is too powerful, too determined, to let such a thing stand in her way for long. When we are returned home, when she can have a physical presence between us once more, well, then I fear things will be different.

Perhaps it is the Gypsy in me that so enjoys sleeping beneath the stars, listening to the creatures of the night, lulled to slumber by the noises of nocturnal hunters and foragers. More likely, I will admit, it is my newfound delight at the pleasure I share with Cai. I wish, now, that we had no home. That we could travel as

Dada once did, roaming the world, just the two of us, all of our lives.

But such freedom as we have lasts only a few short days. On the last Thursday of the drove Cai leaves me to journey into London alone. Here he will attend to the matters of business entrusted to him by the people of Tregaron. There will be transactions regarding sales of property, contracts of work, and letters of betrothal, as well as wills and testaments, and various bonds and investments, all to be safely delivered. I bide the time he is absent in further training the youngsters. I keep a weather eye on Angel, and wonder if Isolda's watching of us extends only to where her familiar is present. I sense her nearby, so it may be that, whilst I have no respite from her all-seeing eye, Cai at least will be rid of her for a few hours. When he returns we sit by the campfire and he tells me of the noise and bustle and vastness of the city and all that he has seen there, and I am heartily glad I do not have to set foot in the place.

And now Friday is upon us and the dealers arrive from London. The red-faced, portly man who comes to buy the cattle does so with little preamble. It is clear to any who care to look that the herd is in excellent condition. Cai stands confidently among his beasts and swiftly conducts the business of arriving at a good price. The transaction is sealed with a spit and a handshake and the two disappear into the inn to exchange money and a bill of sale.

The horse buyer is a different animal altogether. He gives the appearance of a gentleman, with his fine clothes and his airs, and yet there is something sly in his manner, something guarded in his expression, which I do not care for. I observe him closely as he inspects the ponies. This is not a man who loves horses. This is someone who sees them only as merchandise, to be bought and sold, to turn a profit, to pay for his finery. My blood boils at the thought of this man taking our precious ponies. Will he treat them well? Will he see that they are suited to their new owners? Cai senses my distrust and leads the dealer some distance away from me. He is wise to do so, for I am not certain I could contain my anger if I were forced to listen further to the man's casual criticism of our beautiful colts, or his scathing assessment of the fine brood mares. The negotiations stall and stutter, with much head shaking and pursing of lips. Time drags, with hours passing, so that the soft light of evening lends an inappropriately sweet tinge of pink to the proceedings. At last the trading comes to a conclusion. Cai is slapped heartily on the back by the man who is of a sudden full of friendliness and good humor. They conduct the details of their transaction out of my sight, leaving me to bid farewell to the ponies. The smallest foal, his coat still fuzzy, his curly mane not yet long enough to flick away flies, ambles up to me and nuzzles my skirts, searching for tidbits. Where will you find yourself three months hence, little one? Will your new owner be kind? Will they appreciate your wild origins and dauntless spirit? Prince is standing in the shade of a gnarled oak tree, swishing his tail more from habit than necessity, dozing lazily. I cannot resist climbing onto his back one last time. He opens his eyes, but does not bother to move as I jump up and settle behind his snowy withers, letting my hands smooth the fine hair on his strong white neck. It pains me greatly to think we are to be parted forever. I feel ridiculous tears filling my eyes. How foolish. I know the way things are. For Cai's sake, I must not give way to sentiment. I am flustered to see the two men, their business complete, approaching us. I wipe my face with my sleeve, no doubt depositing a layer of grime, and quickly slide from Prince's back. Cai steps toward us with a rope halter which he slips onto Prince's head, gently fitting it behind his ears and setting the little stallion's forelock neatly over the headpiece. I can see by the set of his shoulders that this is hard for him, too. To my surprise he hands me the lead rope of the halter.

"You have said enough farewells on this journey, Morgana. Prince is yours to keep," he tells me, adding with a shrug, "Think of him as a bonus from a *porthmon* to his hardworking drover."

I can scarcely take in what he is saying, but when the words at last make sense in my head I leap forward, throwing my arms about his neck, covering his face with kisses. He laughs, holding me close.

"Well, *Duw*," says he, "if that's the response I get 'tis a good thing I didn't offer such a reward to Meredith!"

16.

The journey home with Morgana is one Cai will hold in his heart as a treasured time. He has decided against taking the stagecoach. Angel might keep up, but the carriage horses would be too swift for Prince. And, if he is honest with himself, he wants to prolong this time alone with Morgana, just a little longer. For four days they ride west, chasing the pale autumn sun through the hours of daylight, finding a place to camp each night. Though they could afford a room at an inn they both prefer the simplicity of sleeping out. Besides, he reasons, they appear less prosperous, and will garner less interest, keeping themselves to themselves and not being seen to have money to spend. He has no wish to suffer the same fate as Llewellyn. The evenings cool quickly, but Cai finds them a warm barn, or a clearing in a sheltered copse where they might light a campfire. They sit close, watching the flames, cooking a rabbit purchased from a local poacher, or fish hooked from a nearby stream, as the horses graze peacefully on their tethers. The cattle fetched a good price, as did the ponies. At last Cai can see a clear future for himself and Morgana at Ffynnon Las. At the first opportunity he will take her to Llanybydder horse fair and they will buy two new mares— the start of the rebuilding of the herd. The notion of a life together, of a shared purpose, fills him with hope and pride. She has just returned from bathing in the bracing waters of the narrow river and leans near the fire, working her fingers through her wet hair to let the smoky air dry it. She becomes aware of him watching her but is no longer overcome by shyness. Instead she smiles, an open, warm, heartfelt smile, and Cai feels his heart lift. He still thinks of Catrin, and knows that he always will. But the memory is not painful now, and his affection for Morgana not tainted with guilt. She shakes her head and droplets of water hiss as they shower the fire. Bracken barks nervously.

Cai laughs. "Be quiet, m'n. What sort of a dog are you, afraid of what the flames have to say?" He rubs the corgi's ears. The little hound has worked hard, his pads worn to bleeding by the end of the drove. He, too, has earned a leisurely journey home. And Cai is glad of his presence beyond the enjoyment of his companionship. He can sleep easier knowing Bracken will watch wakefully for strangers. It would be tragic indeed to have come so far, to have made such a success of the drove, only to be robbed of the proceeds now. For this reason he has chosen a little used route, and is circumspect in his conversations with those they meet along the way.

Home. The idea of it is bittersweet to Cai. What will he find waiting for him back at Tregaron? Many will have attended Dai's funeral. Edwyn will have had weeks to spread his version of events around the region. Will there be people who put the blame for Dai's death on Morgana? Will he be able to convince them of her innocence? The drove was a success; that at least is beyond dispute. He can only hope that the relief of financial security for the farmers who entrusted him with their stock will work in his favor. Morgana is Mrs. Cai Jenkins, wife of the *porthmon,* mistress of Ffynnon Las. If they value him, they must accept her. If they trust him, they must surely accept his word when he tells them she is not at fault.

The water in their little billycan begins to boil, and Cai tips spoonfuls of black tea leaves into it.

"Come," he calls to Morgana, "have a hot drink. I swear autumn gets earlier every year. You'll catch your death sitting with that wet hair. Move closer to the fire. Closer to me. There, that's better, see?" He puts an arm around her waist and pulls her toward him. She grins, pushing him away playfully. "Oh no, my wild one, I can't let you go. Bit of a chore for me, but there we are. I have to hold you to keep you warm, else you'll fall sick, and then where'd I be without my best drover?"

Morgana swats him, not without force, before shoving him onto his back on the leafy ground and quickly straddling him. He laughs as she takes his hands and pins him down.

"Well, you've got me now. What are you planning to do with me, *cariad*?" He raises his eyebrows suggestively.

For a moment she narrows her eyes, considering, and then sets about tickling him mercilessly. Cai laughs until he has no breath left and is forced to topple her off him, pressing her to the floor beneath him, stilling her wriggling with a long, deep kiss. Slowly he feels her change. Her limbs relax, her mouth softens against his, and she returns his kiss with feeling. He pauses, drawing back a little, brushing her damp curls from her face.

"I love you, Mrs. Ffynnon Las. You are aware of this fact, are you not?"

She smiles and nods, and then, the smile fading, more seriously, she nods again, before reaching up to kiss him once more, drawing him down to her, letting him rest the length of his body against her own.

The following morning they travel on slowly, pausing to visit Mair's grave and inspect the headstone Cai had ordered be carved. Morgana plants flowers about it and leaves coins with old Mrs. Roberts to tend the grave. They arrive in Tregaron on the day of the harvest fair. The colors of the landscape have indeed altered markedly since there departure but a few weeks before. The oaks and birches have lost their gloss of green and instead sport leaves of a hundred shades of gold and ochre. Only the ash clings stubbornly to its summer garb. The grass in the high meadows surrounding the town has passed beyond the lushness of late summer and been cropped by hungry sheep eager to fatten themselves against the coming winter cold. In a final salute to the warmer months, and a celebration of the lifesaving bounty of the harvest, the people of Tregaron have gathered in their best clothes for a day of rest and of fun. Cai is conscious at once of what a ragtag and scruffy sight he and Morgana must present as they ride into the main square. Even Angel and Prince have lost the sheen of their summer coats and look homely with their sprouting winter hair, and weeks of mud in their manes. Bracken's fur is matted in places and his paws no longer chalky white. Cai's own duster coat has a ripped sleeve and a thick layer of grease from rubbing against the cattle for weeks on end, or being used as a ground sheet or makeshift cover when sleeping out. Morgana's clothes have fared little better, and both their hats are battered and beaten out of shape. Morgana's skin has been weathered as much as tanned, and Cai regrets not having taken the time to shave off his unruly beard before their return.

They wend their way between stalls and fair-goers, the horses much too tired to gib at flapping bunting or the shrieks of playing children. People turn to stare at them, and a whisper travels around the square: *the* porthmon *is returned*. Although Cai knows better than to expect a fanfare, or any sort of hero's welcome, he is still disconcerted by the reception they receive. Amid all the gaiety of the fair, news of their presence seems to spread an unfitting quietness. A seriousness. A wariness. He urges Angel through the crowd to the Talbot Hotel. Morgana keeps Prince close behind him. Bracken trots quietly at their side, tail low, sensitive to the mood around him. Cai had thought to stable the horses behind the inn and go inside for a celebratory drink, but he changes his mind. This curiously muted response to his arrival is unsettling. He acknowledges those who tip their caps at him. He will, he decides, not linger, but deliver what monies are owing to the cattle breeders and take Morgana home. They tie the horses to the hitching rail at the front of the hotel.

"Come, Morgana." He bids her follow him inside. He knows this is unusual, for it is a place ordinarily reserved for men, but he feels uneasy leaving her outside among such an unfriendly gathering. She hangs back, aware of the strangeness of his suggestion, clearly not wanting to cause trouble where it can be avoided.

A voice from the crowd interrupts the moment.

"Welcome home, Mr. Jenkins," says Isolda, stepping forward. She nods at Morgana. "Mrs. Jenkins, you look every inch the drover."

The onlookers laugh at this. Cai bristles, but is determined to remain as moderate as possible in his reactions.

"Mrs. Bowen." He gives a small bow.

"I am pleased to see you safely returned," she assures him, but something in her manner has changed, Cai thinks. There is a distance, a coldness, a harshness about her he has not felt before.

"Your horse proved an asset," he says. "I am grateful for the loan of him. I will bring him home to you tomorrow when he is rested."

"Do not trouble yourself. I will send a groom to collect him. You must be weary after your hard work. Both of you."

Something in the way she looks at Morgana makes him shiver. He is confused by such an alteration in a woman he had thought he knew better than most. Whilst Morgana has never made any secret of her dislike of Isolda, she herself has always been civil. Solicitous, even. Not anymore, it seems. Looking at his wife he notices her fists are clenched. Can it really be rivalry, some sort of jealousy, perhaps, that sets the women so at odds? Whatever it is, he could have wished for Isolda to choose a better moment to reveal her animosity. The expressions of those watching, their shut faces, their guarded, almost nervous glances at Morgana, are deeply disturbing.

"If you'll excuse us"—he takes Morgana's arm and guides her toward the door—"we have business to attend to."

The situation does not improve when the first person Cai sees inside the Talbot is Llewellyn. The man has evidently been at the bar some time, and his skin is flushed with the effects of strong ale imbibed in quantities.

"Well, well, here's Jenkins Ffynnon Las come to spend his money. We are honored, *porthmon*," he says with mock formality. "You succeeded in delivering the herd, then?"

"Aye," says Cai, "and turned good profits for all. We were fortunate."

"Oh? That's not what I heard."

"What do you mean by that?"

"Fortunate for your farrier to be trampled to death, then, was it?"

"No, of course not. No one regrets what happened to Dai more than I."

"His widow and orphaned sons might disagree with you there."

"I'll see them right. They know that."

"And do they know the person responsible will be brought to task?"

"I sacked Edwyn. Sent him home. If Cerys insists I will refer the matter to the magistrate."

Llewellyn drains his tankard and drags the back of his sleeve across his wet mouth. "There are those as says it was not Edwyn to blame. There are those as believes 'twas your wife was neglectful, and that you only accuse young Edwyn Nails to protect her."

"I was there. I saw what happened with my own eyes."

"Aye, well, maybe. And maybe a husband with a ripe new bride sees what he wants to see."

Cai can stand no more. He draws back his fist and hits Llewellyn a powerful blow on the jaw. The older man is knocked off his feet and falls backward, scattering drinkers and bar stools. He lies dazed, rubbing his face, spitting blood. "Well, *Duw*, Jenkins—touched on a sore spot, did I?"

"Keep your poisonous thoughts to yourself, Llewellyn. There's none wants to hear your drunken ramblings. I know the truth of what happened to Dai. So does Edwyn. If the man has a conscience he'll not falsely blame Morgana again." He turns to face the wary men in the bar. One or two take a step back. "Is there anyone else thinks justice has not been done in this matter? Well? Speak your minds now, or hold your tongues. I won't have lies spread about my wife, see? I hear anyone talking out of turn on this matter . . . well, he'll have me to answer to."

There is a shuffling of feet and a reluctance to meet Cai's eye. Even Llewellyn chooses to stay silent as he hauls himself to his feet. There is a prickly silence until Cai, taking a deep breath and summoning, with some effort, a calmer tone, says, "Right you are. Now, for those of you who have business with me, I'll take my place by the window. Present yourselves. I've brought back good returns for you all, but I'll not tarry here longer than is necessary."

It is as I feared—we are not believed. Edwyn has done his work in convincing people hereabouts of his version of the truth, and it may be we never succeed in undoing what he has done. I know now, at least, that Cai does not doubt me, and there is comfort in this. Also, I am surprised at how pleased I am to be back at Ffynnon Las. I had thought the magic of our time together returning from the drove might be crushed under the weight of public disapproval, and of Isolda's hatred when we arrived back at the farm. But this is our home. How wonderful it is to me that I can think such a thing! Our home. It feels right to be here, with Cai, my husband. The drove was a success. We have a right to our own happiness in our own home.

Mrs. Jones, at least, is pleased to see us.

"Well, *Duw, Duw,* there's a state you are in! Let's have you inside. I'll put water on for bathing. And your poor hair, Mrs. Jenkins!" She cannot resist taking a lock of my tangled curls in her hand and shaking her head. "Mr. Jenkins, you should be ashamed of yourself, using your pretty little wife so badly. Come along, *merched.* We'll soon have you out of those dreadful clothes and looking as the mistress of Ffynnon Las should look." She bustles me through the door and into the warm kitchen, pausing only to bark instructions to Cai. "Fetch the tin bath, if you please, Mr. Jenkins," she calls. "And more coals for the copper, or there'll not be sufficient hot water to get the lot of you clean." She gives Bracken a stern look and I fear he, too, will not escape a good scrubbing before the day is done.

The moment we are alone I set about trying to tell her what I have learnt of Isolda. I know Mrs. Jones has always disliked and distrusted the woman, and she has hinted that she detects a darkness in her. How clever the creature must be at disguising herself, at shielding her true nature from those who would find her out. For now that I understand it is she who is behind everything—Reverend Cadwaladr's taking against me, the sudden thunderstorm that lost us the herd, Edwyn's wickedness, and Dai's death—now I know where the danger comes from. I must tell Mrs. Jones. I fear there must be a confrontation between myself and Isolda one day. Soon, perhaps. I know I am not ready. I am no match for her. I must warn Mrs. Jones and enlist her help.

She has the bath ready for me but I do not undress. Instead I fetch paper, pen, and ink from the dresser. They are rarely used in this house. The ink is somewhat dry and flaky, and my hand feels clumsy as I struggle to form letters.

"What are you about, *cariad?* Come to the bath while the water is hot," says Mrs. Jones, desperate to rid me of my filthy, unbecoming garments. But I bite my lip, frowning in concentration at the unaccustomed action of dragging the nib across the rough paper. Why did not Mam insist Mr. Rees-Jones instruct me properly? I am but half trained. While I bless the gift of reading, how much better would I be able to communicate had I been instructed in the art of writing! Frustration causes me to make errors, so that I must try three times before I can form anything resembling the letters I am striving for. My efforts are not elegant or neat but they are, at last, legible. I pass the paper to Mrs. Jones. She steps to the lamp the better to read it and squints at the lettering, holding the page at arm's length. She reads aloud.

"'I . . . went,' is it? No, 'I wants,' yes, I see it now. So, you mean 'Isolda wants . . . Ffynnon Las?'" She looks at me and then back at my ugly writing. "'Dai ded' . . . yes, *cariad,* I know but, are you saying Isolda had something to do with his death?"

I nod firmly.

"But, he died on the drove. Isolda wasn't even there."

Now I shake my head. Oh! To be able to form the words. To shout them! I snatch the paper from her and jab with my finger at the last word I have scrawled there. Mrs. Jones squints at it, forming the misshapen letters into a sound.

"'W . . . i sh' . . . no, that's not it. Wait a minute. 'Witch.' Witch." She looks me in the eye and holds my gaze sternly now. "Be very sure about this, Morgana. You are saying that Isolda Bowen is a witch. Did she reveal herself to you?"

This time I nod emphatically, with certainty, and with some relief that my meaning is understood. With surprising speed Mrs. Jones steps to the fire and drops the page into the flames where it is quickly consumed. She does not turn back to me until she is satisfied it is completely destroyed.

"I have long suspected as much, mind. Ah, but she is clever. Such a face as she presents to the world, who would doubt her goodness? Who would look close enough to see that she casts the devil's shadow? If it is as you say and she is responsible for Dai's death then there is nothing she will not do to get what she wants. I had always thought it was your husband she desired. But now, what you tell me changes everything. If she wants Ffynnon Las it must be because of the well. And the *Grimoire*! Oh, *cariad*, I do tremble when I think what a wicked creature—a witch who cares not what is right or wrong—I shudder when I imagine what power she might gain from the enchantments that are kept in that book." Mrs. Jones wrings her hands, twisting her apron in them as she considers what this might mean. "I have no spells to guard against such evil. My magic is for mending, not breaking. *Duw*, she could walk in here whenever the fancy took her and take what she wanted. But no, she won't do that. She will want to keep her good name. Her position. It does matter to her that she is respected, that she has standing in the town. Of course it would—a witch will not find a welcome, she must take pride in fooling so many so well. She will turn them against us if need be. The reverend has never accepted you. Was that her doing?"

I nod, signaling a rolling motion with my hand to indicate there is more. Much more.

She looks at me now and I see her eyes are wide with fear. "And now you stand in her way. Oh *cariad,* I do sense such danger as I cannot protect you from . . ." says she, her voice near strangled with emotion.

I hurry forward and take both her hands in mine. I squeeze them tight and hold her gaze, showing her that I am not afraid. Lightly, I touch first her heart and then mine, before turning to point at where the *Grimoire of the Blue Well* is hidden.

"Yes, of course." Her expression brightens. "We will face her together. You and me, Morgana." She becomes quite animated now. "She may know of my limitations, but I do doubt she understands what you might be capable of." She nods firmly. "And we have the *Grimoire*. 'Tis true, I wanted to take longer in your training. To give you more time to come to it. But needs must, *cariad*. Needs must." Noticing my uncertainty, my lack of confidence in my own talents, she becomes brisk and businesslike, as if to give me time to come to terms with what she has just said. "But first, *merched,* we have to get you clean! Come along, off with those dreadful rags and into the bath with you, quick sharp now."

It feels strange to be in the company of a woman and inside a house, after so many weeks on the road as a drover. And as Cai's lover. Mrs. Jones is deft and purposeful in her attentions, helping me to wash the grit and tangles out of my hair, compelling me to bathe in water of such a temperature I feel I will poach like a salmon and emerge just as pink. She finds me a clean slip and one of Catrin's simple cotton dresses. I have lost a little weight, which does not go unnoticed, eliciting much tutting and fussing and muttering about proper meals and a good night's sleep. But all I wish for is to feel Cai's arms about me again. To lie with him. To share passion with him. To fall to sleep with my head on his chest, lulled by the beating of his strong, loyal heart. Will we share his bed this night, I wonder. The bed that was his and

Catrin's. I have not yet ventured upstairs, but even now, even here in the kitchen among the bright lanterns and the cheerful activity, I can sense that other presence. Can I really take up that place, enter that last stronghold of Catrin's love—where she gave herself to him? Where she died for him. It seems that Mrs. Jones's pronouncement that I am, at last, to read the *Grimoire,* to know of its secrets and mysteries, to taste its power, well, the very thought of it stirs in me such a mixture of excitement and trepidation I feel myself at sea and in need of an anchor. And that anchor, that point of safety, is Cai and the love we share.

In the event I am spared making a decision about which room to sleep in. The hour is so late by the time Mrs. Jones has seen to it that we are both clean and fit to reside at Ffynnon Las once more that she elects to stay, sleeping in the vacant room at the end of the hall. Her presence somehow inhibits us both, so that we shyly step into our own rooms. A moment after I have closed the door, while I still stand lost in my bedroom, there is a light knock, and Cai comes in. He takes my hands in his, looking me up and down, smiling.

"Well, there's lovely. Quite the transformation Mrs. Jones has worked. I scarce recognize you without your drover's clothes."

I smile back, self-conscious, but glad he has come to me. As he pulls me close I feel him flinch. His arm still troubles him, though he never complains. I trace the line of the scar through his clean wool shirt.

"It is healing," he tells me. "Thanks to you. 'Tis of no importance."

Disagreeing, I undo his buttons and carefully peel back his shirt to expose the wound. It is dry and clean, but the flesh is horribly scarred. The red welt of raised skin has fixed in a shiny, jagged line from the point of his shoulder to the bend of his elbow. He and I both know it could have been worse. Much worse. Even so, my heart aches to see him so afflicted. I lean forward and plant kisses along the scarred line, wishing I could kiss away the pain the injury yet causes him. As I do so hot tears spill from my eyes, washing over the wound. The tears of a witch. I have no incantation ready to use, only my heartfelt wish that my dear husband be healed. At first I can detect no alteration in the vivid, uneven scar, but then, very slowly, I see it start to blur, to shimmer, and, at last, to fade until, though not completely gone, it has indeed lessened considerably. I smile up at Cai, who regards first the wound and then me with something approaching awe. He pulls me close, kissing me.

"My wild one," he murmurs into my hair, "how fortunate I am to have you to care for me."

I lift my face again to look into his eyes and see such love shining there. He pulls me close, embracing me with such yearning, and I let him hold me, knowing now it matters not where we are, so long as we are together.

Later I awake, Cai sleeping peacefully at my side. I am unsure what has pulled me from my own deep slumber, but sense that I have been disturbed. I listen, and now am certain I can hear a noise outside my bedroom door. It sounds like footfalls. Could Mrs. Jones be up at this hour? The moon shines through the unshuttered window. The silver disc is still high, the night not nearly over. I listen again and hear more faint steps. Mrs. Jones cannot, I decide, be the cause of these noises, for her own tread would be much heavier and accompanied by a deal of wheezing. I slip from under the covers and take up my woolen shawl, pulling it around my shoulders and knotting it at my waist. The door creaks a little as I open it. There is nothing to be seen but empty shadows. But then, looking deeper, I fancy there is a deeper darkness in one corner of the landing, as if those shadows are more solid somehow. Anxiety sets my scalp to prickling. I make myself step forward and experience the now-familiar coolness of the air in this small space. Catrin? Catrin, are you come to speak with me? Do you resent me lying with your husband, even though he is mine now? But I cannot be sure who or what it is that lingers here. At last, feeling oppressed by the presence, and too unsettled to return to my room, I go downstairs and out the back door, seeking the calming air of the night.

The sense of unease stays with me even here. Once again I am drawn to the well. It is sufficiently cold for a frost, but the temperature is not low enough to freeze the running water from the spring, nor put ice on the deep pool. The brightness of the moon is such that it paints reflections on the water's surface. I gaze at the faint image of myself, which gazes back at me. Of a sudden my heart misses a beat, for there, indistinct but unmistakable, another face peers over my shoulder! I spin round to find Isolda standing close enough to touch me. At first I think she is witch-walking, but now I see she is here completely, body as well as dark spirit. Now I can smell her rank, reptilian odor. She can in no way be described as beautiful this night. It is as if the moon has revealed her true nature in her features, and there is a terrifying savagery about her face.

"It is a cold night for wandering so scantily clad, witch-girl," says she. "You should take care not to catch a chill. Your loving husband would be brokenhearted should anything happen to you." She steps back a little, regarding me with a critical eye. "What can he see in such a childlike body, I wonder. Clearly he is not man enough to consider himself worthy of me."

I know different. I know he is a fine man, a good man, far too good for this evil woman.

"Oh, you think me evil, do you?"

I look away, berating myself for having forgotten how at close quarters she is able to read my thoughts.

"Do you truly know what evil means? It seems to me its definition depends on who seeks to understand it. For some it simply means 'unGodly'—but who is to say there is only one Lord worthy of our adoration? For others it signifies merely the opposite of what is in their own interests. Which would appear to apply to you, *Morgana*?" She makes my name sound a loathsome thing. "I had thought to frighten you away, assuming such a little rabbit as you must surely scare easily. But I underestimated you. So I sought to turn Cai from you, to stir up ill feeling on the drove, to hang disaster about your slender neck until he could no longer tolerate the sight of you. Sadly the poor man is so infatuated he will not, it seems, be put off." She sighs, stepping over to the well to dip her fingers in the silky water. "Which leaves me little choice as to how to proceed. For proceed I will, make no mistake about that. Ffynnon Las will be mine, at any price. A pity, then, that it will be your beloved husband who must pay that price. No, don't look at me so. You must accept the blame at least in part, for had you heeded my warning and scuttled back to wherever it was Cai found you, there would be no necessity for me to take this course of action. What? Nothing to say? Is that, at last, fear I smell seeping out of your pores?"

I will not stay a second longer in her company. I turn and make to stride for the house but she springs to stand in front of me, her movement unnaturally quick and noiseless.

"Why, Mrs. Jenkins, do you not know it is the height of rudeness to walk away whilst a person is in conversation with you?"

I try to push past her but she seizes my arm, her grip painful, her touch poisonous, causing my skin to burn beneath it.

"Hear this! Cai Jenkins will never know good health more! His strength will wane, his blood thin, his mind loosen, until he is but a husk of a man. You will watch him, helpless, as he fades and suffers. And when at last he draws his final breath I will be there to sing triumphant! And I will see to it that you are driven from this place, and Ffynnon Las becomes mine."

I wrench my wrist from her clutches and run for the house, but her words follow me.

"I curse Cai Jenkins! Curse him with a slow and torturous death, and your part in it will be to witness his suffering and know you could have prevented it, had you loved him enough to give him up!"

I slam the heavy oak door behind me, my heart thudding fit to burst from my chest, and race back up the stairs and into my room. I struggle to still my ragged breath. Cai lies sleeping still, peaceful, safe, and well. But for how long, I wonder. For how long?

17.

We are to use the *Grimoire*! Now that the moment has arrived I do not know which I fear most—the book's possible power, or my possible failure. Through elaborate mime and the laborious scratching of a few words I was able to convey to Mrs. Jones the encounter I had with Isolda at the well, and the curse she has placed upon Cai. I find myself watching him obsessively now, searching for signs of suffering or sickness. Thus far, two days from the curse being placed, there is little to see, save for a marked tiredness and a dwindling of his appetite. How long will it take before he is gravely ill? Before he is beyond saving, even? The thought is too terrible to hold in my head for more than a fleeting instant. I was all for running straight to the book, wrenching it from its hiding place, and scouring the pages for some counterspell, some way of lifting the curse. I have to believe such a thing exists, for I surely believe Isolda has the power to do what she threatens. But, Mrs. Jones stayed my hand. We must work in secret, and I understand this. She has explained to me that the forces we may unleash by using the *Grimoire* cannot be easily masked or contained. Beyond these vague assertions I can get no more from her. What is clear is that Cai must be some distance from the house before we can settle to our task. Mrs. Jones is adamant it will do no good at this stage to tell him what dark cloud hangs over him. Indeed, she believes his knowing about the curse might even increase its effect. We cannot be sure, but while he is not suffering, she deems it better we keep the truth of his affliction from him.

And today we have an opportunity. The weather has been

achingly cold, and Cai has decided to gather the ewes from the hill and move them to the pastures above the house instead, so that it will be easier to take fodder to them when necessary. He purchased the small flock on our return from the drove. He continued to mutter about sheep being more trouble than they are worth even whilst he was buying them, but he has calculated that they might turn a reasonably swift profit, so that we will be able to increase the herd of cattle further next year. I watched him urging Honey up toward the hill just after breakfast, Bracken nipping at the lazy mare's heels. He plans to check the boundary hedge while he is out, so we can be confident he will not return until after midday.

I retrieve the book from its nest and sit beside Mrs. Jones at the kitchen table. The two of us are silent now, the book in front of us, unwrapped, waiting. Waiting for us to have the courage to open it. I can hear the ticktocking of the grandfather clock in the parlor. I can hear Mrs. Jones's breath wheezing as she draws it, a little rapidly. Her cheeks are flushed and she licks her lips as she places her hand upon the *Grimoire*. Her obvious apprehension heightens my own anxiety. But I must not be timid. My future here at Ffynnon Las, Cai's very life, everything I have left in the world and hold dear, all depend upon me. Upon the step I am about to take. I feel myself on the threshold of a new existence. I know that, once I have crossed that border, there can be no going back. Knowledge cannot be unknown. Experience cannot be unlived.

"I have been permitted to look inside this book but once in my life," says Mrs. Jones quietly. "I was eighteen, and my mother deemed me fit to see, if not to use, what lies within. She herself never used the book, mind. She explained to me, the wisdom, the power, the strong magic of the *Grimoire* is not for hedge witches. Such witchcraft as it contains, see, well, 'tis not for the everyday and the commonplace. And in the wrong hands . . ." She turns to face me. "I do have to tell you, *cariad,* those who seek to harness the forces of this book become not only a danger to others, but a danger to themselves. This is a perilous path, and one we do not set foot upon lightly. Do you understand?"

I do. And she sees that, however dangerous, however hazardous, this is a journey I must make. I *will* make. For Cai.

Mrs. Jones nods. "Very well, then. Very well." Carefully, slowly, and with trepidation, she lifts the cover of the book and opens it. The page revealed contains a statement, which she reads aloud.

"'Let all who wish to consult the *Grimoire of the Blue Well* heed this warning. Only those who have been seen, only those who have been heard, only those who have been judged and deemed worthy are welcome here.'"

She sits back a little and gestures for me to turn the next page. "It is for you to do, Morgana. I cannot enter. You may."

I may, but should I? Have I been deemed worthy? How can I tell? I have been given no sign to indicate that the Witches of the Well did not find me wanting. What punishment lies in wait for one who is not welcome?

I lean forward and touch the gilded edge of the page. It feels cool, and the second my flesh connects with it I hear again the sweet ringing of some far-distant bells, high and pure, as beautiful a sound as I have ever had laid upon my ears. I try to turn the page, but oh! It is so heavy I cannot lift it. How can something so flimsy have such weight? It takes both my hands and all my strength to heave the page over and lay it flat so that the next is revealed. This one bears one word only: *Contents,* but it lists none. There is nothing save blank space beneath the title. I frown, confused. Mrs. Jones touches my arm lightly.

"You do have to tell the book what it is you need. You will be directed to the right place," says she.

I take a breath. I must be succinct, clear. I close my eyes the better to focus the request.

Give me a way to defeat Isolda and lift the curse she has placed upon my husband.

I open my eyes to see the pages flipping over, ten, twenty, thirty . . . too many to count, a blur of gold and vellum, until the movement abruptly ceases. Yet more blank sheets lie before me, but as I watch they begin to fill with swirling color. It is pale at first, hardly there at all, and then becomes darker. Stronger. The bells change their note, shifting to deeper sounds. A cowbell? No, something bigger. On a church, perhaps? I cannot be sure. Mrs. Jones hears it, too, and believes she recognizes the sound.

"'Tis like a buoy at sea," she cries. "A rough sea buffeting and bouncing a heavy iron bell warning ships of rocks or shallow water."

I cannot think that our salvation lies on board a ship, but the water seems relevant. Indeed, the looping washes of blue on the page now form themselves into what resembles a map of rivers, and these rivers flow down to the bottom of the page where they form a broad sea. No, not a sea, a *lake*. Yes, a wide blue lake with mountains rising around it. Soon the blue water fills half the page, and then, to my astonishment, it starts to pour *off* the page. Mrs. Jones lets out a cry of surprise as water splashes onto her lap. We both spring to our feet, chairs scraping against the stone floor which is quickly becoming covered in water. On and on it pours with a speed and force that is beyond reason. It makes no sense that such a small outlet, the width of an open book, could so rapidly produce sufficient water to cover the area of the room, but so it does. And that water rises. And rises.

With a squawk Mrs. Jones teeters and I only just catch her arm in time to prevent her from falling into the deepening pool around our knees. I push at her now, urging her up first onto a chair and then to stand on the table. Still the level of the wild, foaming water rises. It does not seep out under the door as it should, nor force its way through gaps in the windows, but continues inexorably, terrifyingly upward. The outcome appears both horrendous and inescapable. The space will fill with water in less than a minute more, all air will be taken up, and we will drown. Already, though we stand, clinging to one another on top of the table, the level is such that it pushes against my knees.

I doubt I can keep Mrs. Jones on her feet any longer. She begins to wail and cry out.

"Oh! Morgana, do something. Make it stop. Tell it to stop!"

But how? What message should I send? Why is this happening? Such a deluge as can kill us both—how can this be an answer to my request? What dare I ask next? Are the Witches of the Well refusing to help me, and is this their response? I must have failed their examination, been declared unworthy to use the magic of the *Grimoire*. And now it is too late. Their displeasure is fierce indeed! The book is floating atop the water, bobbing effortlessly, still open at the page of the rivers and the lake, endless, unstoppable water continuing to pour from it. I reach to take hold of it but it is too far, so that I am forced to step off the table and swim. But I have never been in such deep water. Bathing in mountain rivers and dew ponds has not equipped me to manage such depths, such swirling currents. As I kick and splash my progress toward the book is pitifully, uselessly slow. I hear a cry behind me and glimpse Mrs. Jones as she topples from the table and disappears beneath the surface of the water.

I draw in as deep a breath as I am able and dive after her. The room is transformed into an underwater nightmare, with chairs and wooden spoons and cloths and pieces of kindling tumbling and spinning everywhere. Mrs. Jones's clothes are waterlogged and the weight of them is too much for her arthritic limbs to propel her to the surface. I snatch at her, grabbing hold of her beneath one arm. She clutches desperately at me, her panic halting any upward movement either of us might have achieved.

I sense that I am going to fail. That I cannot haul my dear friend to the scant air that remains in this unreal room. I cannot so much as kick my way to the door to try to free it, nor smash a window, so strong are the currents against me, and so scarce the breath inside me. For a moment all feels peaceful, and there is a temptation to succumb to what appears to be a gentle end. Simply to stop struggling, to float, to be carried into oblivion by the bright clear water, becomes a curiously attractive option.

But, it will not do. Really, it will not.

I cease my pointless kicking and thrashing about. Mrs. Jones has on her face such an expression of terror that I am almost undone by it. She thinks I have given up, that I am submitting to the water, that we will both die here today, and be found drowned in a kitchen. I will not allow either of us to meet such a ridiculous end. I summon what strength there lies deep within me, and I can feel the power of it building up, pressing on my eyes, wanting to burst from me. Let the Witches of the Well do what they must—I have my own magic in me. Magic blood. I am not some piece of driftwood to be smashed and broken by this unearthly torrent. I wait as long as I dare, as long as my lungs will stand, letting the strength within me reach its height. Mrs. Jones's eyes close and her grasp on my sleeve loosens. Now I act. I flick my head this way and that and the water moves, it parts, it recoils before me, and I am borne up, still holding on to Mrs. Jones, sent racing to break the surface of the water with such speed that I shoot on upward, meeting the ceiling with a thud. I gasp, gulping air, shaking Mrs. Jones so that she quickly does the same. We are afloat, yet the water is still rising. Time is running out.

The *Grimoire* is on the far side of the room, near the window. I scowl at it, willing it to come to me, and it does. As soon as it is within reach I snatch at it, plucking it from the maelstrom, and hold it high.

Stop! Do not test me further. This old woman has done no harm, and nor have I. I tell you, stop!

And, just like that, the water vanishes.

It does not recede quietly, letting us drift downward, but simply ceases to be. In the blink of an eye, in the heartbeat of a skylark, the water has gone and the room is dry, restored to its usual order. Even the fire burns cheerily in the hearth.

And we are returned crashing to the ground with such abruptness I fear for Mrs. Jones. She lies stunned and crumpled from the fall. I kneel beside her, raising her head and cradling it in my lap. She is horribly pale and I fear the ordeal has proved too much for her. What have I done? I was driven to use the *Grimoire* because of what I wanted. Because of Cai. It seemed a selfless desire, but what if this poor, good woman has paid for it with her life?

Wake up, Mrs. Jones. Oh, please wake up!

At last she stirs. Her eyes blink open and she takes a moment to recall where she is and what has befallen her. She struggles to sit up and I assist her.

Then, to my amazement, she smiles at me. Aside from my relief and joy at seeing her recover, I myself see little else to smile about. The power of the *Grimoire* came so close to ending both our lives.

"Oh, *cariad,* what magic!" says she, as if oblivious to the peril we were in. As if she has blotted from her mind the terror we have both just endured. She seems to read my thoughts, for she goes on, "No, I have not lost my senses. I know what happened, *merched.* You called upon the Witches of the Well and they answered you. They tested you, Morgana, and you passed that test. Next time, they will be ready to help you."

Next time! I cannot imagine what would induce me to risk ever consulting the *Grimoire* again. It is too dangerous. Too powerful. Whatever Mrs. Jones thinks, I am not convinced the Witches of the Well have accepted me, and their strength is so great, the potential for destruction so real, how could I ever place myself or anyone else in such jeopardy again?

※

Barely three weeks have passed since Cai and Morgana returned from the drove, and October is only half done, but the weather is already bearing all signs of winter. Trees shed their leaves with indecent haste. Green grass quickly fades and turns to shriveled yellow. Northerly winds bearing icy rain assail farmer and stock alike, driving beneath collars, saturating coats, and chilling bones. Cai has watched the new stock he purchased with funds from the drove lose condition with each passing week. The three brood mares obtained at Llanybydder Horse Fair were quick to grow their dense winter hair, and two have had to be treated for rain scald. He has already been forced to abandon the grazing in the higher pastures in favor of the more sheltered home meadows. The dozen young heifers he bought to replenish his herd of cattle seem shocked to find themselves inhabiting such hostile land, and have lost any spare weight they arrived with. Even the hardy Welsh ewes, bred for centuries to withstand the extreme cold and bitter gales the country of their birth has to offer, are noticeably thinner than when Watson delivered them a month earlier. Cai had reasoned that, with fewer cattle and without the ponies, he could turn a modest profit on a small flock of sheep without too much outlay. He had forgotten, however, that his fences had not been called upon to contain such small and willful livestock, and has spent many hours retrieving the sheep from neighboring farms or lanes. Bracken has taken a strong dislike to the silly creatures and is ineffectual at herding them.

So it is that for the third time in as many days Cai finds himself, short axe in hand, hedging mitt gripping the thorny branches of the hedge, stooped against the relentless wind, as he works to repair yet another gap in the boundary which the restless ewes have widened in their efforts to take themselves somewhere warmer. Ordinarily, Cai would find such inconveniences irritating but inconsequential. But these are not ordinary times. Aside from the freakish weather, there is something else he must contend with. Something so unfamiliar to him that he is at times at a loss as to how best to proceed. For Cai is unwell. He is not sick in any way he has experienced before. He does not have a chill, nor suffer fevers. Nor is he compelled to vomit. This illness is curiously unspecific, and worryingly debilitating. A lethargy began to overtake him soon after arriving home from England. At first he thought it merely fatigue, but no amount of rest would refresh him. Next the malaise manifested itself in a heaviness in his limbs, and was soon accompanied by dull aches in his joints. Mrs. Jones proffered remedies first for rheumatism, and then for arthritis. None gave him any relief from his symptoms. Soon after he started to be troubled by a painful tightness beneath his skull, as if his brain were in the grip of some medieval instrument of torture. Mercifully these bouts of increasingly severe pain visit him only occasionally. Not wanting to alarm Morgana, he has done his best to keep his suffering from her. He has tried to discern a pattern to their onset but can find none. Gradually, as time goes on, he has adjusted to these afflictions, accepting them as responses to a hard life and the onset of a harsh winter. Even so, they weary him, so that the hill behind the house feels steeper than it has ever done, the trek to the far boundary longer, and the weight of a feed of hay for the stock heavier. By the end of each day he sinks gratefully into the chair by the range in the kitchen, tired to his bones.

Now, as he chops at the slim hazel sticks made brittle by the intense cold, he has time to wonder if the decline in his vigor will ever halt. It is perplexing to find himself so debilitated; it is deeply troubling to consider the possibility that the downward slide of his health might not be checked. Could a person die of such a thing? Of nothing, and yet everything, being wrong with him? It is as if each day a little more of his youth, of his strength, of him, indeed, seeps out, leaving him minutely but unmistakably diminished. He feels it with each rise and fall of the blade as he chops the branches. He feels it every time he puts his effort to pulling or bending the thicker boughs in the hedge. He feels it with each step as he trudges homeward, face into the stinging wind, hat pulled low on his head, eyes struggling to focus on the ground a pace ahead in the failing light of the day. By the time he reaches the farmyard he is not walking but staggering. He is slogging his way toward the back door when a disturbing sound stops him. It is coming from the stables where the mares are housed.

Cai feels a chill not brought about by the low temperature flood his body. He has spent his life with horses, and he knows too well the sound of one in extremis. He is not surprised, therefore, to find Wenna flat on her side, her flanks heaving, her breath ragged and labored. The old mare's coat that used to gleam in the sun like polished bronze is dulled with sweat. Cai drops to his knees beside her and puts a hand on her dainty head. Her eyes move minutely, her ears flicker in response to his presence, but he can tell she is barely alive. The severe cold has beaten her. She has seen her last mountain winter. As if she had been waiting for him, she starts to breath more softly until, very soon, all movement has ceased and she has gone. Cai feels her passing as if she were a family member taken from him. He remembers her as a foal, nimble and flighty, as one of the most beautiful ponies his father had ever bred, and as the best brood mare of the herd, producing quality colts and fillies, protecting them as the perfect mother should. He knows she has had a good, long life, but to lose her now, when all seems so bleak and so hopeless, is a body blow.

Clambering stiffly to his feet he trudges to the house and pushes open the back door, all but falling through it onto the cold flags. Hearing him, Morgana and Mrs. Jones fly out of the kitchen.

"Oh! Lord save us, Mr. Jenkins!" cries Mrs. Jones.

Morgana kneels beside him, putting his arm around her shoulders, and helps him to his feet.

"Morgana," he gasps, "Wenna . . ."

She searches his face, trying to understand what it is he wants to tell her.

"Never mind about the ponies now, *bachgen.*" Mrs. Jones helps haul him to his feet. "Bring him to the fire, *merched.* Quickly now. We must get those wet clothes off him. What were you thinking, *bach,* staying out so long in this cruel weather when you are not well?" She bustles through the door, flapping her tea towel at Bracken who has already put himself as close to the hearth as he can. "Shoo, silly dog. Here, sit down now. *Duw,* what are we to do with you?"

Cai fights to regain his voice. "Wenna is dead," he blurts out, regretting he did not speak more gently when he sees Morgana's shock. "She was old, *cariad.* This cruel weather was too much for her."

For a moment Mrs. Jones stops her bustling.

"Dead, you do say? Well, *Duw,* there's a shame," she concedes, seeming to ponder on the information. Cai is surprised, as the woman has never shown interest in the individual ponies, and is as pragmatic about livestock as only the daughter of a farmer can be. Seconds later she is back to the business of bustling about him.

He shakes his head as she stokes up the fire and puts water on to boil. "Don't fuss so, Mrs. Jones. I am only in need of a little rest."

"You are ill, Mr. Jenkins. 'Tis no good carrying on as if you are not, see?"

Morgana helps him off with his coat and hat, sending icy water hissing into the fire as she shakes them, and drapes them over the high back of the settle. It pains him to see the concern on her face. He knows she is worried about him. Knows, too, that she does not believe his casual dismissal of his ailments. At times, somehow, it seems to him she knows more of what it is that afflicts him than he does. He unwinds the wet muffler from his neck. The pitiless rain has even found its way through to his jacket, and this he discards, too. Mrs. Jones snatches it from him, shaking her head.

"I shall fetch a mustard bath for your feet," she says.

Morgana kneels in front of him and sets to unlacing his boots. He watches her as her deft fingers tug at the wet leather. He feels he is failing her, by being ill. There is a hard winter coming. It will take all their best efforts to tend the stock and endure the long dark days ahead. He needs his health. At last he allows himself to form the question in his mind: What will happen to Morgana if he dies?

As if sensing his distress she looks up at him, frowning. He musters what he hopes is a reassuring grin.

"Don't fret, *cariad*," he tells her. "'Twas only the cold caught me unawares. I feel better already. Why wouldn't I? I've got the two best nurses in the valley, see?"

She grips his left boot, tipping back the toe and pulling behind the heel until it slides off his foot. She works quickly, efficiently, her expression still grave. She takes off his other boot and then his woolen stockings. His feet are cold slabs, the toes tinged blue. Cai gasps as she begins to rub them firmly, coaxing blood back to his chilled extremities. Mrs. Jones arrives with a bowl which she sets in front of the fire, pouring steaming water from the kettle onto the ground mustard seeds she has placed inside.

"Now then, in with your feet, if you please," she says.

Cai does as he is told.

"*Duw*, woman! Are you trying to boil me alive?"

"Well, there's a baby you are. No, don't take them out! The Lord knows, Mrs. Jenkins, men do make poor patients."

Morgana nods thoughtfully, picking up his boots and holding them close. Cai sees, with some astonishment, that she is near to crying.

He offers her his hand and she takes it. He pulls her onto his lap, taking the boots from her and dropping them onto the floor.

"All will be well, *cariad*. They breed us tough up here in these hills, see? A few days' rest, some of Mrs. Jones's best steak and kidney pudding. I'll soon be right again. *Paid poeni*."

But she will not be consoled. She lays her head against his shoulder and he feels hot tears dropping onto his chest through his unbuttoned shirt. That she is so concerned shakes him. For all her apparent frailty, he has come to think of her as dauntless, fearless, a fighter who would die sooner than admit defeat. Yet that is, at this moment, precisely how she seems to him. Defeated. It is so at odds with her nature he cannot understand it. He holds her close, allowing her warmth to thaw his numb body. Drawing strength from the vitality he feels within her. Wishing she did not doubt him, for it makes him doubt himself.

The loss of his favorite mare has drained my poor husband of what little strength he had, it seems. The cold has reached deep to his marrow, so that it takes Mrs. Jones and I some hours to completely restore color to his feet and hands, and to stop his body shivering and his teeth chattering. At last we consider we have him warm enough to risk sleep. Before I take him upstairs, Mrs. Jones presses a mug of something hot and aromatic into his hands.

"Now then, Mr. Jenkins. Drink this, if you please."

"What is it?" Cai sniffs suspiciously, wrinkling his nose at the unfamiliar smell, even though it is pleasant enough.

"A remedy for your cold. And a draft that will help you sleep, for there is no cure I do know of can be effective without hours spent peacefully in your bed. Drink, now, *bach*."

Reluctantly, he does as she bids him. It must surely be strong medicine, for barely have I helped him into bed than his eyes close. He fights sleep for a moment, murmuring at me, his words too slurred to make sense. I stroke his brow and plant soft kisses on his face until he lies quiet, his rhythmic breathing indicating sound slumber.

Upon returning to the kitchen I am surprised to find Mrs. Jones wearing her outdoor clothes and lighting two lamps.

"Hurry, *cariad*, there is much to be done," says she, handing me my duster coat and drover's hat. I am at a loss to know why she should want us to go outside, and my surprise turns to alarm when I see her furnish herself with the carving knife. Seeing my shock she pauses to explain.

"*Cariad*, you are a Welsh woman. You well know the custom in ancient times of burying the head of a horse beneath the hearth." Seeing me gasp she holds up her hand. "'Tis no time to be squeamish, *merched*. Our forbears understood that the spirit of a horse is a thing possessed of great strength. Protective strength. You do know the legend, don't you? You will have heard tell of what it is we are about, though none will admit to doing it themselves. 'Tis always the friend of a neighbor, or a cousin's husband . . . But there is powerful magic to be had here."

I shake my head, horrified, as understanding dawns. She wants me to cut off Wenna's head, bring it in here, and inter it beneath the hearthstone! I cannot! I shake my head, backing away from her, my eyes drawn to the lamplight that flashes on the blade in her hand.

"But you must, Morgana. Listen to me." She steps forward and grips my shoulder, just as my mother used to do when trying to make me see reason. Her reason. But this feels like madness. "Listen!" Mrs. Jones insists. "There are dark forces working against us. Winter has come unnatural early and fierce. Cai is ailing. We do know who is behind these terrible things. There is nothing she will not do to get what she wants. She do threaten your husband, your home, your own life, *cariad*. We must use whatever we can to defend what we do hold dear. Fortune has brought us a great gift with the death of this old mare. She served Cai well when she was living, would be a nonsense to let her passing go to waste. You do know the legend, don't you?"

I nod, blinking back tears that sting my eyes.

"'Tis well known," says she, "and for good reason. Generations have called upon the horse spirits to protect their homes in just this way. To protect their homes against witches."

I raise my arms in confusion.

"*Evil* witches," she goes on. "You have nothing to fear, but Isolda, *Duw*, she will not find the air tolerable in this house with the talisman in its place, see?"

Still I cannot bring myself to take the knife from her. To mutilate dear Wenna, to so despoil her body . . . it is a dreadful thing.

At last Mrs. Jones gently takes my hand and places the knife in it, closing my fingers around the handle.

"Do it for love, *merched*. Do it for Cai. You must."

She is right. I know it. I know this is too good a bounty to pass up. We are ill matched against Isolda, I know this also. Who knows if I will truly be able to command the power of the *Grimoire*, or if it will prove too dangerous? We must defend ourselves in all ways possible.

I take up one of the lamps, and together, we go outside. Bracken sets up a squeaking as we shut the door on him, but this is not a job he can assist me with. The icy rain has stopped but an iron frost is already gripping the ground. The air is so cold it hurts my teeth. We hurry to Wenna's stable. The other mares have moved to the far side, instinct driving them to put distance between themselves and death.

"Fetch Honey," says Mrs. Jones. "We must take the mare outside."

Honey is put out at being summoned to work in the night and I have to drag her from her stall by her bridle. I fit a collar over her broad neck and secure the logging chains to it. Mrs. Jones helps me loop the loose ends of the chains around the pitifully skinny corpse. Already the cold is making me clumsy and slow. I wonder that Mrs. Jones can stand it so well, and I know her arthritic legs must be paining her greatly. I heave on Honey's reins as Mrs. Jones slaps her on the rump and eventually she consents to move forward, dragging her uneven load across the frozen cobbles of the yard. We go into the meadow, behind the barn, to a patch of soft mud.

"This will serve our purpose," says Mrs. Jones. "We can cover the body in branches from the kindling pile for now. Cai is not well enough to come out here. We will worry about burying the carcass another day."

I want to protest, but I am all too well aware that this is no time for sentiment. I drop to my knees. One last time I stroke Wenna's pretty face.

Forgive me, little one. We need your help. Cai needs your help just once more.

And now I begin to cut. The first surprise is that there is less blood than I had anticipated. This I attribute to the severe cold, and the slope of the ground on which the pony's body lies. Nor is there any smell, as the carcass is chilled, and the process of decay has not yet started. Under Mrs. Jones's guidance I cut through the skin and the flesh until the blade hits the spine.

"Work in till you do find the join, right at the top of the neck. Take care, *cariad*. Best not to chip nor splinter the bone."

I frown up at her to express my displeasure at this seemingly unnecessary persnicketiness.

"The skull must be complete," she explains. "If the condition of the thing was of no importance we would have brought an axe."

Looking at her now I notice the strain showing on her face. I was wrong to think what we are doing is easy for her. It is difficult for both of us. It is not fair she should also have to navigate my qualms. I concentrate my attention on the task at hand once again. It takes some time to wheedle the point of the blade into the perfect spot.

"Remember how you jointed the rabbit?" she asks. "'Tis just the same, only of greater size. Feel for the gap between the bones."

I have it! The knife plunges deep into the slippery joint and I can feel the skull working loose as I press and prise. Under the uneven lamplight it is troublesome to see exactly what I am doing, so that my eyes begin to water with the effort of it. A long, cold twenty minutes later the head is completely free of the body. It looks so forlorn, lying adrift on the unyielding mud. Away in the distance a fox barks, its grating cry breaking into my thoughts.

Mrs. Jones swiftly wraps the head in an old bedsheet she has brought for the purpose. My muscles ache with chill and exertion as I heave wood from the pile to cover the mutilated corpse. I take the bundled head from Mrs. Jones and am surprised by its weight. We make slow progress back to the house. The fire in the range has gone out, and the cold of the night seems to follow us into the kitchen and cling to our clothes. Our work is not yet done. Bracken comes to sniff and wag as I use a bar to lever up the largest stone in front of the hearth. As I dig at the dry, dusty earth beneath it the dog joins in, thinking this a fine game. Soon his black nose and white muzzle are rendered chocolate brown, and he looks quite ridiculous. So much so that Mrs. Jones gives a chuckle at the sight of him. The sound seems out of place, given our morbid activity, and horribly loud. Instinctively I freeze mid digging, casting my eyes up to the ceiling, listening for any sign that we might have disturbed Cai from his drugged sleep. What would he say if he discovered us now? How could anyone react other than with revulsion at what we are doing?

"All is well, *cariad*," says Mrs. Jones. "The concoction I made for him will keep him wrapped in happy dreams until sunrise."

Soon we have our precious bundle pushed into its new resting place, and the worn and dented flagstone returned to its position. Mrs. Jones sits stiffly on the floor beside me, holding her hands out in front of her, palms up. Her eyes are closed, and though I cannot hear any words, her lips move and I know she is offering up a prayer to the spirit of the horse. When she opens her eyes once more she looks straight ahead, unseeing, and says clearly and firmly, "We are Witches of the Well and we call upon you to protect us from those who would do us harm. Keep them from our home. Keep our loved ones safe, we implore you."

Bracken sits close to me, tips back his head, his mud-caked snout pointing to the heavens, and sets up a thin, eerie keening.

Come Sunday Cai is determined that they will attend chapel. He knows it is as much to convince himself that his illness is no cause for serious concern as it is to convince Morgana. And Mrs. Jones. And all the others who have heard by the unfailingly reliable local whispering that he is not well. They will go to Soar-y-Mynydd. He will stride in to take his place in the front pew with Morgana on his arm in a fine woolen dress, and he will say his good mornings to all and any. He will even sing a little louder than is his habit. Altogether he will present a version of himself no man could doubt will shake off this passing minor affliction and continue to be a successful *porthmon* with his wonderful new wife. He is keenly aware that Morgana is no longer held in high regard in the neighborhood. There are those who still believe she was, at least in part, responsible for what happened to Dai. There are even those who, incredible as it is to him, have swallowed Edwyn Nails's poisonous nonsense about a curse on the drove and ill luck following the new Mrs. Jenkins. They must show themselves at chapel, he has decided, and they must show that they are not people who will be put down by malicious gossip, speculation, or illness.

The journey up the hill is a difficult one. The rain has stopped, but only because it is too cold. Should anything fall from the sky it will certainly be snow. A frost arrived the night before and has elected to stay, so that all about them lies a dully glittering dust of ice. A greyness colors the clouds above, which sit heavily, obliterating an already weakened sun. Ice has made the road treacherous, so that Cai quickly regrets bringing the trap.

"Next time," he tells Morgana as Prince slithers sideways yet again, almost putting them all in the ditch, "we will ride. 'Tis not fit weather for the trap," he adds, somewhat unnecessarily, as they are both forced to clutch at the sides of the little wooden cart while Prince scrambles to regain his footing and make forward progress.

They arrive in good time after all, and find a sizable number of worshipers hurrying into the chapel. Cai ties the reins and offers Morgana his arm as they cross the stone footbridge. To onlookers they are a well turned out couple making their way to morning prayer. In truth, Cai is leaning heavily on Morgana, and finds the short walk to the door an effort. His limbs refuse to move as he bids them, so that by the time they have crossed the graveyard he is dragging his left foot all too plainly. Glancing about him, Cai knows his condition has not gone unnoticed. The good and the faithful have braved the weather to turn out in fair numbers. Fortunately, none is tempted to linger and chat outside. Everyone present squeezes into the small space between the thick, frozen walls of the chapel. There is no fire to bring cheer or heat, but the snugly wrapped congregation create at least a modicum of warmth themselves, albeit a pungent one. It is not until he is inside that Cai notices the absences. Many of the families present are fractured. Many husbands are attending without their wives. Familiar faces are missing. He leans closer to Mrs. Cadwaladr.

"Why are so many absent?" he asks. "Most have found it in them to face the weather to be here, but where is Mrs. Davies? Or Twm the mill? And why does not Dylys Evans have her babes with her?"

Mrs. Cadwaladr looks stricken for a moment and then whips out a handkerchief, into which she weeps copiously.

"Oh, Mr. Jenkins," she wails, "have you not heard? There is sickness in Tregaron. Many are sorely afflicted. Some have . . ." she hesitates, her voice breaking, ". . . been lost!"

Cai is amazed. He has not been into town recently, but these are surely sudden developments. When Mrs. Jones was last at the house, but three days before, she had mentioned only that one or two of the elderly residents had succumbed to the cold. And now he recalls her saying some of the babies were unwell. He had thought it the ordinary winter ailments, nothing more. But now, looking around him, seeing the distress on Mrs. Cadwaladr's face, which is, indeed, shared even by her daughters, he realizes that this is different. He understands why so many have ventured forth in such inclement conditions. He looks into the eyes of those present and he sees fear.

Isolda Bowen arrives late, making something of an entrance. From his seat in the front pew Cai gives a small bow by way of greeting but she does not respond, save to glare at Morgana. He is aware of the alteration in his wife's demeanor at the sight of the woman. It seems their dislike is mutual now. Is Isolda jealous, then, he wonders. Is his own love for Morgana now so obvious as to cause her offense? His head begins to throb and his vision blur. He is alarmed by how quickly, and with how much severity, the episode occurs. He cannot stop himself putting his hand to his head. Morgana leans forward, concerned. He pats her hand, smiling, determined not to let her see how much he is suffering. Has he, too, fallen victim to the illness that is devastating the community? Is that why he has been so unwell? Are they all to endure this disabling sickness? Could he pass it to Morgana?

Reverend Cadwaladr takes his place at the lectern. He lets his gaze sweep over the shivering congregation, nodding solemnly.

"I see that you are cold, my brothers and sisters. I see that you are suffering in this bitter weather, this unseasonable, deadly chill that has had us in its iron grip for weeks now. I have noticed the sheep digging in the frozen ground, hungry and thin. I have seen small birds stiff and dead on the rocky path. I have heard the harsh wind moaning through my house at night. I have watched those who have so little already burning their winter fuel supplies, already running low on fodder for their stock, already afraid that their provisions will not see them through what threatens to be a bewilderingly ferocious and long winter. And I have touched the brows of those who have not been able to withstand the vile disease that has come to our town."

There is a murmuring in the pews. Sounds of assent and shared worry. Sounds of women gently weeping.

"And I know there is fear among you. Aye, it is plain on your faces. And it strikes me here!" He beats a fist against his heart. "It pains me to see such suffering. And I ask myself, why? Why has the Lord seen fit to visit this hardship upon us? Why has He, in His infinite wisdom, decreed that His children should know hunger, should fall ill, should watch their livestock, their livelihoods, dwindle and fade? Why should He see the need to test us by taking our loved ones; the old, the strong, the innocent alike?"

There is a wail from the back of the chapel.

"I have prayed, my brothers and sisters. I have got down on my knees and prayed for answers, and for guidance. And God spoke to me!" His face has become red with excitement and fervor. "Yes, God spoke to me!"

There is a ripple of gasps and amens.

Reverend Cadwaladr leans forward, steadying himself on the Bible in front of him, earnestly regarding his flock.

"He told me there is evil among us!"

Now shock draws further gasps and muttered prayers from the congregation.

"Yes, I'm here to tell you, the Lord said to me, clear as I stand before you, that there is evil among us! Wickedness! The ungodly and the satanic moves in our midst!"

People begin to clutch at one another, shaking their heads, not wanting to hear.

"He has sent us these trials to snuff out that evil. If it takes the death of every man, woman, and child in this parish, then so it will be! Listen to me, brothers and sisters. All is not lost. I tell you, we have it in our power to save ourselves, to save our community."

There are cries of "How may we do this?" and "Tell us! Oh, tell us!"

"Are you willing to do what is necessary? Are you able to do God's work, so that the innocent may be spared?"

"We are!" comes the response. "We are!"

"Then look to your neighbor. Look to those you know. Yea, look even to your own families, and seek out that evil. Find it, and drive it out!"

"Amen!"

"Drive it out! Cleanse our town of the rot that hides at its core, lest it infect us all, and our Lord must continue in His purging. Seek out the festering darkness that lurks among us, brothers and sisters. Are you up to the task? Are you?"

There is a deal of shouting and waving of fists now. Cai feels his head might split open from the pain inside it and the cacophony around him. He has never seen people in such a state of fervor and determination, and it is the most frightening thing he has ever witnessed.

We will not be attending chapel again. Whatever sickness Isolda has visited upon Cai is worse in her presence, and she makes a point of being there. And now Reverend Cadwaladr has stirred up the congregation, exhorting them to search for the evil among us. It is clear to me he is still dancing to Isolda's tune, like a helpless puppet whose strings are jerked mercilessly. She must have demanded he continue to turn the people of the parish against me. How stupid they all are! How blind. They do not see the wickedness of the creature who would crush any or all of them like a beetle beneath her boot if it suited her purposes to do so. They do not smell her reptilian odor, as I do. Do not taste the poisonous air she exhales, as I do. Do not hear her mocking laughter, as I do.

It is terrible to watch my poor husband becoming more ill with each passing day. What must I do to break the curse? What *can* I do? I would pull her arms from her body and dig her eyes from her face with my own hands if I thought it would free him. If I believed she would allow me close enough to do her harm. I must find a way. I must devise a plan that will enable me to get near her, to find how she might be vulnerable. I do not believe there is anything I could do to persuade her to lift her curse. My only course of action, then, must be to kill her. Oh, to think such a thing! But it is the truth. In the end, it will come down to a life; Cai's or Isolda's. And I will not stand by and watch my beloved fade into death. I will hone what talents I possess. I will prepare myself as best I can. I will consider when and where I must strike. And then I will do what must be done.

Until then, all I can do is care for Cai. Ease his pains. Since we returned home from chapel this morning Cai has not stirred from his chair. I have banked up the fire. I offered him a blanket, but he will not have it. It is as if he fears acknowledging how frail he is. As if to do so would make it more true. He is sleeping now. I have fetched one of my father's books—*Treasure Island*—and come to share the window seat with Bracken. It comforts me to hold the book close, to recall the story, to recall Dada. How I wish he were here to help me now. Somehow I am certain he would know how best to defeat Isolda. Bracken and I gaze outside together and watch the grey light of the day dwindle. The cold is such that I feel it coming through the window as if there were no glass at all. I run my hand over Bracken's soft, warm fur and he thumps his tail lazily. The landscape beyond the garden is dull and uninviting, with no pretty sunset to lessen the metallic gleam of ice that covers everything. It is difficult to discern the horizon. It is as if the world is shrinking to only a few frozen yards beyond the house. And now, as my face begins to tingle with the cold, I see them. The first flakes of snow.

"Morgana? Morgana, where are you?" Cai's voice is heavy with sleep. I slip from the window seat and go to him. "You will freeze over there," says he. "Close the shutters and come and sit by the fire with me."

I do as he wishes, pausing for a moment to watch as a snowflake, new and wonderfully intricate, sharp-edged as if made of sugar, sticks to the pane. For a few brief seconds it remains there, beautiful and perfect. And then the scant heat from the house works upon it, and it begins to blur, its definition is lost, before it is absorbed by another flake which lands atop it. And another. And another. I swing the shutters to and drop the heavy metal latch that secures them. I sit on the settle opposite Cai's chair. Bracken comes to lie as close to the hot coals as he can safely put himself. I still have my book in my hand and Cai sees it.

"What's that you have there? Oh, *Treasure Island,* a wonderful story." Seeing my reaction he goes on. "I read it many times as a boy. Scared me then, mind." He smiles faintly. Watching me stroke the worn leather of the cover. "They were your father's books, weren't they?"

I nod.

"They must be very special to you, then. It must give you great comfort, to read them."

I look away, my eyes darting to the intense red of the fire, unable to meet his gaze. I attempt to maintain an impassive, impenetrable expression, but he knows me too well.

"Morgana, what is it?" he asks, shifting to lean forward in his chair, the effort making him draw a quick breath. I cannot help but look at him now, and in doing so I reveal the sadness within. "*Cariad,* I'm sorry, I did not mean to cause you distress by mentioning your father," says Cai.

I give a small, dismissive wave, but he remains unconvinced.

"No, I have upset you. I have been thoughtless," says he. "Is it that you don't want to read the book without him, that it reminds you too much of him? Is that it?"

I shake my head. And I realize that I want him to understand. I want him to see that without someone to share the stories with, they are but half experienced. Oh, how I would relish having him read to me! To journey to all these wonderful, exotic places together, away from here, from the hardship and dangers in our own world. I open the book to a random page and take it to him. I point to the words, letting my finger trace them, and then I look at him and then put my hand to my heart. He watches attentively, and I know he wants to understand. I take my hand and lay it palm down over his heart, and then, smiling, pass the book to him.

"Why yes, it is as I said, *cariad,* I do enjoy such books. I have always loved to read. But what . . . ?" He thinks for a moment, and then his mouth opens as realization blows away the mists of confusion in his mind. He is astonished. "You'd like us to read them together, is that it? For me to read to you sometimes, perhaps?" At once his face brightens. He reaches out and strokes my face, pushing wayward hair from my brow.

"I can think of nothing I would like better than to share these stories with you. Is that what you would like, Morgana?"

So that he be in no doubt as to my answer I shower him with kisses, each one of them a heartfelt yes.

He laughs. "Steady now! Best not get me too distracted, else I won't be able to concentrate on what's written, see?"

I nod, sliding from his lap to sit on the hearth rug at his feet, forcing Bracken to move over to make room for me. I reach up and open the treasured book on page one. Cai smiles down at me for a moment longer.

"You are so very beautiful, my wild one," says he.

And then he starts to read. And as he does so I experience such a muddle of feelings. It is a joy to listen to him, to share the magical journey of the story, yes, but that joy is tainted, for this is a moment I fear may never come again. How long will we have together to enjoy such special times, such precious times, if Isolda cannot be stopped? Will there come a day when all I have is the memory of this instant, a treasured recollection of one occasion when he understood me so well, and we journeyed into make-believe foreign lands and story worlds, the two of us? Are we to be robbed of such a simple pleasure as his strength fails him, until he can read no more? Until he can breathe no more!

Tears sting my eyes as I listen to his soft voice recount the story that is so familiar to me, but I do not let him see my fears. I lean my head against his knee and let the words soothe me, shutting out Isolda as best I can, refusing to let her rob me of even this. An hour later we are both fighting fatigue and I help Cai up the stairs and to bed. His rest is fitful, and I lie beside him watchful and concerned, hardly daring to take my eyes from him in case he should worsen while I sleep.

It is now two days since the snow started to fall, and it has not yet stopped. Cai has taken to the pastime of shared reading with an eagerness that is at once heartwarming and heartbreaking. I feel he does not, as I do, question how long we may have to enjoy this gentle pursuit. Why, he has even promised to teach me to write. My excitement at this idea was short-lived. For a brief moment I allowed myself to think what this could mean; to imagine all the ways I could employ the skill of forming my thoughts in ink upon paper. But even in these few short days I have watched my dear husband sicken further. Every wheezing breath, every wince of pain, reminds me that our future, all that we wish for and hope for, stands hostage to Isolda's wicked desires.

Mrs. Jones valiantly made her way here on foot yesterday and is now unlikely to leave in advance of some sort of letup in the weather. Inside the house, at least, we are snug. There is plenty of coal to keep us warm, and though the pool is frozen the spring itself continues to bubble, so that we have water. Thanks to Mrs. Jones we also have a well-stocked larder. However, there are things which we are in need of, not least some more brandy to ease Cai's suffering. His joints pain him badly now, and are not helped by the cold. Mrs. Jones has also suggested that a bottle of laudanum might be obtained from Dr. Williams. It would, indeed, be a blessing if Cai could sleep more than a few snatched hours at a time, for how can the strongest among us thrive if we are in want of sleep? And at this time, Cai is far from strong. Alas, Mrs. Jones has no more of her own sleeping concoction left. It is decided, after much debate and some resistance from Cai, that I will go into Tregaron and fetch what we need. I will ride Prince and lead Honey, who will serve as a packhorse. I will obtain the medicines Cai has need of. In addition I will purchase more sugar, a sack of oatmeal, some dried fruit, and a ham, if I can find one. Who knows how long we may be snowed in? It is best to make the most of the trip.

I know that Mrs. Jones has plans for us to call upon the strength and magic of the *Grimoire* again. I am fearful of it, but she has convinced me there is no other way, if we are to summon the force needed to rid Cai of the curse, and to rid all of us of Isolda, once and for always. But first we must attend to Cai's immediate needs. We must keep him as well as we can whilst we ready ourselves for the confrontation that lies ahead.

I prepare myself for facing the cruel weather by donning the heavy divided skirt and long duster coat I wore for the drove. They are roomy enough for me to be able to fit several layers of woolen garments beneath them for warmth. I have once again turned to Catrin's trunk of clothes and found some fur-lined leather gloves which will suit my purposes well. I have pulled an old pair of Cai's gaiters over my boots and hose for further protection against the elements. In my bedroom I regard my reflection. The clothes are worn, but will keep out the snow. In order that my broad-brimmed hat fit properly and stay on my head I wear my hair down. I am conscious of how outlandish my appearance will be to the people of the town, but in truth I care little for their opinion. None have come to offer help, though they know Cai to be unwell. They are content for me to manage the livestock on my own. Not for the first time I am thankful for Mrs. Jones, for I would not like to leave Cai alone for the hours it will take me to make my journey. In the kitchen the sight of me makes him smile. He sits up straighter in his chair, the knee rug he has finally agreed to use falling from his lap. I pick it up and tuck it tightly around him once more.

"Never mind me," says he, "you'd best get started. Make use of the daylight. You don't want to be caught out in this when dark falls." He grins slowly. "I had not thought to see my little drover again this season." His attempt to lighten the moment is short-lived, however. He sees the lovespoon whistle around my neck. "Take care, my wild one. Treat the weather with respect, even if it is not deserving of it."

I smile at him and kiss his hot cheek before hurrying out.

Mrs. Jones meets me in the hallway, and sets to winding a fine wool scarf about my neck.

"Now then, *merched*," says she, "have a care. *Duw*, 'tis no weather for you to be going outside. I know, I know." She holds up a hand as if to stop me speaking. "Your husband has need of what Doctor Williams can send him." She finishes tying the scarf, tutting as I pull my hair from under it so that it falls over my shoulders. She looks at me seriously now and I see real concern in her kind brown eyes. "Take heed, Morgana. I do not doubt you and that sure-footed pony of yours will manage the weather, but there are more dangers than snow in Tregaron this winter." She pauses, searching for the right words. "People are scared, *cariad*. And you know a creature is never more dangerous than when 'tis frightened," says she.

I embrace her, closing my eyes briefly to breathe in the comforting smells of lavender and baking, smells of home and hearth, smells of my mother. I use the back door. The front one has swollen in the weather and is near impossible to open now. The smaller door at the rear of the hallway is sheltered by a narrow stone porch. Even so, I have to tug hard at the handle before it moves, and there is the discordant sound of wood scraping upon flagstone.

The snow has not so much ceased falling as paused. As if it is drawing breath for further effort. I must take best advantage of the respite, however short it may prove to be. I stride over to the stables, a sharp squeaking accompanying each step in the snow, which is easily deep enough to cover my boots. I can hear Bracken barking back in the house, but I will not take him with me. His legs are so short and his fur so dense he quickly becomes balled with ice and makes poor progress. He must guard his master and wait with him for my return. Prince, as ever, is willing and more than a little agitated. Honey is reluctant to leave the stable. I tighten the girth on her panniers and the one on Prince's saddle. I have only been outside minutes, but already the cold is beginning to penetrate my gloves, making my fingers clumsy and slow. At last I swing aboard Prince and tie Honey's lead rein to the saddle. We all but haul her out of the yard and onto the track. She objects to the very idea of going abroad in such conditions, and Prince quickly becomes bad tempered at having to drag her along. We have not gone many yards before I decide it is better to let her loose and ride behind her, herding her along with Prince and a springy hazel stick like the old nag she insists on playing. I do not look back at the house as we go, but I feel I am being watched. I can clearly imagine Cai and Bracken at the window seat, following my laborious progress, both of them wishing they were out here with me.

There is neither wind nor sun. The air is thick with cold, and the sky pregnant with the promise of more snow to come. The landscape beneath this heaviness is a dull white. A white tinged with grey. A white that does not reflect prettily, or glisten brightly. A white that suggests merely an absence of life. Nothing can thrive or grow in such bleakness. The birds and animals whose lot it is to exist here, now, in this suffocating cold, can only endure. Only work to survive the bitter ice that would still their hearts and freeze the blood in their veins. As I ride farther along the lane, Prince and Honey are forced to stagger and plunge through drifts that have formed between the hedgerows. Fog descends upon us, so dense and heavy with moisture that it has soon soaked manes and hair alike, and this water in turn quickly freezes. Within a short time, every branch and twig, every stone and fence post, is coated with a bristly covering of ice. As are the horses. As am I. My hair is frozen white, and makes an unearthly tinkling sound as I move. What manner of winter is this? It is unnatural. So much so, that I even begin to suspect Isolda's hand behind it. The notion that she might be capable of bringing out such deadly conditions, blighting not only the objects of her fury but the weak, the vulnerable, the innocent at random, is a heavy thought to carry with me.

By the time we reach Tregaron Honey is puffing and weary and both horses steam as sweat cools off them. The little town is hushed and empty, with few people venturing out. Even so I feel eyes upon me. Suspicious eyes. Wary eyes. Fearful eyes. With my icicled hair and outlandish clothing I must cut a curious figure. The snow-muted hoofbeats of the horses echo flatly against the stone walls of the houses in the square. I dismount, tie reins and rope to a hitching post, and knock upon the door of Dr. Williams's house. Across the street from where I stand is Isolda's imposing home. I know she will be aware of my presence. I keep my back turned and do my utmost to empty my mind.

Dr. Williams's maid opens the door. She looks down her crooked nose at me.

"The doctor is engaged," she informs me with unconvincing haste.

I take the coins and the letter Cai has written requesting laudanum and hand it to her. She takes it from me gingerly, as though it might bite her, and disappears back inside, the door shut firmly against me lest I should force my unwelcome way in. As if I would wish to!

A group of small children has assembled on the stone monument a few paces off. They watch me closely, whispering among themselves. Soon they are joined by an elderly man and two women whom I recall from chapel. They stand and stare at me as if I were a visitor from a foreign land. The looks they cast my way are not friendly. Indeed, they are openly hostile, and I notice the old man spit loudly in my direction, the yellow sputum discoloring the snow for a few ugly seconds before being absorbed by it. Now three more men emerge from the inn, their faces dark. Mrs. Jones was right—these people are afraid. Their loved ones are dying, and they have been convinced, not least by the exhortations of Reverend Cadwaladr, that someone among them is to blame. Someone different. Someone upon whom suspicion has already fallen. Someone with whom an untimely death is associated. And then I hear it, muttered quietly at first, and then again with gathering strength: the word *witch*.

Abruptly the door in front of me opens again and the maid reappears. She thrusts a dark brown bottle into my hand and retreats once more. The door slams, sending snow from the roof onto the street beside me. I hear a heavy bolt pushed home. Tucking the bottle carefully into the inside pocket of my coat I walk as briskly as the going allows to the grocer's shop farther down the street. I sense that the crowd is shifting behind me. Following me. I make my purchases as quickly as possible, planning to call next at the butcher's for the ham and then make my escape. With the dried fruit packaged and nestled in my large outer pocket, a small bottle of brandy next to it, and the sack of oatmeal on my shoulder, I emerge once more onto the square. I need to turn right for the butcher's, but my way is now blocked by three burly youths. They regard me with silent aggression. Someone in the crowd has more to say for themselves.

"Go home!" comes the cry. "You are not welcome here."

"Stay away!" adds another.

"Witch!" shouts someone bolder. "Witch!"

Within seconds the entire mob is chanting at me.

"Witch! Witch! Witch!"

I push past, hampered by the oatmeal but pressing on, refusing to be riled. I must not be drawn into conflict, I must not! To let loose my temper now would only confirm what they suspect and fuel their hatred of me. Prince has sensed the danger and whinnies at me from the far side of the square. If only I can reach him I can leave quickly.

The first stone whistles past my face. And then another. And another. I am close to the horses when a large lump of sandstone strikes my cheek with such force that I stumble, landing heavily in the snow, the sack of oatmeal snagging on the wall, ripping open, disgorging its contents in an instant. The crowd, as if shocked, hesitate, and I seize the moment. Abandoning the oatmeal I untie Honey, grab Prince's reins, and spring quickly into the saddle. Blood trickles from the wound on my face, splashing crimson onto the pony's frosted mane. It is taking all my concentration, all my will, to control the force that rages within me; my own protective instinct which would, given freedom, rain havoc upon these vicious people. I am on the point of urging Prince through the crowd and forcing an exit when I see Isolda come out of her house. She is dressed in fine furs and looks strikingly elegant and composed. How misleading are the appearances of people. How can I expect society to accept a wild harum-scarum such as I, and to doubt the picture of respectability and prosperity Mrs. Bowen presents?

For a moment I wonder if she will spur on my persecutors. Will she openly side with them and reveal her hostility toward me? At this moment she would surely find support for any theory she might put forward which was in agreement with their own misplaced fears.

Oh, Morgana—her voice is inside my head again!—*do you think I would be so stupid, so clumsy?*

She hurries forward.

"Why, Mrs. Jenkins!" she cries, her hands to her mouth, her face the very picture of genuine concern. "You are hurt!" She rushes through the crowd who step back, deferential, more than a little confused. "Come, child," says she, putting a hand on Prince's bridle, standing in front of me so that I would have to ride over her to make my escape. "Come into my home and let me dress your wound. You are in no condition to ride."

I shake my head, digging my heels into Prince's flanks to push him forward. But the hold she has over him is more than merely physical and he does not so much as lift a hoof, instead standing stock-still, as if in terror. What manner of horror has she laid before his bright eyes to affect such a state?

One of the women in the crowd finds her voice.

"Have a care, Mrs. Bowen," says she. "That girl is wicked! To be near her is to risk harm!"

"Surely not." Isolda is a fine actress!

"'Tis true, missus," adds a toothless man. "She cursed the drove. She's cursed this town. *Duw,* she's even cursed her own husband!"

All of a sudden, Prince comes to his senses, but with such a fright, with such anguish driving him, that he rears up on his hind legs, so that I am forced to lean forward and cling to his mane to stop myself from sliding off. He bounds ahead as if I have whipped him, and in doing so knocks Isolda to the ground. She falls with a cry to drag pity from a heart of stone. Prince plunges on. Glancing back I see the terrible woman being assisted by the onlookers. Fists are waved at me, oaths sworn, and further stones thrown. I give Prince his head, and he needs no further bidding to gallop from the town square. Even Honey is startled into action and soon catches up as we hasten toward home.

Cai has rarely in his life felt such fury as he does now. The sight of Morgana returning, bruised and bleeding, and the tale his questioning revealed has enraged him to the point of senselessness. There are gaps in the story which even Mrs. Jones's more careful inquiries could not provide answers to, but they have gleaned sufficient information to paint a dark and ugly picture of events. As Morgana goes upstairs to change into dry clothes he paces unevenly about the kitchen, his face contorted with impotent anger.

"How could they? How could they turn on her like that? What madness drives them?" he demands.

Mrs. Jones shakes her head slowly. "They are afraid, *bachgen*. They are in despair," she tells him.

"That does not give them the right to set upon a defenseless girl."

"They do not see Morgana as defenseless. They see her as dangerous."

"What? What nonsense is this?"

"Many are sick, *cariad*. There is fever in the town and many have died. They believe it comes from here. From Ffynnon Las."

"But, I do not have a fever. Why would they think that?"

"People do say Morgana is responsible."

"For the sickness in Tregaron? Morgana? This is insanity!" He looks at her now. "And you, Mrs. Jones? Is that what you believe?"

Mrs. Jones tugs at her apron and shakes her head again. "Of course I do not! 'Tis cruel unfair, *bach*. That girl of yours is more godly than half of them as attends chapel. But Edwyn Nails has spread his poison. And that *creature,* Isolda Bowen . . ."

"Isolda? What part has she to play in this?"

"In my opinion folk would do better to look to her if they wish to rid their town of evil."

Cai runs a hand through his hair. He cannot make sense of any of it.

"Mrs. Bowen has good standing in Tregaron. She is respected. Well thought of."

"But what does anyone know of her? What do you really know of her, Mr. Jenkins? You do see a wealthy widow, proper and God-fearing. But who ever met her husband? Did he even exist? How did she come by her fortune? Why has she no family as she ever makes mention of, or do ever visit?"

"But why would she hate Morgana so? What has she to gain by setting people against her?"

"Morgana sees her for what she truly is."

"The two dislike each other, I know." He hesitates, then goes on. "Such rivalries between women are not uncommon. Isolda and I were . . . friends."

"Oh yes, Morgana has something that Isolda wants. But it is not you, *bachgen*."

"What then?" He throws up his hands against her answer. "No. Do not tell me more on the subject. I have neither time nor strength to deal with such squabbles."

"Squabbles!" Mrs. Jones is pushed into snapping at him. "*Duw, bachgen,* we are not talking of two silly women making fools because they are pitched against each other in love. Lord save us from the vanity of men!"

"I only meant . . ."

"'Tis true if anything can save you it will be Morgana's love."

"Save me?"

"Open your eyes, Mr. Jenkins, and look at that wicked woman you hold in such high esteem. She is not as she appears. She is not what she pretends to be. She is not what you and every other shortsighted person in the village believes her to be. Every one except your wife." Seeing his confusion Mrs. Jones stops.

Cai senses there is still something she is not telling him, but he is too tired, too weary, too angry to stuggle to understand more.

"Maybe I do not know the woman at all. If you say so, I believe you, Mrs. Jones, but, to be honest, I do not have it in me to worry further about her. Not now. What truly concerns me is the way the people of this parish have turned against Morgana. That they could believe she is somehow responsible for their sickness, for their loss . . . it is inconceivable. How do they think her capable of such a thing?"

Mrs. Jones takes a deep, slow breath and meets his eye levelly.

"They believe she has the skill of cursing. They think she has visited sickness upon them because she is evil and can do so. They even believe she has brought about this terrible weather."

"The weather!"

"Aye, they have convinced themselves of it, *bach*. So much so, that they have given her a name. I've heard it whispered, though most are careful what they say in my presence." She pauses, but forces herself to continue, "They do call her the Winter Witch."

18.

I am astonished, the next morning, to be woken by sharp shards of sunlight slicing between the cracks in the curtains. I slip from the bed, being careful not to disturb Cai. The laudanum brought merciful relief from his pains, and though it took a deal of persuasion before he would drink it, he knows, as we all do, the restorative powers of sleep. He looks so peaceful, his features so untroubled. It is rare to see him thus nowadays.

I dress and hurry downstairs, quelling a shudder when unseen fingers, every bit as cold as the ice daggers that hang from the window ledges outside, scratch at my back as I pass the door to Cai's room.

Mrs. Jones is already risen, and reassuring smells of baking drift out from the kitchen.

"Well, you look a little better this morning, *cariad,*" she tells me, dusting flour from her hands and frowning at the bruise on my cheek. "And Mr. Jenkins still sleeping, is he?"

I nod and peer round her at the griddle on the stove. Half a dozen *picau ar y maen* bubble and steam, the sweet aroma of the traditional Welsh cakes making my mouth water. Mrs. Jones laughs at me.

"Two more minutes and they'll be ready. Got to give them a good dusting of sugar yet, mind. I've mix for another batch. And I've *bara brith* in the oven. Put that dried fruit you fetched to good use. We do have to tempt that man of yours into eating, see? I always used to set to baking when my little Maldwyn was poorly. Now then, *merched*. You sit down and I'll fetch you something to eat. Can't go out feeding the stock with your own stomach rumbling fit to scare the sheep."

But I shake my head. It is many days since I have seen the sun and I am anxious to be out in it. Anxious to be doing rather than thinking, for I am weary of worry. I dart past her and steal a sizzling cake, using my sleeve to stop it burning my fingers. She squawks and swats at me with her cloth but I am quickly out of the room, snatching up my hat and coat as I go, Bracken at my heels.

She calls after me, "Don't be too long, mind. We do have work to do, later."

I pause and turn.

She nods, knowing that I understand, and adds in a whisper, "Time is short, Morgana. We must turn to the *Grimoire* for help."

A mixture of fear and excitement speeds the blood through my veins.

Outside, the morning is glorious, the countryside splendid, and it is easy, just for now, to put from my mind the frightening events of the day before. My cheek still smarts where the stone struck it, and has developed a vivid purple hue. Was there ever a color more suited to hatred? I take up a handful of snow and press it to my skin. Within a moment all pain has vanished. The horses have heard my boots scrunching through the snow and Honey begins to bang her stable door, eager for her freedom and her hay. It is a joy to feel the sunshine and I pause to turn my face up to it. There are no clouds today. I have not seen such a blue sky for weeks. The landscape glitters beneath it, transformed from something lifeless and forlorn to something beautiful and blessed. I open the stable doors so that the horses may stretch their legs in the yard, then fetch them hay from the barn, which I share out in piles. Honey settles to eat straightaway. Prince makes a show of bossing about his mares for a minute or two before they are allowed their breakfast. Next I take a lump hammer from the woodshed. The spring is so furred with ice now that it is reduced to a trickle. Raising the hammer above my head I bring it down with as much force as I can muster onto the frost-covered ice which glazes the pool. With a loud crack which reverberates around the yard the ice breaks and splits, so that the black water laps over it. I do the same to the adjacent trough so that the ponies may drink. Leaving the hammer, I return to the hay barn and move the hurdles which separate the cattle from their feed. The herd is so small they have been comfortably accommodated in half the barn. There is nothing to be gained by keeping them out of doors in such weather, for, unlike the sheep, they cannot find any suitable food, and will lose condition. They shuffle forward with a deal of pushing and shoving until each locates a place where they can reach the hay. Sunshine slants into the bay of the barn, and even the beasts in their thick winter coats seem cheered by it. The sheep are in the meadow behind the yard. I take a pitchfork, jab it in the hay, then heave it to rest on my shoulder and slip through the gate into the field. There is a low, lean-to shelter against the wall, and the ewes mill about as I scatter the hay in it. I count carefully. Twice. Three are missing. I scan the field, shielding my eyes against the bright glare of the sun as it bounces off the frozen snow. The wretched sheep are not in sight. I must go and find them while the weather is benign. Bracken bounds ahead as I make my way across the field. It is not long before I spot a new gap in the hedge. Yet again, it seems, the silly animals have decided there is a better living to be had elsewhere. I stoop down to pass through the low passageway they have created. In the sloping hill field I can clearly discern their tracks, and set off to follow them.

As I slog up the steep incline somber thoughts begin to invade my mind, until the sunshine and prettiness through which I move is no longer sufficient to sustain my mood. There was something most dreadfully ugly in the way the people of Tregaron hounded me yesterday. I know they are scared. I know, too, they are many of them grieving. Yesterday, when, I suspect, they considered me out of earshot, I overheard Mrs. Jones laying some hard truths before Cai. Truths regarding Isolda, though he seemed not ready to hear these. And truths about the way I am thought of in the town. How it pained me to hear his shock, his horror—his disgust, could it be?—at their use of the word *witch*. I had thought him able to bear my singular talents, to accept that I have, as Dada would put it, the magic blood running in my veins. But how can he be at ease with these aspects of me when others around him view me as something dangerous, something wicked, something evil? He loves me, of this I am certain, and I hold the thought to my heart and hear it sing. But this is his home. These are the people he grew up with. The people who call him *porthmon* now. It must matter to him what they think of me. Of him. I remember now, his words to Mam on our wedding day: *She will be well regarded at Ffynnon Las.* How far from true that promise has proved to be. Yet I have more pressing matters with which to concern myself. Cai's health continues to falter. Whilst the laudanum brought brief respite, it will not effect a cure. It cannot lift the curse. Nothing, I fear, will do so until I have confronted Isolda direct. Confronted, and emerged triumphant. For I know, in my heart, this will not stop until one of us is dead. And before that she will take Cai from me. For a second the breath is knocked from me by the thought that he might very well die soon if I do not act. Why must it be that everyone I love is snatched away by death's hungry jaws? Must I always pay for love with the agony of grief? My head begins to pound with too much thinking. I have been foolish to allow myself to be seduced by the mountain, by the white wilderness, by the comfort of Mrs. Jones's cooking and the freedom of walking the hill alone, away from critical eyes. I must hold my attention on what I am doing. Indeed, I have been so lost in thought I have scarcely noticed the change in the weather. Bracken and I have climbed more than a hundred feet, and the sky that was empty and bright such a short time ago is now sullied with dense cloud which descends about me as I watch. Bracken's ears prick; he has seen a hare. I catch movement out of the corner of my eye, and in a heartbeat he is away, after it, lost into the thickening gloom. Within moments the horizon has shortened to but a stride from where I stand. And now the snow begins again, in earnest. There is no wind, and the day is not as cold as some have been recently, but there is something frightening in the nature of this snowfall. The flakes are unusually large, some as big as daisy heads, others fat as dandelion puffs. They fall with such speed and such relentlessness that it is hard not to breathe them in, and I wonder, is it possible a person might drown in snow? All sound has ceased. Not in the ordinary way in which winter weather can stop echoes and muffle noises, but *completely* ceased, as if the whole world has been struck as mute as I. The only thing that tells me I have not become deaf is the rasping of my own labored breathing as I struggle to walk through the rapidly deepening snow. I try to retrace my steps, but my tracks are being filled quicker than I can follow them. Of Bracken there is no sign. I clap my gloved hands in an attempt to summon him, but such soft noise as they make is sucked into the dizzying downpour of flakes and hushed in an instant.

It is now that I sense rather than hear the whispering voices. At first they are distant, as if someone else has ventured abroad and we have stumbled upon one another. But no. I quickly realize, as the words become clearer and louder, that they are not emanating from anyone present. At least, not anyone present in body. A stirring of the thick, wet air around me, an irregular pattern in the fall of the snow, alerts me to the fact that I am not alone in this white nightmare, and yet whoever is with me is here in spirit only. And those spirits are not friendly. As they whip past me, back and fore, and around me, causing me to turn this way and that, searching the whirling snowfall, I feel hot breath upon me. There is more than one. I detect a presence to my right and my left, and now another behind me. It is impossible to count them. All I know is I am surrounded by these dark, invisible entities, and I am in grave danger. I must get away, must descend the hill. But which way should I go? Such is the obliteration of any landmarks, of even the ground farther than a few short feet ahead or behind, that I can barely tell which way is down, let alone in which direction home lies. My tracks, *all* tracks, have been obliterated. A force rushes by close to my face, striking me with real power, even though there is nothing to see, so that the cut on my cheekbone opens afresh and begins to bleed again. I must hold my nerve. This is Isolda's doing, I am sure of it. Now I can detect her rancid, sulphurous odor. The voices increase in strength and number. They call my name. They scream at me. They laugh at me. They wail and plead and badger me in all ways possible. At one point I think I hear the voice of my father, but I quickly understand it is but a trick. I must not falter. Cai will die without me. That is the truth of it. I will not meet my end here on this colorless, lifeless mountain, and leave him to his fate.

It will not do. Really, it will not.

I stand still and steady my breathing. Drawing in as deep a breath as I am able in the suffocating snow I clench my teeth and summon my will. I feel blood dripping thickly from the freshly opened wound on my face. The more I call on the force of my inner strength, the more it flows, splashing onto the bleached ground, spreading scarlet, staining the snow about me, the patch of redness growing and widening until I stand in a bright pool of my own making. I feel the voices recede, fading, growing more distant and less torturous. Even the snowflakes yield to the invisible bubble that surrounds me. I must seize the moment, I must make my escape. Still there is no sign of Bracken. I cannot leave him up here in such weather, alone, distracted by hunting. If only I could call him to me. My whistle! My heart races as I fumble beneath my clothes and pull out the lovespoon. The wood is warm from being next my skin. I put my numb lips to it and try to blow, but can muster nothing by way of sound. I try again, and it emits a damp splutter. Again—this time it works, a shrill noise cutting through the miasma and reaching far beyond what is visible. There is no response. I blow into the wooden

mouthpiece once more. For a moment, nothing, and now, bowl-
ing into view, comes the snow-covered dog, his fur wet with icy
water, his tongue hanging low as he pants and grins at me. I
crouch down, holding his head still, making him look into my
eyes. In my head I clearly picture home. Home and Cai. *Home,
Bracken,* I tell him in my mind, willing the silent words to reach
him. *Home.*

I let him go, and he turns and bounds away through the
snowstorm. I hasten to follow, trusting he will lead me back to
the farm, turning my back and my mind on Isolda's phantoms.

Our descent is speedy if clumsy, and the snowfall does not let
up for one minute, so that by the time I trudge through the back
door and into the house I am sweating from the effort and
coated with snow. The house is eerily quiet. Not bothering to
remove my boots I hurry into the kitchen. Cai is in his chair by
the range, stirring as I enter. He wakes and sees me, shocked by
the state I am in.

"Morgana? *Duw, cariad,* look at you! You are near turned to a
snowman." He struggles awkwardly to his feet. "Come and sit
by the fire. Mrs. Jones will fetch you some broth. Mrs. Jones!" he
calls. There is no answer. "Where can she be?" he wonders aloud,
rubbing his eyes. "I am still groggy with that laudanum. Powerful
stuff, mind. I recall now, as I was drifting off, she spoke of seeing
to the laundry. She would have gone outside to fetch water." He
looks at me seriously now, suddenly fully awake. "You must surely
have seen her as you came in," says he.

But I did not. I dash from the room, flinging open the back
door, all but tripping over a confused corgi in my haste. The
fresh fall of snow is fast masking all traces of feet, paws, and
hooves, but I can faintly discern stout boot marks leading toward
the spring. I hurry to the low wall, still searching the ground for
footprints coming away from the water again, but I can find
none. A lurching sickness stirs in the depths of my stomach.
With mounting dread, I force myself to peer into the pool. The
thick, broken chunks of ice set adrift by the lump hammer have

been fused together once more by a thin, glasslike sheet of frozen water, which has, in turn, been covered by a fluffy layer of snow. I reach down and wipe the sugary coating from the surface. Gazing up at me are the kind, gentle eyes of Mrs. Jones as she lies submerged and drowned in the dark, still waters of the pool.

Cai emerges from the house into the yard just in time to see Morgana plunge, fully clothed, into the spring water.

"Morgana! *Duw,* what are you doing?" He staggers over to the well, the ponies, alarmed by the tone of his voice and the unusual activity, shy away, driven from their hay to stand and snort at the far end of the yard. Bracken leaps up at the wall of the pool, barking frantically. Cai reaches the well and grabs hold of Morgana, who is half submerged and thrashing about in the ice and snow and deathly cold water. Now he is able to see what has driven her to such action. Now he can see she has Mrs. Jones in her arms and is battling to pull her out.

"Oh, dear Lord!" He grabs at the old woman's arm and hauls her to the wall. Morgana pushes, and together they heave the sodden, lifeless body from the water, and over the low stones, so that it slithers onto the snow-gripped ground. Morgana falls to her knees beside the corpse, tears streaming. Cai's heart constricts at the sight of her suffering yet more loss. "She must have fallen in trying to fill the pail," he says, indicating the bucket sitting half covered in snow nearby. He shakes his head. "She shouldn't have come out here alone in this terrible weather. She should have asked me to help her." He realizes how little able he would be to help anyone in his current state. He is wheezing already from the effort of recovering her body, and his limbs are shaking. "I could have come with her, at least," he says, his own eyes stinging with tears. He sniffs, wiping his face with his wet sleeve, clambering to his feet. "We must move her. Find her somewhere to lie." He hesitates. The roads are impassable and may remain so for some time to come. They will have to keep her somewhere outside the house so that the cold preserves her body. He looks about him, forcing himself to be practical, to think only of what must be done, not of how he feels, not of what might have been prevented. "There," he says at last, "we can put her in the end stable. She will be . . . safe, in there." Morgana looks up at him, her face stricken. He helps her to her feet, brushing tears from her reddened cheeks. "We must move her, *cariad*. I need you to help me. Are you able?"

Morgana nods. She is bending down to take hold of Mrs. Jones once more when she notices something clutched in the old woman's cold, plump hand. She touches the unyielding fingers, gently prizing them open, to reveal a flat square of slate.

"What is it?" Cai asks. "What have you got there?" She passes it to him, and he studies it, brushing wet mud and dead algae from it until he is able to see that there are symbols carved upon its surface. *No,* he thinks, *not symbols, but letters.* "*C . . . T?* No, not *T, J,*" he reads to Morgana. "Look, it has the letters *C J* written on it." He feels his innards churn and a chill not brought about by the weather enter his very bones. "My initials," he says quietly. "Cai Jenkins." His mouth dries. "You know what this is, Morgana?"

She shakes her head, frowning, not able to make sense of anything.

"Don't you remember Mrs. Jones telling us Ffynnon Las has a cursing well? She believed in such things, see? I used to laugh at her, to scoff . . . but she was adamant there was truth in the legend." He rubs his thumb over the dull letters on the slate in his hand. "Seems someone else believed in it, too. This is a cursing stone, Morgana. Someone has used this stone, has used my own well, to put a curse on me."

Morgana takes the cold slab from him and stares at it.

"But who?" Cai asks her. "Who would put it there? Who would want me dead? Who would be capable of doing such a thing?"

Morgana looks him straight in the eye, raising her palm in a gesture that tells him he knows, that the answer is plain.

"Mrs. Jones wouldn't have put it there herself!" he gasps.

Morgana shakes her head, rolling her eyes in exasperation. She holds her hand up, suggesting someone taller, then makes a shape describing someone thinner. She leans down and uses her finger to write a ragged letter in the snow. The letter *I*. To underline her point she frowns darkly and spits at what she has written. Now he understands.

"Isolda? You think Isolda did this?" He is incredulous, but Morgana is nodding emphatically, her face imploring him to believe, to accept what she knows to be true. "I know you hate her. And lately I have seen that she dislikes you also. And Mrs. Jones, well, she never cared for her." Now he recalls their earlier conversation, when his housekeeper had tried to tell him, tried to warn him how deep the loathing between the two women was. He hadn't wanted to listen, hadn't been able to take it in. Why hadn't she simply come right out with it? Come right out and said *Isolda is a witch*? Had she seen how frail he was? Had she realized that his fragile hold on what he knew to be real and true was slipping? It had not been easy for him, after all, coming to terms with Morgana's gifts. With what she was. Would he have been pushed into some dark, unstable place to think Isolda Bowen, pillar of the community, his friend for years, was also . . . a witch? Now it all makes sense. Now he understands. And, looking at Morgana's grief-stricken face he understands something more. Mrs. Jones hadn't told him the whole truth because she had been afraid of what he might do. Of what he might *try* to do. He was so angry after what happened to Morgana in Tregaron that day. If his housekeeper had named Isolda as the source of all that hatred he would have walked out into the snow, then and there, to find her, to confront her. And the fact was he was too weak to even saddle his own horse. He would have tried to protect Morgana, and the doing of it might well have killed him.

"Isolda," he says again, almost under his breath.

Morgana grinds her teeth and hurls the cursing stone against the wall of the stable, where it shatters, the slivers piercing the snow as they fall. Cai looks at her. For a moment neither of them is capable of moving, as they process what has happened; what has just been lost, and what has just been found. The snow still pelts, swirling, heavily about them. Cai comes to his senses first, registering that he is outside in his shirtsleeves, and that Morgana is wet to the skin.

"Come," he says. "Let us put her to rest." Together they wrestle with Mrs. Jones's unhelpfully heavy body. They cannot lift her, so are forced to drag her, sliding her over the snow to the stable door, and then haul her inside over the cobbles. Cai fetches some hay and they lay her gently down. Morgana carefully closes the housekeeper's eyes, and Cai takes two pennies from his pockets to prevent the lids springing open. He folds his dear friend's hands across her chest and straightens her skirts so that she might look decent and composed, as she would have wished. He finds that by the time he stands up again he is kitten-weak and shivering. He takes Morgana's hand.

"We can leave her now, *cariad,*" he says. "We must go inside. We must get warm, Morgana." She looks at him now and, seeing how badly he is faring, nods quickly, and follows him back into the house.

In the kitchen the fire is still burning in the hearth but the coals give out insufficient heat to combat the intense cold Cai has begun to feel. Morgana has turned horribly pale and her teeth chatter.

"You are soaked through," Cai says. "Here, take off your wet clothes. Stand by the fire." He drags himself upstairs to fetch her nightclothes and warm towels and blankets. On his return he finds she has removed her coat and boots but nothing more, merely standing, her whole body convulsing with the shock of the cold, and the shock of the awful discovery of Mrs. Jones in the well. She looks dreadfully chilled, not just white-faced, but somehow faded, as if he is watching the life freeze within her. He has seen a man die of cold once, when he was a young boy. He had gone on the mountain with his father and an uncle to gather the herd and icy weather had caught them out. In their haste to descend his uncle's horse had slipped and thrown him, leaving him with a badly broken leg. Cai had been left with the injured man whilst his father rode for help. The cold had helped staunch the flow of blood from the wound, but then it had gone on stopping his blood until it stopped his heart, too. Cai had spent three long hours on the hill with his uncle's corpse, and the pallor and bloodless appearance he had been forced to watch for all that time he recognizes now in his poor, young wife. He must bring warmth back to her body, and he must do it quickly if he is to save her. He snatches up a small chair and dashes it against the flagstones, using all that is left of his strength. It splits and splinters, so that he is able to pull it apart and pile the wood onto the fire. There is a moment's smoldering and spitting and then the dry waxed pine bursts into flame, giving out an instant, ferocious heat. Cai undresses Morgana as quickly as he can, taking off his own soaking shirt, too. He takes towels and rubs her body vigorously, until at last he begins to see some life return to her eyes, some color revisit her face.

"That's better, *cariad*. Soon have you warm, see?" he tells her, keeping his voice level, not wanting to let his own fear for her show through. "Too cold for a dip in the pool today, my wild one." She wriggles into his arms, snuggling against him, so that he leaves off drying her and pulls a warm plaid blanket around them instead. "There now, that's better, isn't it?" He kisses her wet hair, breathing in the smell of her as the fire begins to make them both steam, chasing away the water and snow from the pile of clothes at their feet, and from their own damp bodies. Her soft flesh feels wonderfully smooth and marvelously alive with her inner heat and energy as he holds her close. He kisses her face now, her forehead, her nose, her cheeks, her chin, and then her mouth, long and slow. He gazes into her dark eyes.

"All will be well now, *cariad*," he tells her. "I know, I know, my heart is breaking for dear Mrs. Jones, too. She was a good woman. A kind, gentle soul. We will both miss her sorely." He shakes his head. "You know, I think she went looking for that cursing stone. She must have got the idea into her head that someone had put it there, that that was what is wrong with me. And now, thanks to her, thanks to you, it is over. The curse is gone." Seeing she is unconvinced, he manages a grin. "I feel better already. Truly, I do." It is the first time he has ever lied to her, and it hurts him to do so, but at this moment his concern is that she recover, that she be herself again, that he is able to do anything he can to help her get over what has happened, and to reassure her about the future.

He kisses her once more and feels her nipples harden against his chest. He knows it is no longer the cold that is affecting her body. Morgana nuzzles close to kiss his throat, her lips cool against his hot flesh. Soon he is aware of his own state of arousal, of his own desire. A part of him is appalled that he should be capable of lustful thoughts when a good friend has just lost her life. But it is as if the proximity of death serves as a reminder of his own mortality and drives his desire. As if the only way to triumph over the terror of human frailty, of the fragility of life, is to engage in an act of procreation, an act of passion and of vigor.

He turns, swinging Morgana round, laying her down on the long table, pushing candlesticks and mugs away, not caring that they fall clattering to the floor. She pulls him down on top of her, eager for him, wrapping her naked legs about his body, responding to his need with her own, every bit as ardent, every bit as hungry. As he enters her he feels more powerful, more alive, than he has done in many long, dark weeks. She clings to him, her mouth against his ear, and he listens to her ragged breathing, to her gasps that are so nearly words, so nearly speech. But then, he thinks, they have no need of talking now, not when they are like this. They are as one being, linked physically, emotionally, in every way that matters.

"My love," he whispers. "My love."

His pleasure is startlingly intense, more so than any he has known. Morgana arches her back, throwing back her head, exposing her slender, white neck, moving with him, as fervent and passionate as he is, so that he soon calls out her name, losing himself completely in the moment.

Later, Morgana lies on cushions, wrapped in blankets on the settle, and Cai sits opposite in his chair, unable to take his eyes from her.

"You are very beautiful, Mrs. Ffynnon Las," he tells her.

She gives a small, sad smile, and he knows she is allowing herself to think of Mrs. Jones now, and to begin grieving. How he wishes there were more he could do to ease her distress. At least now that the curse is lifted, he can start to get better, to be strong again, to be whole, to work the farm, and to look after Morgana. The thought has no sooner formed in his head than he suffers a terrible, searing pain in his stomach. It is so fierce and so unexpected that he is unable to prevent himself crying out.

"Argh! Dear Lord!" he screams, falling from his chair onto the floor, clutching at his stomach, his legs drawn up against the agony. "What can it be?" he yells as Morgana throws off her blankets and drops to his side. "Will I never again be well? Is there to be no end to this suffering?" He screams now, a terrible, despairing sound that frightens even him. Morgana helps him back into his chair. She dashes off to fetch the laudanum from the dresser and holds out the bottle to him. He shakes his head. "No! It will make me stupid. I will not lie here senseless while you sit alone!"

But Morgana insists, removing the stopper from the bottle and holding it to his mouth, tipping it so that he might take one large swallow of the bitter liquid. She lets his head fall back against the chair, puts down the bottle, and observes him closely. Soon his breathing steadies.

"That is better," he says. "Be at ease, *cariad*. The pain has passed. I am better."

He meets her gaze and wishes he had not, for the look on her face clearly asks *but for how long?* The unspoken thought hovers in the air between them. *Why is the curse not lifted?* He tries to find words to comfort her, to reassure himself, but he is too dazed from the pain, too weary. His mind becomes dull, a blackness descends, and he falls giddily into a deep, dreamless sleep.

I watch until I am certain Cai will not stir. My body is recovered from the cold, but a chill grips me still when I think of poor dear Mrs. Jones lying cold and lifeless in the stable. How can I have let this happen? How could I have been so slow, so blunt in my wits, not to see that she was in as great a danger as both Cai and me? She must have considered the possibility of Isolda having placed a cursing stone in the well and gone to look for it, knowing that to do so would be risking the witch's wrath. Why did she not wait for me? And now the stone is removed, but Cai suffers still. The curse is not lifted. I cannot say I am surprised, for I have long known that the creature will not stop until one of us is dead. And between now and then she means to kill everyone I have ever loved.

It will not do. Really, it will not.

Cai surfaces from the depths of his drugged slumber to find Morgana in the chair opposite him. He is a little alarmed to see that, though she is apparently asleep, her eyes are open. Her hands are clasped in her lap and she looks serenely composed and still. There is a quality to her stillness that is odd, that unnerves him. He rubs his eyes, shaking his head in an attempt to clear it. He pulls himself from his chair with some difficulty and kneels in front of her.

"Morgana?" He speaks her name softly, but she does not smile, nor move her head, nor nod, nor in any way respond. He leans forward and slowly waves his hand in front of her eyes. They are open, but do not flicker. It is, he decides, as if she has entered some sort of trance. At her feet, Bracken sits up, intently watching his mistress, occasionally whimpering. Cai thinks to shake her gently to rouse her from this unnatural state, but he recalls that a person found walking in their sleep should never be disturbed. Merely watched over. Instinctively, he knows that this is not some random condition, not some ailment which has visited his wife. Rather it is a state she has entered willingly, consciously. For what purpose, to what end, he cannot begin to guess. He sits back in his chair, fatigue, sadness, and worry working with the opium to render him exhausted. He must trust her. Her ways may sometimes be strange, but they are *her* ways. He will watch over her, and wait for her to come back to him.

After half an hour he is having difficulty keeping his eyes open. Darkness has almost fallen, and cold air is coming through the glass of the windows. With some awkwardness, and pain in his joints, he gets to his feet and goes to close the shutters. As he does so he glimpses something odd in the gathering dusk outside. The moon is bright, the sky clear of snow now. A moaning wind winds its way around the house. Trees are pulled and buffeted by it, so that they appear engaged in a mournful moonlit dance. But all this is as it should be, after a snowstorm, the clouds spent, the weather grimly inhaling before the next onslaught. What is strange, what is out of kilter, is the flickering of torches on the road. He peers through the icy glass, frowning to focus. Sure enough, he can just make out shadowy figures proceeding down the drive, spluttering torches and lamps held aloft. He is at a loss. There must be a dozen people marching, with purpose and determination, toward the house. By their gait and size he discerns they are all men. Then he sees them, clearly defined in the blue-grey twilight. He sees that more than half the men are carrying guns. Now he recalls how the people of the town treated Morgana when last she went there. He remembers the stones thrown and the cut on her cheek. He brings to mind what Mrs. Jones said about people fearing his wife, and how frightened people can do terrible things. And he recalls, with a shudder that shakes his entire body, that they consider her to be a witch. Only now can he admit to himself he has been fearing this moment all along. That he has been expecting it. As the figures draw nearer there can be no doubt: They have come for Morgana.

Muttering an oath he slams the shutters closed, dropping the metal bar into place. He hastens to the back door to bar it. The front door is securely shut, having not been opened for weeks. He staggers into the parlor, his breathing ragged, his vision woozy, and fastens the shutters there, too. Back in the kitchen he pauses to look one more time at Morgana. She has not moved the smallest bit, but still sits upright and composed, her eyes open, her soul he knows not where. He kisses her brow tenderly before turning to Bracken.

"Stay, *bachgen*. Guard your mistress well," he tells him before reaching down his gun from its hooks on the beam above the dresser. He fumbles in the drawer for shot, loads the gun, takes as much ammunition as he possesses, and lurches from the room, dragging himself up the stairs and into the front bedroom, where he takes up his position at the window to watch and to wait.

"Let them come," he says under his breath. "Let them come. They'll not touch her. Not while I live."

19.

Although my senses are heightened as I witchwalk, I am impervious to the cold, which is a blessing. With ease I am able to leave my body in Cai's tender care and will myself to the broad, imposing front door of the home of Isolda Bowen. Glancing around I see that the town square is deserted. The night is clear now, the moon a shining disc in a velvet sky. Crisp snow lies thick beneath my weightless feet, but I make no sound as I step forward, and leave no footprints to give away my presence. I am shielded by the cloak of magic which means that in my current, ethereal state, none but another such as I can see me. I pass through the front door and enter the forbidding house.

How perfectly Isolda inhabits the role of well-to-do widow. How completely she fools all who meet her. Even Cai, with his generous, trusting heart. And look how she has repaid that trust! She will kill him if I do not prevent her doing so, I am certain of that now. Just as I am certain that removing the cursing stone from the well has not, for whatever reason, lifted the curse upon Cai. There is no alternative but that I face her. Now. Here. I am prepared. I have consulted the *Grimoire* and asked for the assistance of the Witches of the Well. I am ready at last to stand face to face with the awful creature who would take away from me the one person left in this world whom I love. Who loves me. My magic is my only weapon, the support of my sister Well Witches my protection, and my love for Cai my spur.

The house is quiet, though I can hear muffled voices. These are coming from the rooms at the rear of the house, most likely the kitchen. I assume it is the servants chatting, for I cannot dis-

cern Isolda's voice. I move to the bottom of the sweeping staircase. The newels are delicately carved acorns, with twisting oak
leaves working up the banisters. Small wooden mice decorate
the balustrades. All is given the appearance of gentleness, of
a oneness with nature. Of goodness and Godliness. How false.
What lies! I make my way to the unremarkable door in the corner of the hallway. There is light flickering from beneath the
door. I am drawn to it. I know, without seeing it, that Isolda's
stronghold, the place where she is most powerful, where she will
least expect me to confront her, lies beyond this threshold. I sniff
the air, and can clearly detect her familiar stench. I glide over
the smooth floor tiles and through the locked door. On the
other side there is a narrow passageway and a flight of stairs leading down into shadowy gloom. Gloom which is interrupted by
guttering light, as if there are candles below, rather than lamps. I
descend, and as I do so fear worms its way into my phantom being and accompanies me, a cold, slithering companion, on my
journey into the unknown. The farther I go, the more oppres-
sive my surroundings become. My every instinct bids me turn
around, bids me flee, but I must not. I cannot. Cai's life depends
on me, and on what happens here in this awful place tonight.
I will not fail my only love.

When I at last reach the bottom of the long flight of stairs
a further passageway twists ahead, lit not by candles, but by
torches fixed to the wet stone walls. Far off I hear the sound of
dripping water. A rat scampers past making me start. The ceiling
is horribly low and seems to press in upon me as I proceed. I
venture onward for some distance before reaching another door.
This one, too, is locked, and I am grateful for the lack of substance
which allows me to pass through it without difficulty. On the
other side is a room the like of which I have never seen before.
The ceiling here is high, vaulted stone arching above my head.
There are many torches, I count six or seven at a glance, giving
a garish light that casts jumping, jittery shadows against the blue-
grey stone of the wall. There is scant decoration or furnishings,

except for four enormous tapestries which hang from the walls, large enough to reach from ceiling to floor. They depict scenes of such bawdiness and lewdness I cannot imagine what women might have stitched such images. And there is no natural light, nor air from anything which could be called a window, aside from small gaps in the stonework high up, barred with iron. At the far end of this cavernous space there is some manner of altar, with a wide table mounted on a dais. The table is no more than a slab of stone, upon which are black iron candlesticks and curious items unfamiliar to me. One is a dagger of some sort. Another a stout cooking pot. The room feels as if it is from another time, an age long ago. There is something threatening about the strangeness of the place, and about the way it is hidden here, deep in the earth, shut away from the light and from the world. As I step forward I see that there is a shape inscribed upon the dark flagstones of the floor. It is a star, I think, with five points, drawn to take up the entire space, its points touching the walls at each side.

With a suddenness that makes my heart leap beneath my breast, Isolda appears, stepping forward from the shadows behind the altar.

"Morgana," says she, her voice syrupy, "how good of you to come and visit me. And how clever of you to find my special place. But then, you are a clever little witch-girl, are you not? Perhaps I should count myself fortunate that you are not able to speak, for who knows what tales you would tell, and to whom."

I stand straight and still. I will not let her intimidate me. There can be no running away this time.

Isolda begins to walk around the room and I instinctively circle away from her. I find myself oddly drawn to the center, as if the heart of the curiously shaped star were exerting a force upon me, like that of a whirlpool in a stream sucking at a floating leaf, though with immeasurably greater strength.

"Do you like my pentacle, Morgana? It is precious to me. A place of magic. A site consecrated a very long time ago by one of my forebears. Oh, yes. I came new to Tregaron not many years before Cai fetched you into his life, but my ancestors had been here before. I was merely returning to my birthright. Or at least, *part* of my birthright. For there is somewhere else, somewhere sacred to me and my kind. Somewhere that will soon be mine. The good people of this town love to recount the legend of the well at Ffynnon Las. They think it a diverting tale. A story to scare small children or send an exquisite shiver down the spine on a winter's night. They do not know the truth of it. They little know how powerful, how magical the place is. Nor are they any of them aware of the fact that I am the descendant of the very witch of whom they speak. Such stupid creatures. So easily spell-bound. And soon my hold over them will be complete." Her eyes are blazing now, alight with anger and with a mad desire to have what she wants. "The well is mine. It is my right to claim it! And with it the *Grimoire*."

She notices my expression harden and now she knows that I have seen the book. She knows that I am aware of its power.

"So, that stout little housekeeper revealed it to you, did she? I wonder the pair of you were not burned up by its force. It is not a plaything. It's enchantments are not meant for a silly witch-girl and a herb-boiling hedge witch. If you have seen inside it you know this. You know why I want it. It belongs to the mistress of Ffynnon Las, which, by the end of this winter, I shall be."

I cannot help but look at the lines on the floor beneath me; they are mesmerizing. And as I look the shape begins to rotate, faster and faster. Isolda's noxious odor fills my nostrils, making my stomach heave. Dizziness overcomes me, so that I stumble forward onto my hands and knees. The second I am contained within the angles of the drawing I know that I am trapped. Even though I am present only in my spirit form, it is as if I were solid and corporeal and heavy as lead. I am tethered to the floor by a hundred unseen chains. Fettered at ankles and wrists by invisible iron. I am ensnared. And, like a rabbit in a hunter's snare, the more I struggle against my bonds the tighter they grip me. I fight fiercely against my bonds, turning this way and that, twisting and wrenching at the unseen ties. But to no avail.

Isolda is smiling, a slow, slippery smile. Her face has become more angular, her eyes deeper set, the hollows and shadows more pronounced, so that there is little left in her countenance that can be called beautiful.

"How long can you remain here thus, I wonder. How long before you are unable to make the journey back to your sweet young body? Where have you left it? In Cai's care, I assume. How many hours, how many days, will he watch over you before he accepts he is merely witness to the rotting of a corpse?"

I try to summon my will, to fight back, to exert my own magic in any way that might break the hold of hers. But her sorcery is so strong, so ancient, and so practiced, that it requires a draining effort for me simply to keep my eyes open, so that all I accomplish is the noisy slamming of the door.

Isolda laughs. "What do you plan to do, Mrs. Jenkins? Startle me to death?"

Darkness begins to close in upon me, as if my vision is shrinking. Soon I am immersed in blackness. My strength is fading now, I can feel it leaving me. The dark is comforting, soothing almost. I cannot hear anything now, so that I am left floating, senseless, in this velvety nothingness. How easy it would be to give in, to accept defeat, to allow myself to be swallowed up by this endless night. What hope do I have of defeating Isolda? She is far more powerful than I. If I am a witch, then she is one of an entirely different origin. A different force drives her. A force imbued with all the sinister menace and strength of the devil. How can I match such strength? Such ruthlessness? Should I let her finish me? Perhaps, if I were not in her way, she would relent and allow Cai to live, reverting to her original plan to marry him. She cannot know he has discovered the cursing stone. She does not know that he believes her to be the cause of his illness. But then, if I were dead, and because Cai does know these things, he would resist her. And then she would kill him to get her precious well. And the *Grimoire*. I recall the broken man that the reverend became under her spell. I see the frozen, dead face of Mrs. Jones drift before my eyes. Isolda would be unstoppable should she harness the strength of the magic book. Why would she bother herself with Cai? She would destroy him just as she is set on destroying me. For she knows that only the owner of the well can wield its full power. Others might have use of it in some way, by permission or by slight, but she will settle for nothing less than total control. And what havoc she could wreak then!

I feel so very weak and, oh, so very weary.

Now I hear something. And a pale shape takes form before my eyes. At first it is hard to make out, but now I can see it is a figure. A man. I listen hard and recognize the voice that was once dearest to me in all the world.

Dada!

"Morgana," says he, softly, his features gentle, his smile warming my heart.

Dada! To have found him, at last! After all these years of searching and waiting and hoping. He comes to stand beside me and helps me to my feet. Even though we have no substance, have no tangible forms, I feel his touch, feel his hand upon my cheek as if I were a child once more.

"My little girl. What a fine young woman you have grown to be." His smile turns to a frown. "I can't abide to see you suffering so, child."

I shake my head, for I feel no fear, no pain, no anguish, now that I am in his presence. I let him embrace me, and am enveloped in such peace, such tranquility, I never want to leave the protection and comfort of his arms.

"You are safe now, Morgana," he tells me. "No more struggle. You are safe here with me."

Oh, how I long to stay with him! To follow him wherever it is he will lead me, knowing that as long as I am with him no harm can come to me. But I cannot stay. I force myself to pull away and look up into his dear face. Again I shake my head, but this time my meaning is different. Already he can sense I am drawing away from him.

No, Dada. I cannot stay.

"Do not go back, *cariad*. Come with me, child."

I move away, withdrawing from him, feeling as if my heart is being torn in two. It would be so easy to stay, to remain with him, the father I have missed so very much all these long years. The father who understands me better than I understand myself. But I cannot. There is someone who needs me. Cai's very survival depends on me, and I will not abandon him. My place, now, is at *his* side.

I must turn back, Dada. I have to go back.

Seeing the torment written plainly on my face he smiles faintly and nods.

"I am proud of you, daughter. We will be together again, one day, when the time is right. You have the magic blood, Morgana. Use your power. Go back and tread the path that was meant for you, *cariad*."

And so I force myself back, back into consciousness, back into the room, back to Isolda. There is a roaring inside my head now, a terrible sound, as if the side of a mountain is collapsing. And then I am returned, my eyes opened, my vision restored. I stand firm, holding Isolda's gaze. It may be my fancy, but I believe I discern surprise there, or is it, perhaps, a little fear?

"Well, well," says she, "I did not think to see you put up such a fight, witch-girl."

Her voice is steady, but I sense her nervousness now. I can taste it. And yet still she will not release me. Still she thinks to torment me. To have what she wants at any cost.

I must still my whirling mind. I must do what I came to do. I stagger to my feet and shut out her mocking voice. I shut out the pentacle. I shut out the memory of Dada. I shut out everything so that I may concentrate my thoughts, direct them to call, to summon, to plead with the Witches of the Well.

Help me. Come to my aid now. Assist me in my cause to stop this fiendish, wicked creature, who would use you and your wisdom to her own callous, terrible ends.

I repeat the entreaty, over and over, keeping the *Grimoire* clear in my mind's sight, just as Mrs. Jones taught me. I must not fear its power. It is mine to command now.

I am the mistress of Ffynnon Las! Keeper of the Grimoire *and owner of the Blue Well. Come to me now and wash away the darkness that surrounds me!*

For an agonizing moment there is nothing and I fear I have failed. But now, faint at first, but growing stronger, I hear two distinct sounds. The distant chiming of the sweetest bell imaginable, ringing clear and true, slowly building until the chamber is filled with its ringing. Isolda hears it, too, and I see her glance about her. Her nervousness gives me hope.

The second noise heralds a force unleashed that turns her anxiety into naked fear. Water. Water rushing in. Now it comes! Surging down through the passageway, torrential, violent, unstoppable, it pours into the chamber with such speed that in seconds it is up to our knees. I see it, but I do not fear it. For I am stepping in spirit, and need no air to breathe here.

Isolda lets out a cry of rage. She raises her arms and begins chanting in strange tongues, over and over, whirling and spinning as she does so, causing a whirlpool about her, even as the water rises to her thighs. Pressure builds about us. The pressure not of the elements, but of magic fighting against magic.

Suddenly, with such abruptness that it takes me a moment to understand what has happened, the deluge ceases. Not a drop of water moves. I stare down at the blueness which surrounds me and now I understand. I no longer stand in water, but in ice. Isolda has stopped the flood in its progress in an instant, by freezing it.

She laughs at me now, relief and delight lighting up her face. She looks triumphant.

"Is that really all you have to muster? You have the *Grimoire* at your disposal and this is what you make manifest?" She gives a derisive wave of her arm and continues to laugh at me.

It will not do. Really, it will not.

I narrow my attention so that it is entirely in this moment, in this place, and I summon my will. *My* will. I may be unpracticed with the *Grimoire,* but I have the magic inside me. Dada's magic blood. I bring all my thoughts to one point, just as I did when I restored Catrin's china. As I did when I mended Cai's wounded arm. I pull all my strength to me until I feel the air crackle with it. I listen hard. I sniff the damp air of the chamber. With my senses at witchwalking pitch I can easily detect the presence of other beings. There are so many of them, moving and squeaking and squirming in the drains and the narrow culverts and tunnels that run in a labyrinth beneath the houses and streets of the town. I smell their warm, dirty bodies. I hear their teeth gnawing hungrily on whatever they can find. For they are hungry. Very hungry. This sudden winter has quickly brought them to near starvation. From somewhere deep within me I find the strength to overcome my own fears, my own natural repugnance. And I call to them.

Come, little brothers and sisters. Come to me, and I will give you such a feast, such a banquet . . . your bellies will be full tonight and your fur slick with the fresh blood of your kill.

I know Isolda will have heard me, too, but she cannot know what I have planned. Or if she does, she does not consider me capable of making it happen, for she shows no sign that she is afraid, though in truth she has ample reason to be.

Now I shift my thoughts to the wall behind her. It is centuries old, its stones pocked and water worn, its mortar crumbling. I can shift these stones. I know I can. I narrow my eyes and summon my strength, with more determination, with more ferocity, with more anger than I have ever used to summon it before. At first the task seems impossible. I redouble my efforts, yet still there is no discernable effect.

Isolda watches me with a dry smile upon her lips, amused by

my apparently ineffectual struggles. Almost idly she sways this way and that, diminishing the ice that covers the floor of the chamber, so that it begins to recede. Clearly she no longer considers me a threat.

But I am.

The first stone moves barely an inch, accompanied by a small grating noise as it shifts minutely. Isolda hears the sound, but cannot detect its source. I continue. Now a second stone moves. Now another. And another. She sees what I have done and sneers.

"Do you think to bring my own house down upon me, witch-girl? Do you seriously believe yourself capable of such a thing?"

No, I let her read my thoughts, hoping it will buy me a few moments more. *I do not.*

"Ah! Only now you decide to communicate with me. What a shame you did not think to do so sooner. Who knows what arrangement we might have come to, had you shown some spirit of . . . cooperation," says she. But neither of us believe there is any truth in her words. She walks over to one of the holes I have made in the wall, putting her head on one side to examine it.

"Poor Morgana. Such hard work, for you. Why bother? Why not just lie down and sleep. So much nicer, so much more dignified than all this futile struggling."

At last another stone moves, this time from several feet up they wall. It dislodges with such speed and force that it flies from its place and crashes to the floor next to Isolda. Mortar and mud and stone shatter and spread to her feet. In quick succession, four more stones do the same. But the gaps they leave remain empty, nothing more than dark spaces letting in cold air and the occasional trickle of icy water. For a moment I think they have not heard me; that they will not come. I call again.

Come, little ones. Hurry, my hungry friends. Hurry to the feast!

The first grey-brown nose pokes from a hole behind Isolda, so that she does not see it. It drops from its tunnel, its skinny body and hairless tail close to the ground as it begins to circle her. More whiskers appear in the same hole, and then, quickly, myriad snouts and beady eyes begin to emerge from all the spaces I have created, so that within seconds the floor appears alive with rats. They scamper and scuttle as they pour into the chamber, raising their heads to sniff for food, exposing their long yellow teeth as they do so.

At first I think that they ignore me because I am here in spirit only, and therefore do not offer a potential source of sustenance. But I notice that they take care not to put one wet claw over the outline of the pentacle. Indeed, they avoid it as if it were drawn in fire. There are hundreds of them now, and still more stream forth from the gaps between the stones. Isolda curses and stamps her feet to shake off the first few bold ones who have already begun to nip at her toes. One, particularly large, even in its reduced state, with dense black fur, drops directly onto Isolda's shoulder. It clings on as she grasps it by the neck and pulls at it. It is determined, digging its sharp claws into the fabric of her dress, but she wrenches it from her and hurls it across the room with such strength I hear its spine snap. Its corpse falls into the melee of its cousins, who, scenting fresh blood, fall upon it, biting and nipping. It is as if a signal has been given for the frenzy of feeding to begin. Suddenly, as if they were one many-headed beast, the rats surge forward and swarm over Isolda.

She lets out a furious scream, snatching at the rodents as they climb and crawl over her, plucking them from her to fling them this way and that with unnaturally swift and forceful movements. But there are too many, too many for her to fend off, they come at such a rate. Soon she is entirely covered in the squealing, stinking creatures, as they hang from her fingers, from her bodice and skirts, from her hair, burrowing into her clothes, biting and clawing, sensing the feast that is theirs for the taking. And still more rats tumble into the room, so that the flagstones are a writhing mass around me, revealing the shape of the star in which I crouch.

Isolda continues to shriek and rage, flinging her arms, shaking her head, kicking and staggering about, but she is completely covered with pulsating, chattering creatures who hang on with teeth and claws, taking every opportunity to bite and chew. Repulsive noises fill the air—sounds of flesh being torn and blood being slurped. As the smothered figure blunders about the room trails and spurts of blood splatter over more hungry rats which fight for a taste of what their kin have found. I watch in horror at what I have brought about. I am compelled to watch, though I fear it is a vision that will haunt my dreams for the rest of my days.

Just as it seems she will be overcome, will be pulled to the ground, savaged, and devoured by hundreds of hungry mouths, Isolda ceases her flailing and stands motionless, save for the undulation of the living fur coat she wears. She utters a long, low sound that chills my soul. It is neither a cry of pain, nor a scream of rage. It is very clearly a summoning, a calling, an asking. Of whom or of what I fear to fathom, but the temperature in the chamber drops dramatically. The discordant, rising note is sustained for an impossibly long out-breath, strong and unwavering, flat and droning, menacing beyond imagination. Even the rats seem to sense danger in the stillness that follows. Some of them drop from her body and slink away. Others pause in their frenzy. There is a small moment of total calm where all movement, all sound, all life, it seems, is stilled.

And then the beast is unleashed.

The rats still clinging to Isolda, or what *was* Isolda, are flung to the far reaches of the room, smashing against the stone walls. From beneath them emerges a twisting, throbbing shape that grows as it shakes and convulses, ridding itself of its parasitic passengers, contorting and enlarging until it, until *she,* is completely transformed. For it is no longer a woman who stands before me but a green-scaled, monstrous serpent. It raises its colossal head high, its yellow eyes glowing in the torchlight, its forked tongue flicking in and out of its cruel, lipless mouth. It fills the chamber with a deafening hissing, surely loud enough to wake the dead. The terrified rats turn and flee, scrambling over one another in their haste to escape, clawing at the wall to reach the holes through which they entered. But the giant snake strikes with deadly speed, snatching mouthfuls of the panicking creatures, swallowing them in great, wriggling gulps. In a matter of seconds the chamber is cleared, the rats gone, either eaten or fled. Only I remain, my spirit still imprisoned in the pentacle. And the coiling, bulging serpent, which slides silently around the room, never for one second taking its eyes from me.

It is a further shock to hear Isolda's voice coming from this terrible apparition.

"Your actions are tiresome in the extreme, witch-girl," says she as she slips past me.

"You must know you cannot vanquish me. Why persist in delaying the inevitable conclusion? Desist in these pointless attempts upon me. Nothing will come of your efforts. All that is required of you now is that you give in, submit to the inevitable. To the end. To me."

The creature's muscles ripple as it propels itself round and round, gathering speed. For a moment I think she plans to coil herself around me and crush the life from me, but I realize, of course, that in my witchwalking state she cannot harm me physically. All the evil animal strength of her repulsive form is useless against me in my spirit state. She has tried to send me to another place, to weaken me, and to tempt me with my dear father. Was it even truly him I saw? Or was it merely a trick, another spell cast by Isolda to suck me to my death? I will never be certain. What I do know is that, without my body here to destroy, there are few ways she can bring about my end. Indeed, her only option would seem to be to hold me here, captive, until I am stayed too long from my body and have not the strength to return. But how long? How long can I exist a stepping soul, disembodied and wandering? She asked me the question, but I myself do not truly know the answer. I know that I am weakening. That I feel increasingly weary. Increasingly faint. I do not have much time. I must use it wisely.

I sit, drawing my knees up under my chin, wrapping my arms tightly about myself.

You are right. I lay my thoughts clearly in front of her. *I know it now. Forgive me. Have pity.*

"Pity? Ha!" Saliva spits from the snake's jaws as Isolda laughs at my pleading.

I keep my eyes cast down.

I care only for Cai, I tell her. *Please, show mercy. If I . . . die.*

"*When* you die. For die you will."

Please, let him live. I open my eyes and hold the gaze of the lurid creature that bobs its great head before me. *I beg you, let him live.*

I have never before seen a snake laugh, nor heard such a cruel noise as this one makes.

"Beg me! You have caused me no end of trouble, *Mrs. Jenkins.* Were it not for you I could have won round that soft husband of yours. Could have made him mine. Then I would have been the mistress of the Ffynnon Las well, and all the power that goes with it would have been mine. I would have been invincible. I *will* be invincible. But I do not feel inclined to mercy, not now. Why should I? You will be dead very soon, and Cai will join you in a shared grave up at Soar-y-Mynydd chapel, and the farm will be put up for sale and *I* will buy it, naturally. So beg all you like, I am deaf to any request that might further delay my finally obtaining my birthright."

I nod carefully, resigned to my fate.

Very well, says I, *I cannot change what will happen. I will meet my love in the afterlife. We will be together then, and he will suffer no more.*

The snake pauses in its slithering, regarding me closely.

One thing I ask. Let me not leave this life in such terror, with only the company of a creature from hell. Will you not at least return to your womanly form so that my last sight will be of something beautiful, and so that you can meet my gaze as it fades to nothing?

Isolda laughs again and the serpent begins to shimmer and

twitch. I have appealed not to her humanity, nor her charity, but to her vanity, and there I have found her weakness.

With much flexing and twisting and slapping against the stones the snake diminishes and slowly shrinks and reduces until Isolda herself stands before me once more, with scarcely a scratch from the rats to show for her ordeal.

She puts a hand up to her hair, concerned that it should be in place.

I do not stand, but remain, small and still in the very center of the star. I look at Isolda, trying to keep myself from trembling, willing myself to stay awake and alert, even though I feel myself fading.

Won't you step into the light so that I can see you properly? I ask her. *You are in the shadows, so that I cannot see your face.*

With only a small sigh of impatience she walks a short distance to stand between the two large sconces, the flames of the torches lending a warm glow to her handsome features.

"Quickly now, little witch-girl. Drift away and be gone. I am tired of this game," says she, her hands upon her hips, her head on one side, watching me as a crow watches an ailing lamb.

This is my moment, my one last chance. She need only wait and I will die. But she cannot damage my body in here. In that respect I am not vulnerable. But she is.

I suck in a deep, slow breath, filling my lungs until they must surely burst. I summon all the strength of my love for Cai, all the adoration I have carried with me all these years for my father, all the love I felt for my mother, and all the wildness of the mountains. I feel magic fill my soul, feeding it, until I am aglow with it. And then I exhale. A great tumult disturbs the air inside the chamber as if a tempest were raging. My hair flies upward and outward as if billowing in a gale. My clothes are likewise disturbed. The flames on the torches flare and spit, growing in an instant to twice their size. Isolda looks about her, disconcerted. She turns her gaze back on me and with a wave of an arm sends a blow of energy to try to stop me. But I remain unharmed.

Soon the room is filled with a howling, circular wind which chases round and round, faster and faster, growing in strength and ferocity, roaring as it blows, snatching up the heavy tapestries as if they were gossamer, causing them to fly and flap. And as they fly and flap they are licked by the flames of the torches. Within seconds the first one has caught fire. And then the second. And then another. Now all of them are ablaze, the racing air feeding these new, terrible fires until the entire space is a whirling mass of flame.

I hear Isolda shout oaths and curses. She rushes to the door, pulling at the handle, but I have shut it, and shut it will remain.

"No!" she screams. "No!" She runs about the room, pointlessly, for there is no other exit. Unlike me, she is here in body as well as soul. And whereas a spirit may wander at will through walls or doors, a body may not. Whereas a soul might remove itself to a place of safety without the use of stairs, a body may not. A soul will withstand the intense heat of the fire and emerge unscathed. A body will not.

Soon Isolda's screams have turned to shrieks. I listen not with horror, nor with triumph, but with a calm acceptance, with a knowledge that I have done what I can and that Cai will be safe. And now, as the furnace engulfs every part of this stone tomb, I wait.

※

It is properly dark by the time Cai opens the upstairs window and rests his gun on the sill. Below, the men have reached the front garden. Under the bright moon Cai recognizes familiar faces: Edwyn Nails, Llewellyn, the Reverend Cadwaladr, and many more. Some have guns, others axes. One carries a coil of rope. Cadwaladr steps forward and hammers on the barred front door.

"Jenkins!" he bellows. "Cai Jenkins, open this door!"

Cai shifts his position carefully. Even resting the barrel of the gun as he is, it feels almost unmanageably heavy. He has always been a fair shot, but now, feeling so weak, his body wracked with pains, he wonders if he will be capable of so much as lifting the gun to fire straight.

"You cannot come in, Reverend," he calls down, causing the mob to turn their gazes up to him.

Edwyn shakes his fist. "We're come for Morgana, Jenkins," he shouts, his face twisted with hatred. "Send her out!"

"This is my home." Cai keeps his voice as level as he can and fights back a gasp as pain grips his chest. "Leave us be!"

Reverend Cadwaladr calls up to him, "You are bewitched, Mr. Jenkins. Bewitched by that creature."

"She is not a creature, Reverend. She is my wife. A good woman."

"She is wicked!" yells an old man from the back of the crowd. "She has brought death to our town."

"That is not true." Cai shakes his head, appalled at how easily they are prepared to believe terrible things of Morgana.

Llewellyn steps forward. "People are dying because of her. She has turned the land to ice! She will have us all dead."

"No, you're wrong."

"'Twas she brought the terrible sickness to us," cries another.

"Not she!" Cai insists. "If it's wickedness you're looking for try that fine house on the square. Look more closely at Isolda Bowen."

"What?" Cadwaladr is incredulous. "What nonsense is this? Mrs. Bowen is a respectable, God-fearing woman."

"You are wrong about her, just as you are wrong about Morgana," Cai tells them.

Edwyn won't be put off.

"We mean to take her, Jenkins. You'd best open this door. You're sick, m'n. She's made you sick."

"I'm not so enfeebled as I can't protect my own wife. I'm warning you, stay back!" He raises his gun.

Llewellyn laughs at him, daring him. "You can't fight all of us, Ffynnon Las."

In reply Cai fires his gun, the blast hitting the snow-covered ground close to the rear of the crowd. The sound is cacophonous, bouncing off the frozen landscape and echoing on and on down the valley. Men leap and scatter in all directions, flinging themselves out of range.

"You'll have to kill me before I let you take her," Cai shouts down at them. "Are you prepared to do that? Are you, Reverend? She's done nothing wrong, I tell you."

The men clamber cautiously to their feet but keep their distance. The reverend puts up his hands, half a gesture of surrender, half of prayer.

"We mean you no harm, Cai Jenkins. We will leave you now, so that you may have time to consider. We will return for her. We must return." For once the stout man's voice falters and breaks. "God will not allow such wickedness to thrive. He is punishing us all, Jenkins. My own darling daughters . . . !" He cannot finish the sentence.

Cai sees the man's despair and shakes his head sadly. "I am sorry to hear your family is suffering, Reverend, truly. If you wish to save them turn out Isolda Bowen. Do what you must to that wretched woman, and maybe God will look favorably on your actions. But he will not thank you for persecuting an innocent person such as my wife."

There is much muttering and shuffling of feet. Fists are waved and oaths sworn, before the mob reluctantly turns and heads back toward Tregaron. Cai waits at the window, watching them go, wanting to be certain they will not change their minds and turn back once more.

He is startled by the sound of frantic barking coming from the kitchen. Bracken, who had kept quiet throughout all the noise and excitement outside, is sounding the alarm. Grabbing his gun, Cai staggers from the room, all but falling down the stairs. He bursts through the door to the kitchen to find Morgana fallen from the settle onto the hard stone floor.

"Morgana!" He drops to his knees beside her. Bracken leaps and whines and barks, clearly aware that his mistress is in trouble.

Cai takes her in his arms. Her eyes are open yet she appears blind to his presence, as if she is still in some far-off place, witnessing something terrible. She begins to struggle violently. She writhes and flails with such force he has difficulty holding her.

"Morgana, *cariad,* stop," he begs her. "Please, my love, please."

At last she gasps, her body stiffens, and her arms stop beating at the ground. He looks into her eyes and sees recognition flicker there. And terror, her pupils wide, her mouth opening and shutting in silent horror at some unseen calamity. Her gaze fixes on the fire in the hearth and she scrambles backward, fighting to get away from the flames.

"Hush now, *cariad.* You're safe here, safe with me," he tells her, pulling her close, holding her gently and rocking her to and fro.

Now her limbs relax and she allows him to help her up and back onto the settle. He takes her hands in his, kneeling on the rug before her.

"Where have you been, my wild one? How I wish you could tell me."

She leans forward so that her brow is touching his and he feels how utterly exhausted she is. Even so she squeezes his hands tightly and then pulls back so that he might see her expression. He is surprised to find she looks . . . *happy.*

"Where would you go?" he asks himself as much as her. "I was ill, and you went somewhere to try and help me. To try and find a cure? No, that's not it. To stop someone hurting me! Of course. Isolda. Did you go to find Isolda?"

Morgana nods calmly.

"Such a brave girl you are. Did she hurt you, *cariad*?"

She looks frightened for a moment and hesitates before shaking her head very slowly.

"What happened? Oh, dear God, Morgana. You must tell me. Is she coming here?"

She shakes her head again.

"You stopped her? You made her stop?"

She nods, meeting his eye with a look of such seriousness that it scares him.

"*Duw,* Morgana, did you . . ." He cannot bring himself to speak what is in his head. "Is she . . . is she dead, Morgana? Is Isolda dead?"

She nods, her eyes filling with tears. She nods and flings herself into his arms, sobbing, clinging to him as if she will never be able to bear to let him go, so that Cai can only wonder at what she must have been through. But Isolda is dead. However it was done, it is done, and they are free of her at last!

Cai kisses Morgana's hair, allowing himself to all but collapse against her as he holds her, his body weak with relief.

"Hush now, *cariad,*" he tells her. "All will be well, my wild one. Hush now. All will be well."

But all is not well. A day and a night have passed since we found and destroyed the cursing stone, and since I watched Isolda burn, and yet Cai continues to ail. At least the townspeople have not returned, and for that we are thankful. Perhaps, without Mrs. Bowen to incite them, they will not pursue me further. Surely, if she was responsible for the sickness in the town it will now abate. I dare not venture to Tregaron to discover what is happening. All I know to be true is that Cai continues to suffer. To suffer and to weaken, so that I fear for him still. We are both at a loss to understand this. Why is the curse not lifted? Can it continue, even after Isolda's death? Am I to lose him, then? After all that has happened, after all we have endured, am I to lose him? He will eat no breakfast, but drink only thin broth. I leave him dozing by the hearth and go upstairs to fetch the brandy from our bedside. As I reach the landing I am assailed, once again, by the chill, menacing presence that lingers there. Catrin? But why? Why would she project such ire, such anger, such dark emotions toward me? Can she not see that I love Cai? That I wish only what is best for him? That I am striving, in every way I can, to help him? And now, just as my mind is aching from confusion and from strain, it is another of my senses that alerts me to the source of the phantom entity. I smell sulphur. Isolda—*still*! Or at least, Isolda's evil. There must be another curse, then. Yes, that might be it. She has hidden some talisman or corn dolly in the house. Somewhere near. Where? Where would she place such a thing for it to have the greatest effect? I steel myself, for I know where I must go. Catrin's bedroom. The room she shared with Cai when he was her husband. The room where she died. I force myself to throw open the door and stride in. But there is no presence here. I touch the unused coverlet on the bed. I wander about the clean, pretty room. I open the wardrobe and even gaze into the mirror. Nothing. There is nothing here to harm anyone. The presence at the top of the stairs, Isolda's presence, not Catrin's, cannot, it seems, penetrate further. And yet, *it is still there*! What must I do to be rid of the woman's evil influence? She used the well to curse Cai, knowing the power it had, but I smashed the cursing stone myself. I saw it break into smithereens. Surely it cannot hold sway any longer? The stone has been removed from the magic water. The object destroyed. But the spell is not broken. Indeed, it has not let up at all. It is as if it still lies in the pool, still working its wickedness, undisturbed. The thought strikes me like a blow to the head. Perhaps it is still in the pool! What if the stone we removed was not the only one?

I turn on my heel and run down the stairs. Bracken, sensing the urgency in my footsteps, dashes out of the kitchen and follows me as I slam out of the back door. Behind me I hear Cai calling my name having been woken by my noisy exit.

The gusting wind that has blown ceaselessly since yesterday now has hard, mean, snow in it. They are not so much flakes as tiny pieces of ice which sting my face and prickle my gloveless hands. The noise of the wind fills my head as I stare down at the ice-covered pool. I do not have the hammer in hand, so I snatch up one of the coping stones from the wall around the spring. I raise it high above my head and bring it down with all the force

I can muster. The ice splits and cracks, but only a small hole appears. I raise the stone again. And again, and again, and again, until at last the ice crust gives way, shattering and dispersing in the oily water. Above the whining of the wind I hear Cai calling from the back door.

"Morgana, for pity's sake, what are you doing? Morgana, you have no coat. There is plenty of water inside. Come back to the house."

His words are swept away by the relentless wind. I cannot stop now. There is something more to be found here, I am certain of it. I plunge my arms into the black water, my breath catching in my throat at the intensity of the cold. I grope and grasp, running my benumbed palms over the slimy stones, searching, seeking, testing gaps and crevices. Where could it be? Where? Where?

Cai has battled his way against the wind and crossed the yard to stand beside me. He sees that I am looking for something.

"What is it? What do you think to find? We took the stone out, Morgana, don't you remember?"

I have not the time or the strength to attempt to explain myself, and he knows me well enough to understand that I will not be put off doing that which I have set my mind to. So he sets to helping me, pulling great slices of ice from the water and casting them out, so that it is easier for me to search. My hands are beyond feeling now, and the water has soaked through my sleeves completely, so that my arms are aching with the cold. And yet I search on. Here and there I find a loose stone, one which has become dislodged from the wall, but with nothing inscribed upon it. I pass each one to Cai and he checks them, but can detect no letters. I fumble on, digging in unseen corners and slender gaps in the interior wall, gouging ancient mud from the floor of the pool. And then I find it. I know, even as my cold-clumsy fingertips reach it, I know I have found another cursing stone. I lift it out and show it to Cai. It is slate, as the first one was, a small rectangle. And on it are scratched initials. Three letters this time— *CTJ.*

Cai stares at me. "My initials. *My* initials—Cai Tomos Jenkins. This stone curses me." He pales at the realization of the truth. Pales first, and then colors with anger. "The first one was not meant for me. Dear Lord, the first one cursed Catrin!" He reels back as if struck. "That witch! That evil, Godless creature! She cursed Catrin! She killed her, and did for my baby, too!" With a cry of rage he grasps the slate in both hands and brings it down hard onto the edge of the pool wall. It splits and shatters, dashed into a dozen harmless pieces. Cai stands panting with the effort, the wind moaning about us, a full blizzard raging now, so that we can scarce see the house across the yard. I put my frozen hand over his. When his eyes meet mine they are filled with tears. I stroke his cheek, wishing I could take away his pain. We share a moment of such stillness, it is as if the wild air and ice that assails us does not exist. But then, into this intimacy, into this instant of remembrance, of loss, and of hope, comes a sound that causes my scalp to crawl. It is a small sound, but it is out of place and unnatural.

I turn toward it, peering into the white maelstrom, searching for the source. Beside me I feel Cai's whole body tense as a shape starts to emerge through the swirling snow. Slowly, something blurred, a vague figure, approaches, accompanied by sounds of dragging, of slithering over the icy ground. There are no footfalls. There is no breathing. And yet this is, this must be, something living. As it draws closer I have to fight the urge to flee, for whatever it may be is possessed of such a terrifying presence that every part of me longs to run as far and as fast as I can. I hear Cai gasp and call for God's protection as the figure lumbers into view. It is Isolda. Or rather, it was once Isolda, for the creature hauling itself across the frozen earth can scarcely be described as human. Her clothes are melted and fused into her horribly burned body. Her hair has gone, so that her scalp glistens wet and black, mercifully obscured to some degree by the blizzard. The flesh on her face and arms is red and charred and hangs from her in shreds, as if some sharp-clawed demon has attacked her. She does not so much walk as progress in painfully awkward, lumpen movements, flopping heavily onto the snow with each yard of ground gained.

When she speaks, it is through a hideous, lipless mouth.

"Well, what a pretty pair you make," says she. "Morgana, I see you found the little gift I left for Cai. A pity to disturb it when its work was so nearly done." She hauls herself closer and Cai brings his arms around me, instinctively drawing me to him, even though we both know he is weak beyond defending even himself.

"Did you think I could be so easily vanquished?" Isolda hisses at us. "I will suck the final breath from each of you, restore my body with your blood, and then let the buzzards feast upon your carcasses!"

So saying she flings her melted, fingerless hand out in Cai's direction. The pain he receives is such that he is thrown across the yard, crashing heavily against the stable wall, where he lies moaning, clutching at his head. I find myself, once again, unable to move. Something protruding from the newly drifted snow catches my eye. I can just make out the handle of the lump hammer! Gathering what strength I have left, knowing that not to act will mean the end for me and for Cai, I cause the hammer to fly from its resting place and hurtle through the air. It reaches Isolda with sufficient force to break her bones. But it does not. It merely passes straight through her. Now I understand! This is not Isolda's earthly form before us, but a mirror of it. She is witchwalking. Her body must lie trapped in the ashes and cinders of her cellar, but her spirit escaped and came to find me. She lunges forward and I feel her phantom hands gripping my throat and pushing me back over the wall of the pond. How can I fight what is not here? I wriggle and squirm, but she has me as in a vise. I feel the water soaking into my hair, dragging my head backward, so that I might snap my back on the wall, or drown, or be throttled.

"Morgana!" Cai calls to me. "Morgana, here!"

I twist in Isolda's grasp so that I can see him just as he throws something to me. Instinctively I catch it. It is a sharp-edged piece of slate and I think perhaps he means me to use it as a weapon, not understanding that Isolda's rotten spirit cannot be harmed by such a thing. But now I see that he has scratched something on it. Letters. Initials I force myself to attend, to think, to recall—yes, letters—*IB*. With one last effort of will I wrench myself from Isolda's choking hands. I lean over and plunge the cursing stone into the water, all the while holding her loathsome gaze. Then I form the words clearly in my head, words that I know she will be able to hear.

I curse you, Isolda Bowen! I curse you to hell, now and forevermore!

The air is rent with a hideous shrieking, all the sounds of a nightmare visited on one brief moment, as the dreadful apparition before us writhes and squeals and reels and crashes and spins, smoking, until suddenly, it is gone. And the snow stops. And the wind stills. And there is silence. Nothing but stillness and silence.

Tomorrow is Christmas day. I take Cai's hand and we walk across the meadow and up toward the high pasture. The sun shines softly, low in the sky. There is snow lying on the ground, but it is of a variety so gentle, and so appealing, that I am happy to see it. A dusting on the trees helps relieve their winter bareness. A frosting on the grass beneath our feet lifts its drab December color.

It is wonderful to see my husband restored to good health once more. The second Isolda was cursed and banished, his suffering stopped, just like the snowstorm. Likewise, the sickness that had been plaguing the town disappeared. Any who were ill rallied and recovered, including Reverend Cadwaladr's daughters. General opinion was that, after all, I was not to blame. It seems that the fire that destroyed Isolda's house revealed the existence of the basement. The charred remains of its contents had been examined closely, and the reverend, along with others versed in the practices of the occult, had identified items which spoke of sorcery and magic. The conclusion was drawn that it had been Isolda who had visited sickness and starvation upon them. The rest of the house was cleared away and disposed of. Isolda's remains were buried beneath a heavy slap of stone well beyond the boundary of the town, and without sanctified ground.

As we lean into the steepness of the slope, our breaths white clouds in the cold winter air, Cai turns to me, smiling.

"I didn't think to see you without your drover's hat and coat ever again," he laughs.

At last the weather is fine enough for me to be dressed in the more becoming woolen coat that Cai has bought me, and I have no need of a hat. I like to feel the fresh breeze tugging at my loose hair. I swat at him playfully, tipping his cap over his eyes. I know he cares not how I dress, but he is happy to see me out of the swathes of clothes the brutal weather required. Neither of us will forget what we have endured, any of it. Nor will we ever be able to shake from our minds the unnatural winter that near stilled all life hereabouts.

As if reading my thoughts, Cai pauses in his walking, casting his gaze over the valley below, his expression grave, and says, "Do you think she would have stopped at nothing, Morgana? I do. I believe she would have killed every man, woman, and child without flinching, just to get what she wanted."

I squeeze his hand tighter. We both know how close she came to succeeding.

"She hadn't reckoned on you, mind," says he. "She took you for a slip of a girl, see? Didn't know what she was taking on when she went against you, Mrs. Jenkins. None of them did." The seriousness leaves his face again, his eyes softening. "Mind, there's not a person within twenty miles hasn't heard of the new mistress of Ffynnon Las now. They saw you stick by me, saw how tough you were, how determined. They saw us come through that cruel weather together. And they found the right place, in the end, to lay the blame for their losses. You have earned the right to be here, Morgana. No one will ever question it again."

We complete our climb and decide to take in the view, settling on a sloping flat rock that protrudes from the snowy ground. From where we sit, up here on the hill, we can see the valley in all its prettiness and know that everywhere people are busy with thoughts of new life, and hope, and good will to all men. The weather has improved so much we have been able to put the sheep back up here on the hill, and behind me the ewes dig about, finding roots and tender twigs to nibble. From here I can make out Prince in the pond meadow, pausing in his own idle grazing to round up his mares, nipping one smartly on the rump just to remind her who is in charge. The cattle, fattening again at last, have the run of the barn and the yard.

Bracken comes back from tracking a rabbit and sits next to me, licking my hand.

"Daft dog," Cai tells him, putting his strong arm around my shoulders and pulling me close.

No further mention was ever made of any accusation of witchery against me. Cai was all for demanding apologies and there being a public clearing of my name. But I persuaded him to let things be. I am no longer feared or reviled, but accepted. Respected, even. I am content with that.

Besides, how could I have him stand up and deny what I truly am? It would make liars of us both. I am not simply Morgana who goes witchwalking, or Morgana with the curious talents—I can no longer think of myself as such. I am Morgana Jenkins, Keeper of the *Grimoire of the Blue Well,* Mistress of Ffynnon Las. With Mrs. Jones gone the *Grimoire* has passed into my care. Just as the well is now mine, so is the book, though it is true to say no such things can ever be owned. I am their protector, their guardian, as much as they are mine. I will use the healing properties of the well for those who might need it, though I will have to do so secretly. I will daily thank the Witches of the Well who came to my aid when I needed them most, and who permitted me to use the fearsome power of the *Grimoire* to save Cai and to, ultimately, rid us of Isolda. And, in the years to come, if we are blessed with children, it may be that one of them is a girl, and then I shall have someone to school in the ways of the Blue Well. I shall raise my own little witch, and show her how to witchwalk, and teach her to respect the magic blood that runs in her veins. The *Grimoire* and the Blue Well will be her heritage and her birthright, and I shall hold them safe for her until she comes.

And now Cai and I can be happy, here at Ffynnon Las, *porthmon* and his wild wife. Of course, our happiness is tinged with loss, for Mrs. Jones is sorely missed. Given the extreme weather we had all been experiencing, no one questioned that she had fallen victim to the cold. We are both doing our best to learn to cook, and often wish she were here to scold our hopelessness. I readily admit, Cai will make a better housekeeper than I.

I snuggle against him, taking in the beauty of the landscape below, warmed by his presence, by his love for me, and by the comforting happiness that comes from knowing I belong here. That this is my home. Cai puts a finger beneath my chin and turns my face to him. He looks at me with such an expression of tenderness as could thaw the most frozen of hearts.

"My wild one," says he. "I love you, Mrs. Jenkins Ffynnon Las. You are aware of this fact, are you not?"

I look at him and I see the love shining out of him, and know that I am safe and wanted and adored, and that I always will be. I feel the pressure building inside my head, and hear a noise like the winter winds raging through the dark pine trees, and my thoughts and feelings fall forward, tumbling over one another, and my blood, my magic blood, sings in my veins, and I take in a long, quenching breath, and my tongue feels heavy against my teeth and clumsy in my mouth, and my lips part, and there is a thickness in my throat, and I open my jaw, and my heart lifts, and . . . I . . . say . . . "Yes!"

Y Diwedd

1. What did you think of the arranged marriage between Cai and Morgana? Which of them did you sympathize with more?

2. How do you feel about Morgana's speechlessness? How do you think it helped or hindered her developing relationship with Cai? Did it make it harder for you as a reader to connect with her?

3. Mrs. Jones became a very important person in Morgana's life. What did you think of her? How might the story have been different without her?

Discussion Questions

4. Superstition and the supernatural (arguably!) played a much bigger role in society in 1830 than they do now—how did they impact Morgana's new life at Ffynnon Las?

5. Did you find the landscape around Ffynnon Las attractive, threatening, or perhaps both?

6. Isolda uses her magic in very different ways from Morgana. Which of them do you think more closely conforms to most people's idea of a witch? Why?

7. Did you see Reverend Cadwaladr as a victim, or a weak man who should have known the right thing to do?

8. The weather was almost a character in its own right in this book—would you agree with this statement? How much were you affected by it as you read?

For more reading group suggestions,
visit www.readinggroupgold.com.

ST. MARTIN'S GRIFFIN

THOMAS DUNNE BOOKS

Turn the page for a sneak peek
at Paula Brackston's new novel

Available April 2014

1.

London, 1913

The dead are seldom silent.

They have their stories to tell and their gift of foresight to share. All that is required for them to be heard is that someone be willing to listen. I have been listening to the dead all my life, and they never clamor more loudly for my attention than at a funeral. This is in part due to proximity, of course. Here I stand, beside an open grave, somber in black, quiet, watching, waiting, pain constricting my chest more tightly than the stays of my corset, and all around me souls stir. But they must wait. Wait to be called. Now is not the time. I know they are eager to speak to me, and I value their trust in me, but wait they must.

It is always important, what the dead have to say. At least, they consider it so. As if departing this world has conferred upon their every single utterance a dignity, a value, that was not present while they trod the ground instead of sleeping beneath it. There are times their insistence and their self-importance tire me, I admit. Times such as now, when I am far too consumed by grief to want to hear them. Even so, I can never forget, *must* never forget that sometimes their words are indeed of great value. Necromancers through the ages have known this; we have learned to listen to their bold prophecies and their whispered warnings. What would the genteel lords and ladies assembled here today think, I wonder, if they knew that among them now are those who summon spirits from the past to divine the future? What would they think of me if I were to tell them I am most at ease in a catacomb, or sitting in a graveyard cloaked in darkness, talking softly with those who have crossed the Rubicon and dwell in the Land of Night? That I find comfort and solace in the companionship of the dead, as my ancestors did before me? What would they say if I told them I have always harbored a secret fondness for coffins? There is something about their sleek lines, the rich tones of the burred walnut, the gleam of the brass fittings, the comforting thought of a place of rest and safety, that appeals to me.

Now, though, as I watch my father's coffin being lowered into its grave, no amount of admiration for its workmanship can distract me from the loneliness I feel. My father was not an openly affectionate man—most thought him rather cold and aloof—but he loved me, and now he is gone. At twenty-one I should be excited about the future. Instead I feel only the sadness of loss, and the weight of duty upon my shoulders. My brother will inherit the role of duke and all that goes with it, but I am heir to my father's other title. A position that bestowed upon him both immense power and fearsome responsibility. And now it is my turn. I am to become the new Head Witch of the Lazarus Coven.

As I stand at the graveside I let my gaze sweep over the gathered mourners. Hundreds have turned out to pay their last respects to the late duke, but only a handful among us know that the coffin which is the current focus of attention, and which is now being lowered into the damp, dark earth, is, in point of fact, empty. The August sunshine has warmed the soil so that its musky scent drifts up from the open grave. To me the aroma is familiar and stirring. It smells of long ago, of ages past, of loved ones moved from this world to the next, of death and rebirth, of rot and regeneration. As the smell fills my nostrils I identify the presence of cleansing worms and busy beetles, and under it all, from nearby newly filled graves, the subtle beginnings of sweet decay. I am not the only one to detect the presence of disintegration. From the branches of a majestic cedar comes the agitated cawing of sharp-beaked rooks.

The heat of the summer afternoon is starting to tell on many of the mourners. The pool of black the gathered company presents seems to ripple as women sway unsteadily in their heavy gowns, their restricting corsets robbing them of much of what little air there is. Here and there fans are worked listlessly. The men fare no better beneath their top hats, and some pluck at their starched collars. The relentlessly high temperatures of this summer of 1913 are not conducive to comfort for anyone dressed for a society funeral. Even the gleaming black carriage horses, despite standing in the shade of an ancient yew tree, fidget, causing the blackened ostrich plumes on their bridles to shudder and flutter in the inappropriately cheerful sunshine.

I feel my mother's grip on my arm tighten. Her gloved fingers dig into the night-black crepe of my sleeve. She looks worryingly frail.

"Mama?" I whisper as close to her ear as her elaborately veiled hat will allow. "Mama, are you quite well?"

"Oh, Lilith, my dear. I do feel a little faint."

The dowager duchess teeters alarmingly.

"Freddie!" I hiss at my brother, who stands only a few paces off but wears an expression that places him in another world entirely. "Freddie, for heaven's sake, help Mama."

"What? Yes, yes, of course. Now then, Mama. Steady as she goes." He smiles weakly, slipping his arm around our mother's tiny waist. "Not long now," he murmurs. "Soon be over," he adds, as much to himself as anyone else.

I take in the pale couple that comprise my family and wonder if I am equal to the task of looking after them. They need me to be strong. To take Father's place. But how can I? How can I? My mother's very existence has been defined by her husband for such a long time. She was a duchess for so many years, and now she must alter her view of herself, of her position, to become Lady Annabel. She finds this modern, fast-changing world confusing and illogical, and overhanging us all is the possibility of war. She is adrift, and I must be her safe haven. It is so typical of Mama that she insisted on such a grand and lengthy funeral. She has overseen every detail—from the number and variety of lilies, to the breed of the carriage horses, and the funereal livery of the footmen. I understand that she is sure in her mind that she knows precisely what her beloved Robert would have wanted. She believes it is expected of her as the duke's widow to carry out his wishes. However keenly she feels her grief, she will not let it show. However lost she knows herself to be, she will present a small point of stoic dignity at the center of the cortege. Only those closest to her will be aware of how much she is suffering. I know the truth of it. My mother is burying not simply an adored spouse, but the greater part of herself. Freddie and I will go into the world and have lives of our own; she will remain in privileged purgatory, from now until the moment of her own death, no longer duchess, no longer wife, no longer with a purpose of place around which she can shape her existence.

And Freddie. Freddie has singular problems which require singular remedies. Perhaps he can be persuaded to move out to our country estate in Radnorshire, far away from the destructive temptations on offer in the city. It would be a solution of sorts. But how will I succeed where even Father failed? Freddie knows what he would be giving up if he went back to Radnor Hall. I fear he would as soon jump into Father's grave.

That brother of yours will bring you to ruin!

Who is that? Who speaks to me unbidden, uncalled, unsummoned? What spirit would venture to do such a thing? Who is there?

One who watches you, Daughter of the Night. One who knows you, and your worthless brother, better than you know yourselves.

I must close my mind to this unwelcome, unfamiliar voice! Despite this relentless heat of the day I feel a sudden chill. Spirits may become restless, may long to communicate, but still they wait to be called. I will not listen. Not now. Now it is the living who need me. Freddie, perhaps, most of all.

Watching him now as he attempts to support Mama he appears almost as insubstantial as she does. His skin has about it a transparency that seems to reveal the vulnerability underneath. Tiny beads of sweat glisten on his brow. He leans heavily on his cane, as if he cannot bear his own weight, let alone that of anyone else.

I remember the first time Father brought us here, Freddie and me. It was gone midnight, and the house was quiet. He came to the nursery, and told Nanny to get us up and dressed. I could have been no more than nine years old, so Freddie must have been seven. It was certainly strange, to be roused from our beds in the dark hours, and to leave in the carriage with only our father. I recall Nanny's anxious face watching at the window as we left. Did she know? I wonder. Did she know about Father? Did she know where he was taking us?

He had the driver park the carriage at the gate to the cemetery, and then led us through the narrow paths between the graves. He walked quickly, and Freddie and I had to trot and scamper to keep up. I remember feeling a little excited at such a mysterious outing, but I was not afraid. My poor baby brother, however, was so dreadfully scared. By the time we reached our destination—this very spot—he was crying quite loudly, so that Father had to scold him and insist that he be quiet. We stood still then, among the tombs and statuary, letting the dark settle about us. I heard an owl screech, and several bats flitted past, their wing beats causing the warm summer air to stir against my face. Father said nothing, gave us no instructions, told us not a thing about what was expected of us. He merely had us stand silently among the dead, wrapped in the night. Freddie fidgeted the whole time, stifling his sobs as best he could. But I was quite content. I felt . . . at home.

I take Mama's arm once more and hold on firmly. The vicar presses slowly on with the service, his voice flat and monotonous, like a distant bell, weathered and cracked, echoing the dying heartbeats of the man whose body we commit to the earth, and whose soul we commend to God. Except that his body is absent, and his soul will linger a while yet.

❦

Beside a mournful statue of an angel, sheltering in the relative coolness of its winged shadow, and at some remove from the main company attending the duke's funeral, Nicholas Stricklend, Permanent Private Secretary to the Minister for Foreign Affairs, waits and watches. He has no desire to engage in small talk with others in attendance. Nor does he wish to give his condolences to the chief mourners. He wants merely to observe. To witness the interment. To assure himself that the leader of the Lazarus Coven is indeed dead and gone, once and for all, no longer occupying that privileged position of power and influence.

A squirrel scampers by close to where Stricklend stands. The quick movement of its claws on the dust-dry ground scuffs up fallen pine needles, some of which land on the senior ranking civil servant's spotless shoes. He regards the needles with distaste. Their presence offends him. He does not consider himself unrealistic in his expectations of life; he is aware that perfection, however sincerely strived for, is often unattainable. However, it is his habit to aim for nothing less, so that even when his attempts fall short, a high standard is maintained. What he finds irksome almost beyond endurance is the way in which the actions of others on occasion cause his cherished ideal to be compromised. Focusing on his shoes he exhales firmly, directing his breath effortlessly, as if it were within everyone's capabilities, the distance to his feet so that the pine needles are blown away as on a zephyr, and his shoes regain their matchless shine. The squirrel, sensing danger, freezes. Its face registers first fear and then pain, as it drops to the ground. After one small gasp it is stilled forever. The nearby rooks fall silent.

Stricklend returns his attention to the family of the recently deceased duke. He met Lord Robert's widow several times when she was still the Duchess of Radnor. No doubt she would remember him, just as she would remember all her guests. She would naturally value her reputation as an excellent hostess but now, even so soon after the duke's passing, she appears to Stricklend diminished. Her husband's illness had been protracted and his death prepared for, but still the shock of it shows. Though her face might be veiled, her demeanor, her deportment, her seeming lack of substance are plainly visible. On her right, her son, Frederick, presents a picture of almost equal frailty. The young man is tall and good-looking, with the family's black hair and fine, aristocratic features, but he is painfully thin, and there is a restlessness about him that gives him away. Stricklend doubts the youth will make a good duke. He will not come close to filling his father's shoes.

The person who is of real interest to him, however, is the slim figure to the left of the dowager duchess. Lady Lilith Montgomery, only daughter and eldest child of the late Lord Robert Montgomery, sixth Duke of Radnor, wears her striking beauty casually yet with dignity. She does not flaunt the head-turning loveliness with which she has been blessed any more than she would flaunt her position of privilege as the daughter, and now sister, of a duke. There is about her an air of seriousness. An earnestness. A self-contained strength, that Stricklend finds both admirable and attractive. He witnessed her coming out into society through the summer with careful attention. But it is not her feminine attributes that matter to him. Nor her social standing. What is of concern to him, what he is keenly interested in, is her ability to take on the mantle of Head Witch in her father's place. Only time will tell if she is up to the task. If she is not, it will be a bad day for the Lazarus Coven. A very bad day indeed. It will also be a singularly good day for Nicholas Stricklend.

Despite the weight of his valise, the bulk of his knapsack of artist's materials, and the awkward legginess of the easel he carries on his shoulder, Bram Cardale traverses the cemetery with a vigorous step. Being tall and strong means his luggage is less burdensome for him than it might have been for others, added to which a sense of purpose lends energy to his stride. He is glad of the shortcut, for he has walked a mile or more already, but he could happily travel until sunset, for today he begins his new life. Behind him lie burned bridges, disregarded offers of secure employment, and the comfort and stability of his family home. Ahead lies nothing certain, save that he is to lodge with the renowned and feted sculptor, Richard Mangan, and he is, at last, to attempt to become the painter he believes himself capable of being. Such a leap of faith shocked his parents. His father took it particularly badly.

"But, lad, you've a position waiting for you at the factory. You'd throw it all up to . . . to what? Paint pictures?"

"It's what I was meant to do, Father."

"All of a sudden our life, what we do, that's not good enough for you?"

"I don't expect you to understand."

"You're right about that."

"Can't you be pleased for me?"

"Pleased you're going off on the rim of your hat to live in a house of adulterers and heaven knows who else instead of taking your place here, where you belong? Oh, aye, I'm certain to be pleased about that."

Bram had not attempted to win his father round to the idea of his chosen future. He had dried his mother's tears and promised to write. There had been a moment, when she had looked deep into him in the way only she could, when he had faltered. She had touched his cheek with such tenderness, such concern . . . but if he did not go now he feared he would remain forever living a half-life, his talent, his art, his need to create, stifled and smothered. He could not tolerate such an existence. True, there could be no guarantees of success, and he might end up alone in London, a failed nobody, his talent exposed as an illusion. He risked one manner of madness if he went, and another, a slower, more tortuous insanity, if he stayed. He had caught the evening train from Sheffield that very night. Guilt dogged his footsteps, but with each passing mile his certainty that he was doing the right thing grew.

The energy of London, the vibrant hum of the place, the sheer scale, all speak to him of possibilities and of freedom. He could not paint properly while still living under his father's shadow, living a provincial life, where he was hampered by his family's expectations of him. He knows he is acting selfishly, but if he must paint—and it seems he is driven by some irresistible force to do so—he must find a place and a company conducive to artistic expression and endeavor. He had written to Richard Mangan scarce hoping for a response, so when he was invited to take rooms in his house he knew it was an opportunity he could not pass up. Here was his chance to give vent to his ambition.

As he approaches the halfway point on the path to the east gate of the graveyard, Bram is struck by the number of mourners attending a burial. Large funerals are not uncommon in Sheffield but he has witnessed nothing of this kind before. He pauses in his journey, sliding his easel to the ground for a moment. He can make out several funeral carriages, all drawn by very fine horses, each black as coal, and draped in heavy velvet. The hearse itself might no longer be in attendance, but the remaining conveyances are no less impressive or flamboyantly liveried. Each has painted on its doors and embroidered on the drapery of the horses the emblem of a dragonfly, delicate and slim, its body shimmering green. Mourners stand a dozen rows deep, at least two hundred of them. Close to the grave the chief mourners look to Bram to present a touchingly small family. The young woman wears a broad hat with a long spotted veil, but he can discern elegant deportment and fine features even so. And a graceful, slender neck, the only part of her not swathed in black. Bram finds the whiteness of this small, exposed area of flesh somehow startling. Erotic, almost. A shaft of sunlight cuts through the branches of the lone cedar tree to illuminate the trio at the graveside, so that the fabric of their clothes, though cellar-black, reflects the light with such brilliance that the glare causes him to squint.

He wonders at once how he would paint such a phenomenon, how he would capture on canvas the strength of that light in the midst of such gloom. A familiar excitement stirs within him at the idea of the challenge. His pulse quickens. Images flash through his mind, light upon dark, dark upon light, blocks of color and bold brush strokes. In that moment of inspiration all is possible. He drops his luggage to the ground and scrabbles in his knapsack, pulling out board and paper, digging deeper for dusty shards of charcoal. He supports the board with one arm, pinning the paper to it with his fingers at the top. In his right hand he grasps the charcoal and turns to stand facing the scene he wishes to capture. He is in the full glare of the sun, and can feel perspiration beading his brow, dampening his hair. His hat offers more heat than shade, so he pushes it from his head, letting it lay where it falls on the parched ground. He frowns against the glare of the blank page, hesitating only a moment before beginning to sketch. A passing couple comment sharply on his inappropriate behavior. He is immune to their criticism. He knows he is witness to the grief of strangers, and he knows his actions could be seen as callous or disrespectful. The small part of him that still pays heed to such conventions, however, is stamped down by the urgency of his desire to depict what he sees, to immortalize that moment. It is not merely the juxtaposition of shapes, of sunlight and shadow, of patterns and elegant lines he wishes to show. Nor is he interested in recording a comment on society and its cherished traditions. It is the very essence of his subjects he strives to transpose to his picture.

To show what cannot be seen one must first represent what can be seen, he tells himself.

His mind works as swiftly as his hand as he draws. Deft, energetic marks begin to fill the paper.

It is my lot to spend my life in pursuit of the impossible. To reveal what is hidden. But am I able? Am I equal to the task?

He continues to work even as he feels his head spin with the heat of the day and the intensity of his concentration. Even as curious onlookers pause to peer over his shoulder. He works on, seeking to show the brilliance of life in the midst of a ceremony for the dead. Even as the vicar closes his good book. Even as the beautiful, slender girl beside the open grave raises her head and finds herself to be beneath his fervent gaze.